QUEST FOR A QUEEN
The Falcon

QUEST FOR A QUEEN
The Falcon

Frances Mary Hendry
illustrated by Linda Herd

CANONGATE KELPIES

First published in Great Britain in 1989
by Canongate Press,
14 Frederick Street,
Edinburgh EH2 2HB

First published as a Canongate Kelpie in 1992.

British Library Cataloguing-in-Publication Data
A catalogue record for this book is available from
the British Library.

ISBN 0 86241 365 6

The publishers acknowledge subsidy of
the Scottish Arts Council
in the publication of this volume.

Printed and bound in Great Britain by
Cox & Wyman Ltd, Reading, Berkshire.

CANONGATE PRESS PLC
14 FREDERICK STREET, EDINBURGH

Other titles by the same author
published by Canongate

Quest for a Kelpie

Quest for a Maid

Quest for a Babe

The Falcon is part of the *Quest for a Queen*
trilogy which spans the life of
Mary Queen of Scots.

To Iain, with love.

Contents

Author's Note

My grateful thanks to all the people who have helped me; in especial, to Dr Rosalind K. Marshall, presently of the National Portrait Gallery. Her books *Virgins and Viragos* and *Queen of Scots* have been of enormous importance in my research. In addition, she has been kind enough to check the historical accuracy of this book. She points out that there is no evidence of any trick letters sent to Queen Mary; though in England Mary herself protested, "I came to England on my cousin's promise of assistance against my enemies and rebel subjects."

In the same way, Alistair McKissock, Mains of Moy, Forres, who kindly checked the falconry, says that the catching of the carrier pigeon as I describe it is just barely possible, but most unlikely.

But they make a good story!

Leezie and her dad, Peter Matheson, Ina, Sandy, the Pattersons and Frasers, and the mews apprentices, are pure invention; but every other named soul in the book actually lived when and where, and approximately how, I have described them. Their characters may not be accurate; if not, I apologise to their departed spirits.

There is no evidence that Kate Lenton was black; but there were several black people in Edinburgh about that time, so I thought it would be interesting to make her one of them. Mary's grandfather, James IV, did indeed take the part of the Rough Knight in a tournament at Stirling, when the lady in whose honour it was held was the Black Queen.

The quotations from John Knox's speeches and letters — not the one Kate produced, of course — and the words of Rizzio's and Darnley's murders, are as far as possible accurate to the records of the actual events, only modernised enough to be intelligible.

I hope you enjoy reading the book as much as I've enjoyed writing it.

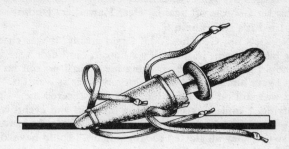

Master Matheson

Out of my whole life, if the Queen's Messenger had tried to pick a worse minute to find me, he couldn't have. Up to my knees and elbows in the burn, my shirt tail draggled round my backside, bare head, bare legs, filthy all over, hair in stinking rats' tails down my neck, washing out pig guts; and a strange voice calls, "Where can we find your mistress, laddie?"

At the first word, of course, I'd spun crouching round, my hand at my wrist where my knife was aye strapped. I backed off across the stream, cursing the ripple of the water for drowning their horses' hoofbeats, and abandoning the trail of pink and white gut to the swirl of the current. . . But then I recognised one of the men, and then some more behind him. Hepburns. Our own clan. I was safe — well, fairly. I stopped, and straightened up warily.

Geordie Dalgleish, the Earl's agent, laughed like a drain. "Dod, Leezie, but ye're a bonny sight!" he wheezed, his chins wobbling. "Sweet an' cuddly as a wee lamb! Sure an' I'll wed ye, just as soon's my wife obliges me by dyin'!"

His guard of half a dozen blue-bonneted mosstroopers, shaggy in their tattered sheepskin jerkins as their own ponies, grinned obligingly, but the stranger in the dark red doublet frowned and leaned forward.

"A lassie? My god! Never fear, lass, we'll no harm ye."

This set Geordie off again. "Her? Harm her? Dod, the last man tried it's still runnin'!"

"No, he's no, Geordie Tod," I said grimly. It was cheeky, using his nickname in front of a stranger, but I didn't see why he should get away with scorning me. "He'll no run far wi' what I gave him. An' it's waitin' for any other as wants it." My hand was still on my knife hilt, and they cheered me — very satisfying. I smiled sweetly, raising my chin and eyebrows at him — then a bit of drying muck tickled my nose. As I sneezed and swore, they all started to laugh again. I could have killed the lot of them, especially the fancy stranger, who didn't smile; even looked a bit shocked.

"Are all your lassies like this one?" he asked Geordie. "Or is she —"

"No, no, sir," Geordie spluttered, waving a feeble hand. "Leezie's no what ye might call the regular run o' the still. She's a rare brew is our wee Leezie! Fifteen, an' no even kissed yet! A rare wildcat kittie — eh, Leezie?"

I tossed back my sticky hair. No sense in letting them know how their laughter and teasing hurt me. Better they admired my toughness. "Aye, Maister Tod. There's no many about like me."

"Thank the Lord!" he returned as usual, his wee fox teeth twinkling in his black whiskers. Then, glancing at the stranger, he sobered up. "But we've no time to waste, Leezie, lass," he announced importantly. "Where's yer dad?"

The stranger raised his brows. "Her dad?"

"Aye, sir. She's daughter to the man ye're seekin', no his servin' lass."

He frowned again. "It's Mistress Hepburn I'm seeking, Master Dalgleish."

"Aye, aye, but that's no how we do things here, sir! This isnae Embra town! Ye must speak the man before ye have dealin's wi' the wife here, Maister Matheson. Where is he, Leezie? We need a few words wi' him — on the Queen's business, see you!"

Queen's business with my dad — or my ma? I thought back

10

ten years. Maybe. . . But as for my dad — "Well, Maister Dalgleish, ye'll have to wait till the morn, I'm fearin'. For he'll no be fit to speak to nobody till then."

They looked at me in surprise; then at the pig guts snagged bobbing round a rock; and the faces of the local men, at least, showed comprehension. "Aye, sir," I explained to the stranger, "we've been at the pig-stickin'. He was fair bleezin' when I left, an' he'll likely be asleep by now, past wakin'. But wait while I come up wi' ye, an' we'll see."

As I gathered the long, slippery coils up from the burn — Queen's Messenger or no, I wasn't going to leave them for any buzzard or wandering fox — Geordie was explaining to the stranger, in enthusiastic detail, how the pig was aye killed in November. Once it was bled for the black puddings, the man of the house scalded the carcase to scrape off the bristles and get the hooves off, then heaved it up on a rope to the door lintel, gutted it, cut it down the middle with an axe into halves, and butchered it. The women — ma and me — cleaned out the gut and made sausages, salted the hams and sides to be hung later in the chimney to smoke, made brawn of the head and innards, and the house had meat stored for the winter. But once the danger and excitement of the sticking was bye, all this was heavy, dirty, smelly work.

Geordie paused there. They were all eying the stranger, hopeful he'd show disgust or nausea so they could jeer at the finicky city man, but he just nodded. "Aye, aye. I'm from Meigle in the Sidlaws mysel'. I helped wi' the Martinmas work every year, an' I know fine a man has need o' a good draught o' ale to wash the stink out his throat. But a drink's one thing, an' a skinful's another. Why should this man Adam Hepburn get so drunken?"

All the men laughed again. "Dod," wheezed Geordie, "it'd be simpler to ask what for he shouldnae, eh, Leezie? He likes his drink, does Adam. Aye."

"He does that," I agreed sourly. "An' his friends dinnae discourage him."

"Now, Leezie," he protested, "he's a big man, yer dad, an' if he offers a man a wee sup o' a good ale, ye'd no have us insult

11

him by refusin', would ye?"

"Aye, would I!" I snapped, rinsing my hands and face, and shoving my hair back with my fingers. "If ye insulted him that way a time or two, he'd maybe no drink so much, an' there'd be a bit siller left in the house. An' he'd have less sore heads in the mornin's." As I hauled on my breeches, still damp where I'd rinsed the blood off, but they'd do, the men laughed and joked, praising dad's head for drink, and his generosity with it. They paid me no heed, of course. Women aye complained their men drank too much.

I studied the Queen's Messenger as I trotted up the hill beside the horses, and he eyed me back with some wonder. "Are you no cold, lassie? It's a lazy wind, this." As I frowned, not understanding, he grinned. "It doesn't take time to go round you — it just cuts straight through!"

"No, sir, I'm fine." Soft, I thought him, dressed warm, shirt, quilted doublet, fine slashed moleskin trunks above long brown boots, and a thick cloak wrapped tight against the raw wind that I scarce noticed, even in just my shirt and breeches. But yet, there was a firmness about the wide mouth, and a sideways kink he'd not been born with in his nose, and a shrewd, wary look in the grey eyes. A royal messenger had to cope with all kinds of trouble; not a few had been killed for their letters. More to him than on the surface, then.

When we turned the corner of the hill he drew rein in surprise. "But — sure this is never where Mistress Hepburn lives?" His face showed his disbelief, that a Queen would send a message to anyone who lived in such a desolate ruin, the dry-stane dykes broken down, their stones lying scattered among the rushes on the thin, sour soil of the tiny fields.

I laughed. "What did ye look for, sir? The house has been burned four times in the last ten year. Was it Holyrood ye were expectin'?"

"The English?" he asked.

"Once," I nodded. "The Earl's men once, Geordie Dalgleish there," Geordie grinned, not ashamed or offended, "when we couldnae pay our taxes for payin' protection money. The Armstrongs once, when we didnae pay them protection money

12

for payin' the taxes. An' the Elliotts. They're no friends o' the Earl o' Bothwell, an' we suffer for it, even this near the Hermitage."

He kicked forward again to the gateway, slowly, taking in the uneven, badly turfed roof, the blackened walls, the single bunch of scarlet berries brave on the scorched branches of the rowan, the door off its leather hinges to make a table for butchering the pig in the middle of the yard.

But one of the trestles was thrown over, and the board down. And in the far corner dad's great wolfhound was busily, guiltily tearing at a whole leg of the pig that was to keep us fed this winter.

Reivers again. In broad daylight! I dropped the guts and drew my knife.

Ma was in a corner of the yard, huddled against the stone wall, crying. I ran to her. She was as dirty as myself, dirtier, save where tears had washed away some of the blood, grit and dust. Her cap was off, and her fading fair hair had fallen over her dress that had great new rents among the darns in the skirt and shoulder. As I put an arm round her, she cried out in pain.

After one experienced glance round, the men had fanned out, spears and swords ready, to find the raiders. They returned to the yard angry and puzzled. The horse was still in the stable. The cow and sheep were grazing safe away up the outfield. The hens were pecking about. No reiver would have left them.

I tried to get ma to tell me what had happened, but she just clung to me with her right hand, and sobbed. She cuddled her left arm protectively, and new bruises were rising on her face blue-black among the old purple and yellow ones and the red grazes.

At last it came to me. "Dad! It was dad done all this!"

Ma tried to control her sobs. "No! No!" she whispered desperately.

"It's past time for hidin' it, ma!" I snapped at her. "They can all see nothin's been stolen — it wasnae reivers this time. It was him, was it no?"

"Aye." It was just a tiny whisper. She'd hidden the truth

from the neighbours for so long, from shame and loyalty, and need, for we'd nowhere else to go, that it was hard for her, but once started between sobs she couldn't stop. "He knocked over the ale-cask an' spilled it all. So he drank down the whisky flask. An' then last week's brewin' o' ale. I told him it wasnae ready yet. But he wouldnae listen. It gave him a sore belly, and he said I'd tried to poison him. An' he hit me, an' knocked me down, an' kicked me. I hid under the table, but he shoved it over on me, an' kicked me again. An' I felt my armbone snap, just at the elbow there, an' I screamed, but he wouldnae stop. He wouldnae stop. He just went on an' on, kickin'. Till he was tired. An' then he went away."

"Where?" I asked. "When?" My eyes were fixed on the gleam of the blade in my hand, and my head felt stuffed full of red till I could scarce breathe.

"I dinnae know. No that long bye. Oh, Leezie, Leezie, dinnae leave me!"

I started to stand up, to do something. The knife. Dad. Aye. Dad. A path opened through the redness. I screamed it out — "I'll kill him!" But ma clung to me, and suddenly a hand gripped my wrist and twisted hard, and before I could react my knife had slipped out of my greasy fingers onto the stones.

As I jumped up, the stranger grasped my other wrist. "Now hark to me, Leezie Hepburn! Listen to me!"

"My name's no Hepburn!" It was desperately important to me. "He's no father o' mine! He's ma's second man, no blood kin to me! An' this isnae the first time, nor the hundredth, but by God it'll be the last! He's aye at ma an' me — I'll kill him, the brute! Drunken animal! I'll —"

He held on until I stopped screaming at him, and again until I'd stopped struggling. He wasn't a big man, and I was a tall, tough, wiry lass, that could best any of the local lads in a tussle, but somehow he kept me from breaking away, or from hurting against ma again. His hands were horseman's hands, or wrestler's, quick and strong, and I couldn't free myself however I fought. The smears of pig fat and dirt from my shirt spread over his fine dark-red broadcloth doublet, and I rejoiced, but my bare toes came off badly against his boots. At last I had to stop, gasping, furious and ashamed at being worsted.

Gradually I became aware of the other men, setting the yard more or less to rights, chaining the snarling hound with a yelp and a curse for a bitten hand, gathering with a grin for me and a frown for ma's sobs. "I'll put a man over to Isa at Yethouse, Maister Matheson, she's the nearest, to aid Janet here. That's likely where he's went anyway, to get more ale, or a draught for his sore belly," offered Geordie, grinning.

The stranger shook his head. "You do as you wish, Master Dalgleish. But I have a message from the Queen for this lady, an' I'll just give it to her now." He held me off and looked down at me. "Lassie, if I let you loose, will you bide still, an' no be runnin' off to kill anyone?" Fought out, I nodded, and resentfully sank back down by ma as he loosed my forearms and turned to his horse. I rubbed my bruised wrists, and put an arm round ma's shoulders.

Luckily one of the men was a bonesetter. While I helped hold her still, he quickly straightened ma's left arm and with a strip from her apron strapped on a broken stool leg as a splint. As I gently fastened the rest of the cloth for a sling, her cries and gasps slowed and stopped. After a minute she started coming a little back to herself. She looked round for her cap, to hide her hair decently, and reached a trembling hand to draw together the tear in her dress.

I looked up at the men. "Likes his drink, eh? Carries it well? Ye wouldnae care to insult him?" I spat, and they looked angered, but what could they say?

Then Master Matheson produced the letter from his saddlebags. Ma blinked at its seals, and sighed deeply, stirring painfully and sitting up. "Would you have me read it to you, mistress, if your eyes are sore?" he asked gently. That was tactful, in case she couldn't read.

She sighed again. "My eyes are bad, sir." They were all swollen, and her thin, tired face was puffy with blows and weeping.

He nodded, and looked round at the clustering men. "This is a private matter between Mistress Hepburn an' the Queen's

Grace," he said pointedly, and as they didn't take the hint, added, "Move back there, an' give us peace!" There was enough authority in his voice that even the tough mosstroopers moved. I wished I had the trick of it.

As they edged back reluctantly, their ears fair flapping, I began to rise, reluctantly too, but sank back pleased as ma put out a hand. "No, you bide, lass," he said. "Your mother has need o' you. Now, then." He knelt by us, showed the unbroken seal on the ribbon binding the letter, broke it and began to read. His low voice took on a kind of ring as he read the long, sweeping sentences.

"Mary, by the Grace o' God Queen o' Scotland and France, to her dearly beloved Janet Sinclair or Hepburn, near the Lieutenant o' the Border the Earl o' Bothwell's Castle called the Hermitage; we greet you well.

"Remembering kindly your good care and affection, an' the loving kindness that you had o' our person in our bairnhood, we request o' you that upon receiving this letter you do straightway repair to our Castle o' Edinburgh; there to join our service in the post of Nurse attendant upon the child presently expected o' us and our husband, Henry Darnley, King o' Scotland, if such be the will o' God. And this you fail not to do, but any delay or restraint whatsoever, as you will make us thankful service.

"Master Robert Rychardson treasurer, that you take this letter as warrant to the abovesaid Mistress Hepburn for the sum o' ten pounds for her expenses o' the journey, which shall be thankfully allowed to you in your accounts. Subscrivit with our hand, at Edinburgh, the vi day of November, anno 1565."

And he showed us the swirling signature; Marie R.

For a long minute we sat stunned. Then ma started to laugh. Crying and laughing together, she gestured at herself, her ruined dress, her draggled hair, her bare, dirty, calloused feet. "Can ye no see me there? Am I no the very pattern o' a nurse to a royal prince? I cannae! I cannae! Never again! Oh God, why should ye make mock o' me?" The tears started to flow again down her cheeks, whose only colour was from the bruises dad had laid on them. Her shoulders sagged again, and she turned

16

her head into my shoulder like a bairn.

I was angry for her. Had she not enough to bear, without this kind of bitter joke being laid on her from outsiders? How could she get away from dad, to be a nurse to this babe? How could she? Look at her — how. . .

How could she stay? With dad trying to kill her whenever he got drunk?

He'd not let her leave. Not if we stayed till he got back sober. . . .

I eyed the Queen's Messenger. He was looking at ma, pity and regret in his eyes; yes, this looked to be a good man. He'd not let us down; if he agreed to help. I aye hated asking for anything, and specially him, but. . . He was shaking his head, folding up the letter. I reached out and touched his arm. "Sir, is it true? The Queen — Queen Mary — really is callin' my ma to Embra town for to be nurse to her comin' bairn?" He nodded, his gaze still on the heavy parchment. "Then will ye help us, sir? For we cannae do it wi'out ye."

Ma's hand clutched convulsively at mine, and she murmured desperately, "No, Leezie, I cannae. I cannae." I shushed her.

Master Matheson eyed me searchingly. "What d'you mean?" he said, but I could see he was judging me witless. I had to convince him.

"Sir, if he finds out, Adam Hepburn'll no let her leave. He'll kill her first. He's tried already. Just see her bruises. She couldnae get away before, for there was no place else to go. But here this is her chance. Her only chance. But she has to go now, right away, an' no wait for dad, whatever Geordie Dalgleish says. Will ye no help her? To save her life?"

He frowned again. He'd an open face, not handsome, clean-shaven with a knob on his chin, the light brown hair starting to shrink back off his brow. As he thought, he whistled through a gap between his front teeth. He looked at ma's state, and round the yard again, and shook his head doubtfully. He mustn't refuse! If he said no, it would be harder to change his mind. "It's the Queen's command, sir, is it no?" I said desperately. "Ma was the Queen's own nurse when she was wee, when she was sent over to France to save her from the

17

English. She wasnae aye as ye see her now. She was bonny an' blithe, an' cuddly, that any bairn would love. An' that'll be why she's wanted now. If the Queen wants her own nurse for her bairn, should she no have her? At once, like she says?"

He decided as I spoke, and nodded decisively. "Aye, lass, you're right. It's a royal command." 'Request', the letter said; for Geordie's benefit he smoothly changed it to 'require'. That, and 'without delay nor restraint', were used to counter Geordie's argument that he'd no right to take a man's wife without his consent. Master Matheson made great play with the bright red seals on the letter. But the Queen's writ was worth little here, far from Edinburgh. . . I was biting my fingers.

At last silver chinked, and Geordie slapped him on the back. "Aye, sir! As ye say, who are we to stand in the way o' the royal will? The Earl o' Bothwell wouldnae be best pleased if his men angered Her Grace, an' him new pardoned home an' ridin' high in Her Grace's favour. A braw time he had in Paris, by all accounts! A wild rogue that, heh, heh! I'll just tell Adam when I see him that his wife's away to attend on Queen Mary, an' if he's a complaint he can aye take it up wi' the Court. After all, he wasnae here to argue, was he — an' we cannae keep back the Queen's affairs for every wee mannie wi' a skinful."

All this time, ma was arguing with me in a whisper. "I cannae, Leezie! How can I? What'll your dad do?"

"He'll no can do nothin', ma! We'll be far away out o' his reach! Ye'll be safe! Safe from him at last! Ach, come on, ma, can ye no see it's the best?"

"But see the state o' me! I've nothin' to wear — I'm no fit! An' my arm — how can I manage?"

That one was easy, and my heart singing. "Ye cannae, ma. No on yer own. I must just come wi' ye, to look after ye. Maister Matheson'll find us lodgin's in Embra, sure, an' we'll buy cloth, an' I'll sew it up for ye."

"You? You couldnae make me a gown!" ma gasped. "You couldnae say which end o' a needle the thread goes through!"

I'd have sworn all Master Matheson's attention was on the men, but he'd heard his name, and turned to us with a smile.

"Aye, wife, you needn't fret yoursel'. If your lassie can't sew, there's plenty in Edinburgh can an' will, for a plack or two, an' you've ten pound, mind! The Queen's Grace is a good mistress, an' generous." While my jaw dropped at the idea of such luxury — getting a gown made for you! — he knelt again beside ma. "Can you ride, think you, mistress? I'll take you up before me — you'll go easier that way."

Ma was flustered at the courtliness of his attention. "Ye cannae — I'm clairty!" she protested, but fell silent as he gestured to the mess I'd already made of his doublet. Foiled that way, she made one final attempt to argue. "But what o' my man? Who'll look after him?"

All my fury burned up again. After the harm he'd caused her, and me, her main worry was about Adam Hepburn! As I drew breath to curse, Master Matheson cut in smoothly. "No, no, mistress, you've no reason to fret. Isa at wherever it was can see to him rarely, I've no doubt." Aye would she! "Come away up, easy now." He helped her gently to her feet, supporting her on one side while I steadied the other. "You're comin' wi' us, Leezie? Did I hear right?"

At my nod he smiled, but Geordie started to howl with mirth. "Leezie in Embra? Dod, man, I'd give a gold royal to see it! Lord help any lad as looks sideways at her! How'll ye do in Embra, lassie, wi' all the ministers there glowerin' at yer breeks? Ye'll have to be civil an' quiet as a nun's hen, an' go to the kirk regular, an' mind yer manners, or they'll duck ye for a scold, or set ye on the stool o' repentance. Oh-oh, could I be there to see!"

"Ye ill-thoughted old billy!" I snarled at his open-mouthed glee.

He just laughed the more. "Now, now, Leezie, lass, that's no way to speak to yer elders an' betters! Ye'd best start to practise manners, had she no, sir? Dod! Leezie, in a cap an' high-heeled shoes! An' a farthingale an' a pair o' bodies!" He went off into a gale of laughter, and all his men with him.

I started to seek my knife, lost in the stones somewhere, but Master Matheson interrupted. "Leezie, will you ride behind

19

my man Danny there till we can get you a mount?" he asked civilly.

"I'll take our own cuddy!" I snapped, but Geordie put his foot down at that. Taking a man's wife was one thing; taking his horse was another, and out of the question. They laughed even louder at my annoyance.

"Have you anything to fetch wi' you, mistress?" asked Master Matheson.

Ma shook her head. "Nothin' o' value, sir." True enough; everything she had had been stolen or burned, or sold to pay for dad's drink. "But my plaid — Leezie, will ye fetch it for me? An' put on yer skirt."

"My skirt? I'd be better ridin' in my breeks, ma," I protested.

To ma's surprise, and mine, Master Matheson agreed with me. "Aye, breeks would be that much better, lass. That's good thinkin'. I've men wi' me, but five men an' a wife is less likely to be set on than four men an' two women. Aye, lass, your breeks. You can carry your skirt."

As I turned, pleased to be still in my lad's gear for a while — though the unwelcome thought came to me that I'd have to put on skirts in Edinburgh — I caught sight of my knife, and slipped it into its soft sheath strapped inside my left forearm as I went in. I'd taken it from a dead mosstrooper three years back. It had saved me from the Elliotts once, and when a drunk man had tried to attack me in Langholm, I'd put a hole in his shoulder with it and driven him off. After that, the knowledge of it had kept all men at a safe distance. I was never without it, and having it back I felt better.

It was dark in under the turf roof, with the fire right down, and the mess was incredible. Ma's pot of oatmeal and onions for the black puddings, the box of precious salt and the big basin of blood were all spilled over the earth floor and trampled in. Someone — dad, of course — had been sick. The jar of honey was smashed and running into the blood — after all the stings I'd had getting it! — and the hay we'd stored in the butt end of the house for wintering the beasts was scattered and trampled into everything. The plaids were a mucky, sticky huddle by the heather bedpile. Feuch!

Well, let dad right it all. I was done with here.

I climbed the ladder to the shelf where I slept and pulled down my skirt and plaid. What would the city man think of them, patches on patches, and darns in between? But I'd soon have new! What for did I need a pair of bodies, I wondered, dropping back down and going over to lift ma's plaid, hoping it wasn't too dirty. Was my own body not good enough — What on earth. . .?

Under the plaids, half-burrowed into the heather, lay my dad. Drunk? Blind drunk. Dead drunk. Not even a twitch as I tugged him out of his cocoon to flop bonelessly onto the earth floor, snoring through his greasy whiskers.

I looked at him, and considered.

My knife was to hand. Nobody knew he was there. I could stab him; throw burning peats from the fire onto the heather and roast him; twist his plaid round his face to smother him. Nobody would know. Here was my chance.

But my rage was burned out, and I was going to a new life in Edinburgh. With two bodies. No, I'd leave dad. He'd suffer worse, with nobody to cook and clean for him, or mend his clothes, or look after the beasts. Or stand for his beatings and all. I spat on him, picked up ma's wrap and turned away.

In the doorway stood a dark figure. I jumped. Master Matheson moved forward, and looked down at dad. "Your step-father? Well, Leezie? Are you no goin' to use that sharp wee cuttie?" Resenting his interference, I shook my head, and went to pass him. He stretched out a hand. I tensed, but he stopped before he touched me, nodding approvingly. "That's a good lass. I'm glad you've the sense. It's a hard enough life, without addin' murder to it."

My mind suddenly went red again. Him, this soft stranger, to approve me? He'd not lived in pain and fear and hatred of dad, listening in horror and guilt to ma whimpering and crying, to the thud of blows I couldn't stop, to the footsteps stumbling closer and closer to my ladder. He'd never lain under the rafters clutching a knife, praying for the strength and courage to strike down if the ladder creaked under a man's weight. How dare he pat me on the head, and tell me I was a good wee lassie, as if I was a bairn?

I wanted to hit him. But he was going to take ma and me away. I couldn't.

With the hot rage on me, I had to do something, or my head would burst.

I went back out and gave ma her plaid. Then I crossed the yard to where the guts I'd dropped lay trodden and muddy in the dust. I picked them up, all greasy, and went back in, the men crowding curious behind me. They whistled as they saw dad. Lifting his head, I carefully draped the squelchy guts round his neck. I rubbed them stinking into his hair and nose and beard. I poked the dripping ends in his ears and snoring, snorting mouth.

Round me, the mosstroopers were choking with laughter, reeling about and holding each other up as they imagined his waking. I led them back out to the light like a queen myself with her train, and smiled sweetly again at Geordie Dalgleish, who was laughing till he took three tries to mount his horse.

"Dod, Leezie!" he spluttered at last through the guffaws. "That's the best joke I've seen this ten year! What an afternoon! Wait till I tell the Earl! He'll be sorry to lose ye, he will that! A lassie wi' spirit like yours should go far, Leezie, far! I wish ye good fortune, lass! A' the luck in the world!"

"Maybe it's Embra town ye should wish luck to, Geordie!" a voice howled from the back, and he guffawed again.

"But what'll ye do there, lass? There's few pigs' guts in Embra!"

"I'll find somethin', Maister Dalgleish," I assured him. I felt grand — till I turned and saw ma. She was already mounted before Master Matheson, warm in his cloak and cradled sideways in his arms to favour the break, but sniffing miserably. I ran over to her, while the rest climbed on their wiry ponies. "What's wrong, ma? Is yer arm that sore? Is there anythin' I can do?"

She and the man in red looked down at me, and together shook their heads. "No, lassie, no," ma murmured. "It's just — ach, it's nothin'."

Master Matheson settled her more comfortably. "Cheer up,

22

Mistress Hepburn," he said. "It'll be different in Edinburgh. More civilised. There'll be a big change, you'll see." She nodded and gave him a watery smile.

Change in what? In me? Why? There was nothing wrong with me!

As my temper rose again the man I was to ride with called me. I leaped up astride behind him, scorning the hand he offered me, gripped his belt, and we galloped whooping out of the yard, the hens scattering and one or two flapping wildly in a hard fist here and there in the crowd, Master Matheson following gently with ma. I didn't bother to look back.

Mary

At the Hermitage Water Master Matheson drew rein and shouted us back.

"Master Dalgleish, I'm thinkin' we'd best part here. Master Hepburn will no doubt come up to the Hermitage seekin' his wife, will he no?"

"Like enough, sir," Geordie nodded, his wee eyes all bright with interest.

"Well, sir, you see for yoursel' how Mistress Hepburn feels about that." Ma was shivering and white at the very thought. "So if I go a longer way round, an' head for Hawick, sure enough, but by the Rule Water instead o' by Stobs, it'll throw him off the scent, maybe. An' at the least, the Earl wouldn't be put to the trouble o' lyin' that he doesn't know where we went, eh?"

Geordie stared for a moment, and then started to laugh again. "The trouble o' lyin'? My God! Wouldnae put him to — Dod, man, ye dinnae ken the Earl! He's the biggest rogue in Scotland! On my oath, sir, if Jamie Hepburn o' Bothwell told me the earth was under me, it's up I'd look to check! No, no, sir, ye neednae fear the Earl givin' ye away, but I'm bound to say yer plan's a good one. You go on up the Liddell, an' over the Note o' the Gate, an' Adam can seek ye up an' down the

24

Limekilnedge way till he's sick as a nun's cat. Aye, that's best. An' I'll even let ye have a beast for Leezie. Ye can return it to the Earl's stables when ye reach Embra."

"Most thoughtful an' generous o' you, sir!"

Geordie was grinning. "Aye, sir, an' it'll cost ye but four testoons."

Master Matheson's smile didn't alter at the quibble. Maybe his eyes narrowed a touch, but he was all affability. "O' course, sir!" How much would the Earl get of it, I wondered. "An' I pray you permit me offer you a wee token o' thanks for all your help." He could have saved some breath there, I thought, show Geordie a glimpse of silver and his hand would beat yours to your pouch.

They galloped waving off up the side of the Hermitage Water. We waved back, and started up Liddell-side; but the second they were out of sight, just as I was about to speak up, Master Matheson stopped and grinned at me. "Can we trust them no to tell your dad, Leezie?"

I grinned back. "Geordie Dalgleish's nickname's the Two-legged Tod. Geordie Tod. Aye, an' he's sly as any fox. He'd set dad after us for a plack, no trouble to his conscience — if he has one." As we turned back, ma sighing with pain and weariness already, towards the road to Canonbie, I was both glad and sorry that he'd seen through Geordie. I'd not want to be caught, sure; but it was disconcerting to find the city man so shrewd.

We went away south and west, far from any road we might be expected on, and kept good watch. If we saw anyone on the road, which wasn't often, we drew off to hide till they were by. There would aye be a herd lad or gangrel body that we'd miss, but with a bit of luck word of us wouldn't come to dad's ears.

It took us near three weeks to reach Edinburgh. We stayed in a flesher's house in Sanquhar for ten days, and ma slept near the whole time. I worried about her, but Master Matheson said not to; "For it's just the strain liftin' off her, Leezie. She's fair worn out. If I'd known how bad she was. . . But no, she's better away. I didn't reckon on bein' out this long, but Sir James'll just have to do without me a week or two yet. There's men enough to do Her Grace's biddin', an' I'm needed here. You could do wi' a rest yoursel', lassie."

I didn't feel tired; more full of joy and energy. At first I spent hours watching the road for dad following us, but after a few days the fear wore off me. I sat with ma till my restlessness drove me out. I couldn't join the women of the house in their cooking and sewing, for I knew nothing about that. But I got on fine with the men Master Matheson had hired to guard us, and spent a lot of time with them. They were a hard lot; Danny, whose father and brother had been hanged last year, was their leader. Each had killed his man, or men, and I was pleased that once I'd proved myself, by spitting farther than any of them, they accepted me. They taught me how to throw my knife better, and I listened happily to their tales of raids into England and the Lowlands.

They'd bet on anything, I discovered. I won Danny's old sheepskin jacket at dice, wagering against a kiss. They all laughed at me, for they knew by now I'd not let them touch me, but I'd have paid if I'd lost. The jacket was so fine and warm, in spite of the holes, and I was so happy to win, I gave him a quick peck anyway, and taught him some French swear-words to sweeten the deal. He didn't grudge it to me; he'd get a new one off the next sheep he stole.

The next day the rain poured down. It was too cold and wet for even me to go out, as I couldn't wear my fine sheepskin. I'd sunk it in a stream overnight to drown the fleas and it was steaming dry at the hearth. The men chased me from the stable where they were swopping lies about Girls I Have Known, for they said my catty comments cramped their style. Ma was sleeping, as usual, in one room. In the other we were all on top of each other. The flesher, who had a nasty cold, was steaming next to my jacket, with a towel round his head and his feet in a hot mustard bath, near wishing the lot of us well away in spite of the silver he was getting for our lodging. The goodwife was sewing at ma's dress by the fire with her daughters.

I fidgeted about the house till she came near crowning me with the spit. At last, to save everybody's temper and probably my skull, Master Matheson said, "I'm away to see to Betsy,

Leezie. Would you like to learn how?"

"I've tended the cuddy this six year, sir," I replied, huffed.

He laughed. "Betsy's my pistol! I'm goin' to clean an' reload her. Well?"

I jumped at the chance, of course. It — she — was the newest make, plain, but good and heavy and longer than my forearm. She had two barrels, with a flintlock for each barrel. He told me about a pistol he'd seen with only one barrel, but three locks, spaced along it. You loaded powder, ball and a thick wad three times down the barrel, and if you'd judged the thickness correctly, there was a load opposite each touch-hole. Then if the front loads didn't blow back and set off the ones behind, you had three shots instead of just one or two. "Too many ifs for me, lass," he said, carefully reaming out the old loads. "Betsy'll do me. See the screw here's brass, in case it should spark against the inside o' the barrel? I can do without blowin' off my hand." He was joking, but I knew it was really dangerous, and he puffed out with relief when the old powder was all out in a wee black heap on the stool top.

"It looks all right, but you can't aye tell. I'll just try a wee drop."

Lighting a splinter at the fire, he touched it to a tiny pinch of the powder. It suddenly flared up and gave me a start. He grinned, but shook his head. "No, it's no as lively as it should be. It's done for wi' the damp."

I watched fascinated as he cleaned the barrels, adjusted and snapped the flints over and over till the tiny sparks regularly showered glittering into the flash-pans. He showed me how to hold her firm, in both hands, point and fire, and let me cock the locks, aim, and snap the trigger. The great ball at the end of the butt balanced her in your grip, and then when you'd fired your shots, he said, or she had missed fire, and you were left with just a lump of ironmongery, she made a grand club. She had saved his life more than once.

He told me about some of his adventures. The most common message he was sent was to carry a legal letter of arrest or recovery of debt, and he was often very unpopular with the folk he was seeking. Sometimes, too, he had to carry money, and then had to beware of thieves. It was exciting, and I quite lost my ill-feeling towards him.

In the middle of one story he looked up and broke off. Ma had wakened. We gave her some broth, and she lay quietly smiling over at us as we went on working with the pistol.

"Mind, she's no a toy!" Master Matheson warned me sternly. "Never point her at a man you're no ready to kill, an' if there's nobody in sight be even more careful. Last year I was near killed when a lad in the next room fired by mistake, an' the ball went through the wall within a foot o' my ear. He didn't know it was loaded, he said, gormless gowk! An Armstrong; you might guess. Them an' the Douglases are as daft as they come. And the Kerrs. No enough brain to keep their ears apart, an' wild as polecats. I half-killed that one in return, though; he'll mind better in future." I promised him I'd be careful and watched him measure out fresh powder from the ram's horn flask and reload.

When the last wad was rammed firmly in to hold the ball in place, he showed me how to put a pinch of powder on the flash-pan and clip the cover down over it. "Then you pray your powder's dry, an' doesn't get blown away by the wind, or wetted by the rain, or tipped off when your hand joggles," he said ruefully. "She's a braw piece, Betsy, but she's like most women — no that reliable." I started to get huffy with him again, until I saw he was teasing me in a gentle, friendly way. Unused to this, I didn't know what to do, but I decided to grin, and he nodded. "Aye, lass, you'll learn fast."

"Thank you, sir," I said, pleased at the praise, but a bit puzzled. "But your pistol's that interestin', anybody would learn."

"Aye." He grinned even wider. "Now take care an' no tilt your hand when you cock her, or you'll lose all the powder in the flash-pan. An' mind an' lift the cover to the pan, or she'll no fire at all!" he said. "The times I've forgotten that! It's — it's disconcertin', when there's a dozen men howlin' at your tail. Now I'll put her away, an' your ma can rest easy again."

"Aye," she murmured, "I must admit I dinnae like them.

They're modern, I suppose, but — I prefer the older things, whiles."

"Aye, you'll like me, then," he smiled to her, "for I'm no callant."

"Ye're never more than thirty-five, sir? Maybe thirty-eight?"

"Merci du compliment, madame! I'm forty-four," he bowed.

She laughed. "De rien, monsieur! Your years rest light on ye." I couldn't understand it; forty-four? That was ancient! But then, ma was aye polite.

Ma asked him if he knew how the Queen had learned where she was.

"Now that I couldn't say, Mistress Hepburn —" he said.

She raised a hand quickly. "Sir, pray ye do me an obligement an' dinnae mention that name. It's my belief I'd be better no usin' it. My man'd find me too easy, an' — an' I dinnae want that. So if it please ye to cry me by my own maiden name, Sinclair? An' you as well, Leezie. Will ye do that for me, sir?"

"Aye will I, mistress, an' gladly. Mistress Sinclair it is. An' Leezie Sinclair, eh? Fine. Well, like I say, I don't know how Her Grace learned your whereabouts. Did she know your wedded name?"

"Oh, aye, sir! She sent me gifts for my weddin' — both my weddin's. A length o' fine yellow fustian for a gown, an' a silver spoon. Not that I kept them long. They went the first raid." She sighed wistfully.

"No, they didnae," I told her. It was time for me to tell what I'd seen. "It was dad took the spoon. He telled me no to say a word or he'd kill me."

Master Matheson's lips tightened in anger, but ma just sighed again and shrugged. "Aye, well. That's Adam. But aye, sir, the Queen knew my name."

"Well, then," he said, "that'll maybe explain it. She'd time to talk wi' the Earl o' Bothwell on the Chaseabout Raid —"

"The what?" I had no idea what he was talking about, nor had ma.

"Did you never hear? Perched away up your hill there like hares, no, you mightn't. Well, you know the Queen wed in the summer there? A Stewart, Henry Darnley, son o' Meg Douglas an' that twisted rogue the Earl o' Lennox, that's changed sides from Scotland to England an' back that often he has to look at his breeks to see which way he's facin' the day. This lad's by way o' bein' a cousin o' Her Grace, an' o' Elizabeth o' England as well, an' weddin' him would bring the both o' them closer to the English throne that Mary's aye claimed, so he came up to Scotland — well, his mother sent him up, she's that ambitious for him she'd send him to Tartary if she thought it would do any good. He's a handsome long lad, an' minded his manners, an' Mary fell in love wi' him. An you know, mistress, Her Grace has a soft spot for weak, sick folk?"

Ma nodded. "Aye, sir, her first husband, the wee King o' France, was aye sickly, an' she nursed him kindly. Did this Henry Darnley fall sick?"

"He did that, wi' the measles. So he could lie there, lookin' pale an' grateful for her visits —"

"When the spots had worn off!" They laughed, and I felt warm and pleased.

"Aye, lass. Or maybe it was Elizabeth forbiddin' the match as settled her on it, for Mary's aye been used to her own way, so the opposition just set her mind on him. Whatever, she wed him. An' she's regretted it ever since."

"Why that, sir?" Ma looked as puzzled as I was.

"He's — he's just unbearable. He's arrogant, an' lazy, an' sulky, an' insults even the lords that's been Mary's closest advisers, her half-brother Moray, Morton that's his own uncle — he's set them all against him. An' he's greedy, an' if he doesn't get his wants he's like a stoat wi' the toothache. He said Moray had too much land, an' Moray accused Darnley o' plannin' to murder him — their servants were fightin' in the streets, mistress. It ended up wi' nobody for Darnley but his daft friends — that Italian they call Seigneur Davie, that's the Queen's secretary, the jumped-up rascal, an' the others — why the Queen takes in all these foreigners, struttin' an' lordin' it over their betters, as if Scots weren't good enough. . . Anyway. Them. An' o' course the Queen.

"Well, the finish o' it was that Moray an' a many more rose in revolt against the pair o' them, Mary an' Henry Darnley. But she raised an army — no him, he couldn't raise his fork to his mouth without somebody told him how — an' the two sides were nippin' in an' out o' Edinburgh at each other's backsides like a pair o' terriers. That's why they cried it the Chaseabout Raid. In the end o' it, Moray ran away down to England to Elizabeth, an' Mary came chasin' down after him, wi' her man beside her in a right fancy suit o' gilded armour that took six lads to polish for him, right down to Dumfries. That would be — September. Aye, near three month back.

"But anyway, one o' the men as supported the Queen against the rebellion was your own James Hepburn, Earl o' Bothwell, no that long back from France, his conscience all new-minted fresh after bein' outlawed. An' Mary put him back in his place as Lieutenant o' the Border. She maybe mentioned to him that she'd had a nurse married a Hepburn. Thinkin' to please her he'd seek news o' you. That'll be how she got the word, an' it put the notion in her head."

"Ye're most likely right, sir," ma murmured. She was looking tired again.

"Sir," I asked, "a man as is just pardoned from outlawry — how can he be made a great officer? To be a general for the Queen that outlawed him before? It doesnae make sense."

Master Matheson shook his head. "It's his right, Leezie, his hereditary right, like bein' Lord High Admiral o' Scotland, pirate that he is! But the Queen has no better servant, for all he's a wild rogue. He was outlawed for some trouble over a lass, nothin' treacherous, like some, just natural wildness. But Bothwell's clever, you must admit. A right fly man. Did you hear how he made his fortune? Stealin' one o' the loads o' gold that Elizabeth o' England sent up to help the Protestant nobles against the Queen's mother, while Mary hersel' was still a lassie in France. Ten thousand pound, English pounds, no Scots, they say — but that's puffed a fair bit, I'm thinkin'. Aye, he was rich a while on that, till he gambled it all away. An' now he's Sheriff o' Edinburgh! Him!" He looked over at ma again. "Sh, Leezie, she's asleep again."

No surprise either, I thought, my head spinning with all the news and names. Strange how like Geordie Tod he sounded when he spoke of the Earl of Bothwell. Neither of them would trust him, but both admired him.

A day or two later we rode on to Edinburgh, by easy stages for ma's sake. As she slowly recovered, she gradually blossomed into smiles and jokes, as I could just remember her from long ago, and kept us all cheerful. Not all the time; often she'd shiver and snap at us, and the fear came back into her eyes. But she was improved. Even her speech became more ladylike again.

To please her, and now that dad wasn't there to beat us both if I tried what he called putting on airs, I started learning how to behave in a way that no longer drew amazed stares. I didn't swop dirty stories or wrestle with the serving lads. At table I didn't shout or swear, or spit, or pick my nose, or scratch my backside. Practical jokes were banned. My knife was hidden except at meals, and I tried a daft thing called a fork that dribbled sauce all down my front. Fingers were far easier. I tasted wine, and didn't like it as much as ale, for it was thin and sour, but it was strong; I learned why dad's temper had been so bad, some mornings.

Though I still rode in my breeches, I gradually collected new clothes, gifts from the wives in the houses where we put up on the road; a cloak, shoes, a skirt. By the time we saw, and smelled, the reek of Edinburgh's coal fires, I felt every inch a lady, fit to serve the Queen herself.

The road through the busy farmlands to the Cramond Bridge over the River Almond was thronged in the mild, damp weather, and we passed sleds and packhorses taking goods to and from the city, droves of pigs, sheep, cows, geese and ducks going in to market, and many folk walking with high-laden backs. Sometimes there was a galloping horse, or a message runner, and once another Messenger-at-Arms who stopped to whisper in Master Matheson's ear for a few seconds before he raced on again. Master Matheson shook his head.

"What's wrong, sir?" asked ma. With her arm still in a sling and unable yet to turn or move her hand, she couldn't draw on reins, and still rode with Master Matheson, tucked in before him in the shelter of his arms and cloak.

"Nothin', mistress," he replied with a smile. "The Queen's Grace isn't awaitin' your arrival just as eagerly as I'd been expectin'. She's been no well, but she's racin' about like a cat wi' a burned tail, gallopin' as if she was daft. They're wonderin' if she's wi' bairn at all, Alec says. For if she was —"

"She'd take more heed?" ma asked. He nodded, frowning, but suddenly peered down the hill. I looked where his eyes led. There was a company riding up the road towards us. A fine company, with soldiers behind and before it, and ladies in brilliant dresses, and — it couldn't be! Not the Queen herself!

"Come by!" called Master Matheson urgently. We drew to the side, to leave room for the bright cavalcade sweeping gaily towards us.

First there were six men running, with long staves, who shouted to us to clear the way. We moved right off the road onto the field beside it. About fifty yards behind them came a score of soldiers, in red like Master Matheson, but with helmets and body-armour over their doublets, and long hackbuts slung on their backs. They looked carefully at us, but passed without stopping. Then behind again, far enough to feel separate, cantered a group of young men and women, one man with a fine deep voice carolling a thumping tune in time with the beat of his horse's hooves, the others laughing and joining in the chorus. At their head rode a tall woman, not much over twenty, dressed in black and gold on a white horse, a huge ruby holding the white feather nodding in her flat-crowned, gold-beaded hat. Laughing, she cantered towards us, great brown eyes in her white face turning for a swift glance as she passed, one hand in a red glove lifting in a light response to our bows. Then they were by, with a rattle of hooves and a glitter of gold, a snatch of melody and a flash of embroidered skirts and slashed sleeves.

But just up the road, as a second group of running men in red livery passed us, the riders swung in a circle and drew up. A man rode back a little towards us and called, beckoning. Master Matheson immediately set ma down and galloped up the hill to them. I slid down too, and we stood forgotten, staring, as the rear-guard in turn stopped in front of us.

"What the deil is it this time?" a voice growled above our heads. "Four times already — the baggage carts'll reach Linlithgow before us at this rate!"

"Shut yer gob, ye blatherskite Gordon! We've all day, an' if ye'd drunken less ale last night ye'd be enjoyin' the pleasant ride. Cheer up, man! It's no that bad a day, an' no that far till yer dinner!"

A third voice chimed in. "It's no drink that's the matter wi' the Gordon, sergeant! He'd a boil on his bum lanced yesterday, an' his saddle's kissin' him hard as Kate Lenton!" They whistled and laughed, paying us no heed.

Suddenly the sergeant stiffened. "Look out, lads!" They all straightened, gazing up the road, to where a white horse was galloping full tilt back down the rutted path. Ma drew in her breath with a hiss at such risk.

The Queen herself — the Queen! — skidded her pony to a halt, slipped down unaided from her embroidered saddle, and while her friends raced after her and a runner leapt to take the reins, she lifted ma gently from her knees, took her in her arms and kissed her. "No, no, Janet," she murmured, "don't kneel to me, my dear!"

She led ma to sit on the bank by the road. One man, the ugly one who had been singing, leaped forward to lay his frilled and braided russet cloak with a flourish for a cushion and was rewarded with a smile and a nod. The Queen spread her own cloak and skirts smoothly, sat beside ma, and took her hand. "That is comfortable now, Janet, no? Fine. Thank you, Davie." The ugly man bowed again, with a flashing smile, waved the soldiers and our men back, and strutted to join the glittering group staring surreptitiously from just up the track. "Now," the clear voice went on, "tell me how did you come to break your arm?" Her voice was Scottish, with little of the foreign accent I'd expected. It was rather high, but pleasant to listen to, and I stood by the horses, staring mouth and eyes agape at my own mother talking to the Queen of Scots.

Ma was fluttered by the attention, and flushed brightly, but stammered that she'd had an accident. "Aye," Her Grace said, half smiling, half grim, "but Master Matheson told me different. We'll see can we no do somethin' about that sometime." There was a flash in the heavy-lidded eyes. Her gown was laid with swirls of black and gold cord all over the body and sleeves — on just a riding dress! "Aye me, my dear Janet, it fair lifts my heart to see you again! I'm sorry I can't wait now, but later there'll be many times we can be comfortable together, as we used be years bye, is that no true?"

"Aye, Your Grace," ma whispered. "But you're a bittie big now to sit on my knee for songs or riddles to keep you from cryin'."

The Queen laughed again. "Bee, baw, babbity, babbity, babbity," she sang softly. I was astonished that a Queen should have been hushed with the same songs as myself; but then I saw how foolish I was. "But I need no riddle-me-rees now. No from you, at any rate, for I have more than enough o' my own! But mine don't aye stop my tears." Bitterness burned behind her smile. Somehow she was speaking to ma easily and intimately as if they'd never parted.

It was maybe that ease that made ma say, "Aye, Your Grace, you have riddles. One I've heard is whether or no you're wi' child? For the way you're actin', racin' about like that, I'd wonder. The bairn I nursed had more sense."

The Queen's eyes frosted for a moment. She looked over at me, but ma said, "My daughter Leezie, Your Grace. She knows when to keep her mouth shut." I did? About this, anyway. "Well? Is it true?" There was a firmness about ma that I'd not seen in years; not since the last baby had died. I wondered again, how ma could speak so to the Queen; but maybe it wasn't a Queen ma saw, but the wee bairn she'd nursed years before.

For a moment there was a tension, as if anger wasn't far off. But then Queen Mary's head sank, and she looked away from the love in ma's face. "Aye," she whispered. "I'm with child. And whiles I wish I wasn't."

I saw ma's knuckles whiten as she gripped hard on the

Queen's hand. "You must never wish that! You hear me, Your Grace? Never! If you've a babe within you, it's because the Lord willed it; an' dare you set yoursel' up against the Lord? Just you mind, Your Grace, that your bairn'll be a fine lad an' a great King. An' take proper care o' yoursel' now, like a clever lassie." In her urgency she beat the red-gloved hand gently on her knee.

The white feather waved in the cold wind, and the great ruby flashed as its wearer bowed her head. "Like a clever wee lassie!" she murmured, and sighed. "Aye, Janet, that was long ago! You'll no coax me wi' that now!"

"More's the pity, Your Grace," ma said quietly.

The plume nodded gently, sadly, for a moment, and then the Queen braced her shoulders. The plume lifted gallantly, and she smiled. "You sound like Knox, Janet, you know that?" She mimicked someone. "It is the will o' the Lorrd, grreat Jehovah, who smites kings as easily an' frreely as the commonalty!"

"Aye, Your Grace? A preacher? A bother to you, is he?" asked ma.

"Ach, an itch, Janet, an itch that needs scratchin'! An arrogant rascal. But he's no the only one o' them I have round me!" She smiled, sighed again, and glanced round. "I must away, Janet. I'm stayed for." True enough, her courtiers, dismounted politely out of earshot and straining to lip-read, were fidgeting restlessly, and their laughter was high-pitched and brief. I wondered if any of them had boils. Suddenly I realised the Queen's eyes were on me. "Your daughter, you said? In breeks? For better safety, aye. The roads aren't as safe as I'd like them, but. . . Aye, they're more comfortable, lass, no?"

I blushed, my throat choked with delighted consternation, stammering something about breeches being easier to ride in. Her smile warmed and charmed me. I felt she cared about me, even me, Leezie. I loved her.

"Aye," she said. "Leezie, is it? Aye, then, Leezie, I've worn breeks often, for masquin', an' wanderin' the streets at night as a jest. I've the figure for it, no?" She had indeed, tall and energetic. "An' this side-saddle's elegant, but me, I prefer the freedom o' ridin' astride. It was my good-mother — my first husband's mother showed me how. Aye, the Queen of France, Catherine de Medici herself, she rode astride. You'd no think it, would you? Here in Scotland I can't do it often. Just when I'm out hawkin' wi' my friends." She looked over at the gay group of men and women waiting for her. I noticed some carried hawks on leather gloves on their left hands, and one of the running men had a rack slung on his shoulders with six hawks perched, hooded and leashed in red and gold. The Queen sighed at a thought of her own. "This isn't France. . ."

I nodded, astonished to find myself sympathising with her, and wishing with all my heart I could do something to help ease her of her cares.

She shook her head to clear the troubling thought. "Now, Janet, you're no to come runnin' about after me wi' that arm. Go in to Edinburgh an' find yoursel' lodgings. Master Matheson'll look after you well — tell him I said he was to take special care o' you!" Her true affection for ma was clear.

"He's doin' that now, Your Grace," ma smiled, and the Queen smiled back.

"I'm glad to hear it. He'll find you a good place. You'll be more comfortable in the town than in the castle till — till my time comes to bear the child there." Her voice wavered slightly, and steadied. "But as soon as may be you'll go down to Robert Rychardson, that's my treasurer. He'll see you right for silver. You'll make ready everythin' for the bairn, all its napkins an' vests an' wee soft things. For there's a crowd o' noble folk will fight for the honour o' seein' to the rich things, the tapestries an' cloth o' gold coverlets, but none I'd trust like you to remember that inside the velvets there's a wee babe that has to be kept cosy an' happy. That's what you did for me, Janet, an' that's what I want you to do for my bairn."

"And welcome, my dear," said ma. She nearly hugged the Queen, and I watched as Queen Mary smiled at her, seeing the urge, and knowing with regret why she stopped herself. But ma wasn't finished. As the Queen started to rise, ma held her back.

I heard a shocked hiss from the group on the far side of the road. "An' you'll take heed to yoursel', now, an' to the bairn within you?"

The Queen freed her embroidered sleeve and rose slowly to her full, tall height. She looked away towards the town for a long moment before she spoke. "Aye, Janet. I will take care." With a bright, brittle smile, she added, "On my honour as a Queen!" and as ma stood and curtseyed again, she walked over to her waiting horse, was put up to the saddle, and then, to the surprise of her followers, she walked it away up the road. Before she turned the corner of the brae out of sight, she lifted a hand and waved back to us.

The courtiers and soldiers exchanged startled glances with each other, and eyed ma strangely as they reined back their horses to the new pace. Who were these tattered folk who had such an effect on the Queen?

Babs

As we rode on towards the smoke of the town rising grey before us, Master Matheson pointed out the landmarks. "See there, Leezie? There's the Castle o' Edinburgh, away up on its rock."

Ma nodded round at me from her perch before him. "Aye, lass. The town's like the bones o' a herrin'. The castle's the head, an' the High Street an' then the Canongait's the spine runnin' down the ridge, you can just see the house tops, an' the arches — see them? — that's the crown on the Kirk o' St Giles."

"They call it the High Kirk now," he warned us.

"Aye? Well, there's dozens o' wee lanes an' wynds runnin' down from the High Street on each side o' the ridge like the ribs o' the herrin', an' all packed full o' wee shops an' stalls."

"Like lice on Leezie's sheepskin!" Master Matheson said, and she flapped a hand back at him, laughing to make me grin too.

"Ach, you! Look, Leezie! The city's well protected. On the north here there's the Nor' Loch to guard the town, an' from the Castle Rock round the south there's the wall, an' the Burgh Loch an' all the marshes there."

Master Matheson turned serious for a moment, over his

happiness and relief at nearing the end of his long mission. "Watch out if you go round by that way, Leezie; Johnny Faa's the King o' Little Egypt down there, an' the gypsies aye like to keep theirsel's to theirsel's. There's too many folk about for their likin' now, for a good bit o' the trees there are cleared, an' the front o' most o' the town houses built up wi' the wood. The English burned it all about fifteen year back. The wall was damn little protection then."

Ma tut-tutted and shook her head disapprovingly, her eyes bright as she looked across at the city she'd known so long before. "See the crags at the far side there, Leezie, an' the hill? That's Arthur's Seat, it's a park for the Queen to hunt in. An between that an' the ridge, at the far end o' the Canongait, like at the tail o' the fish, there's the Palace o' Holyroodhouse."

"That's where you'll find Rab Rychardson, mistress, if you can see him under the heaps o' papers. How he doesn't drown in them the Lord knows." The two of them laughed together, their breath puffing in a single white cloud.

We rode right round the Nor' Loch to the end of the city wall that had been built to keep the English out, and hadn't succeeded. It was tumbledown in places, with houses built right onto it, and some even sticking out over it. We came in by the leper hospital and along busy Leith Wynd to the Canongait, where the priests had lived till not so long ago. Many of the court now had houses there to be near the Palace of Holyrood at the far end of the street.

At the crossing we turned right to the Netherbow Port that led into the town, and Master Matheson paid off the guards. I promised Danny I'd take good care of his sheepskin for him. They galloped whooping away down the road with their silver, Danny turning in the saddle to blow me kisses as they went.

"Daft gowk," said Master Matheson with a scowl and a smile. "Come on, lass." He whistled piercingly through his teeth and waved to the gatekeeper.

"Aye, ye're back at last, Patey!" the man cried to him. "We've missed ye! Who's that ye've got wi' ye? A bonny bird, that one! Ye've good taste, man!"

Ma smiled and blushed. Master Matheson shook his fist,

grinning. "Has old Babs Martin got a new tenant in her wee top rooms yet, Johnnie?" he shouted.

The man shook his head. "No to my knowledge, Patey. No since David Couper was banished. Just the Pattersons. No, the rooms should still be free."

"Thanks, Johnnie!" Master Matheson called. "I'll see you again!" As we rode through, ducking under the portcullis in the big stone arch, he warned us that the gate was shut at sunset, and we'd have to rouse the keeper and pay a fee to get in or out after that. "An' Johnnie Galloway's a hard man to waken. Snores like a hog, does John, an' sleeps like the dead."

I stared as we threaded through the crowding traffic up the High Street. It was cobbled, and far wider than Langholm; three men linking hands could scarce span it, and there was room for a many busy stalls. The houses towered three and four storeys high, wee wooden roofs and galleries jutting out all over them. The windows had bright-painted shutters, and some had glass above the wood. All the ground floors were shops, but I'd neither time nor peace to look at the goods, nor up at the castle lowering above us.

In front of us a man driving a pig tried to pass a lass herding five geese up the street. He tripped over one of them and fell, dropping the rope on the pig's hind leg. The young pig, squealing wildly, charged down the street towards us, and the crowd erupted in shouts and yells. Immediately an inquiring head popped out of the hole in every shutter.

There was a wild carry-on for a minute while they chased the pig and the geese. One flapped away under my pony's belly. The astonished beast reared and kicked, and I was near off for a minute. Then a tall lad dived at the pig, flat on his face, to grab its back legs, rise to his knees and hold its trotters up off the ground, so that when it tried to kick or bite him it fell over. He'd a fair strength to hold the writhing animal, I thought, as its owner ran up to grip its tether again. The lad was looking for a plack reward, and the lass bewailing the loss of one of her geese, stolen in the confusion. We left the man and lass arguing who should pay the lad, and rode slowly on.

I'd seen crowds at the Martinmas Fairs in Langholm, but

there were more people here than at a dozen fairs. I was near smothered with folk's closeness, the noise of their chaffering and shouting their wares, the stink of the gutter and the piles of rubbish silted in every corner, with dogs and pigs and half-naked bairns scratching about in them. I couldn't breathe. I was near panic.

"Do you remember it, Mistress Hepburn?" Master Matheson shouted to ma.

"Aye, sir, but no — no as crowded," she replied, rather faintly. I wasn't the only one to feel overwhelmed, then. Somehow that calmed me.

"Aye, there's a good few folk lives here," he called proudly. "Near twenty thousand, they say. A many o' the lords lives down there in the Cowgait, the next street down, Leezie. There's no like to be a place for you there. But there's a wife just round the corner here has rooms at the top she lets out — an' her last tenant lost his gear, an' near lost his life, for darin' to go to the Mass. Aye, if you don't attend regular at the kirk, you'll have the elders at your door, an' be hauled before the Kirk Session. An' no argy-bargy, Leezie."

He reined in his horse. "This is it, just below the fleshers' stalls. There was a house o' the Black Friars down this way. They were driven out years back, but it's still cried Blackfriars' Wynd." As we dismounted, the lad who'd gripped the pig seemed to pop out of the cobbles with a wide, friendly grin, ready to hold the horses.

We turned down the path, shadowy between the tall houses and so narrow I could almost touch both sides just by stretching out my arms.

"Mind you turn in by Sandy Bruce the flesher's," Master Matheson said. "Above him there's Sir James Balfour. Blasphemous Balfour, they cry him. Keep clear o' him. An' this second house we're passin' — Leezie, watch out for the folks here as well. Tam Paterson — Katy's Tam they call him — he has the sword shop there. There's no harm in him himsel', but he's a boozy deil, like his friends. An' the first floor, it used to be the Earl o' Moray's, but he's gone, an' it's James Ormiston lives there now — Black Ormiston. He's a friend o' Balfour, an' the Earl o' Bothwell. An' there's no that many villains to beat him — him an' his uncle Rab both."

"If he's friend to Bothwell, that goes wi'out sayin', sir," I said, trying to seem cocky. "Why come here, if it's that dangerous?"

He grinned at me. "Wi' all the rogues in Edinburgh, lassie, I'd be hard put to it to find ye a street that has none! But Bassandyne the printer at the top's a good man, an' the third house there, that's where the Master o' Maxwell lives, an' he's honest. Well, fairly. An' on the ground floor below him there's John Stirlin', servant to the Roman Archbishop o' St. Andrews, an' his wife. Well, no his wife. Men in holy orders aren't allowed to wed these days. But there's many churchmen disagrees wi' that, an' still has their wives unofficial-like. They're as respectable as they come, in spite o' what the Kirk says about them. There's a tailor in the garret. He'd maybe make you a new gown, for meanin' no offence, Mistress He — Sinclair," ma smiled at him as he hesitated, "you're no dressed as you should be." She nodded agreement. "An' he's cheap, for he's no in the guild. Anyway, this is Babs Martin's, right opposite. You bide here a minute till I go in to her."

He ducked under a low, narrow lintel. A warm, savoury smell made my mouth water, and I sighed. "A pie shop, ma! I wish I'd a plack. I could eat a horse!"

She smiled back, stretching to ease her back. "Aye, let's hope we get settled here. At least we'll no starve. An' we'll no be bored — a pie shop's as good as a barber's to get all the gossip."

Just at that a scratchy voice came from the shop door, arguing fiercely with Master Matheson. "No, no, Peter! I've never had a lone wife in the house before, exceptin' Kate, an' look at her, an' I'm no havin' another! Aye pryin' an' peerin', an' askin' wee favours, an' criticisin', an' pokin' her long nose into other folks's business! No, no, sir, I'll no do't, an' that's flat!" A tiny wee woman skipped out of the shop and peered up at us, white hair wisping from under her snowy cap, shrill and determined as she railed on. I glanced at ma to see should I be angry or amused, but she was swaying slightly, and Master Matheson was supporting her.

The old wife's scolding stopped. "What's wrong wi' ye, lass?" she snapped.

"My man broke my arm near a month back, an' it's no right yet," ma said faintly. I was surprised to hear her speak of it, her that had always been so set on keeping it all from the neighbours. But this was Edinburgh, of course.

The little woman frowned, smoothing her apron. "Yer man? Aye. Men! An' no set yet? What have ye been doin' — usin' it? There was never a woman yet could leave an arm to mend in peace. Come away in and have a seat, then, mistress — ye're as white as my linen kerchief, an' I dinnae want ye fallin' on my doorstep — folks might think it was one o' my pies had done for ye!"

As she ushered ma in the door, Master Matheson grinned and winked at me.

I jumped as I entered, for there was a woman sitting just inside the door. A big wife, older than ma, all bundled up in shawls and plaids in spite of the heat that hit me like a blast from the oven. But this woman was scarfed to the forehead and mittened to the knuckles, sitting there grinning at me. Then I saw the staring eyes, too wide-set, and the hanging lips, and sighed with mixed relief and pity. A daftie. I knew such a lad in Canonbie. Poor wife.

Ma was already seated on a stool by the counter where a fine display of pies was spread. Plump. Steaming. My mouth filled urgently with sweet liquid at the heavenly scent, and I sniffed long and longingly. Mistress Martin was talking to ma and Master Matheson. If I could just. . . She'd not miss a wee one, surely. . . I started to edge towards the counter, but suddenly from behind me there was a great grunt, and a violent push in my back. I whipped round.

The old wife laughed heartily. "Ach, never heed her, laddie. That's just my daughter Ina. She'll do ye no harm — unless ye're at stealin' my pies!"

I denied it hastily and heartily, and tried to smile at the great bulk sitting hunched up by the door. "Good day, Ina," I said cheerfully. "I'm pleased to meet ye." She grunted again, her

44

eyes glinting above the scarves — was she laughing at me? The top half of the heap of shawls bowed to me, over and over.

"Stop that, now, Ina!" Mistress Martin said. "She's no daft, son, though she looks it. She knows every word we say, an' every soul that steps up the wynd. She's just — she cannae move hersel' right, that's all." The big woman grinned loosely, her full mouth sagging open, her shallow, far-apart eyes intent on my face, and nodded. As the action repeated and repeated, Mistress Martin again snapped, "Stop that!" The great head jerked obediently to a halt and the fusty heap of shawls settled into stillness again.

I tried to think of something to say, to cover my awkwardness. "D'ye work here, then, Ina?" I asked. There was another grunt, and the broad face leaned forward again into the light from the door. She said nothing, just grinned at me, mouth agape, breathing heavily, not blinking. I began to feel I was in a nightmare. Then I shook my head. Nonsense, of course she couldn't answer. Even if her mother thought she had all her wits, it was clear she hadn't. How daft was she, I wondered. Maybe she'd not notice, if I went slow enough. . . But as my hand started to inch towards the pies again, the shawls leaned forward threateningly, the smile vanishing, and I moved my hand up to scratch my nose instead. Oh, well.

I looked round to find the others watching me. "Well?" asked Master Matheson. "Do you want a pie?" He knew fine well I did.

"Aye, just take one, then, one o' they broken ones at the end there," squeaked Mistress Martin, "an' we'll nip up to see the room. Will! Will!" It was a second before I realised she was calling someone else. A tall, heavy-set lad in a filthy apron looked up from a table in the dark at the back of the room, where he was rolling out dough. "Have ye no that done yet? The oven'll be stone cold! See to the shop, Will. Mind all the pence goes in the drawer, now! Ina'll keep an eye on ye!" He nodded, stretching, scratching his armpit through a hole in his vest, sneering at me with lips as flabby and bulging as his belly. I disliked him on sight, as I'd not done with the daftie.

The old wife tutted at me as I hesitated over the pies. "On ye go, then," she snapped, "I've no time for gormless gowks as cannae make up their minds. Are ye wantin' one or no?" She helped ma up from the stool, muttering to herself. I smiled nervously at Ina and gingerly reached for one of the broken pies. The huge head just nodded and smiled, and with a sigh of relief and anticipation I lifted the juiciest, crispest, flakiest pastry I'd ever set tooth into, and followed the others in a chin-licking ecstasy of oyster gravy.

The stair was inside, first a stone flight rising in a corner of the shop behind the door, and turning up and across one wall. From the upper corner it spiralled in wood past a fine big door on the first floor, and on up another tighter circle. Underfoot it was warm; "Aye, son," chirped the old wife, "that's from the oven. It's built in under the stair itsel', wi' the flue right up the centre there. It heats the whole house, an' all the folks pays me a wee bittie towards the firin'. A groat extra a week for the rooms, but it'll save ye on wood. It's a real bargain." Ma smiled, and nodded, too occupied with struggling up the stair to answer.

On the landing at the top were two small doors. "Here's yours. The other's taken by Mistress Patterson. An' five bairns. All wi' fine, strong, well-exercised voices. Her man's a hammerman in pewter down in Tolbooth Wynd. He's a Kirk elder, an' he's seldom in. A pity the bairns aye are. But when he is in he sings hymns. I wouldnae care, but he sings near as tunefu' as the bairns howl." I spluttered with mirth, and the crumbs flew. "Aye, an' if ye scatter my good pastry like that we'll have every rat in Embra up the stair. Take a bit heed, son. My cat Tibbie's got enough to do in the kitchen." Ma started to laugh helplessly as our door was creaked open.

There were two rooms, sheer luxury. The first was big, about eleven feet by twelve, right against the wall of the stairs so that we got the warmth from the oven. In summer it might be unpleasantly hot, but for the winter it was wonderful. There was a window onto the street and a proper wee fireplace, a row of pegs in a beam at one end to hang things on, and an old cupboard. "See the door's broken and it's too big to get down the stair easy. It's the only thing o' the last tenant's that the Kirk Session didnae take."

The back room was smaller, with a mattress leaking chaff onto the floor under the roof beams where they dipped down on one side. A tiny window looked out through the hole in the shutter over the drying green and away out to the hills south of the town, well away from the crowds. There was an old apple tree down there, and a robin singing. I could breathe there.

Mistress Martin looked round. "Aye, I'll hang a curtain across the room. That'll give you an' yer son a bit privacy, mistress."

I giggled again. "My daughter, Mistress Martin," ma smiled.

"What!" She collapsed into screeches of horrified glee. "Ye're never a lassie? My certes! In breeks! I've never seen the like in all my born days! No, no, lassie, this'll never do! Get them off, get them off, an' get into decent gear before ye set foot in the street again, or I'll tell Maister Knox on ye mysel', that I will!" Him again! Who was this Master Knox, then? Her screeching laughter echoed back to me as she clattered down the stair.

"Well, Leezie?" ma asked. "It's no grand, but Peter — Master Matheson says Mistress Martin's honest, an' if you're too tired to cook for us we can aye buy a pie for the dinner." My mouth full of the last joyful scraps, I nodded enthusiastically, wiping my greasy fingers on the sheepskin jerkin. Ma's face showed pain for a second — did I imagine it? — but then she nodded too.

"Aye, I think so," she said quietly. "It'll do fine. An' at a testoon a week it's within our purse. I thank you, sir." She and Master Matheson smiled at each other.

After that evening, when Mistress Martin introduced us to Master Patterson and his family, I seldom set eyes on our next-door neighbour. I heard him often enough — too often, indeed, for Mistress Martin was quite right about his voice, and he was enthusiastic in his religion. I also heard and sometimes met his thin, tired-looking wife and children, with whiny voices and sly faces. Like slugs, I avoided them as far as I could. I never even learned their names — maybe the wife was called Maisie? But in the two years I lived there I only ever met Jaikie Patterson himself four or five times.

I did meet the tenant of the rooms below, though, that very afternoon.

Ma and I had been out for a look at the shops and stalls, to buy a blanket, a pot, two bowls and some oatmeal. When we found our way back to the pie shop again with these basics for living in our new room, there was Master Matheson blethering to a group of soldiers and Babs Martin at the door. He had just called by, he said, with word that the tailor would be round later.

Willie Grey the scullion was firing up the oven again, and picking his spots to turn your stomach. He didn't improve on further acquaintance, staring and smirking at my skirt and my shirt till I checked for holes or stains, but it was quite clean — cleaner than his, anyway. I suddenly realised what was wrong; it was him, not me, the ill-thoughted lout! I was just going to tear a strip off him, literally, when there was movement at the head of the stair.

A sweet voice, deep for a woman, said, "They'll all be here this night, sire, for sure, for entertainin' you's aye a pleasure as well as a privilege!" Four men started trooping down the stair, more elegantly dressed and richly jewelled than any I'd yet seen, looking back to call something about a new set of strings for the lute. Master Matheson's hand suddenly tugged me down. He was bowing, and trying to make me curtsey. I fell over, my bare legs flinging.

The men stared down at me and guffawed. I scrambled to my feet, ignoring Master Matheson's hand and warning hiss. I could have murdered the lot of them, strangers, Master Matheson, Willie sniggering beside me and all. One tall youth of about eighteen, handsome in a pale kind of way, in rich purple and a lather of jewels, started to sing the old song, 'John, come, kiss me now," but changed the name to 'Joan', and all the others joined in, laughing and gesturing rudely at me. My face was scarlet. My mind started to turn red too.

I was just opening my mouth and drawing breath to swear at them when another person came onto the top step of the stair, above the men. The rich voice called, "What is it?" A woman, in carnation red velvet and damask, stood smiling down at us. Tall, smiling, vivid, elegant. Her skin was black.

I screamed.

All the faces, that had been turning up to her, turned back to me. I screamed again. "It's a deil! Run, sirs! There's a deil after ye! Run!"

Automatically, as I hadn't done for years, I crossed myself, and the small act gave me courage to move. I whirled round, picked up a pie from the counter in each hand, and hurled them with all my strength at the devil, to give the men time to get away, all the time roaring, "Avaunt, Satan, Jesus Christ aid me an' give me thy strength, Oh, Christ save me, save us all. . ." The pies hit, one on the wall above the devil's head, one actually on its shoulder, splattering minced mutton and raisins all down the gorgeous dress. Terrified, triumphant, I reached for another two pies just as Master Matheson flung his arms round me.

I don't remember a great deal about the next few seconds. There was a scream, a lot of laughter and swearing, Master Matheson explaining rapidly that I was just a country lass, I didn't know. . . It all filtered faintly through the hot, buzzing mist that filled my head. Then a hand slapped my face, and the sting of it brought me to my senses.

The black-skinned woman stood in front of me, absolutely furious, her white teeth and dark eyes fairly snapping at me.

"What the hell d'you mean by that, you jaud! I've ne'er been so insulted — never! Would you look at my sleeve there — it'll never be the same again! Four pound an ell, that damask cost! Hell mend you, you hizzy, you'll pay for that! If you've a penny to your name, you'll pay!" She turned a raging black gaze on the men around us, all helpless with mirth. "Aye, sirs, it's a right laugh to you, but it's no you that's had your best gown ruined! Look at the stain — it'll never come out! I'll take it out o' your hide, you wee besom! Deil, am I? I'll deil you! Ach, an' it's right down the front o' my petticoat as well! Ohh!" She was speechless with fury, a pink-palmed hand drawn back to strike again.

Master Matheson held my arms, or I'd have struck out at the dark face before me in sheer terror. There was a scrap of mutton stuck trembling on a pearl on the brim of the fine lace-edged cap. Oddly enough, that was what suddenly made me realise that I'd made a mistake. A dreadful mistake.

Ma and Babs, who had been thrust to the side as the soldiers rushed in the door, pushed through and in front of the woman to where Master Matheson held on to me, though now there was no need — except to keep me on my feet. "What are you at, Leezie?" ma cried. The woman gripped her arm — her sore arm — to tug her away, but let go when ma screamed with pain.

For a moment there was silence. I wriggled out of Master Matheson's grasp as he stepped towards ma in concern, and we helped her to sit on the stool that Babs set for her. He knelt by her, steadying her as she gasped, slowly recovering from the shock, and the eyes turned back to me and the black wife.

She'd calmed slightly, taken aback by the hurt she'd done ma, but was yet in a fine temper. But the callant in embroidered purple satin touched her sleeve, still laughing, and instantly she turned all her attention to him.

"Katie, Katie, be at peace! She's right enough, my fine lady — are you not a true devil, eh?" He slipped an arm round her waist, giggling, and at once she changed from a spitting wildcat to a sleepy puss, purring and curling into his shoulder. He pulled her in tight to his side. "Never mind your gown — no, no, Katrin, I'll get you a new one!" She kissed right into his ear, murmuring something, and his arm tightened again. "Here, then, my sweet devil!" His hand, groping vaguely at the neck of his doublet, with some difficulty pulled a heart-shaped medallion of gold and rubies over his ruff and up over his head, knocking off his flat, plumed hat. One of the other men caught it for him. With yet more difficulty, even though the woman helped him by a sinuous movement of her neck, he looped the chain over her head and slid the jewel slowly into the low neck of her crimson gown, grinning sly and wet-lipped as he jiggled it up and down. She straightened her cap that he'd knocked awry, a look half smile, half irritation, on her face as she watched him watching the medallion. He smirked at her. "Will that content you, then? Are you not a devil, then, my lady? Would we all be your faithful admirers if you weren't, eh?"

As he looked round, the others applauded as if he'd done something clever. I saw Willie's face behind him; they were queerly alike. The woman disengaged herself slowly, ignoring me now as she curtseyed deeply and somehow luxuriously to them all. "If this is the way you pay me for it, sire, she's welcome to spill gravy on my gown any day o' the year!"

Unexpectedly his face changed, and pettishly he pulled away from her. "Aye, that's all you want! All any of you ever want! Just my gold! Well, you'll be disappointed!" There was an immediate chorus of anxious denial from his friends. He reached out his left hand to grasp the thin chain and jerk it, while he slapped her face viciously with his right.

The lady yelped as the chain snapped, and her eyes flashed angrily. Then she cried out, pretending to more hurt than she really felt. "Sire! Ah, sire, what have I done that you should harm me?" She leaned towards him, pouting and pointing out the red line on her dark skin. He peered at it doubtfully. She turned again into his arm. "But I'll forgive you, sire, if you'll forgive me for angerin' you!" Smiling, she unhooked the cord from his lax fingers. "An' as for only wantin' your gold, see here!" She stepped aside, whirled the medallion glittering round her head and hurled it straight into the open oven, where it disappeared in a puff of red ash. We all gasped. Willie reached for the poker, but she stopped him dead with one scorching glare. Her gold-embroidered slipper kicked the door firmly shut. She turned back to the youth. "Now, sire, will ye credit it's yoursel', no your gold that wins all our loyalty an' love?"

After a tense moment the man smiled and pulled her back to him. All the other men seemed to relax. "Now, sir, now, sir," she scolded him smilingly, "mind you've Maitland an' the English Ambassador waitin' on you!"

"Let them wait!" the man muttered thickly. "Is Maitland not my subject, like all the men of Scotland? An' all the wives too, by God! Except my own!" He glowered round, but our blank faces made him lose the thread of his complaint. It took a second for him to recall what he'd been speaking about. "Yes, Maitland! Yes! Waitin' on me, eh? Then let him damn well wait for his King!"

I swear before God that it wasn't till then I realised that this was the King of Scots, Henry Darnley, husband of the Queen that I'd spoken to earlier that morning. And now here he was, the King himself, cuddling this black wife in the wee pie shop.

No wonder the Queen was unhappy. But he looked no happier.

The black woman's lips tightened briefly again, till she broke away from him, smiling sweetly. "An' what about my lute strings, then? How can you be entertained as you should be, Your Grace, if I don't get my new lute strings?" She laughed throatily and her spicy scent wafted over me in a heady cloud.

He gripped her wrist. "Damn your lute strings, Kate Lenton, an' damn you as well! You're my subject too, an' don't you forget it! If I want to spend an hour wi' you, then Maitland can damned well wait my leisure! And damned Elizabeth of damned England's man as well! But if you're more interested in their damned feelings than in mine, I'll take my gold back now! Well?"

She twisted her arm quickly out of his grasp, laughing, and laughing ran towards the stairs. "You're that determined!" she called back. "Come away then, sire, if you've the strength for it!" Her eyes met mine for a second with a strange, angry resignation in them under the smile. Or did I just imagine it?

The King staggered as he followed her up the unrailed steps. He skidded on the broken pies, near fell off the edge, teetered as the others all rushed forward to catch him, recovered, gave us a regal wave of his hand, hawked, spat, cried "My subjects, damn you all!" and vanished round the turn of the stair.

Babs Martin spat.

The Merlin

There was a nasty pause. The oldest lord noticed the soldiers, and before his glare they trickled out. They didn't snigger till they were through the door.

Looking both appalled and delighted, Willie reached for the oven door, but Mistress Martin held up a hand to stop him.

"Will it no be ruined? The pendant?" whispered ma.

"No, a bake-oven's no near hot enough," Master Matheson returned quietly.

One of the lords was counting under his breath. "Ten, eleven. . ."

"A royal the maid's down before twenty," said another with a giggle.

He nodded, and went on, "Fifteen, sixteen, seventeen. . ."

A sour-faced wife clacked down the stair, glowered at us all, snatched the poker from Willie, raked the medallion out of the fire, bobbed a sketchy curtsey to the lords and rattled away up again, juggling the hot gold and polishing the ash off in her apron. A gold piece was silently handed over.

The three lords exchanged looks. "Aye," said the giggler at last. "Never misses a trick, Kate, eh? He'll no be leavin' for a while yet. Charlie, run down to the Palace an' find Maitland. Tell him he's to tell the ambassador the King's no well, or some excuse."

"It had better be good. He's had a many excuses this past week," Charlie replied. The third, the oldest, hushed them both, and they went out together, to chase the spectators and talk quietly for a minute on the steps outside before Charlie hurried off up to the High Street.

The other two came back in, nodded to us, and were heading for the stair when Master Matheson said, "Sir John? Will that be the end o' the affair, then? For these ladies lives here now."

They turned as one on the bottom step and studied him. And Mistress Martin. And ma. And me. At last the elder sighed. "Who's to say, man?" he said quietly. "I'll tell you, lassie; go out an' buy Mistress Lenton a set o' new lute strings, for God's sake, an' she'll forgive you."

"Aye, that's it," piped up Mistress Martin. "She's no a bad lass, Kate, for all she has a wild temper. She'll no hold it against ye that long, if ye dinnae anger her again. But the Lord help ye if ye do!" They both laughed admiringly.

I finally found my voice again. "Sir — sirs?" As the lords looked over at me, I cleared my throat and asked, "Sirs, was — was that the King?"

"Aye, lass," said Sir John, rather grimly, I thought. "That's him. No what you expected, eh?"

I couldn't answer that; I'd not expected anything. Ma was shaking her head sadly. Mistress Martin spat again, and turned with disgust on her face to chase Willie back to the pastry.

I had to ask. "An' her — who's she? The — the black wife?"

"Have you never seen a black woman before?" the young lord asked. As I shook my head, he shook his also, with another giggle. "No, nor ever heard o' one neither, eh? That's Kate Lenton." I knew the name. Something about a saddle. . . "She's famous from here to — to London. Paris. Rome, even!"

"Where does she come from, sir?" I asked.

They shrugged. "Stirlin', I think," said the elder. "Oh, aye, I see what you mean. Her grandmother was a princess o' Prester John's Land. She says. The Duke o' Venice sent the lass — the grandmother, that is — as a gift to James the Fourth o' that name, Queen Mary's grandsire. I can't mind on her name. He held a great tournament forty year back, an' to avoid pickin' one o' the ladies o' the Court as Queen o' Beauty, an' insultin' all the rest, he picked this black lass. The King himsel' fought as the Rough Knight, her champion. He broke my grandsire's jawbone at it, an' the old man never ate nuts again. There's three grandchildren o' hers about the place. One's a journeyman in the Hammermen's Guild, a silversmith in the Cowgait, an' a good one. The elder lass is wed on a saddler in Stirlin'. This is the youngest — an' the blackest o' them all. She's a — a lady o' varied an' engagin' talents. She sings an' dances, an' entertains the King, as you saw —"

"An' a good many others," said the young one. "Music for all tastes, has our Katie!"

Will sniggered. His mistress frowned him silent.

The elder lord frowned too. "She's a rare favourite here in Edinburgh, wi' all the nobility." Babs Martin was nodding at her table. "You'd be well advised to make your peace wi' her, lass, an' be her friend rather than her enemy."

The younger one giggled again. "Aye, an' that's just what Knox'll learn, if she has her way, eh?" The other raised a hand in warning, but the young man was laughing so hard he brushed it aside. "Ach, John, she'll find out soon enough! Mistress Lenton, lassie, was accused o' harlotry wi' the French Ambassador no three weeks past."

Master Matheson stood up by ma. "That would be after I left, sir. What did she say? Did she deny it?"

The young man giggled so much he had to sit down on the steps. "Deny it? She boasted about it! 'You're hell-ordained, a scarlet woman as goes wi' men for siller!' croaks Knox." Knox again? The man saw my puzzlement. "He's the minister o' the High Kirk, lassie, a damned cantin' rogue. 'Never in my life, sir!' she snaps back at him. 'Would you insult me? Gold, sir, gold!' An' all the spectators tryin' tae hide their grins. 'Does the Good Book itsel' no say that the price o' a good woman is far above rubies?' she says. Knox is taken flat aback. 'You'd dare call yoursel' a good woman?' cries he in horror. It's just what she's waitin' for. 'Well, sir,' she says, all saucy-like, 'I've never had any complaints!' We near split oursel's laughin', an' the old man fair foamin' at the mouth! There's no that many gets the better o' Knox in an argument."

"Aye, an' it didn't help her any," said Sir John.

I was enthralled. "What happened, sir?"

"She was condemned to have her hair all shorn off, an' stand at the Cross in the branks three hours. The hair-clippin' was for bein' cheeky, I'm thinkin'. So she's no that pleased wi' Master Knox. If looks could kill, he'd have melted like a rush dip in a furnace there and then. But she couldn't melt the sentence. Last Saturday, it was. There was the biggest crowd for years — an' never a stone nor an egg thrown, in spite o' all the ministers preachin' against her."

"What else, man?" said the young lord. "Wi' twenty armed men standin' by, ready to deal wi' any man dared lift hand to her? An' nobody can say whose soldiers they were, official-like, but their faces were fair like some o' the King's bodyguard. He's no wise-like, whiles."

The older one nudged him hard. "Wheesht! Come away up. If we're no there wi' his damned hat when he's ready to leave you know what he'll be like."

"Aye, you're right. God, is it worth it?" With a bow to ma and Mistress Martin, and a nod to Master Matheson and me, they went off up the stair.

We all looked at each other. "Aye, well, Leezie," said Mistress Martin. "That's the King an' his friends for ye. An' Kate. I never thought to say. . ."

"I thought it would be a surprise," said Master Matheson.

"It was that all right, sir!" I said, and Babs Martin laughed squeakily.

He grinned. "Aye, I'm sorry. But you've a grand knack o' makin' friends!"

"I'm sorry, ma," I said. "I didnae know."

"No, Leezie, it's all right," she murmured, and raised a brief smile for me. As she rose with an effort, we both reached to help her, but it was Master Matheson she leaned on. She ignored Will, still sniggering at the back of the shop, but smiled over at Ina, sitting lumpy and absolutely still by the door. "We'll away an' let you get on wi' your trade, lass. I'll see you later, Mistress Martin. Leezie, clear up that mess on the stair before someone breaks their neck." She took a deep breath. "It might even be somebody important."

"I'll do it, mistress," offered Will, but I'd not be in his debt. I got a cloth and cleaned the steps myself. As I wiped, I dreamed of the day I'd be as rich and stylish as that burning beauty. But I'd not entertain the King, I thought with a grue of disgust.

Within three days I'd flatly refused to wear a pair of bodies when I saw the dreadful iron cage, with its hinge at the back. But I had a grand new dress, thick and warm, of deep blue wool; to bring out my eyes, ma said. It had a tight waist and a wide skirt that took four petticoats, but no fashionable train because we decided I'd not pay enough heed to it to keep from tripping when I turned. I had two pairs of separate sleeves to tie on, one full and tight-cuffed, blue like the dress, for everyday, the other pair straight black velvet for my braws for the Kirk; and two chemises with little frills like ruffs at the neck that were a right bitch to keep clean. I was near as fine as ma in her new damson red — she'd laughed herself silly when Master Patterson from next door, who had come to call and offer advice and a prayer of Christian fellowship to the newcomer, told her that the Kirk recommended sad grey or sad brown as the most suitable colours for women. "Sad, sir?" she cried. "No, no, I'll no wear a sad colour ever again, for I'm that happy I could near fly!" And chased him out. He wasn't best pleased. The hymns fair echoed that night.

No, ma was free of dad, with money, with a task that she loved to occupy her, with a position of some importance in the town, with all she'd ever dreamed of. She was aye flying about, seeing folk about linens and embroidery, wool and knitting, or else there were folk coming to the room at all hours to see her with samples or work — or bribes. Blankets, sheets, a quilted coverlet, a feather mattress, a carpet for the table, a carved chest, a stool, two steel forks; wood and pewter cups and plates; wine and spices; clothes, too — coifs, gloves, slippers, belts — she took all they offered her, or they'd have thought her a fool, and then picked the ones she'd have picked anyway.

Our stair was busy with visitors from dawn to midnight, even more than came to Kate Lenton's door. Not that Mistress Martin minded, for many of them bought pies in the passing, or while they were waiting. Ma was happier than she'd been in years.

Master Matheson kept calling, too, whenever his duties allowed. His excuse was that the Queen herself had commanded him to see that ma was safe and well, but visiting twice a day whenever he was in Edinburgh was greater devotion to duty than was needed, I felt.

But what did I have to occupy me?

I had no friends. When I bought the new lute strings for the lady down the stair, and hoped to apologise to her, it was her elderly maid that took them in at the door, and said with a face like a nippy sweetie that her mistress was out. We heard music and laughter rising from her rooms every day, as she entertained people or rehearsed with the royal musicians, with their viols and shawms, lutes and flutes, new songs and new dances; but we seldom saw her, even passing on the stair. I met some of the neighbours, but I was too shy to speak easy to new folk. Ma said I was aye too loud and brash, trying to cover it, and put them off. She was right; but what could I do?

Then, I couldn't work, for I could do nothing useful. There wasn't much call for long-distance spitting or throwing a knife here. When the bed was made, water fetched up from the well and the room tidied, I'd nothing to do all day. Bake a leathery scone on the fire, maybe, or walk over to the Nor' Loch to wash a grubby shift. I tried sewing, but was all thumbs. In Liddesdale I'd spent happy dreaming hours just watching the clouds and the birds. Stinking coal smoke, and the pigs rootling in the middens and kennels, weren't the same.

Exploring the streets was interesting, once I'd grown used to the crowds and the stink, and learned to keep an eye and ear alert for rubbish being emptied out of the upper windows — against the law, of course, but who'd take the trouble to carry it down to the middens, and who cared to check? The horse-holder lad, Sandy, showed me round when he'd no errands to do. He knew everybody round all the wynds, up and down the

High Street from the Castle at the top, down through the Lawnmarket with its linens and laces and second-hand stalls, past the fleshers' stalls at the High Kirk and the lane they called the Stinkin' Style for obvious reasons; he knew the fish and fruit-mongers, the clothiers and hosiers, candlers, saddlers, jewellers, hammermen in iron or silver or gold or pewter, the tailors, the perfume and wig and hat and glove and fan and shoemakers, right down to the gates of the Palace at the far end of the Canongait, in every stall and shop, round every corner, up every stair. The goods on sale were unbelievable, from all corners of the world. Silk from Cathay, glass and armour from Venice, cut velvets from Florence, spices from Zanzibar, ivory, amber, furs, great sugar loaves, ostrich feathers — it was all marvellous. For a while. But when I'd no silver to buy the sugared fruits or the silver-embroidered collars, it soon lost its charm.

The town was cold, colder than the Liddesdale hills, and harder on my feet, for ma made me wear my new shoes out of doors. Even after I'd worked them into a left shoe and a right, they hurt for a long time.

There was the Kirk twice on the Sabbath, of course, dressed in our braws. Ma liked to go down to the Canongait Kirk to hear Master Brand, or round to gentle Master Craig at the Tron Kirk. I preferred the High Kirk, where Master Knox preached. He was more exciting. He'd been a Catholic priest, they said, and converted by the preacher George Wishart, who was burned to death by Cardinal Beaton in spite of Knox being his bodyguard. When the Cardinal was murdered, Knox preached in favour of the killers, and for taking part in their rebellion was sent to the galleys in France. He was freed after two years, and went to study under Calvin in Geneva. He'd been condemned to death in his absence, and his straw effigy had been burned. I wondered if the sentence might still be hanging over him; if so, he was brave to come back at all, especially preaching so openly against the Queen.

He'd come into the Kirk leaning on a staff, and be near lifted up into the pulpit by two strong servants, for his health had been damaged in the galleys. But in half an hour he'd be warmed by his passionate raging against the sons of Belial and slaves of the Roman Antichrist. The staff would whistle through the air as if he saw them right there before him, the pulpit shook under his pounding fists, and after maybe three hours' preaching he would leap nimbly down the step a different man from the decrepit old soul that had arrived. Not that I could often have told you what he was talking about, mind, for the High Kirk echoed badly and the floor was distractingly cold where we women sat on our hassocks — the pews were for the men — and I paid more heed to trying to make out the pictures on the walls that the Reformers had whitewashed over, or watching the nobles from the Palace fidget as he charged them and the King and Queen with blasphemy, vanity and greed. But he was a good show. On weekdays I had nothing to do. I started to moon about the pie shop all day. At least it was warm. When Mistress Martin asked what I was at, she and Ina had a good laugh at me, for they were aye busy. Then they sobered.

"Aye," Mistress Martin agreed with me, "life's dull these days since the Kirk declared declared Christmas a pagan festival, and stopped the Twelfth Night celebrations. The Queen has them still at the Palace, o' course, for she's Roman. But there was a merchant fined last year just for givin' his apprentices a Christmas holiday, can ye credit it?"

She laughed fondly. "In the good old days the 'prentices would pick one lad as Abbot o' Unreason, for just the one day o' any sort of wildness. He'd ride backwards through the town on a donkey, half-drunken, an' make everyone he passed drink with him or pay a forfeit. Stand on his head, or kiss the donkey, its mouth or below its tail, or sing a rude verse, or strip to his drawers. Good fun that, specially if it was a bailie or a bishop. An' then he'd preach a wild sermon in St. Giles' Kirk, wi' all the priests tryin' to smile an' take it in good part. But no nowadays, eh?" she sighed. "The new Kirk men dinnae take kindly to jokes. Even the Robin Hood celebrations on May-day has been banned — though mind you, they were often enough just a riot. But now — well, life's far duller. But dinnae tell anybody I said that!"

I started helping some afternoons to prepare the vegetables for the next day's pies. I could handle a knife as well as Willie, and after a bit practice found I could near keep up with Mistress Martin herself, her cleaver flying through the turnip and onion that pattered in even wee chunks into the firkins under the counter. We blethered away, and I learned all the town's gossip.

"The King was out drinkin' again last night!" I'd tell ma. "That down the stair was nothin' out o' the ordinary. Him an' his vicious hangers-on attacked a wee servin' lassie in the Grassmarket, an' stabbed her father when he tried to stop them. There's no a soul in the town can stomach him."

"Hush, now!" Ma would say, pretending anger, but listening avidly, tut-tutting and shaking her head.

But all this just passed the time. I found I hated Edinburgh.

It must have been about a week after the New Year that I finally broke out. After ten miserable days of rain, a fine, crisp frost beckoned me to the window, to throw back the shutter in spite of the chill and gaze out over the white-rimed roofs to the white hills beyond. I felt caged, prisoned, pressed by the mass of people. I had to get out, away, free for a while.

As the door shut behind ma I rummaged under the bed for my old breeks and sheepskin. Had they shrunk, or was I getting fat? I slipped away down by the Cowgate Port, out into the countryside. At last I could breathe again!

I ran for near an hour, stopping only to ease a stitch. I was horrified to find how soft I'd grown — and not just my feet; I was panting after only a few minutes on level ground and a smooth path! I ran south, away past the Burgh Loch and the gyrss women gathering the dead grasses to sell for fodder, out past the farms and gardens that fed the town, the pastures where the town cows grazed in a cloud of sweet white breath as their herd lads waved to me, out by the old nunnery of Sciennes and the Wrychtishousis, Merchiston Tower and the Bore Stane, where the Scots army had gathered before marching out to the catastrophe at Flodden. I nearly ran right into Little Egypt, but the barking of the dogs warned me, and I turned away and ran for my life as soon as I saw the rounded hummocky tents of the gypsy camp, with the smoke oozing out from every crack. All day I roamed the Burgh Muir and the Braid Hills, and when near sunset I turned back I felt I could face the crowds again.

Ma understood, of course. She'd been worried, but when I returned safe she didn't scold. Indeed, she suggested the best idea I'd heard in weeks.

"Why no earn some silver catchin' coneys? There's a good market for them here in the town — sure Mistress Martin might buy some from you, for her pies. It would be a good venture for you, I'm thinkin', for it's plain you're half stifled here." I kissed her in relief and gratitude, and whirled her laughing off her feet round the room.

The very next day I bought twine, and for a while was out before dawn every morning, happy and busy, to set my traps. There were many coneys burrowing in the hills, and I worked out a round of snares in the woods about the Braid Stane. I got a good price, too; ma had been right. A penny for three well-grown coneys, and a plack for six cleaned skins; I'd soon be rich.

I knew fine that ma didn't expect me to carry on with this. She hoped I'd settle, grow more civilised and soft, and become a real daughter to her. I'd no intention of it, but why should I spoil her hopes? We were both happy now.

For a week. Then I came through the trees on my trap-line, and found a man taking a rabbit from one of my snares. He was a big man, ragged and rough. Well, too bad, it was my coney. And I'd my knife. I crept up behind him and yelled, to scare him. "Put down that coney, ye thief!"

He didn't drop it and run as I'd hoped. He spun round, still crouched. When he saw it was just me there, he stood up. And up. And up. Not a big man; a huge man, dirty and wild, a long thick staff in his fist. My knife came unconsciously into my hand. His reddish eyes flicked to it, and scorned it. I began to wonder myself if it was enough.

Put a good face on it. "That's my snares ye're stealin' from!" I screeched.

"What the hell d'ye mean, stealin? Ye as walks in here, takin' the bread out o' our mouths? This is my ground, ye wee deil! I'll learn ye to steal off Johny Faa's men!" He swore hoarsely as I backed off among the bracken and heather, away from his swinging staff.

I suddenly realised what I should have seen before, that this place wasn't like half-empty Liddesdale. Each part of the hills near the town would have its own trapper, making a bare living for himself and his family out of the coneys and birds he could snare. And I was unlucky, for this one was one of the Egyptians, Lord help me! I decided to apologise, not fight, but he didn't want to talk. I tried to shout to him I was leaving, but he wasn't listening. Against another knife I could make a stand, but not a staff. Especially in this man's huge fist. He lunged at me. Throw my knife? If I missed. . . I turned and ran for my life.

His feet were pounding the stones behind me. I tripped on a root and fell, and the staff cracked down just where my head had been as I flung myself sideways, rolled to my feet and kept running. I had neither time nor breath to shout now; if I fell again he'd have me. He yelled a curse as the staff whoomed again, just behind my head.

I was gasping for air. Why was I so soft? Too many pies, not enough exercise. When I got away, I'd toughen up again. If I got away.

I raced across a bare slope, going down, not up, to keep that long stave from tripping my heels. The pad of his rag-wrapped feet fell back a bit. I dodged away up a burn side, through some birches, leapt the water, and up the rise on the far side. Dear God! In front of my toes the hill fell away in a steep rock slope, and disappeared twenty feet down over the edge of a cliff. I was trapped.

His breathing behind me was drawing closer. I couldn't stay here. Oh, God!

I started down and along the slope at top speed, my bare feet holding the rock well. He shouted behind me, and then I was too busy to hear any more, for suddenly my feet hit a strip of gravel and slid from under me. I rolled helplessly over the edge of the drop, crashed swearing through some bushes onto a nearly sheer rock face another nine or ten feet down, luckily feet first, skidded, rolled again and thumped to a stop against a boulder.

Every drop of air was knocked out of me. I lay in an agony of pain and fear and frustration, trying to make my chest work again, but silently; trying to make my arms and legs obey me and move, but without rustling in the bushes that covered me. The man was shuffling about above me, muttering. Could he see me? Or my white, gasping breath melting the frost on the leaf edges above me? My ribs hurt when I breathed — was one broken? I'd banged an elbow, and wanted to cry and laugh together with the exquisite agony, but I thought the bone was whole. My left leg was all scraped raw. Where was my knife? Not far — I could see it over to my left. Thank the Lord I'd not fallen on it.

My ears strained for the sound of him pushing through the bushes. Nothing. I started to breathe more freely, mouth open to cut down the noise. Where had he gone? Silence. Was he lying in ambush for me? Still silence. Just the wind, and water trickling, and at last, to let me know there was no one about, a robin singing.

I moved gingerly as my limbs came back under my control. The pain in my side wasn't a cracked rib, but a coney I'd caught earlier taking its revenge; a leg bone had snapped and stabbed me right through my jacket, but not badly, thank goodness. I'd broken nothing, nor even strained an ankle. My sheepskin jerkin and coney bag had cushioned my fall, and saved me from the worst of the damage I was due in such a tumble. I was, it seemed, safe.

I lay resting for a while, till the sweat was chilling me as it cooled, and I started to grow stiff. At last I gathered myself, rolled over gasping with aches and bumps, picked up my precious knife and carefully, listening all the time, moved to find a way out of the narrow crevasse I'd fallen into.

Uphill or down? Which way might he be waiting? Down was easier, and I'd been going that way. He'd expect me to carry on; I hoped. I turned up.

It was hard going, with whin bushes and brambles catching

at my jerkin. At last I found the easiest way was to kneel down and crawl under one particularly thick clump. And there, right in under the bushes, I found it. And my life changed direction.

At first I didn't know what the tinkle and the rustle in the dry grass was. I froze, scared in case it was the gipsy, but after a moment I saw it was something small, tight in by a gorse stem. I thought it might be a coney until I saw a bright black eye, and a wee hooked beak hissed and snapped at me viciously. It was a hawk. A merlin.

Rubbish. What would a hawk be doing down under all these bushes?

It was trapped. The strap on one of its legs had a tiny silver ring at the end, which had caught over a kinked stub of root, and the hawk couldn't get free. Feathers were scattered about, probably from the bird it was chasing in here when it got itself trapped. A thrush. A trickle of water ran just by it. It had food, shelter in the dry grass and bushes from rain, frost and mobbing birds; the only question was how a wandering stoat hadn't found it. How long it had been there I couldn't guess.

Well; what now? A hawk was worth silver, especially a trained one. Could I take it back?

I'd be surprised if I couldn't.

I stood up carefully, to peer out over the bushes again; no sign of anyone. Right. Slip off my coney bag and empty it. I'd put the hawk in there.

The merlin had other ideas. It hissed again, and as I reached for it, it dived in under the whins as far as it could go, its bells jingling. It was rather smaller than a pigeon. It cowered against the bank, and then flipped over onto its back right under a strong branch, claws up. It stayed there, hissing and clawing at me as I strained in through the whin thorns to grasp it. I got a good pricking as I jumped back, and I swore at it. It was a tame hawk, wasn't it? I wasn't going to hurt it, but take it back to people who could look after it. So why couldn't it relax and let me help it?

Five times I tried to reach in beside that bird to release its strap, and each time it tore at my hand, hooked beak and needle-sharp little talons stabbing and tearing.

Resentfully, I sucked the blood off my fingers. Drat it! I'd not be beaten!

Try something different. I slipped off my jerkin. I couldn't get through the whins to throw it over the hawk, and if I did I might well hurt the bird while I bundled it up. I offered one corner, woolly side out, to the bird. As it had done before, it struck up, but this time I didn't draw back. Its claws struck deep into the fleece, and before it could disentangle itself I drew it out and had a hand round its back, and never mind the neck bending incredibly far round, and the sharp wee beak ripping at my skin. Its wings flapped desperately, the feathers rattling against the twigs round me, but I hadn't a hand to spare to hold them steady. It was amazingly strong, twisting inside the smooth, shifting coat of feathers, and I was scared I'd break something, so it nearly got away from me twice; but I decided that it was safer if I handled it firmly than if I was tender with it, and after that I got on better.

Talking soothingly — I hoped — all the time, I freed its leash, untangled its claws from the fleece, held one wing down now I'd a hand free, opened my bag with an elbow and slid the bird in. I closed the bag over before I let go my grip, but in the dark of the bag it seemed to give up, and stopped fighting. The bag heaved a second as it folded its wings, and it lay still. I'd done it!

Dear God, what a mess my hands were in! For such a small bird, it had a fierce temper. I couldn't help admiring it even as I licked the scratches and stabs.

Carefully, warily, I picked up the bag and the coney, and started back to the town.

Master Kerr

I decided to try the Queen's own mews, in White Horse Lane. Even if they couldn't say who the owner was, they'd know best what to do with the bird. I found the door, just after noon, and knocked. There was no answer. I knocked again, and then went in, to find myself in a small empty hall with four doors.

Suddenly one of the doors opened and a heavy-built, heavy-jowled lad bounced in. He glanced at the coney in my hand. "Away, we've plenty rabbits!" he said rudely, and was diving out through another door when I found my voice.

"It's no coneys I'm here about — it's a merlin!"

You'd have thought I'd hit him. He stopped in mid-bounce, swung round and gaped. "A merlin? Ye've found a merlin? Wi' jesses? Master Kerr! Master Kerr! Bide here, you!" He raced away, and I stood for a minute waiting.

Nothing happened. At last I lifted the latch of the door he'd gone through, pushed gently, the door opened without a squeak, and I stepped in.

The first thing that struck me was that the big room was clean, cleaner by far than the pie shop. The floor was thick with fresh, bright sawdust. The windows along one wall and at the far end were close barred vertically, and covered with sacking to give a steady light, not very bright. Long poles, thin treetrunks with the bark still on, were fastened along each side of the long room at about waist height, with sacking tacked to them so that it hung down underneath in a loop, and weighted firm. From the droppings under them, that must be where the hawks perched. But there was only one there, on a stump on the floor in one corner. It sat fluffed up and sick-looking, sheltered from draughts by cloth screens. There wasn't a soul about.

Staring all round me, I quietly walked the length of the room, the hawk eyeing me, shifting uneasily. Some stools stood before a fireplace between the windows, and the shelves of a big cupboard were full of pots and bags. A pile of leather hawking gloves lay on a heavy chest. On one wall, on rows of pegs, hung tiny things like half-made golfballs, of rich dyed leather and cloth, with feather plumes and tassels. I picked one up; a hood for a hawk, of course! It took a minute for me to work out how it would be put on, with the beak out there, so, and the thongs tightened at the back to hold it. But how could you get it on and off with a hawk on your wrist? I tried it; you needed two hands. But you only had one. I looked again, and thought. . . what else did you have? I tried it out, using my left hand as the hawk's head, and found I could work the double thongs, so cleverly arranged to pull both open and closed, with one hand and my teeth. Dod, I told myself, you'd have to be damned careful you didn't get your eye taken out when you were at that.

"No if you do it right," a voice quietly answered my thought.

A man stood behind me, smiling slightly, a hawk perched on a heavy gauntlet on his huge left fist. A big man, but not clumsy. A bit older than Master Matheson; well over the forty. Brown clothes, brownish skin, not much hair. Quiet in his manner, so that he didn't frighten me, even though he'd caught me fiddling with the hood. The hawk was beautiful.

It suddenly struck me — "Was I speakin' to mysel', sir?"

He nodded. "Aye, son, that you were. But that way somebody's sure to be listenin', eh?" We smiled at each other, somehow at ease. "That's a peregrine hood you have, like for this fine lady here. You can tell by the size. Here's a big one for a saker, an' this wee one's for a merlin." He picked up each hood as he spoke, his thick fingers neat and sure. The hawk on his glove suddenly flapped its wings wildly and screamed harshly, but he soothed it and smoothed its wings gently. I stood still, not to scare it, and he nodded at me approvingly. "Did you work out how to use the cords yoursel', or have you seen a hawk flown?" There was a piercing quality to his look, like a hawk himself.

"No, sir, I've never seen it, no close up," I said. "Just the Earl out wi' hawks by my house. I thought they were grand, fair grand." The hawk on the stump sneezed, and without thinking I said, "Bless you!" as if it was human.

He smiled slightly, and nodded again. "Aye, well, it's no bad then that you could understan' the hood so quick. I've had lads in here take long enough, even after I showed them. Aye, well. Rab says you've found a merlin?"

With a start, I remembered why I was there. "Are ye the hawker here, sir?"

He threw his head back and laughed, but aye quietly. The hawk on his fist tensed, but relaxed again as he stroked its breast feathers with a thick, gentle finger. "Hawker, eh? That's a good one! I'm the head falconer here, son. That means I'm charged wi' all the Queen's hawks here at Holyrood, wi' their care an' their trainin'. Aye, Matthew Kerr, Head Falconer an' Austringer, Master o' the Royal Mews at Holyrood to Her Majesty Queen Mary, God help her, that's me. Now, about this merlin. Had it jesses? These straps on its legs?"

"Aye, sir. One was caught fast, an' it couldnae get free."

He moved at once, but smoothly, to set his hawk on the tree-trunk and tie its leash. "Is it hangin', lad? Can you take me to it right away?" His voice was urgent and worried. Clearly he cared for this bird, even without seeing it.

"No need, sir," I assured him. "I have it here." I held out my bag.

He finished the one-handed knot that held his hawk safe before he looked at the bag. "Aye? Good lad. On the shelf there. Gently, now." He pulled a glove on his right hand and slid it, still sure and quiet, inside. In a moment he lifted out the bird and sat it on his left fist, where it gripped automatically, startled and beginning to flap again, but already he had slipped over its head the tiny hood that he had shown me. The hawk instantly stopped fluttering, and stood still and steady on his hand as if it had grown there.

He studied it a few seconds, his hand smoothing the tattered remains of the strap — the jess — on its left leg. "Aye, aye. I never thought to see you again, lassie." His voice was full of affection and wonder.

"D'ye know it, then, sir?"

"I do indeed, son. For she was lost three days past by one o' my lads here. It was her first day out on the hill. We saw some larks, an' unhooded her, an' Rab lifted her to let her see them. But just at that very second a starlin' flew by. The gowk hadn't a right hold on her jesses, an' she just lifted away an' dodged round the side o' the brae out o' sight after it. When we ran after, there was no sign o' her. She didn't come to the whistle nor the lure, an' we couldn't hear her bells nowhere. I flew another merlin over the place, thinkin' that would bring her out, but no. Nothin' worked. I was that angered! For I took her mysel', a passage hawk, an' manned her, an' she learned fast as any bird I've ever handled, sweet as a dream. Her name's Diana, after the heathen goddess o' huntin', an' she's one o' the Queen's own hawks!"

He had lifted a dead mouse from a box, and rubbed it on her feet. When she felt it, one set of tiny talons lifted and clamped it tight, and she bent her head and tore eagerly at it, the plume on her hood tossing as she tugged. All the time Master Kerr was speaking, he was examining her, gently so that he didn't disturb her feeding, running his hands softly over her chest and lifting the feathers of her wings and tail. "Aye, her feathers are damaged, but a drop hot water'll sort the most o' that, that's no grave. Apart from that, she's in fair shape. Thin, mind. I'll just fit her wi' new jesses while she's busy."

"She'd killed a thrush, sir," I said as he buttoned fresh thin straps on her legs, and then had to explain how I'd found the bird and caught her.

"Well done, son!" the man said approvingly. "I couldn't have done better mysel'. Let's see your hands — dear Lord, what a mess! Come here an' we'll put some balm on." He tied the little hawk on the narrow end of one treetrunk, fastened the remains of the mouse to a staple beside her, and removed her hood when she was still. She startled, and tried to fly, to be brought up short by the new jesses and fall, dangling. I was about to lift her, but he held up a hand and I stood still. With claws and beak she caught hold of the sacking looped below the branch, and clambered back to her perch, to rattle her plumage back to smoothness and glare at us in irritation.

As the merlin settled again to her food he drew me down to the end of the room, lifted a pot from the shelves and started to rub the cream from it onto my scratches. Some were quite deep, and rubbing the punctures left by the hooked claws was painful, but I bore the stinging ointment without wincing. His light grey eyes, shallow-set among netted wrinkles, kept glancing keenly up at my face as he rubbed and talked. "Aye, there's a reward due you for this. An' I'll see you get it. We'll go up in a minute to Robbie Rychardson, or whichever o' his clerks is in the office, an' I'll tell him. Aye will I."

Something had been puzzling me. "Sir, where's all the hawks? I thought —"

"Outside, son," he said. "You don't think we keep them indoors all the time? No, no, they'd get soft. Just while they're sick they bide in here."

"Like that one wi' a cold?"

"A snurt, we call it. Aye."

"What do ye do for it?"

"Keep it warm, rub on a drop resin to ease its breathin', an' feed it a few cardamom seeds." As I looked puzzled, he explained, "They're heatin'."

"Like mustard, ye mean? Or is that too hot? Ye could aye try boilin' it first, though, that bursts the seeds, an' they're just spicy an' warm." I looked over at the one he'd carried in. "What's wrong wi' this one? Her eye looks bad."

He was watching me thoughtfully. "Aye. She was flown at a hoodie crow that was flyin' wi' its brood, an' got beaten up,

71

poor bird! Deil take all daft Highlanders that doesn't know enough no to over-match their birds! She could have killed it on a straight stoop, lad, never fear, but a hoodie's clever. It dodges to the side, see, an' then if the hawk attacks the old one on the level, as you might say, an' they bind an' fall together, the young ones sometimes come back to aid the parent bird, almost like good Christian folk. An' a crow has a right strong bill. Poor Ellen here near lost an eye."

I nodded, entranced by the birds, their yellow feet and the great black talons. It never struck me how strange it was that this man, the expert and master in his own place, should spend so much time on me. He sat still, studying me as I studied the hawks, not watching them straight on for I could see it made them uneasy, and then said, "The rest o' them gets handled an' trained every day, but they pass the most o' their time outside at the back, weatherin'. Unless the day's too bad. Would you like to see?"

"Oh, sir, would I no!" We went out through a small door I'd not noticed, and I stopped and sighed in delight. For on stumps and low perches on the grass behind the mews, fenced off from the hill behind, stood about fifty hawks of all kinds; peregrines, tiny hobbies, kestrels, goshawks, sparrowhawks, merlins, a huge golden eagle, some I couldn't identify, their bells jingling gently as they preened, tugged at a bone or meditated. All turned to stare with their fierce red or yellow eyes at this stranger in their training area.

It was starting to snow, and the man considered the sky. "Rab! Rab! We'd best bring them in," he called quietly, and the heavy lad, at the far end of the field with two other lads and some dogs on the leash, looked up, nodded, and they went to pen the hounds. "You'd like to watch?" He didn't need to ask.

He and his lads slipped a gloved hand behind each hawk's feet, lifted it up under the train of the tail feathers, and pressed gently against the back of the bird's legs so that it had to step back onto the hand or fall off. Then, gripping the bird's jesses firmly in the gloved hand, they untied it from its perch and carried it inside to fasten it to its accustomed place on the trunk.

After I'd watched them bring in about twenty, I asked, "Can I try, sir?"

The head apprentice snorted, but his master, after another considering look, agreed and gave me a glove. "Try Magog there, the merlin in the corner. He's maybe the quietest," he said. I'd been watching carefully, and approached smoothly. The first time I reached in to him, he tried to fly away, but was held by his jesses. The lad sneered as I drew back, but Master Kerr said nothing, and when the hawk had settled I tried again. This time it worked. The little bird stepped onto my fist with no more than an uneasy shuffle of his wings, and I lifted him quietly.

"Hand up, son. He'll sit on the highest part o' your arm," Master Kerr advised me, turning away to pick up another hawk himself. "Imagine you're holdin' an egg between your elbow an' your waist, an' go easy, easy." I glided along, holding my hand high and even, and my heart was singing as I carried in the beautiful bird, and was shown the special falconer's one-handed knot to tie it to the perch. And another after it. And then another.

"Aye," the falconer said thoughtfully, fastening the last leash. "You like the birds, eh? Aye, well, son. Come away an' we'll see to your reward." He didn't move. I think maybe he knew what I was going to say before I said it.

"Sir — sir," I stammered. "I dinnae want any reward. I just — I just want to work wi' the hawks. They're marvellous. That would please me more than any siller. Can I no stay an' help ye? Sweep up — or anythin'!" Big Rab and the other lads grinned jeeringly.

His master nodded consideringly. "Aye, son, I could see you were drawn to them. An' I must admit I've no often seen a laddie wi' a better way wi' them. For they're chancy birds; there's some folk they'll just have no dealin's wi' at all, do what you may. But it seems they like you. Aye. An' you're no daft, that can tie the knot on just the one showin', for it's a tricky thing, that. Aye, well. Tell me a bittie about yoursel', an' if there's nothin' against it, I'll 'prentice you. Will that satisfy you, eh?" Rab stopped grinning.

73

"There's no much to tell, sir," I said, biting my lips anxiously. I'd never in my life wanted to impress someone as I did this quiet big man. "I came to Embra wi' my ma — she's to be a nurse to the Queen's babe. I've nothin' holdin' me, no master nor nothin'. I can come anytime."

"Aye, aye. That's fine, then. An' what's your name, eh?"

"Sinclair, sir. Leezie Sinclair." Oh, daft, daft, daft!

He nodded. "Sinclair — that's a common name. Where are you from, Leezie?" Then suddenly he saw Rab's dropped jaw and seemed to freeze. "Leezie. Leezie!" He started to turn purple. "A lassie! You're no a laddie! An' here me speakin' you as a laddie all this while, an' you never said a word! Cozenin' me, lyin' to me! A lassie!" Rab's grin was back, doubled.

"I never lied, sir! Folks aye thinks I'm a lad when I'm in my breeks, it's no my doin', I just never think about it," I protested, but it seemed to make him even angrier.

"Breeks! Get out o' here, you wicked hizzy! Tryin' to be what the Lord never intended! Get into a skirt, an' act the lassie, you jaud! An' if you come near me or my birds again I'll have the skin off you!" The change in him was incredible. He was panting with fury, and the hawks, sensing his anger, were ruffled and uneasy, screaming and flapping their wings. Another door opened, and a man and two more lads stuck their heads in to see what was going on.

"But ye said I'd a way wi' the hawks, sir, like ye'd no often seen! Why will ye no take me? I'd do anythin' for ye to take me as 'prentice!" I was near swearing again, but it would put a final end to my hopes. This wasn't right! I'd be good with his hawks, and he knew it. "Ach, sir, it's no my fault I'm a lassie! What can I do for ye to take me?"

"What can you do?" The veins were standing out on his forehead as he struggled for control. "Nothin'! Nothin'! Get out o' here!" He tried to calm himself and be fair. "Aye. An' about your reward, I'll see you get it! I'll speak to Robbie Rychardson this very day."

"But ye said I could be yer apprentice. That's the only reward I want!"

"I did not!" he snarled. "A lassie be a falconer? Never!"

"Maybe a word from the Master o' the Household would change yer mind!"

His fury died at the ridiculous threat. "You'd need more than Rab Beaton's word for that!" he snapped, snorting in annoyance and amusement at my nerve in thinking of going to such a high official with a complaint. "It's me that's in charge o' these mews. There's nobody can give me orders here but the Queen's Grace hersel', an' she'd think twice about tellin' me a thing like this. Aye. But I'll make you a bargain, Leezie Sinclair. You leave here wi'out claiming a reward, an' the day Queen Mary her own sel' tells me she specially wants you to be apprenticed here, I promise you I'll take you! But till then, clear out!"

There was nothing else for me to do.

I slammed about the room all evening. Ma couldn't get a civil word out of me. I knew it wasn't her fault, and I was sorry to be hurting her, but I just couldn't stop myself snapping and snarling at her whenever she spoke to me. I couldn't even bring myself to tell her what it was all about, but at last Master Matheson came in and told her what had happened.

"Ach, Leezie, Leezie! What'll we do wi' you, my dear?" she sighed. "Is it no just like you, to set your heart on what you can't get?"

I sulked on my stool. "Why can I no get it? It's no fair! Just because I'm a lassie! I'd do well wi' his hawks, I know it! An' so does he! It's no fair!"

They both shook their heads at me. "Life isn't fair, Leezie. You just have to accept that," Master Matheson said.

"Ach, blethers! Why can I no do what I want? I'm no breakin' any laws!"

"Leezie, even the Queen hersel' can't aye do what she wants," he said. That gave me an idea, but he saw it rise in my mind. "An' before you ask, no, your ma'll no beg her to order Master Kerr to take you."

As I sulked deeper, he leaned over to me. "See, lass, the Queen's Grace is the mistress o' us all, but under her each man has his place, with its duties an' its rights. She can't interfere an' damage his authority for no good reason. Well, she could, but all her staff would be up in arms against her, an' all the ease o' the palace would vanish. An' the poor wife has enough grief outside wi'out losin' what peace an' loyalty she has in her home. No, she'd no interfere in the mews for you wi'out good cause. You must just resign yoursel', I fear."

That didn't help me much. I sat sullen as ma looked up from her darning. "Has she more troubles than normal, then, Peter? Her man, as usual?" He nodded.

"Why did she wed him if he's that bad?" I asked rudely. "Nobody forced her. Sure no woman would wed a man that'll treat her bad — or is she daft, then?" Ma bit her lip, and I felt worse for reminding her of dad.

Master Matheson's lips had tightened at my tone, but he decided to answer to cover ma's discomfort. "No, she's no daft. She was just set on havin' her wish, same as aye." 'Same as you,' his eye said.

Ma sighed. "Aye. There's a sayin', 'Be careful what you wish for, for you might get it.'" As she too glanced at me, I sulked deeper yet.

"Anyway, she's regrettin' it now," said Master Matheson. "He's a petty, vicious, arrogant peacock. An' worse than all that, he's stupid. They've had to make a stamp o' his name, for he was too lazy to sign official documents. An' he wants the Crown Matrimonial, Lord defend us, so that if the Queen died he'd rule by himsel' as rightful King. But she's no like to be that daft, no now. But there's a many discontented lords in Scotland will praise him up for their own ends, an' he's fool enough to credit anythin' he's told, if it's well sugared."

"Will the bairn no bring them together, Peter?" ma asked.

"Maybe. Or it could be Mary's ruin. Knox says a woman's rule is against the laws o' God. An' there's nothin' the Scots nobles likes better than a bairn for a king. If this babe's a lad, there's many would think to put Mary in prison, crown the babe, an' have another twenty year wi' no hand over them but a regent — maybe Darnley, that would do as they pleased for a sweet word."

"No wonder she's worried, then," ma commented softly.

"None at all. That's why she's so great wi' her friends from

France, an' her secretary. At least he's loyal to her, even if he is the King's friend too!"

At last he'd said something that interested me. "Her secretary? Davie Rizzio? Seigneur Davie, they cry him? Was he no the man singin', that day we met the Queen? Aye, well, I saw him yesterday, buyin' a sword at Katie's Tam's."

"Buyin' one? That's a surprise. There's that many given him — as presents, they say, aye, an' I'm an Aberdeen fish-wife. But he's fair daft on swords. He's got near two dozen. Too many airs, our Davie, an' takin' too much in bribes. See his grand clothes? He's puttin' folks's backs right up, as much as the King."

"Ye dinnae credit all they say about him an' the Queen?" I asked.

Ma was furious. "Gossip! Evil, mischievous blethers! I'll hear none o' it from you, Leezie Sinclair! There's no word o' truth in that vile talk, I'll have you know. He's a friend, no more; he writes the letters she dictates, an' sings to ease her, an' makes her laugh wi' his tales an' jokes, an' that's all. My God, I'm in an' about the Palace every day, an' you'll no stop maids gossipin'. If there was the slightest familiarity, do you think I'd not hear o' it? Me an' the whole town?"

Master Matheson shook his head. "Maybe so, Janet, but it's believed all the same. He dines wi' her in her own room, an' her husband no there —"

"But aye her sister, or her brother! An' a score servants round them! Ach, Peter, it fair makes me wild that the nasty, evil tongues can — "

There was a knock at the door, and a woman came in with a down pillow ma had ordered. Master Matheson slipped away, and though we spoke of the Palace often again, we somehow never were as open about it.

When Bothwell came to town, though, we spoke freely enough of him, and the way he was getting on in the world. For early that February, he was wed. The bride was Lady Jane Gordon, the rich — of course — sister of George Gordon, the young Earl of Huntly. Their mother was a royal lady-in-waiting. Huntly was one of Mary's most sincere supporters, and delighted to wed his sister to another — and one of the most powerful, if not most respected.

Bothwell was a wild man, especially with women, and had been chased, outlawed and jailed in Scotland, England, Denmark and France for his escapades. He'd promised to wed the King of Norway's niece, they said, but as soon as the dowry was paid him he'd sailed away, leaving the lady on the quayside, insulted and furious, vowing vengeance. But he did support the Queen loyally, and so she arranged this marriage for him.

It was whispered the Lady Jane wasn't any too happy, being a Catholic where the Earl was a strong Protestant, and in love with another lad, but she'd not much choice when it was Mary's wish, so she agreed without argument — at least in public. The Queen gave her a length of cloth of silver for her wedding gown, a handsome gift.

It was a grand wedding, with wine flowing in the fountains, and dancing and masquing in Holyrood that lasted five days. Kate Lenton was fair exhausted, with taking part in the festivities from dawn — well, nearer noon — to past midnight every night. The Canongait was one huge hangover.

The King turned up late for the service that was held in a corner of the Abbey, and sulked about all the first evening. As the Queen danced with this one and that one, her husband obviously avoided her. At last she herself went up to him and smiling asked him to dance. "Are there not enough men here for you, madam, that you should be forced to ask me as well?" he snarled. As everyone gasped, and Mary tried to hide her shock and hurt at being so insulted, Darnley's own father, the Earl of Lennox, reproached him for speaking so to his wife. "I speak as I see myself used, sir!" the King snapped, with feebly blustering defiance, and flounced out.

"It fair spoiled the gaiety," commented Master Matheson, who had been on duty that night. "An' he wasn't asked to any o' the other celebrations." We felt sorry for the Queen; but he was her own choice, after all. The new Countess of Bothwell hadn't had that freedom. The general opinion was, though, that she had a better man than the Queen's, choice or none; Bothwell might — might? would — break his vows, but he'd more pride than insult her in public.

As the days went by and my mind and my temper eased, I started to go in and about the pie shop again. It was aye busy. Every morning, long before dawn, Willie took out the trays of dough and dried fruit that had been warming gently in the cool oven, and started the fire again with faggots, bundles of twigs and branches that burned fast and hot, and heated the oven in about an hour. His mistress readied the meat she'd bought last thing the night before at the fleshers' stalls in the High Street, all the offal and meat a bit too high or gristly to be sold. Ina, still in her chair by the door, took a chopper in each powerful hand, and they set up a heavy, thick table in front of her; she couldn't bone or sort the meat herself, for the fine movements were beyond her, but the great cleavers fair thudded deep into the wood, one two one two one two, as her mother moved the meat in under them, threw on the salt and spices to mix in, and scooped away the mince after a few seconds. The whole wynd and the closes round us echoed to Ina chopping the meat, and the trestle table booming like a drum. Some folk cursed her for waking them early, but most were glad of it, for the watch that should call the hour were often behind and she never was. She saved many a 'prentice a beating for sleeping late.

Willie meanwhile kneaded the dough and made the pastry of flour and fat on the board at the back of the shop, his own knives flashing as he cut and turned it. They cut out the rounds, and filled the first pies before four o'clock. Meat mostly, for the first batch, with fruit and vegetables; the oyster, fish and cheese ones went in later, being quicker to cook.

When they were ready the oven door was opened for Willie to rake out the ashes and wipe down the soot off the sides with a wet cloth on a long-handled wooden spade, called a peel, hissing and then singeing as it touched the burning hot walls. Then the peel slid the trays of pies and loaves in on their ledges, and in half an hour, ready for journeymen to break their fast on their way to their work at five, the first pies and butteries were steaming on the counter, the next ones in the oven, and another batch being prepared.

I never went down that early, but when ma was away, the water brought up and the room tidied, I often gave them a hand with the afternoon's work. I was paid sometimes a plack, but most often in pies, which suited ma and me fine, for my cooking was near as good as my sewing.

The only trouble was Willie. He started to be a nuisance. He was aye leering at me, making excuses to rub past me, touching my hand or my skirt or my shift, making rude jokes and suggestive remarks. Never too bad when Babs Martin or anyone else was about, but if ever she went out and there was only silent Ina there, he'd close in on me. I knew fine well how I'd have dealt with it in Liddesdale; rapidly, roughly and thoroughly. But one riot in the shop was enough. I didn't want to land with a reputation as a rowdy, for ma's sake; I felt the neighbours were scorning her for her useless daughter already, and didn't want to make it worse for her, so I practised patience. I trod hard on his toes accidentally-on-purpose, elbowed him when I had to, once slammed a bowl of oyster shells rattling and pattering and scratching over his head — I told Geordie Tod I'd find something! — and tried to keep out of his way. He was just another of Edinburgh's drawbacks.

It was odd, then, that he should help me forward. Not that he meant to.

Sandy

Now Bothwell was in Edinburgh, he often came up from his house in the Canongait to visit his mother who lived just down from us across the Cowgait, by the old houses of St. Mary's in the Fields, that they called Kirk o' Field nowadays. He'd sometimes come up afterwards to see Sir James Balfour or the Ormistons, next door to us, and one day about a week after his wedding he turned in to the pie shop. I was just going out, and paused on the stairs to watch as he came in.

There was a lively, hardy air about him, like a fighting cock. His yellow doublet was in the French style, bright with slashing and gold clasps and embroidery, and the black plumes of his flat hat were held by a jewelled clasp. His small ruff, the latest fashion, jutted his wee beard jauntily forward as he strutted into the shop and sniffed appreciatively. I knew him for a thorough rogue, a ruthless liar, a gambler, a cheat; but he had a bright bravado, a restless, eager energy, that made every other man in town, all the sincere, religious, good souls, look dull and half-dead in comparison.

"Man, wife, that's a grand smell!" he cried to Mistress Martin. "What have ye got, dame, that can give me a wee tasty nibble before I go home, eh?"

"I'm feared I can but offer ye a pie, my lord," she laughed up at him, for though he wasn't tall he still had eight inches more than her. "It's more than twenty year since I've had what might tempt ye to a nibble o' yer fancy."

He laughed delightedly at the bawdy joke. "Away, dame, no as much as that, sure? Ye're never above ninety?" She screeched with laughter, flapping a dishcloth at him, and even the dour, skinny servant trailing after his master smiled. Bothwell leaned down confidentially to her ear. "But from all I hear, if I did fancy more than a pie, I might well find it just up the stair, eh?"

"Ye might find more than ye bargained for, lad," she warned him. "Kate's a lass wi' her own ideas. She'd maybe no take kindly to ye visitin' so soon after yer weddin'. An' what would your good lady wife say, eh?"

"She'd say naught, dame, an' smile as she said it!" he snapped, his own smile fading as he spoke. He turned to peer up the stair, and saw me gazing. "Aha, who's this? A friend o' Kate's, eh? A right toothsome nibble!"

"But no for you, sir!" I smiled down at him from about six steps up. "I lodge wi' my mother, one o' the Queen's servants, no wi' Kate Lenton."

He wasn't put off, laughing again. "No for me? Is that a challenge, lassie? I warn ye, Bothwell never refuses a challenge."

I didn't know how to answer that. I felt awkward, all elbows. To make a jest of it, I drew my knife, and knew as I did so that it was a mistake. "No, it's no a challenge, sir, it's a fact. I can defend mysel', see?" I should have had more sense.

Laughing still, in a flash he'd stepped forward and tugged hard at my dratted skirt. I came off balance with a squawk, and fell flailing into his expert arms that were ready to catch me. He held me firm for long enough to kiss me, then stood me on my feet again and slapped my backside smartly. "I told ye I never refused a challenge! Now, never do that again, lassie," he warned me, rocking contentedly back on his heels as they all laughed at me, even Ina, and Willie giggled. "Ye only ever draw knife on a man if ye're ready to use it on him. You weren't; ye were jokin'. A man can aye tell." He chuckled at me, grinning, his hands ostentatiously behind his back, daring me to strike an unarmed man, knowing I couldn't. Clutching my now-useless knife I wished desperately for the nerve to stick it right through the gap between his front teeth. He knew just how I felt, blast him! "Now, put it away. Ye're a nice enough lassie, an' no hardship to look at, but as the dame says, I'm but new-wedded. It's a wee thing public here, anyway. But if ye'd like to continue the acquaintance, just tell French Paris there, an' he'll arrange it —"

Scarlet, near retching, I ran back up the stair away from their mirth, scrubbing my mouth to rid myself of the smell and feel of his lips, abandoning my shopping for the moment, wondering if I should tell ma about the kiss.

I didn't. She found out, though, and about me drawing my knife on him, and sternly forbade me to carry it any more. "You'll have no need o' it here, Leezie, this is Edinburgh! It's civilised! You'll just get yoursel' into bother if you carry it. Think, if you'd drawn it on a Kirk elder!"

"I'd have more sense, ma!" I protested, but she was determined. So, reluctantly, I left it in the bedroom next morning when I was going out. What the Earl had said about me being no hardship to look at had niggled in my mind all night. I wanted to buy a wee mirror with my coney silver, to see if he was right.

At the foot of the stairs, Willie stepped up and blocked my way. "Why the rush, Leezie?" he asked, his tongue sliding wetly over his lips, scratching soggily at his soft, wobbling belly. Far too many pies, I thought. "Ye'd do better wi' me than wi' an earl, lass, he'll no care for ye, but I do. I've fancied ye ever since I first seen ye!" He said it as if it was a compliment. "The auld bitch is away out an' she'll no be back before noon — we can have a fine time ere she gets back — eh, Leezie?" His hand was reaching for my waist.

But this was no expert. Before he could touch me I swung a punch to his spotty nose that knocked him off the step and down on his bulging backside in the dust, greasy hair, wet lips, filthy apron and all. As he cursed and the blood dripped, I jumped over him, shouting "Smelly jelly belly!" and ran out

83

with a smile to Ina's grin and grunt, thinking I'd really have to tell Mistress Martin. He was getting past a joke.

It didn't take me long to find a wee mirror in one of the shops in the Cowgait, and I headed right back with it. I was fairly itching to see myself properly for the first time. A reflection in a pool or a pail of water was well enough, but a silver mirror was far better than —

The door of the pie shop was shut.

In the middle of the morning? With the High Street full of customers? I reached through the hole for the latch-string to lift the bar. It wasn't where it aye hung, just inside the door. This worried me even more.

Sandy, the callant who had grabbed the pig that first day, was aye about, hoping to earn a few coppers running errands, clearing the rubbish off the cobbles for a lady to pass, fetching water or holding folks' horses. He saw me puzzled and ran down from the High Street corner. "What is it, Leezie?" he asked, and when I'd told him, grinned. "Never fear, Sandy's here!" he joked, and shoved his skinny arm in through the hole that was far too small for my full sleeve. With a bit of a struggle, he reached down to the bar and scrabbled at it with his nails till it came up and the door swung open. "It's as well I'm honest, eh?" he said, and waited on the doorstep as I entered cautiously.

Ina wasn't in her place. It was as if one of the walls was missing. Ever since I'd come, she'd lived in that chair by the door, all hours, night and day, as if she was rooted there. What could have happened to her?

Two great furrows were scored in the sand of the floor where the back legs of her chair had been dragged across to the door at the back, which led to the wee room where Mistress Martin slept. I followed them uneasily. As I tapped gently, I heard loud grunts and movement inside. Ina? Was she ill? I pushed at the door. Could I help?

The door swung silently open. On Mistress Martin's bed lay Ina, moaning and kicking, her chair tumbled on the floor, her greying hair spilling from her cap over the edge of the mattress. Willie was bending over her, pulling at her clothes. For one disgusted, stomach-churning moment I wondered if I should just leave, if she was enjoying it, but then one thrashing arm thumped against Willie's head and he cursed and slapped her. "Will ye stop fightin', ye daftie? I'll murder ye if ye hit me again, ye great daft lump! Bide still! I'll have ye, aye will I, an' that wee bitch up the stair, aye, her too, so I will. Who else would, eh? Quiet! Ye're all the same! Will ye stop yer kickin', ye damned —"

I could indeed help.

I don't know how the big wooden peel from the oven came into my hands, but I hit at him with it. It broke on a joist. The flat end bounced off his back and clattered on the floor. I struck again with the four-foot long pole handle. He shouted, and fell off the bed. I kept on beating him as he scrambled blindly for the door, screeching, hands over his head to protect it. The pole was too long, it kept hitting the walls or joists whenever I tried a proper swing at him. Somebody was screaming in rage. It was me.

Something outside the roaring red fog in my brain took time to wonder quite clearly why I was using this daft bit wood instead of my knife. Oh, aye, ma had made me leave it behind. Civilised Edinburgh, eh? Well, I'd just have to do my best with the peel. I did.

Sandy was holding my arms, trying to make me stop. I hit out at him, but then a crowd of other folk came in from the street and pulled me away from Willie. There were too many of them. I slowly relaxed, shaking still with rage, and as the crimson mist cleared away, my knees started to tremble.

Sandy was trying to tell what had happened through their shouts and questions when suddenly a clear, deep voice cut through the babble. "What the deil's all this carry-on? Can a body get no peace in this town at all?"

The men's shouting stopped, and we all stared up at Kate Lenton, towering above us at the top of the stairs. Her eye fell on me, still held by three of the men. "God have mercy on us, it's the Borders lassie at it again! What kind o' savages do they rear down Liddesdale way, that you should aye be creatin' havoc all round you? Well? What is it this time?"

She was dressed in white that showed off the rich near-black of her skin, a gleaming ivory velvet robe trimmed lavishly with white fur, pulled tightly round her. As she moved, the front opened enough to show a high-heeled white fur mule, and one dark leg to the knee, and the eyes of every man there swung to the gap. In the awed, admiring silence, she calmly twitched the robe straight and waited for somebody to gather strength to answer her. There was a white silk cloth wrapped round her head, giving her an extra three inches of height that she didn't need. Suddenly my heart ached to be tall and beautiful and sure of myself like her — and might Willie Grey burn in everlasting torment for making me look a fool in her eyes again!

Strangely enough, once she'd sorted out what had happened, she didn't scorn me. She told two men to watch Willie, sent another running for Mistress Martin, and called me in to see to Ina with her. We found Mary Crockett from over the road there already, and Ina lying snorting and heaving, trying to rise. "Never heed, wife," Kate told her. "Your mother'll be here soon. Now, hush your cryin' an' tell us are you all right?"

Mistress Crockett snorted, but Kate raised an eyebrow at her and she stopped her muttering and finished straightening Ina's shawls. I lifted the chair. Ina was shuddering and moaning, tears slobbering down her face. Kate knelt down by the bed and gently took the great distressed head in her arms, holding her comfortingly firm, not caring about the marks of tears and spit on her fine robe. After a long minute the tearing sobs stopped. Ina managed to nod when the question was repeated, and even to stop nodding after a few seconds. She thrust an urgent hand out towards me.

"Leezie? You want to see Leezie? Come here, lass." I moved to the bedside. "See, she's here. What d'you want wi' her?"

I took Ina's hands, trembling even more than mine. "Are ye all right, Ina? Did he harm ye?" The clumsy head rolled from side to side, but the anxious eyes never left mine, and her clasp tightened. She shook one of my hands, grunting. "Me? Ach, I'm fine. He never laid a finger on me."

"Never had the chance, from what I hear," Mistress Lenton added briskly. "Is that folk comin' in?" She rose as the door flew open and Mistress Martin rushed in, praying and scolding all at once. Kate quietly drew me and the other woman out, to leave them alone for a while.

Willie was sat whimpering on the bottom step of the stair, nursing his bruised hands and having his greasy apron wrapped round his head to stop the bleeding. Mistress Lenton, after a shrewd look at me, told the men to set me the stool, and when it was found to be broken called to her maid, glowering even sourer-faced than normal at the top of the stair, to fetch a fine oaken stool and a cushion for me.

The provost had come down with Mistress Martin, and took charge. It was soon established what I had done, and why, for Sandy had come in just behind me and seen what Willie was at. There was a roar of anger as the news was relayed to the crowd all down the wynd, for all the folk shoving and peering in the door knew Ina. Willie cowered in his place. Mistress Crockett insisted on making a statement; she lived right opposite, and she'd just that minute fed the twins when she heard screeching and yelling, and straightway she dropped the bairns into the cradle and ran straight over, and the lassie there — me — was still hitting him. . . . Every detail was gone over and over.

All the while I sat still, trying to get back to calm. I was angry with myself. Every time this red mist came over me, I lost my head. Maybe there had been no need to half-kill Willie, much as he deserved it; if I'd just shouted, someone would surely have come in to help. But then, I thought, did I not have to stop him right away, before he hurt Ina? Ach, it was beyond me. But I wasn't sorry for hitting him. I was glad!

When Mistress Martin came back into the shop, furious and upset, the crowd had all the facts. "How's your daughter, Babs?" Kate asked.

"In the deil o' a state!" she snapped. Willie cowered again under the cuffs he got from the men watching him.

"But she's no harmed?" said the provost.

"No thanks to that rogue!" snarled the old wife.

He pursed his full lips. "Aye well, then, Babs, it's for you to decide what's to be done. Do you want him charged wi' assault? An' Ina go through a court trial? If she's no harmed,

87

I'd say it's no worth it."

Mistress Martin scowled at him. "I'll have nothin' to do wi' lawyers unless it's vital," she muttered.

"I'll no say you're wrong, mistress. What, then? Will you keep the lad on?"

"Him? I'd as soon keep on the branks!" exclaimed Mistress Martin so fervently that the audience laughed.

"There's another thing. You, lad!" Willie looked up sullenly. It was the first time anybody had actually spoken to him. "D'you want to charge Leezie here wi' battery?"

My jaw dropped. What on earth . . .? But —

But cowering below many raised fists, Willie shook his head vigorously. "Aye, you've that much sense, you wee rat! Well, you've lost your place, an' it's no more than your due."

He seemed satisfied, but Babs wasn't. "Ye'll let him off scot-free? Lose his place, an' that's all?" She was furious. "What d'ye say, wives? Is that right?" A general screech of anger answered her. "Well? What'll we do wi' him?"

It was Mistress Crockett, that gossipy wee busybody, who screamed the answer. "A duckin' in the Nor' Loch! That's what he needs, to cool him down!"

The women in the crowd leapt enthusiastically at the idea. "Aye! The Nor' Loch! Come away! Up wi' him!" They grabbed Willie whimpering from his seat and dragged him yelling out and away up the hill, cheering, shouting and capering, hitting him as they went, the men trailing after, gathering all the crowds from the High Street to join in the fun. Kate grinned wide as she watched them go, and tightened the belt of her gown with an air of satisfaction.

Peace fell in the wee shop. Babs Martin came over and took my hand. "I cannae thank ye enough, Leezie. Ina says he's been a bother wi' her an' ye both for long enough. Ye should have said."

"I didnae want to cause ye trouble, mistress," I said.

"Would it not have been less trouble to complain than have this happen?" commented Kate drily. "But you're well rid o' him now, Babs. Come away, wife, sit ye down. Leezie an' Mistress Crockett there'll give you a hand to put the shop to rights, an' get Ina back to her chair. An' then you can think about your trade, an' get another lad in. There's no lack o' them about, seekin' work."

"Aye," the old wife said bitterly, sitting stiffly down on the stool as I rose stiffly, "but how do I know the next one'll no be just as bad?"

I saw Sandy standing at the door jamb, trying to pluck up the courage to speak. "There's yer lad ready, mistress," I pointed out to her. "He helped me. He's strong, an' a hard worker. An' he's aye civil an' pleasant in the street."

As the smile spread like sunlight over his face, she considered him for a minute, and nodded. "That's true, lass. Ach, I'm that upset I cannae think straight! But aye, son, I'll give you a try. Same as Willie — your meat, an' a bed in under the counter there, an' a groat a week. Well?"

"My God, mistress!" he sighed. "I'd give my right hand for the place. Food an' warmth an' a place to sleep regular! It's paradise, mistress! I cannae thank ye enough! An' ye, Mistress Sinclair!" That was me! "Ye'll never regret it, I swear to ye!" He kissed Mistress Martin's hand, and then mine, to my embarrassment and Kate Lenton's amusement, and seized the broom to start sweeping up even as the old wife was saying, "Ye can start by settin' the shop straight. They gannets has stolen the half o' my pies. Damn that villain!"

The dirt flew harder than Willie ever shifted it, and Kate Lenton smiled at me from the stair. "Aye, you've a kind heart, Leezie Sinclair," she murmured musically. I was pleased at her praise, until she added, "Under it all." Under all what? But I was starting to have an idea what she meant.

Some day, I promised myself, watching her swaying elegantly back up the stair, some day I'd be a burning beauty like her. . . But I'd Ina to see to first.

Ma was pleased I'd saved Ina, and to the rest of the Wynd I was almost a heroine. Everybody stopped me to speak to, and I found myself suddenly with more acquaintances, if not yet friends, than ever before. To my surprise I found that they all had known me, and liked the look of me, though they'd not spoken to me. I wished they had; it would have made life much more pleasant. At last, though, I had folk to chat to. Mistress Crockett had me in to see the twins, and ask if ma could advise her on how best to cure cradle cap. Katy's Tam offered me a nip of brandy, and roared with laughter when I took an unwary gulp and it exploded inside my ears. I refused a second. Geordie Bruce, whose shop at the corner of the Cowgait sold all kinds of dry goods from sugar loaves to sacks of oatmeal, gave me an apricot stewed solid in sugar, that was the most delicious thing I'd ever tasted. The printers from Chapman and Myller's at the corner of the Cowgait, who bought Mistress Martin's pies for their dinners, even presented me with a printed picture of Jael, the Hebrew woman who saved her people by killing the heathen Sisera. I laughed myself silly, but it was very flattering.

The Earl of Bothwell, riding past me in the Cowgait one day, shouted over to me, "Hey, Leezie! I was lucky to get away so light, eh?" and his friends laughed as he spoke to them, turning in their saddles and eyeing me with interest as they rode on down to the Netherbow. I'd have been pleased if they hadn't been the Ormistons, that no sensible lass wanted to be noticed by.

Even Master Kerr knew, Peter Matheson told me, and had laughed and said he'd not put it past me. He was still determined not to have me, but not because of anything personal; just the fact that I was a lass. I brooded about it for a while again, but eventually shrugged it off. I'd find a way somehow.

Sandy got on fine in the shop. His early lack of skill was more than balanced by his willingness. The shop was cleaner and better kept, with fresh sand on the flagstones, and his apron was as white as Babs Martin's own. He suggested she put a board on trestles outside the door to serve folk quicker at the busy hours. Mistress Martin was very pleased with him.

He was a nice big lad. Ten years before, his father had been kicked by his horse, and his broken leg festered till he died of it. Next day Sandy and his mother had watched silently as the laird, the Earl of Dunbar — or rather his agent — took the horse, the most valuable possession of the dead man, as death fee. The priest took the cow, the next most valuable item. Then the agent demanded a transfer fee of four times the annual rent, so that Sandy could take over his father's tenancy, but there was no money, and no-one who would lend to a young lad and his ailing mother. They were thrown out of their home, and went to the local friary for shelter; but when the Reformation became the law, the friary was closed and they were turned out again to wander, earning and begging as they could. Sandy's mother died of starvation beside the road one cold dawn, and he could do no more than see her laid in a pauper's grave.

Nine years old, he headed for Leith with a dream of becoming a sailor and going to find El Dorado, but he had no money, and without a bit silver no captain would take on a landsman. He tried stowing away, but was found and thrown overboard with no inquiry whether or not he could swim, which put him right off the sea. He'd come in to Edinburgh and scraped a living as a horse-boy and caddy, carrying goods and messages all round the town, sleeping among the beggars huddled against our stair wall in the pend for shelter and the last warmth of the oven.

He was fair, grey-eyed, wide and open of face; tall, with a breadth of hand and shoulder that promised a big man when he filled out. His head was aye full of dreams; sometimes he'd slow and stop while he was cutting the pastry and gaze away as if he could see through the back wall, away to the far lands across the ocean, muttering to himself and his hands twitching. "Sandy!" Babs would screech at him, and he'd start, grin, and get on with the work again as ready as you please. She was quite happy with him, though she never said so, of course. "Ye're that clumsy whiles, ye break half the pies — to get more for yersel' to eat, I'm thinkin'!" she'd scold him. He just grinned again.

The nicest thing about him was his gentleness with children. He was a great favourite already with every bairn in six closes, and now they started to come into the shop looking for him to tell them stories or whittle them toys as he'd done before. He made some wee pies, child-size fruit pies for only a farthing each, and they turned out a great success. Mistress Martin raised his wages to sixpence after only a week, and it wasn't long till we went up to the flea market and bought him doublet, breeches and shanks, that only needed a bit darning and a good wash, and patchable boots for the Sabbath. I had to drag him sharp away from eyeing the stalls with the lords' cast-off velvets. When he was rich, I said.

He was kind and considerate with Ina, too. He put wee wheels on the legs of her chair, and sometimes when business was slack he'd take her out, huddled in her shawls, and push her up and down the wynd. It was like a new world for her. Everyone spoke to her, and she fair loved it. He took her to services in the the Tron Kirk, too. He could understand her better than anyone else, and helped her stop the repeating and repeating of her actions. She grew brighter every day, the number of shawls gradually shrank, and so did the fusty smell that rose from her whenever she moved. We were all happy at the change.

One sunny afternoon, when he'd parked her by Mistress Crockett's door for a while, Mistress Martin looked out. Ina was smiling at the twins playing by her feet, and suddenly to our horror the old wife burst into tears. "Oh, what'll become o' her?" she sobbed. "What'll happen when I'm dead? It fair worries me sick to think on it." We assured her that it would be a long while yet, but she'd not be comforted. "She needs looked after, all the time. She's no daft, but my sister'll no care for her. A right bitch, Bessie, that selfish an' self-righteous! She'd just throw her some food, an' no clean her nor nothin'. What'll happen to her? There's times I pray for her to die before me! Lord help me!" Sandy and I took long to calm her down.

When I told ma about it that night, she nodded sympathetically. "Aye, it's aye a worry for mothers wi' such bairns. Maybe Babs could see a minister about it. They'll know what can be done. I'm sure if Babs leaves money to the Kirk, they'll take care o' Ina for her," she said, and it did sound sensible.

"God bless her, that's the very thing!" Mistress Martin

approved next morning. "But I'm far too busy to spend a day hangin' about waitin' for Master Knox to find time to see me. You run up an' arrange a meetin', Leezie."

My jaw dropped. "Me?"

"Aye, why no? It's your idea."

I was appalled. Me go up to see Master Knox? He hated women, especially bossy ones like me. He'd even written a book about it, against the Monstrous Rule of Women, that had got him into trouble with four queens. He was one of the most powerful men in the town. If he took against me, he'd preach a sermon at me in the High Kirk, naming me in public, ranting and waving his stick at me — he'd done it to other folk. Me? No, not me. Would Master Craig not do?

But she insisted. It had to be Master Knox. For Ina's sake.

I went. What else could I do? And besides, there was something I'd maybe find courage to ask. . .

It took me long next morning to gather my courage even to knock on Master Knox's door. I'd combed my hair smooth under its cap, brushed my dress, put on my shoes and a fresh white apron. I walked up to the High Street, and over to the house, and back and fore past it three times before I could bring myself to mount the steps. I was ashamed of myself, but I'd rather have faced Kate Lenton in a rage again than the fierce old man with the sharp black eyes, who dared attack the nobles themselves so violently from his pulpit. But at last, calling myself a coward, I took a deep breath and lifted the great iron knocker on the heavy, nail-studded door.

A young woman opened it. She looked near ages with myself, about sixteen, square and somehow heavy of face, with thick, creamy skin above her dazzling white collar and apron that suddenly made mine seem grey.

"Could Master Knox spare me a minute o' his time, lass?" I asked politely.

She eyed me calmly. "Pray you come inside an' wait till I ask my husband." I blushed with shame at the insult I'd given her, though she didn't look offended. But how could I have known such a young lass was the mistress of the house? Of course, this would be Master Knox's second wife; Mistress Martin had told me he had caused a fine scandal last year by wedding a lass so young, and a relative of the Queen's, and himself a commoner and near sixty. Her dark eyes were wide-set, large and cow-like, reminding me somehow of Ina's, and her gown, though it was of the correct sad grey colour, was thick, rich wool. No pious poverty here; but maybe the money came from her father.

I stood in the passage while her slippers padded up the stair, and she tapped and opened a door; a few seconds later, after a murmur of voices, I was called up. She passed me, placid — or vacant — faced as before, on the stair, but then stopped and put out a hand to make me pause. "You'll no can stay long, mistress," she said. "We're near time for breakin' our fast. Five or ten minutes, just, if the Lord wills."

She padded gently on down to the kitchen. I swallowed, lifted my head high and walked up.

Master Knox

Master Knox was in his study, a tiny room built out over the street at the front of the house. It had shelves with letters, paper and several expensive books, and a sloping desk at which the old man sat, pausing for the moment from writing, but no room for a second stool for visitors. Well shawled as Ina over a furred robe, he peered at me over round pieces of glass held in a frame on his nose with a ribbon round his ears; then in irritation he raised his hands, warm in fingerless gloves, and took the glasses off, skewing his cap; laid them on the desk by his inkwell, knocked his quill off onto the floor, tutted, put his cap straight again, thanked me absently as I recovered the quill for him, and scratched his nose with it. He acted as if in his dotage; but his eyes on me were piercing.

"Well, lass?" he asked, hitching up a shawl. "What is it? Dinnae be feared. If it's the Lord's business, you need but ask, an' I'll do my best for you." His ruddy face and long dark beard looked kinder here than in the pulpit.

With a gasp I dragged my eyes off the glass circles, and bobbed my best curtsey. "I've come to ask if ye'd be willin' to see my friend sir. Some afternoon. She's aye busy in the forenoons, so I came to ask if ye could —"

"If I could see her in the afternoon. Aye, I understood that."

I bit my lip. Why had I said such a silly thing? He held up a hand to stop me apologising. "The facts, lass. Just the facts, eh? First your own name."

I took a deep breath to steady myself, and told him. Oddly, he laughed, not what I'd expected. "Sinclair, eh? Ech, aye, Leezie Sinclair, before you tell me o' your friend's need, tell me a wee bit about yoursel'. For why, my mother's name was Sinclair, an' I've used it mysel' at times, if it wasn't — eh — tactful for me to use my own. So, Leezie Sinclair, where's your family from?"

"I'm from Liddesdale, sir, mysel', but ma's family — it's ma's name we're usin' — they're from Lothian. She was a single bairn, but her dad had a sister Jean moved over Haddington way when she was wed, an' they lost touch."

He beat his hand down on the desk, making me jump. "Haddington! That's where I was born! It's possible, Leezie, it's possible! My mother's name was Jean, an' she told me o' a brother Alexander —"

"That was my grandfather's name, sir!" I was as excited and pleased as himself. This meeting wasn't going as I'd feared at all! He was a friendly, pleasant man, not the tyrant I'd expected.

He asked about ma. I told him, eagerly, that she had a good position as a royal nurse, and the air suddenly chilled. His smile vanished, his hand clenched. "Nurse in that house o' Satan!" His voice was cold, with a suppressed rage in its tone. How could he change so quickly? "Is she a heretic, then?"

"A heretic, sir? Do ye mean a Catholic?" As he nodded brusquely, I protested, "No, sir, she's a good Calvinist! We go to the kirk every Sabbath, morn an' afternoon — most often to the Tron, but —" I thought I'd try a bit of flattery — "I prefer it when we go up to the High Kirk to hear you preach." Well, it was true, and no need to tell him why.

He examined me for a minute about my faith, and found me woefully ignorant. I blamed dad, who'd not let us go out to the kirk at all, and that distracted his temper. And it gave me the chance to ask the question, the real reason I'd agreed to come here today. "Sir, can ye tell me how it's possible for a marriage to be broken? Like old King Henry did in England?"

"Does your dad want to divorce your mother, then? On what grounds?"

"No, sir," I explained. "It's ma. How can she div — divorce her man?"

His face was full of shock. "A wife — wantin' to — ech, aye! H'rrm. Well, it's possible, but. . . Tell me all about your parents, an' how they were wed."

I gulped. "Everythin', sir?" I couldn't. . . Ach, well. "Well, sir, ma went to France wi' the baby Queen when she was sent to be wed to the wee French Prince Dauphin, for to save her from the English in — er — in forty-eight, it would be?" He nodded. "Well, ma met one o' the Scottish Company o' Archers, as is the French King's bodyguard, an' she wed him. But dad, that was my true father, died o' the plague when I was five year old."

"What faith was he, lass?"

I didn't know. "Protestant, sir, o' course!" He grunted doubtfully, and I continued quickly. "Well, ma could have wed one o' dad's friends, but she met Adam Hepburn. He'd been a travellin' merchant there, round about Krackow in Poland, he aye telled us, when he got word that his dad an' elder brothers were killed fightin' the Elliotts. So he'd inherit the estate, he cried it, an' himsel' a bonnet laird. An' he met ma, wi' her bit siller, an' he fancied her. An' it. An' he was a fine man then, strong an' handsome, an' masterful — a braw, braw man, ma says, wi' grand tales o' foreign parts an' outlandish ways that would keep ye in stitches for a year. An' he courted her finely. So ma fell in love wi' him." I couldn't help the bitterness. "Bonnet laird! He was a crofter! An' she didnae keep her siller long once she was wedded, for in a month it was gone, wi' two lots o' death duties to pay, an' then the drink on top o' all. An' if she tried to argue wi' him, an' make him take more heed, he beat her nigh to death! She's lost three babes wi' his beatin's." I didn't tell him that ever since the third, she'd taken medicines to be sure it would never happen again.

I'd expected him to be shocked, but he just rubbed one hand across his mouth. "Aye. Were they related? No? Were they wed by Catholic rites, or the rites o' the True Kirk?"

"Protestant, sir. Aye, it was a Huguenot preacher in Dieppe wed them."

He grunted in approval, sat back in his chair and studied me again. "An' your ma wants a divorce from him?" His mouth was twisted in distaste.

"Aye, sir." Well, probably, now she was away and safe; and if she didn't, she should, and I'd soon talk her into it. "He's been that cruel, an' he's tried to kill her —" Why did I feel I had to repeat it?

"Has she witnesses?"

"Aye, sir. Me."

He frowned and shook his head. "How old are you, Leezie? Fifteen? An' his step-daughter. Aye. Old enough for some things, but no for this. Your evidence cannot be accepted. I'm no sayin' you're lyin', mind, just that you've no the experience to judge clearly what's the truth here." As my anger rose — who else had the experience of dad? — he asked, "Has he committed adultery? Had relations wi' other —"

"I know what it means! Aye, sir, wi' every slut in Liddesdale!"

"Again, lass, have you witnesses?"

My stomach crawled. Could I tell — no. Not even for ma. "There's nobody would dare bring witness against him."

"Then in law I can do nothin' for ye," he said with finality and relief. "You must consider, lass, that you may think your dad's tryin' to kill your mother when he's but exercisin' his legal right, an' his moral, God-given task, Leezie, to chastise an' discipline her if she's no properly respectful to him as head o' the house, an' her master an' guide in all things before God an' man. An' since she sees fit to consort wi' that sink o' corruption an' iniquity in Holyrood, I must say she seems to stand in grave need o' such discipline!" As my mouth opened to protest, he raised his hand again. "Now I have every sympathy for your mother, lass, if what you say is true. If. But there's nothin' in what ye've told me to give your ma just cause in law — in law, Leezie — to divorce him. Though your father may well be a hard an' stern husband, an' a bit heavy in the han', that is no more than his duty in these tryin' times, an' your mother's duty before the Lord is no to be seekin' to leave him, against God's ordained order an' natural justice —" Justice! What justice? I thought furiously — "but to return to him an' be a good, loyal an' biddable wife. As yours is to be a dutiful an' obedient daughter." His mouth shut like a rat-trap above his flowing beard.

I was so angry I could scarce speak. Heavy in the hand! I was shuddering with rage. "An' what — what when he kills her?" I finally managed to say.

He frowned again. "If he does, he'll be charged wi' her murder."

"On whose evidence? For he will, be sure o' that, but there'll be nobody about to see. An' even if he is, an' found guilty, an' hanged, that'll no be much help to my mother, will it, sir! An' will ye say a prayer at her grave, an' admit then ye were wrong, an' ye helped send her to her death, you an' yer 'natural justice', an' 'legal rights'? An' you maybe her kin!"

As I stared at him in red bitterness and hate, he suddenly rose to his feet. "Aye, Leezie. I will pray for you, an' for her. An' for him as well. You'll all be in my prayers this very day, for I can see you believe what you've said to me." The kindness in his face, and the worry, were quite unexpected, and surprised me from the worst of my fury. "I can do nothin' for you in law, for the law binds us all, even a cousin o' mine. An' I can help no woman, even — especially — my own cousin, to rise up against her natural master wi'out the gravest reasons. But maybe my intercession wi' the Lord may bring you to see that the way o' the Lord may seem hard, but it is the only road that leads to eternal happiness. An' your dad's heart may come to be softened by your ma's return, an' he also will come to kneel by the throne o' God in true submission an' lastin' joy. You don't credit it, but I know what I say is the truth."

He must have seen I was neither convinced nor consoled, for he shook his head. "If it should come to pass that your father's fury roused him to that abominable deed o' murder, your mother would be welcomed in Heaven as a martyr for the Will o' the Lord. An' be sure your father would get his desserts at the Day o' Judgement, even if that is beyond our sight here in this sinful world. I will pray, Leezie, for a happier end to your troubles than you or I can see at this minute. But though we cannae see it, be sure the Lord does."

I didn't know what to say. One second he was condemning ma to return to dad's brutality, the next offering to pray for her happiness. The old twister! But he looked and sounded sincerely concerned. He surely must believe what he was saying. It was beyond me.

As if he was tired by the tension, he sank back down to his chair. "Ech, aye. It may be, lass, that your mother is my cousin. It's possible. If I've time, I'll come down to see her, an' pray wi' you both. But there's other things takes up my time, an' I must admit I haven't the strength I had in my youth — though the Lord lends me His power whiles, blessed be His name. An' if I mind right, you didn't come to see me about yoursel' anyway, but for a friend, an' her needs shouldn't be forgotten for that you and I, I fear, are heated wi' emotion. Now bring yoursel' back to calm, lass, an' tell me about it."

It took all my strength not to throw the inkwell at him. For a start. But after a minute, I could control my voice to tell him civilly about Ina. I didn't tell him about Willie, but he'd heard something of it.

"Is that no the woman was attacked by her mother's servant lad? Aye. An evil thing, that. But wi' the example o' that Jezebel, that daughter o' Satan at Holyrood there, encouragin' the hellish rites o' Rome, it's no wonder that the common folk act in such devilish fashion," he commented. Before I could protest, he was away, his voice rising and the pen waving in my face as he spoke. "Music an' dancin', laughter an' sports an' all forms o' idolatry an' evil, silks an' jewels an' gold tassels an' wee bells, an' never a thought o' their immortal souls, or —" With an effort he stopped himself, drew a calming breath, and smiled up at me. "But here I'm no settin' you a very good example, eh? I tell you to calm yoursel', an' then I let mysel' get

carried away by my feelin's about that morass o' wickedness —
ech, aye! Now, what was it that Mistress — Martin, was it?
Aye, Mistress Martin was seekin'?"

When I explained, he nodded thoughtfully. "She'd leave
money to the Kirk, for the maintenance o' her daughter, eh?"
He mused a moment. "Well, I'll no deny the idea has its
attractions. You know how little silver the Kirk has, eh? A
sixth o' the income the Papists had. That's all. It's but by the
grace o' God that the True Kirk has any power at all to save the
sufferin' souls o' this land from the fearful abominations o'
heresy." He stopped pounding the desk, coughed, and sighed
again, rubbing his eyes wearily with one hand. "Ech, aye. Pray
you forgive me, lass; I tend to preach at folk as if they were a
whole congregation. I'm forgettin' you're but a single lassie, no
responsible for our ills. Ech, aye. Now, I'll —"

He was interrupted as the door opened and his wife stepped
in. Calmly as ever she said, "Come, now, Master Knox, I told
you when the lass came up your dinner was near ready. It's on
the board."

He nodded. "Aye, Margaret. I'll come just in a wee minute."

She didn't move. "We're all waitin' now for you to ask the
blessin' on the meat, husband." Her face was as bland, white
and smooth as her apron.

"In a minute, Margaret," he repeated, and turned to me.
"Tell Mistress Martin to come see me — the afternoon, you
said? — at two hours after noon the morn, then, an' we can
arrange matters then. Or maybe — aye, I've no been out this
while. I'll come down to see her, an' maybe your mother'll be
in as well. Aye, aye, Margaret, I'm comin', I'm comin'. . ." As
he spoke, she was smoothly, with no emotion at all on her face,
taking the pen from his fingers, slipping her hand under his
arm and lifting him to his feet, turning him towards the door.
He spoke faster and faster as he gradually was drawn out and
down the stair. His "God bless you, lass, I'll mind on you an'
your mother in my prayers," floated back up to me as I stood
and gaped, at a total loss.

Immediately, Mistress Knox reappeared, still calm of eye
and blank of broad, placid face. "He'll come see your dame the

101

morn, then, lass," she said quietly, standing aside to usher me out. "You'll forgive me, I'm sure, but Master Knox forgets the world when folk visit. Good day to you, God's blessin' on ye," the black door shut and I was walking back to Blackfriars' Wynd, my mouth open, my anger at him quite evaporated, wondering just how she'd managed it. I felt like a bit driftwood swirled gently but implacably away by the tide.

If she's like that all the time, no wonder Master Knox can't abide the rule of women, I thought. And what about his legal right to be her — what was it — master and guide before God and man, and his duty to make her an obedient wife? And her but sixteen! I was still laughing as I entered the shop.

Both Mistress Martin and my mother were nervous about the promised — threatened? — visit next day. Ma was so bad she near refused to try to get time off to see Master Knox, but I persuaded her she should. I felt that if he saw her, and she was his cousin, he might relent and change his mind about the divorce. There was a wild tidying-up and cleaning that night and next morning.

They had agreed that Master Knox should see Mistress Martin first, and then come up to us. As we waited, ma was so tense with fright that it spread to me. At last, to calm our nerves, ma brought out a bottle of wine from France and we took a wee glass. It was the first time I'd ever had it with no water added. It fair relaxed us, and gave us fresh strength and courage. It was long, waiting, and another wee droppie wouldn't hurt us, ma said. And then, after another while, a refill. And then it was all gone, and we were looking at each other with a guilty glee, for we knew fine well we shouldn't have drunk it all.

"I'd better hide the bottle away before he arrives," I said, "and not let him shee. See." We near collapsed with giggles.

Ma found us each a clove to chew to hide the smell on our breath. "We're as bad as your dad!" she said, chuckling.

Maybe we were. But if it hadn't been for that wine, there might well have been a tragedy in the house.

When Sandy ran up to tell us Master Knox was ready to come up, we went out, balancing cautiously, to greet him politely and escort him up the stair. He climbed slowly, helping himself with his stick, as Mistress Martin nodded and winked behind him that her business with him had gone well. He was nearly at the first landing when the shop door opened and Willie Grey stumbled in.

He'd been back two or three times, begging and stealing, each time dirtier and thinner than before. His nose was red-raw, and his eyes bloodshot. He stood blinking, trying to smile ingratiatingly. "Mistress Martin, will ye no —"

That was as far as he got before Ina's fist thumped him in the back. He staggered forward, bumping into one of the counters and half-deliberately knocking half a dozen cheese and onion pies to the floor.

As Mistress Martin cursed him and Ina shouted formlessly, he fell on his knees and grabbed two of the pies, stuffing one desperately into his mouth. He was half-starved.

As Sandy bent to pick up the other pasties, the lad on the ground struck out at his legs, and kicked at him, trying to drive him away. Sandy hauled him to his feet and started to throw him out as usual.

Babs looked in disgust and some pity at the wretched boy. "Easy, son. Ach, let him keep those two he's got, but get him out o' here before I'm sick!"

As she smiled up at the minister in embarrassed apology and Sandy shoved Will towards the door, Master Knox stopped him with a wave of his staff. From halfway up the stair he cursed Willie, condemning him to the bottomless flames of hell for his devil-inspired attack on his mistress's helpless daughter. Ina sat there, her jaw even more dropped than usual, while the old man ranted at Willie at the top of his well-practised and far-carrying voice.

The door behind us opened. "God, she's at it again," Kate Lenton's voice chuckled musically.

"No, I'm no, Mistress Lenton!" I hissed at her. It wasn't my fault this time! Ma's lips were twitching, and she bit them to hide her sudden mirth. Folk from the wynd, drawn by the well-known voice, were starting to seep in. Master Knox, encouraged by his growing audience, reached new heights of

103

invective, and poor Willie couldn't get away for the crowd pushing in at the door.

I started to feel sorry for him. It surprised me. I'd never thought to feel anything but loathing for that dirty lout, that stupid violent —

"It was her fault!" His frightened screech rose above the minister's preaching. "Her up there! It wasnae my fault! She made me do it!" His eyes met and fled from mine. The rat! The foul, stinking midden-raker! I gulped in rage.

There was a hush in the shop. Knox, interrupted in full flow, drew breath to blast the lad, glanced up the stair towards us, and then paused. He seemed to settle down on his heels, his shoulders sank, his staff thumped gently down on the step instead of brandishing emphasis to his curses. "What was that? Who made you do it? How?"

You could practically see Willie's heavy brain struggling to think. What had he said that was so interesting? What did the old man want? What should he say to please the minister, to get out of this?

"Her there. Up the stair behind ye."

Knox turned. "This wife?" He pointed to ma. "No? Surely no Leezie here?" His voice showed his disbelief, and Willie obediently shook his head. "Then you mean her — this woman?" He pointed to Kate. I remembered the trial when Kate had made folk laugh at him. His enmity rang in his voice. If he'd shouted, "Aye, this one!" he couldn't have made it plainer who he hoped Willie would blame.

And of course Willie did. "Aye, sir, her! Kate Lenton! She's —" in triumphant inspiration — "She's a witch!"

There was a gasp from the crowd jammed at the door. Master Knox's eyes lit with satisfaction.

Suddenly I lost touch with sense. I found I'd been afflicted with the hiccups; Master Knox was glaring; I didn't care. The wine was working in my head. I laughed out loud. "A witch?" Any sympathy I'd briefly had for Willie he'd driven off again. "A witch? Ye louse, ye mucky big pile o' pigsharn, who in God's name would bother bewitchin' you? D'ye think any self-respectin' witch would waste a spell on ye? Hic! Dinnae blame other folk for yer own filthy rotten mind, ye gangrel! Ye thing, ye!" My mind began to turn red.

Knox furiously banged his staff on the stair. "Witchcraft is an abomination before the Lord! Thou shalt not suffer a witch to live, thus sayeth the Lord o' Hosts! It must be examined fully —"

I interrupted him. "Ach away, sir, there's no witchcraft here! If ye credit anythin' that big rotten scruff says ye've less brains than God gave ye!" In my wine-flown confidence I never noticed the gasp from ma and the crowd. "He's been botherin' at Ina an' me for weeks, an' d'ye think Ina's a witch? Hic? If she was, would she no mend hersel'? She'd no bide like she is, that's for sure. An' I know fine I'm no a witch. So why should Kate Lenton be one?"

"She inflames men's minds in an ungodly way —"

"Ye mean she's beautiful? Aye, so she is. Is that a sin? Where in the Good Book does it say that all women should be ugly? If men want her, that's their doin', an' their fault, as much as hers, an' anybody as thinks different is a daft dottle! Or jealous, that his wife's no as fine as her!"

I hiccuped again, and saw the horrified glee in ma's face. It started to bring me to my senses. I heard myself, and my stomach shrivelled up in me. 'Daft dottle.' 'Less brains than God gave ye.' 'His wife's no as fine as her.' To the great John Knox! Oh my God! But my wine-flown tongue carried itself on. "That louse-ridden creepy-crawly dare accuse anybody else o' anythin'? My God —" thank the Lord I'd not called on the devil, as I might quite well have done, I must stop this swearing, it would get me in bother yet — "My God, what gowk's daft enough to believe him?" Something came back to me. . . "If he said the earth was under me, it's up I'd look to check! Hic!" Who had said that? There was a smothered laugh from the crowd. Was I convincing some of them?

Certainly not Master Knox. "The accusation o' witchcraft has been made —"

Again I interrupted. "Aye, but see who made it! If it was a respectable man, then aye, examine her. Hic! But that vile rogue — no man o' sense could credit him for a second! It's just

105

— just evil an' black wickedness, hic, an' sent by the deil himsel'! An' any man as pays any heed to him is fallin' in the deil's own trap! Like Willie! An' doin' Satan's work for him!" Suddenly I too was inspired. "If ever there was a follower o' Satan, it's him, the way he — I'd no like to say in public the way he's carried on in this very room! But, hic, if it should come to a trial, I would! Ask Ina, if ye dinnae credit me!"

All eyes turned to Ina, sitting by the door, Sandy protective beside her. "She's a daftie!" Willie tried to protest, but was shouted down. Master Knox waved to Sandy to push her chair into the centre, and began to question her. She nodded and grunted and gestured vigorously, thoroughly enjoying being in the centre of the action, and Sandy interpreted for her from time to time. It was clear she understood, and she corroborated everything I'd said — even my hints about Willie's dealings with the devil. Daft she surely was not.

I stood back, trying to silence my hiccups, smiling at ma who nodded approvingly, and at Kate, silent and self-contained. The red mist, and the wine, had almost cleared from my head now, and I could look round. We were the only ones who saw Willie sneaking out the door through the legs of the new folk jostling in to find out what was going on. I glanced at Kate again, but she just closed her eyes and stood still. So I said nothing either.

After a minute or two, Master Knox turned to Willie, asking, "Well, sir, what have you to say?" But Willie wasn't there.

The whole thing turned into a comedy.

Master Knox demanded furiously, "Where has the accuser gone?"

Nobody could say, except Kate Lenton and me, and we kept quiet.

Babs Martin suggested in a carrying whisper, "I'm thinkin' the deil's transported Willie straight to hell to save him from Master Knox's wrath, eh?" There were several sly grins. The minister started to turn red.

She started quietly stirring up the back of the crowd, "It's a damned shame, so it is, when honest women's accused just because they're a bit bonnier than the rest. Who'll be next, eh?"

'Honest women'! Kate Lenton! The murmured joke spread. And every pretty wife wondered. . .

Ina was shouting and waving her arms in agreement with her mother.

Sandy was whispering, "Anybody as believes Willie knows what truth is, is daft."

Kate, fortunately, was modestly dressed today, in dark blue, and though her lace was rich it wasn't outrageous. She simply stood there looking noble and tragically martyred. Master Knox was turning puce.

The men of the crowd, and even more the women, who had been maliciously enjoying the thought of the local harlot suffering for her sins and her beauty, started in equal malice to enjoy the thought of someone making the Kirk look a fool for once. She brought a bit of life to the place, they muttered, and profit, with her visitors. Disgraceful, immoral, certainly headed for hell-fire; but did anybody honestly think she was a witch? There was some argument, and several sour faces, but on the whole they were agreed. They liked her, they didn't like Willie; the buzz of comment turned in her favour.

Suddenly a new actor entered the scene. Kate's door opened again, and a man came out on to the stair. James Hepburn, Earl of Bothwell.

He stared round arrogantly. "What the deil's all this, then, Kate? Are ye holdin' a masque for the neighbours?" As we all laughed, his eye fell on the minister. "Master Knox? Are ye here for a pie, sir, or a visit to Kate?"

In the horrified, delighted, breathless silence, Master Knox turned from purple to white as bleached linen. He stared, started to speak, stopped, opened and shut his mouth. At last he drew breath, bowed to the earl, who nodded casually back to him, and said, "In the service o' the Lord, your lordship, I must even interrupt your entertainment. This woman has been accused o' witchcraft, for which the punishment is death by hangin'."

The Earl's brows rose. "Witchcraft? Kate? Havers! She doesnae need it. Master Knox, I must inform ye that I should be deeply, an' personally, offended by any man who thought fit to name Mistress Lenton a witch." His cocky wee beard bristled hopefully.

It was a challenge, but Master Knox avoided it. Feeling that the crowd was with Kate and the nobleman, and against him — or maybe just because he thought it was the right thing to do — he thumped with his stick for silence.

"Mistress Lenton, it seems that your accuser has absconded, havin' been himsel' accused o' bein' in the service o' the devil. In these circumstances the accusation must be considered gravely impaired." He sounded as if he had to force the words out. There was a murmur of approval. "I must take the matter up in prayer to the Lord whose humble servant I am." Who, his tone suggested, would hear all about it for failing to come up to his humble servant's expectations. "This accusation havin' been made, it will be taken under advisement, an' I charge you no to attempt to leave the town until you shall have been informed whether the Burgh Council will proceed wi' it or no." Kate bowed acknowledgement.

Knox drew himself up to his full height, and cried, "Lord, Thou seest the truth o' this an' all matters. Guide Thou Thy servants through their confusion an' doubt, to do Thy work justly accordin' to Thy word an' will. Amen."

The hiccup I'd been trying to choke down all through his speech exploded loudly. Ma snorted with strangled laughter, the sound not quite covered by the immediate, enthusiastic chorus of Amens. Knox was ushered courteously out, and stumped up the wynd leaning on his staff, shaking his head angrily. As soon as he turned his back, the whole crowd was writhing in almost-silent mirth.

Suddenly, unexpectedly, Bothwell ran down the stairs, with a kiss on Kate's lips and a slap on my bottom that took me quite by surprise so that I yelped to make everyone laugh aloud — it cured my hiccups, though — and he hurried up the wynd after Knox, taking his arm familiarly. They paused at the High Street corner together, and turned together; into Sir James Balfour's door? Ach, it couldn't have been.

Slowly the crowd thinned, buying a good few pies as they went. At last they were all gone, and we had freedom to draw a deep steadying breath, shut the door over for some privacy, and catch Kate as she fainted down the stair.

Kate Lenton

When Kate came to herself, her face was grey, not its usual dark browny-black, and she looked dreadful. She gripped at my hand as Ina had done a week before, slowly recovering, trying to get back her spring, her lift of the heart. "My God, Leezie, I'll never say another word against you!" she finally managed to murmur. "You Borders savage — thank God for you!" I blushed.

Ma could scarce make out why she was so much overcome. "But Mistress Lenton, what could they have done to you? You've done nothin'."

She gave a tiny, shaky laugh. "Done? Have you no heard o' the witch trials in Geneva, Mistress Sinclair? Calvin's tortured an' burned hundreds — hundreds! An' Knox is a Geneva Calvinist! If he has his way it'll come here too! An' I might well have been the first, for that I'm a loose woman, I'm different, I'm black, an' you mind what you thought on your own first sight o' me? No, Leezie, I'm no meanin' to scold you. My God, after what you've done for me this day you could throw every pie in the shop at me an' I'd no say a word!"

Mistress Martin snorted. "Well, I would! Come on, Kate, ye're makin' too much o' it! It's no that bad! We're reasonable folk here. An hour or two in the stocks, an' a few sermons

110

preached at ye — nothin' there ye cannae bear!"

Kate shook her head, struggling to sit up. "No, Babs, you're wrong. I've a friend wrote me." She could read, too! "They're torturin' folk till they confess, guilty or no! An' they'll accept no proof o' innocence, no the finest piety an' goodness, they just say it's Satan's cunnin', an' torture harder. It's hellish. Ach, I can't understand it, but it's just as like to happen here as there, wi' Knox an' his like. There's a — a madness o' righteousness in some folk. You'd best mind yoursel', for he hates the very sight o' me. I've made folk laugh at him, an' he can't stand that, an' he'll mind on you takin' my part."

"What'll you do, Kate? Leave?" asked Sandy. Suddenly I started again to hear what they were saying. Leave? Oh, no!

She started to lift herself to her feet with her maid's help. "Aye, I'll no stay to be burned. It's the one thing scares me. Next time he'll no be so easy turned aside. But I'll find a way. An' now I'm warned, my friends at court can keep him off me a while, till I can arrange a safe place quietly. In the Low Countries, maybe." Finally upright, she took my arm. "Lassie, lassie. How can I ever repay you?"

I bit my lip. It was the wine had done it, not really me. And how could I ever tell her that all I wanted from her was to be like her?

Maybe she read my mind. "Well. Give me a hand up the stair, lass," she said. "We'll talk about it up there. My thanks to you all. I'll see you later." I felt the tremor deep in her hands as she leaned heavily on my arm.

I'd never been in her home before. She had the whole floor, with three big rooms instead of the four wee ones in the attic. The first was her great reception room, beautifully painted and panelled, where her guests were welcomed and fed, amused and entertained. A citterne lay on the bright carpet on the table, gleaming in the sunlight that streamed through the glass in the top half of the window. Somehow I felt that room would always be full of sunlight. Cards, playing cards, that Master Knox called the devil's picture books, lay by a great silver candlestick. Six padded stools stood round, and brilliantly cushioned chests. In one corner, under a fine tapestry, a carved cupboard fair glittered with pewter plates, and glass and silver drinking cups.

Her bedroom was smaller but just as colourful. The huge bed stood high against one wall, with carved posts and gorgeous red taffeta hangings and tassels, and by it a red-dyed sheepskin on the sweet herbs to cuddle her toes.

"Fetch me a cup o' sack, for the love o' God, Alice!" As the maid bustled about the tall cupboard, Kate sank into her chair by the fire. "Come, Leezie, sit you down, an' tell me what I can do for you."

"Nothin'," I said, standing gangly and awkward, hopelessly longing.

"Nothin'? Well, we'll see." She tossed back the glass of wine, coughed, sighed deeply, and looked more like her old self. I stared at a long silver mirror beside the fireplace; no, a strip of four mirrors, one above the other, on the wall. Noticing, she drew me over to them. "Aye, look at yoursel', lass."

I looked. The silver was well polished, and we both showed clearly. I was surprised to see that I was only an inch shorter than Kate. But she was slim, I was skinny; she was — she was — I turned away in despair.

"What's wrong? You're no beautiful?" My head drooped woefully. "Well, that's true. But you're too hard on yoursel'. You're no worse than most lasses; you've the makin's o' beauty, if you care to try. You'll need to work at it, mind, for you look like a ewe that's been on the hill all winter, but — come here again." Reluctantly, but with dawning hope, I moved back, and she turned me this way and that, pointing out my good and bad points as if I was on sale. Resentment flared and died as I saw she wasn't trying to hurt my feelings.

"You've good skin, clear an' fine. Your teeth — open your mouth — wider — well, they could do wi' a rub wi' salt every night, but I've seen far worse. Your eyes are brighter than mine. Your hair's short, but look here!" Smiling, she pulled off her french bonnet, with its fine curve of linen and lace above her dark brow. Her tight black curls were far shorter than mine. Of course, she'd been shorn just four months back. "Aye, you'll need to do somethin' wi' that. But we'll trim it, an' brush it, an' it'll grow. Alice has dyes. Red's the fashion these days. It would take fine on your brown, d'you no think, Alice?"

The sour-faced maid, magically transformed into an ally, smiled and nodded. "No much to start wi', mistress, or all the folk'll be mockin' her."

"Or accuse her o' witchcraft! Aye, just a wee bit at a time, eh, Leezie, an' we'll give you the recipe that you can keep on by yoursel'. Can you read? No? I'll learn ye." Reading, even! My head whirled. "Now, your clothes." She shook her head. "Well, we can do somethin' there the day. Get that dress off, an' your petticoats. Come on, we can't see you right wrapped in that horse-blanket."

Horse-blanket! My new blue gown! Shyly I unlaced it while she and Alice raided the racks and chests in the corner. My petticoats were draggled, and my toes had come through both my hose. I was scarlet with shame, but they paid no attention to the dirt or holes.

"Aye, a fine slim waist. Don't slouch. Head up — up! Shoulders down. Look proud o' yoursel'. That's better. Slip off your shift, an' put on this one." It was fine soft lawn. "Now here." It was a pair of bodies; not iron, like the ones I'd refused before, but strong linen, with something stiffening them. "Whalebone, that is. They'll help you keep straight. Don't lace them tight, Alice, the first time. Now, that's no bad, eh?" Not bad? I could scarce breathe, let alone bend. They tied three more petticoats round my waist, the last one with two hoops of the whalebone in it to hold it out. All of them were finer linen than my own, but they stood out far more. "Starch. Alice'll show you how." And then a black quilted satin skirt. "No, it's no a dress, it's a top petticoat! To let your gown rustle an' slip."

"Dear God, Alice, cut her toenails! It's a farrier she needs, no a hosier!" Black, knitted wool stockings, with embroidery on the front of the foot to show when I walked. Embroidered garters — with a wink, "Take care who undoes these for you!" I'd have blushed again, if I'd ever stopped.

A dress, of black taffetas. It rustled sumptuously. "An' no

113

nonsense about no takin' it. I owe ye far mair nor a gown, an' besides, I never wear it. Black doesn't suit me. You'll have to learn how to manage the train." They padded the empty fullness at the front with a scarf. The neck was low, to show off the fine shift, and a two-inch wide starched ruff tied on at the neck. "No wide, for a young lass. Keep it out o' the rain, mind! An' the gown, or it'll spot."

Shoes. Not high heels, which needed practice or you staggered. Besides, I was tall already. "Most men doesn't like women that's taller than they are. Poor wee souls!" We all laughed. Black silk slippers, with thin silver buckles.

A new cap. The French style that the queen favoured, with its fall of white linen behind, to hide the shortness of my hair, and its prettily curved white band to frame my face. "Aye. It's simple an' severe, but it suits you. No much lace. You're no the frilly type." True.

"A rub o' flour to whiten your skin — Alice'll give you cream for it, an' your hands. An' a touch rouge, on your cheeks an' lips. No too much, Alice! We'll just darken your eyebrows, so. An' your eyelashes — will ye stop gigglin'! An' don't cry, or it'll smudge. Now, come an' see yoursel'. Stand up straight!"

As I came in front of the mirror again they stood back smiling, admiring their handiwork, satisfied and pleased. I stared, silent.

At last Kate had to ask, "Well? Do you like it? Is it no an improvement?"

I just sighed. This tall, elegant figure — it wasn't me at all. The curved seaming on the bodice — the low, pointed waist — the swirls of black cord on my sleeves, unobtrusive but rich — the huge eyes — the bright face cupped in its white cap and high ruff on the long, slender neck — this was a beautiful lady, not me! I couldn't say a word. They smiled, understanding.

I changed back before I left, and ran up the stair with it all piled in my arms, scarcely thanking them. I laid it out on my bed, touching it, remembering, dreaming. . . Then I packed it all away before ma saw it.

I spent the next two weeks, all day and every day, in at Kate Lenton's. She had the patience of a saint to bear with me and my clumsy ignorance of the style and charm which were crafted bone-deep in her; or maybe she liked playing with a real-life doll. But she and Alice between them transformed me into some faint resemblance to the lady I'd thought I was, coming into Edinburgh so long ago. Dear Lord, only three months!

They made me practise with a sheet trailing from my waist, to curb my long stride and teach me how to turn with poise and grace in a train, kicking it smoothly round with me. I could glide when I tried, of course, from carrying heavy water-tubs home on my head since I was six, and I just had to do it all the time now. Alice's clever needle improved my blue gown, but not to the match of the black. I learned how to bleach my hair with the contents of my chamber-pot, and dye it with a herb from Africa, called henna. I washed all over — Kate washed every month, she said, whether she needed it or not, and though it seemed ridiculously unhealthy I did the same. I'd even have done it every day if she had said so! I trimmed my nails and started to buff them to a polish. Kate forbade me to bleach out my hated freckles; "Fernytickles? Maybe the lads did tease you, but the men like them." It was her only touchstone of good or bad. Sharp lavender, she decided, should be my scent, not her warm musk or rose or violet.

I also started to learn my letters, and I worked away at my hornbook till I could name them all in less than a week, and start to make out simple words in two. And I practised talking like a lady. We were all proud of my progress.

In the afternoons I met some of Kate's friends, and learned more from them. Two of the court musicians, John Lauder and his son, discovered that my singing voice was quite fair, a light, high, sweet tone that chimed well with Kate's deep bell, and the four of us started to practise songs together. They taught me to dance, too, which I did well, being light on my feet. I enjoyed a fast galliard, or a volta, especially the part where the man whirled his partner high in the air. Master Knox, who had never been back to find out if he was indeed ma's cousin, would have been quite horrified.

I was never allowed to drink brandy, that Kate called eaude-vie — not that I wanted to anyway. And Kate always firmly sent me up home when she had guests to entertain, or if she was going out to the nobles' houses. "No, I'll no have you wi' me, lassie," she said. "You're no good enough a singer yet, an' your ma wouldn't like it." I sulked a bit, but she was quite right.

It came near to putting the hawks out of my mind. Ma surely hoped it had, for she smiled on my friendship with Kate; mind you, she was so busy she'd have smiled on almost anything that kept me occupied. But still, in the back of my mind, while the front was busy with b or d and p or q, or different kinds of lace, or the rhythm of stamping and clapping that rang your wrist and ankle bells in time for a moresco dance, there was the wee niggle; 'This isn't helping get you into the mews!' And I'd answer it, 'I'll do it yet!'

On the ninth day of March, Sandy shouted me down to the shop. Master Matheson was there, with an arm round ma's shoulders to support her. "What's wrong, ma?" I cried, taking the last flight of steps in two jumps, skirt or no.

She shook a hand weakly at me. "Nothin', Leezie, nothin'. I'm fine. Aye, Peter, I am so. Leave me be. If I sit down a minute I'll be fine. It's no harm done to me, lassie. Just — I've had a shock, that's all. Thank you, son."

She sipped a cup of ale while Master Matheson told us quietly what had happened. "She was walkin' up the Canongait just behind one o' Queen Mary's friars." He looked over at me. "You said your dad used pay protection money to the Armstrongs?" I nodded. "Aye, well, there's a crowd o' them in the town, an' Johnny Armstrong an' three o' his friends beat the friar wi' staves, an' stabbed him. An' when your mother tried to help him, they knocked her down."

Ma started to sob. The ale trembled in her hand till Sandy took it from her, patting her shoulder worriedly. "An' nobody would help us," she sobbed. "That was the worst. I was lyin' there, an' the men were shoutin' at me, an' kicked an' spat on me, an' struck at the man, an' I don't know how many folk were by, but they just watched. I cried on them for God's sake

116

help, but they didn't." She clutched Master Matheson's hand and mine.

"I'll get her to her bed," I murmured to him, and he nodded agreement.

"Aye, lass," he whispered above her head, "she's upset, but no hurt. She'll be fine the morn, or maybe the morn's morn. I'll tell Master Beaton what's happened, an' that she'll no be back for a day or two."

Ma sagged on the stool, babbling on. "He's near dead, Leezie, I'm sure o' it. He cried for mercy, Leezie, an' they just laughed an' hit him harder, till he lay still. An' they had knives, Leezie, an' sticks, an' a sword, an' —"

As her voice rose and rose, her head writhing and her eyes wild, Master Matheson drew back from her, looked hard at her twisting face, and slapped her firmly on one cheek. I started angrily, but Mistress Martin held me still. "Aye, son, that's right. She's no need o' a fit o' hysterics on top o' all." And indeed, after her first cry, ma seemed calmer. She dropped her head to my shoulder as I knelt by her, and started to weep noisily but normally.

Master Matheson put an arm round her. "Come on, Janet, my dear," he said. "I'll take you up the stair." He slipped the other arm under her knees and lifted her. She nestled into his arms, soft and relaxed as a sleeping babe.

'Janet, my dear.' It echoed in my mind as I ran up the stair to open the door for them, and I suddenly felt jealous. It had been me and ma for so long alone against dad; how could this man think to join in with us so easily?

I stripped ma of her dress, she sitting on the side of the bed helpless as a doll, and as she rolled back in just her shift onto the mattress, clinging to my hand, she was asleep already. I covered her and sat with her for a while. All my dislike of Master Matheson was back in a flood. Dislike? Hatred.

I jumped when there was a knock at the door. Thinking it might be him again, I slipped my hand free and marched over angrily, but in fact it was Mistress Martin, panting from the stairs. "How is she, Leezie?"

"Sleepin'," I whispered, my anger deflated. "Come in by the fire."

"I cannae bide," she replied softly, but she came in anyway and sank on the stool with a sigh of relief. "They stairs! I'll rest a minute, but no long, the rush'll be on soon. But Sandy's there. A fine lad, that. A hard worker. An' honest. I'm glad I thought to give him a chance. What do you think, Leezie?"

I looked at her rather blankly, my mind on other things. What was it to do with me? "Aye, he's fine," I agreed.

She nodded in satisfaction. "Aye. He's far better than that — that hellion. Away wi' the fairies sometimes, but a right cheery callant. An' Ina likes him."

It came to my mouth without my willing it. "Ma likes Master Matheson."

Her head tilted like a bird's, and her beady wee eyes peered shrewdly up at me. "An' ye're no happy about it? Why? He's a good man, Patey Matheson. He likes her fine. An' respects her. What's yer trouble? No yer dad, for sure."

It was an excuse, at least. "She's wed. How can she —?"

"Love another man?" The word was shocking. "Lassie, lassie! Lovin's nothin' to do wi' laws! Yer ma, no harm to her, God bless her, she's one o' the women as needs a man by them. Wi'out a man, she feels somehow lost, off balance, like. I'm no like that, an' from what I can see nor are you. We can manage fine oursel's. But there's others no like us, an' yer ma's one o' them. I'm no sayin' nothin' against her, mind. She just feels happier when there's a man about to look after her. An' for her to look after."

I thought about it. Maybe there was more than one reason why ma hadn't run away from dad. Sure enough, she had worried about him. Needing a man — "Ye mean she's like Kate Lenton?" I asked defensively.

The old lady laughed out loud. "Kate? Kate need a man to look after her? My certes, lassie, dinnae let her her ye say that, or she'd have the hide off ye! That one needs no man, nor ever will. It's that wildness, that independence, draws the men to her. Some o' them, anyway. Some men prefers meekness. Patey Matheson, for one. Kate'll play at it, whiles, to get her own ends, but in truth she's her own mistress. No, lassie, yer ma's no like Kate any way at all. She's a good woman. No that Kate isnae, in her own way, but. . . An' she knows her man, an' lucky for her, he loves her. An' ye've no to feel bad about it."

Not feel bad? Daftness! How could I help it? I sulked on my stool.

The old wife studied me shrewdly. "Will ye be wi' her all yer life, eh?"

I jumped at the change of subject. "No, o' course not," I said, puzzled.

"Well then, would ye have yer mother bide alone an' unhappy till she dies just because ye were jealous o' her now? Is that reasonable?"

"No," I admitted doubtfully.

She grinned quirkily at me. "But it doesnae help ye feel better, eh? Ye're an honest lassie, Leezie, kind an' thoughtful, an' ye see clear. You think about it. Ask yersel' does yer mother no deserve a bit happiness at the last, an' will ye stand in her way? An' she's picked a fine man this time, her match every way. Aye. How she'll get him I couldnae say, but I'll help her all I can, for I love her like my own daughter. An' if you love her too, you'll do the same." She sat up, looked at the sky, and yelped. "My certes, look at that, it's past time for the rush, an' here me sittin' fast as a broody hen." As she opened the door, she grinned back at me. "The next sermon from the Reverend Martin will be. . ." she joked, blew a raspberry, and pattered away down.

As I sat by ma in the twilight, I mumped, and thought, and wondered, and eventually decided Mistress Martin was in the right of it. I'd no business to stand in ma's way, or make her feel bad. It might be — it would be — hard at first, but as I got used to the idea. . . It had been coming a long time, I could see that now. I just hadn't noticed. Hadn't wanted to notice. I liked Master Matheson. He'd shown me how to fire his pistol. I laughed at myself — what a childish reason for liking someone. How much older I'd grown since I came to Edinburgh! I felt all mature and wise. And then laughed at myself again for conceit, checked ma was sleeping, and took up my book to practise my reading.

It must have been an hour later that ma woke, in a state. "Leezie, come an' help me dress!" she gasped, staggering as she reached for her gown.

I took her fluttering hands and held her still. "What is it, ma? What's troublin' ye? There's nothin' that urgent, sure, that ye —"

"Aye is there!" she protested, trying to escape, and then collapsing on the bed as her legs folded under her. She looked up at me pathetically. "It's Lady Jean, the Countess o' Argyll. She came by the store-room an' admired a bit lawn trimmin' wi' wee roses embroidered on it. She asked me special to get her some, an' I was comin' up the street for it when —"

"Aye, ma, aye," I said soothingly. "Can it no wait till the morn? She'll be at supper soon, an' no wantin' to bother wi' linens." She shook her head desperately, and tried to stand up again. I could see in her state there would be no peace for her till the errand was done. I sighed, for I wanted to study my book. However. . . "Never fret, ma, if ye're that set on it, I'll take it down to her. Where'll I get it? And how much?"

She sank back in relief. "You don't mind, lass? It's old Meg Hamilton, she lives at the top above the knife shop in Riddell's Close. She promised me another ten ells the day, an' I was goin' to give that to Lady Jean, at six shillin' the ell, an' get Meg to do ten more for the babe. It's a good deal for Meg, an' there's time, for the babe's no due for three month yet —"

"Aye, ma, aye, I understand," I said, pushing her down on the bed again and drawing the blanket up round her. "Here, let me tuck ye in, an' I'll run straight away an' fetch it, an' seek out the lady, an' give it to her."

"Into her own hands, now!" ma whispered. "Promise me, now! No thievin' servant! I'll no have it stolen, an' be blamed for its loss! Promise me!"

She was getting worked up again. I promised, with no intention of keeping my word. Lady Jean's steward would do me fine, and a note of receipt. Would I change into my black taffeta dress? No, not for a steward, even if it was in the Palace. Ma's anxious eyes followed me as I left, and as I went through the shop I asked Mistress Martin to look up at her from time to time.

"Aye, sure, lassie," the old wife said cheerily. She and Sandy were both white from stacking tubs of raisins and sacks of flour, and sneezing she announced with glee that they were using seven sacks a week now, the silver was fair rolling in, and Sandy's wage was going up again. They grinned at each other in content, and Ina grunted and nodded smiling by the door.

"Where are ye off to, Leezie?" asked Sandy, brushing himself down.

"I've an errand to run for ma," I said. They looked at each other again, frowning this time through the drifting mist of flour.

"It's past curfew, Leezie," Babs Martin warned me, "an' it's right dark. I dinnae think it's safe."

"In civilised Edinburgh?" I laughed. It had become a joke for all of us. Truth to tell, the prospect of a night walk, that I'd not done in weeks, attracted and excited me.

"Civilised? Ye can say that, after what happened to the priest the day? An' all they Armstrongs in the town? An' Kerrs. An' more Douglases than I've seen in years." The old lady was scandalised and worried. "Ye're no settin' foot out o' this house alone. Sandy, ye'll leave that an' go wi' her."

I protested, showing her I'd my knife with me — I'd not told ma, but just took it anyway. But she insisted. "There's been an awfu' queer feel about the town this past two-three days. Last time I felt it was just before Moray's revolt. Somethin's brewin'. I dinnae want ye out in it. But if ye must go, then ye'll take Sandy wi' ye. An' put off yer white apron, lassie, an' take my shawl. It's dark, no light fawn like yer own. God keep ye, then, lass."

As Sandy and I went out, I was surprised how intense she'd been. I suggested that the windy weather must be affecting her, but Sandy shook his head doubtfully. "Maybe," he said, "but she's lived in the town all her days, an' she's no daft. I'm thinkin' we'd best get yer errand done quick as we can."

"Well, I'm no that keen on stayin' out long in this cold blast anyway," I agreed. "Come on, then — race ye to the corner o' Riddell's Close!"

It didn't take long to get the wee roll of linen. The Netherbow gates were shut, of course, since it was after sunset, but Sandy knew a place where the wall was broken to only about seven feet high, and giggling like bairns we slid down, hung by our hands and dropped, to get out without paying our toll. A good thing I'd not put on my black! Getting back would be more difficult, but he knew a place where the cracks in the stone let you climb up.

It was strange, I had to admit, how few folk were about the Canongait, but we enjoyed the freedom. I tucked up my skirt and we swooped down the cobbles, clattering right to the palace gates.

The guards stopped us. Sixteen of them. When we explained our errand, one tried to cuff Sandy's ear and told us to clear out. Sandy dodged easily, and when I'd have argued, he took my arm and led me firmly away. "Ye've no sense, sometimes, Leezie," he said, exasperated, when I objected. "Never argy-bargy wi' an armed man! Have ye never seen all the wee houses at the back o' the Palace? We'll get in there somewheres no bother." And so we did.

I'd been in often with ma, and Sandy had taken several messages there; the palace was usually crammed, near as bad as the High Street. But now the whole place was deserted. It was eerie. We were heading for the kitchen to ask directions to Lady Jean's chambers when a man came hurrying round a corner behind us with two bottles of wine in each hand. As he passed us, I put out a hand to his sleeve and said, "Sir?"

He jumped a yard, tripped on the edge of a flagstone under the rushes and, with a baa-ing noise like an aggrieved sheep sank gracefully to the ground, the bottles flying from one hand. Sandy managed to save one of them, but the other smashed on the stone, and the wine splashed up all over the man's cream-coloured doublet.

"Mort de ma vie!" swore the man through clenched teeth. "I 'ave twist my foot! Aagh! Bon Dieu, regardez mon gilet!" He swore again as I apologised, vainly trying to rub off some of the red stain with my shawl. The man was nearly weeping with rage. "Voilà Sa Majeste 'oo attend ze wine of Burgundy, an' but eight bottle zat remain, an' you make me to break one of zem, an' I none can serve her wit' ze ozzer — ah, nom d'un nom d'un nom!"

We stood awkwardly, getting irritated as he cursed in French. It wasn't our fault he couldn't keep his feet. "W'at is it you do here?" he demanded.

"I'm seekin' the Lady Jean o' Argyll's steward, sir. I've a packet for her ladyship. But we couldnae — couldn't find anybody to ask." I spoke politely.

"Non." Suddenly, for all the pain of his ankle, he struggled to his feet. "No, is true. Il n'y a personne. Is nobody." He looked all round, and his face changed. He looked wary. Sandy offered him the bottle of wine he'd rescued, but the man paid no attention to it. He glanced at me again. "You search Madame la Comtesse d'Argyll?"

"Her steward, sir," I said.

"Wiz un packet? Eh bien, I not know where is ze servant, but I tell you where is la maitresse. An' you can to her deliver your packet en person."

Well, it was what ma had told me to do anyway. Sandy was shaking his head, but I thanked the man kindly. He grinned at me unpleasantly.

"Oui. She take souper wiz Sa Majesté. La Reine — Queen Marie." I gasped. "An' since you 'ave cause me do bad to my foot, an' destroy my jacket zat I not can serve 'Er Grace, you weel do so for me! Voici." As I gaped, he thrust the two bottles in his left hand at me. "Go to ze end of zis passage 'ere, an' mount ze stair at right. Mount two stair, make knock on ze door, an' enter. Zere weel be a man zere weel tell you w'at to do."

Something in his voice told me just what he expected the man to tell me to do, but I didn't refuse or argue. "Aye, sir," I said, took the bottles and dragged Sandy away before anybody else came by to take over the errand.

As we turned the corner, the man started to hop away, muttering, "Alors, qu'est-ce qu'il y a qui arrive ce soir?" I paid no attention. Whatever was happening that evening, it suited me down to the ground. Funny how the French language, that I'd not heard since I was five, came back so clear to me.

Sandy gripped my arm to hold me back. "What the devil d'ye think ye're at, Leezie Sinclair?" he demanded. "We cannae go on a message to the Queen! Are ye wandered in yer wits?"

"No, I'm no!" I snapped at him, and pulled free. "Ach, why did I no put on my good black? Listen, Sandy. I must do it! You know I want into the mews! Ma'll no ask the Queen to aid me, but this is my chance to ask her mysel'! It's as if it was meant!"

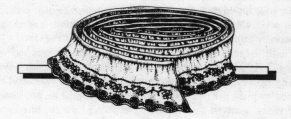

Rizzio

"They'll jail ye!" Sandy argued. "Ye're no a royal servant! Ye cannae interrupt the Queen at her supper!"

"Aye, can I! For I've the wine to deliver! D'ye no see, Sandy!" I took his bottle and brushed past him, the bottles tucked under my arm, and hurried up the stairs, beckoning him urgently as he dragged unwilling behind me. The whole place was eerily deserted. Sure enough, there was a door on the landing at the top. Sandy hung back, and I made a face at him for cowardice as I smoothed my gown and hair, drew a deep breath and knocked gingerly. How hard should you knock at a queen's door? As I'd been told, I walked in.

I was in a big room, with a panelled, painted ceiling and walls. In the corner opposite me a spiral stair ran both up and down, and all the dozen or so folk in the room were watching a serving-man scuttling down it, his ears fair frizzled by a bombardment of French oaths. "Idio'! Besteer ze feet or I steer you, like ze soup! Ze crayfeesh she mus' be serve boiling 'ot! Go! Now! Mon Dieu, 'ow can one produce a meal feet for a queen een zees dog-kennel! Regard zat pan! 'E steek! Attention au petit pot!" There was a crash. "Ze oystaire sauce she taste good off ze floor, no?" It took no great brain to deduce that that must be a kitchen up there, with another of the Queen's

French servants. Where, then, was the Queen's room? Through the door on my right?

As I nervously followed the servant towards it, a burst of music rose beyond. A flute, a viol, a lute, and two fine voices I knew well. I hesitated till it shut behind the man, and then, as someone noticed me and started to ask, "What the devil —?" I hurriedly braced myself and knocked again. It opened on a young lad, a page about nine inches shorter than myself, staring up at me. He gaped, as taken aback as I was, and then started to push me out. He'd no chance, not till he got another four years' growth and weight. He shoved away, but I stood my ground as he whispered desperately, "Get out, get away! This is no place for you! What d'you think you're doin' —"

The music raggedly lost tempo and stopped. Someone inside the next room called, "What is it, Tony?"

He turned rapidly. "Nothin', sir! Just — just — Can you come, sir?"

"Just what?" The lad stepped aside as steps crossed towards us and the door was pulled wider. "A lass! Wi' the wine? Who in God's name are you, lass? An' where's the man should be here?" a tall man in the red and gold uniform of the officers of the Queen's household snapped angrily at me. I knew him, though he'd not remember me. I'd come with ma to carry a bale of fine wool to him just a week before; Master Beaton, one of the Queen's stewards.

I took a step back from his anger. "Careful, sir, ye'll make me drop the bottles, an' there's but four left!" I said anxiously, and he tut-tutted at me.

A woman's voice called, "Bottles? Wine? Grace a Dieu, my Burgundy wine at last! Master Beaton, Master Beaton, bring it in! We're dying o' thirst! Let's see this lass, anyway!" I knew that high, clear voice.

Another face appeared, dark, ugly, a dazzling white smile of pearly teeth above an equally dazzling row of pearl buttons on the gold-trimmed black satin doublet. An agile eyebrow shot up. "A lass? Santa Maria, how comes it a lass is bring up ze wine? Entair, entair! Mastair Beaton, you 'ave need to take ordair in your pantry zis night, it seems me!" He waved me into the room.

It was a bedroom, the walls all bright tapestries, with a huge yellow-curtained bed against one wall. I'd never seen so much embroidered damask. The floor was sweetly covered with lavender and rosemary instead of rushes, and a fine carpet beside the bed. In one corner sat Master Lauder and his son John, nodding and smiling at me in a puzzled way, with six or seven more maids and menservants standing about the room. I was ushered hastily over to yet another door on the far side, and there was a chorus of laughter as I entered.

Flushing with excitement, I nearly dropped the precious bottles while I curtseyed as Kate had taught me to the people round the small table. It was a squeeze for them, for the little room with the rich tapestried curtains and the painted panelling on the walls and ceiling was only about twelve feet long and not as wide. The Queen herself was in the centre of one long side, her chair with its royal canopy in the embrasure of the window facing the fire. She was smiling and beckoning to me to place the wine before her. At the far end of the table the lady I'd actually come to seek, her half-sister Lady Jean, Countess of Argyll, was frowning and amused. On the Queen's left, between her and her sister, sat a man I didn't know. On her right sat her half-brother, Lord Robert Stewart, that I'd seen often in the town, and at this end by the door was an empty chair where the ugly man had been sitting. I knew him well, for he was David Rizzio, Seigneur Davie, perhaps the most envied man at the court, and most hated; the Queen's secretary and favourite.

He laughed behind me as I rose from my curtsey and carefully placed the bottles on the table among the dishes. "A most unusual servant, eh, Roberto?"

Master Beaton flushed again. "Your Grace, wi' your leave I'll —"

"Ah, pray you be still a moment, Master Beaton!" she smiled. "Don't I know your face, lassie? We've met before this, surely."

I was flustered and delighted she remembered me. "Aye, Yer

— Your Grace!" I must speak politely! "With my ma — my mother. We met near Kirkliston, Your Grace, she's Janet — Janet Sinclair as was! You said you sometimes wore breeks like me."

Everyone started to laugh again, and I blushed, but the Queen shushed them, waving down their laughter with her hands. "Hush, now, my friends! I mind on it fine. How is Janet these days, lass? I've no seen her about?"

"She's fine, Your Grace, but tired," I said. Why worry her by reminding her about the attack on her man?

"I tire easy mysel' these days. Tell her I do sympathise," she smiled. She stretched back from the table a bit, the rounded swell showing under her loose white overgown as she eased herself in the chair. As a man in a black gown, one of the servants crowded at the door to watch, stepped forward beside me, she raised a hand to stop him. "Non, non, Monsieur Nau, tout va bien, ce n'est rien! My physician," she explained to me kindly. "He's aye worryin' about me, but I'm fine. Now, lass. Would you tell us how you came to be here?"

All the rest leaned forward attentively. I explained, to growing frowns.

"Did the guard on the stair no stop you, then?" asked the man on the Queen's left. Hearing there was no guard on the stair, he shot to his feet.

"Aye, Mastair Erskine, you 'ad best be about, to see w'at 'as happen, no? It seem zere is a severe lack of discipline in your guard zis night!" Seigneur Davie's voice was sharp and his rings flashed as he waved the man to the door. Master Erskine's lips tightened with annoyance. "An' in ze kitchen also, Mastair Beaton! Are you not responsible for ze service in ze Palace? Zen go you bot' see w'at 'as cause zis — zis disgraceful state of affair!"

Master Beaton stiffened behind me, and his breath hissed through his nose. He bowed to the Queen. "If it please Your Grace to give me leave. . ." The stress on 'Your Grace' was clear.

"Your Grace. . ." bowed Master Erskine, at the door already.

"Aye, go you, my friends, an' return quickly — or there'll be no wine left!" the Queen cried gaily, trying to make amends for Master Davie's arrogance. As the door closed, she frowned at him, and he bowed floridly.

"My sole care is for ze safety of Your Grace, Madonna!" he protested.

Lord Robert leaned forward. "Then allow others the same concern, sir, an' don't insult them." His voice was harsh with annoyance.

The Queen tapped the table with a finger. "Enough, Robert!" He fell silent at once. She was the Queen, after all, even if she was but twenty-five. She frowned at Master Rizzio. "Davie, that was uncalled-for."

He pretended to be terrified, hiding behind me and peeking out over my shoulder. Being smaller than me, he had to stand on tiptoe to do it. "Ah, Madonna! Perdone me! W'at can I do to make amend of my fault?" he begged, switching from one shoulder to the other, lifting my arms to make faces under them, I embarrassed and nervous as the little man played the fool round me. "A song? A new canzo? Compose but zis very morn by Your Grace most 'umble obedient servant, to please Your Grace most delicate, exquisite ear?"

His face was so tragical, and yet so full of glee, that they couldn't help laughing, though Lady Jean snorted as she smiled in spite of herself. "Later, Davie, later," the Queen promised him, and he bowed again, lavishly, hand on heart, and sat, beckoning for more wine. The music started again outside.

I sighed with relief. To ease the moment Lady Jean asked to see the lawn, and I unrolled it before them. They murmured in admiration. "Fine an' soft. Aye, I like the wee rosebuds. Your mother has good taste, lass," approved the Queen. "But then I knew that, when I asked her to come see to my babe's cradle. But what about yoursel', lassie? How are you settlin' in here?"

This was what I'd dreamed of. As I rewound the strip of linen, I told them how I'd chanced to find the Queen's hawk, and how I longed to join her service in the mews. I didn't dare ask, but looked hopefully at her as I ended.

She sat back, thoughtfully cracking a crayfish claw and drawing the pink flesh out of it. "What do you think, Robert? Can I help?"

He shook his head decisively. "No, madam, you must not!" He smiled over at me, friendly enough but quite firm. "I'm sorry for the lass, but you can't countermand your head falconer's decision wi'out good reason." My heart sank. That was just what Master Matheson had said, and the Queen was nodding.

She looked regretfully at me. "You hear, lass? Lord Robert knows better than mysel' in a matter o' the customs o' the country. I'm sorry, as well —"

Suddenly there was a stir in the bedroom behind me, and a kind of hiccup in the music. I looked round quickly, to see the tapestry lifted in a corner of the room. There was a small open door behind it there, and a man walked across from it and entered the Queen's dining room past me. A tall young man, somewhat younger than the Queen, more richly dressed than even Seigneur Davie. As they all rose to greet him I knew him; the man from Kate's that first day; the King! I joined the others, except the Queen, bowing or curtseying to him.

It seemed everyone was surprised. He looked round, smirking and cracking his knuckles nervously. "Sit, sit down! I didn't mean to interrupt you!" he said. "No, no, I won't take anythin'. Well, maybe a glass o' wine, eh? I've had supper already, I'm not hungry." He sat down beside the Queen in Master Erskine's place, expansively smiled round at everyone else exchanging baffled glances, for we all knew where he usually spent his evenings, rubbed his hands, and said importantly, "Well!" As we all waited for the announcement we felt was coming, he grinned, fidgeted, and said plaintively, "It's a cold night, eh?"

The Queen blinked, put down the crayfish shell, and smiled in a puzzled way at him. "It's aye a pleasure to have your company at supper, Henry," she said, rather dryly. "A rare pleasure." Lady Jean glanced up rapidly. She noticed me, and motioned me out with a small gesture of her hand. Glad to get away, I started backing out of the door, as the King coughed, eased his tight ruffed collar with his forefinger, and slipped his arm round the Queen's waist. Her eyebrows rose, and she seemed to stiffen, but then she relaxed and smiled at him more fully. "Aye, I'm truly glad to see you here, my lord," she said.

Everybody seemed to sigh with relief, and movement returned to the table. One man came forward with the wine jug, another offered a napkin for the Queen's fingers. My legs bumped the bed, and I turned to go. Behind me, Rizzio was saying, "Your Majesty, may I tell 'er Grace about our match of tennis zis morn? Nevair 'ave I observe you in such strengt', I swear! My poor hands still pain me of returning your cannon-ball strokes!" Darnley was laughing.

Suddenly the tapestry was flung up again, and a horrifying figure lurched into the bedroom. It was a tall man in full armour, grey-faced, red-eyed, clutching the tapestry to keep from falling, clanking over to the dining-room door. The music faltered and stopped and one of the maids screamed as they all rose to their feet and scattered from before him.

"Ruthven!" cried Lord Robert. "God, man, what are you doin' here? I heard you were on your death-bed!" The intruder was the Earl of Gowrie, then, who had been one of the Queen's advisers till a few months back; and he certainly looked dead, or next to it, swaying, leaning on his drawn sword. But no-one except her guard was allowed to bear arms in the Queen's presence! Surely a former Privy Councillor would know that! What could he want? Was he mad?

The dreadful figure drew a deep, rattling breath. "May it please — Your Majesty," said a voice of doom, pausing often, "to let yonder man — Davie — come forth o' your presence! He's been too — too long here!"

The Queen drew back in dismay for a moment, but then faced the figure firmly. "He's here at my own wish! What offence has he done you?"

There was another pause as Lord Ruthven gathered his strength for speech. "Great offence!" at last he grated, staring eyes fixed on the Queen's face.

The Queen was as white as her own collar, and turned on

her husband. "What do you know o' this, Henry?" she demanded, as he backed off from her wrath. "He's come up the private stair from your own room. My lord, you must know what's the reason behind this!"

Darnley stood still by her, trembling, shaking his head and hands feebly against her glowing rage and fear. It was Ruthven, panting and heaving with the strain of staying upright, who answered. "For this man's sake — madam — you have put aside all — all the Protestant lords — your advisers — you listen to a crafty vile stranger — not your own men — nor your own husband! And what else God alone knows! The disgrace — to the King — that you spend so much time wi' a servant! An' for his sake — you'll no grant yer husband — the King here — the full Crown Mat- matrimonial — as is his due!" Darnley's head was nodding agreement.

Rizzio shrank back along the side of the table to shelter in the shallow window embrasure behind the Queen's chair. He had no weapon but a table-knife, against Ruthven's sword. While everyone was watching Lord Ruthven in a kind of trance of horror, I thought I could slip away and call the guard. Master Erskine must have found some of them, surely? I glided backwards round the bed and reached back for the door handle, ready to race out and yell for help.

Suddenly the huge man cried out, "Sir!" Darnley jumped, his mouth open. "Take the Queen's Majesty — your sovereign an' wife — to you!" Darnley's mouth closed convulsively and as Ruthven thrust the Queen at him, he clutched her in his arms. All the others came to life at the shout, and dived at Ruthven, but he pulled out a pistol and waved them back. "Lay no hands on me, for I'll no be handled!" he yelled wildly.

The shouting must have been a signal. The door knob turned under my hand, and a dozen men rushed in from the outside room, knocking me forward and carrying me with them right back to the door of the dining room. More came up from the King's room, and others were swarming up the kitchen stair; thirty at least.

The Queen screamed as the table was knocked off its trestles, toppling all the dishes, cups and bottles clattering and crashing to the floor. The candlesticks went, too, but Lady Jean grabbed one as it fell and held it up in the far corner to light the scene, her other hand at her mouth for fear. As the men pushed in, Rizzio huddled back in the window, and the Queen twisted in her husband's arms to protect him, but Ruthven shoved past her and grabbed him.

One man aimed a pistol at the Queen herself, pressing it to her stomach. In horror I snatched at my knife and lunged forward, but I knew I was too late. . . With relief I heard the click of a misfire even as a sword hilt clouted me aside behind the door, my head buzzing.

Someone seized Darnley's own dagger and stabbed right past the Queen as Rizzio was dragged out. The Italian's blood spurted onto her white gown. He gripped her skirt desperately, but Darnley held her back while the others dragged and kicked the little man out, screaming, "Justizia, justizia! Save my life, madam, save me!"

I pressed back against the wall, trying not to be seen. Against all these armed, violent, desperate men I could do nothing. I'd tried to save the Queen, and escaped once. I'd not risk my life again, for Rizzio. They heaved him out of the dining room door and across the bedroom, stabbing him over and over. He fell among the lavender by the outside door. Darnley let go of the Queen and crossed uncertainly after the murderers, to be welcomed by them and pulled into the group. They went on striking for a long while after the screams stopped.

After a pause a voice in the crowd — Darnley's voice — said, "Get him out of here! Throw him down!" I closed over the door, to muffle the thumping of a body trundling down the stair, and shut out sight of the murderers.

The Queen stood by the window of her tiny dining room, rigid and as white as her gown. Lady Jean, handing the candlestick to one of the servants, ran to take her in her arms. "Madam, madam! Are you all right? They've no harmed you?" One of the maids was sick in the corner, but after a moment came over with her companion to help the Queen.

They set her chair upright again for her and settled her in it, fluttering round her with wine, medicine, a damp cloth for her brow, anxious inquiries, as she didn't answer them. Her hand smoothed over and over the red smear on her skirt, and when they wanted to rub it away she stopped them. "Non, laisse-le. Leave it," she muttered, the first words she had spoken.

She lifted her head. "Who was there?" she asked in a dry whisper, and took a sip of the wine her page held for her as they all looked at each other.

"Lindsay. Lindsay o' the Byres," said Lord Robert.

"Aye. An' Kerr o' Fawdonside. He held a pistol to my side, but by God's grace it misfired." They all gasped, for this was the first most of them knew of it. "He tried to kill my priest, the first Mass ever I held in Scotland."

"George Douglas, the Earl o' Morton's half-brother."

"Aye," she agreed, "my — my husband's uncle. He struck first."

They all joined in with more names. She nodded, dead-faced, to all of them. "Mind them all. I charge you, remember them, in case that I forget. Sir James Balfour? No? No, he'd no be here; but he planned it. You understand, do you not, it was me they meant to kill. Me an' my child." Her hands went protectively to the swell of her skirt. "They didn't dare do it wi' steel, no quite, but they hope to do it wi' the shock. But they'll no succeed!" Her voice was stronger now and determined, but her hands were trembling, and she was shivering with reaction. They drew her nearer the fire.

There was a tentative tap at the door of the bedroom, and the page laddie opened it. Darnley came in, looking scared and triumphant, sneering and nervous, all together. The Queen roused herself. "My lord! Why have you done this wicked thing to me? You were but a commoner, an' I made you my husband! What offence have I done you, that you should do me such shame?"

He burst out at her defiantly, sulkily, a long rambling speech. She didn't treat him right. Since Davie became such a favourite she spent less time with her husband, but sat playing cards with Davie till dawn. . . On and on.

"If you mislike the way I treat you, my lord, you've but

yoursel' to blame for it!" she interrupted him, snarling. "Spent little time wi' you? I'll spend even less in future! I'll never be wife to you again, till I make your heart as sore as mine is now!" He was overwhelmed by her fury, losing all his bombast.

The door opened again, and as we swung round the steel figure of Lord Ruthven lurched back in. He collapsed clanking on a chest and called for wine. After a moment's hesitation, Darnley gestured to one of the servingmen, who lifted a bottle and a cup from the floor and poured for the sick man. The Queen pushed herself to her feet, to stand over him. "Is this your sickness, Lord Ruthven? Are you drunk, rather than a traitor?" she demanded fiercely. "You were once my adviser, an' I trusted you. But now — I warn you, sir, if either mysel' or my child should come to harm through this night's work, I have friends will avenge me! I warn you, sir!"

Panting, he heaved himself up from the seat and out to the door. "An' I warn you, Your Majesty. I — the King an' I — we have friends too. Don — don't think to cheat your husband again. No. Never. For there's Douglases enough are his friends to — to prevent you!" He swung out an arm to Darnley, who took it nervously, and the pair of them supported each other out of the door.

One of the men giggled, and it ran in a kind of nervous twitch round the room. Only the Queen never noticed it, and it died as she sank onto the same chest where Ruthven had sat. "Douglases enough. Aye." Her whisper was bitter. "More than enough. You mind the Cardinal, Cardinal Beaton, said he'd rid the realm o' Douglases, if it killed him? He didn't do it, an' they killed him right enough. Them an' Knox. But I swear they'll not kill me. Whatever I must do — I'll do it. But they'll not beat me." Her defiant head sank. Lady Jean came to her, and supported the Queen's head again on her breast.

I wished I was well away. And where was Sandy in all this?

"Where is he?" The Queen's voice, an uncanny echo of my own thought, made me jump. "Is he dead?" She meant Davie Rizzio, of course. No-one answered. We all knew the answer, but who could bring himself to say it? "Go an' see. One o' you — go an' see. Tony! You." Reluctantly the lad went to the door and looked out. After a moment he slipped through, to return after a few seconds white and sick-looking. "Well?" she demanded.

"Aye, Madam, he's dead," the lad whispered. As her eyes beckoned him on, he blurted out, "The King's own dagger's in him! An' the porter's jeerin' at him that he's lyin' on the same chest he slept on when he first came here!"

There was a long pause, while the Queen mastered her faintness. Suddenly her head swung up. "Huntly!" she snapped. "An' Bothwell! My best supporters! They're at supper here, in Huntly's rooms! Those murderin' rascals will kill them too if they catch them! They must be warned!"

All her servants looked at each other, and her brother Robert spoke for all. "How, Madam? We can see now why the servants were few, an' too many guards — Douglases all, no doubt! The palace'll be swarmin' wi' them, an' all our faces are well known to be your servants, an' here wi' you. There's none o' us can pass the Douglases this night. D'you want us killed?"

"Try!" she urged desperately. "We must try!"

"We can't! It's no use, madam!" he argued. "Even if it's no too late already. The stair's full o' men. An' if we could get past them, we couldn't pass the corridors." He hadn't helped Rizzio much, either.

"There's the wee stair there," I offered, forgetting to take the back seat in the urgency of the moment. "Could ye no — go — down —" I trickled to a stop as they all turned to stare at me.

"That's the King's own chamber!" said Lady Jean in disdain, and I bit my lip.

But the Queen nodded. "Aye, it is, an' it's maybe the one way they'll no think to guard. An' Lord Robert's right, none o' my own folk can go. It'll have to be you, lass."

"Me!" They were all staring again. "But — I can't!"

"You must!" Lord Robert was grasping fast at the idea too. Easy for him — it wasn't him that would have to go.

"I don't know the way!"

"We'll tell you. You must try, lassie, for my sake, an' the

sake o' your unborn king within me!" The Queen was overwhelming in her urgency. "An' you must go now, before they think to come back. Now! Please, lassie! It's your Queen is askin' you! Beggin' you!" They all looked horrified.

Oh, how did I aye get into trouble? But what could I say?

Bothwell

They told me the way four times, describing the whole palace to me, drawing wee maps on the floor — but not where the blood-stains lay — and at last it sank in. I hoped.

I slipped under the tapestry and down the narrow stair in a state of wild excitement. As if murder and treason weren't enough, I had to go on a rescue mission for the Earl of Bothwell! Well, I thought, if this wasn't a good enough reason for the Queen to help me get into the mews, what was?

There was a man smoothing out the great canopied bed in the king's room. I peered cautiously round the edge of the door, waited scarce breathing till he was hidden on the far side of the embroidered purple hangings — purple velvet round your bed? Not my notion — what a daft thought just at this moment! I slid across the room as silently as I could to the door on the other side. There were men in the anteroom.

The servant turned behind me. "Here, who's that? What're you doin' here, me girl?" His accent was English. I turned at bay, ready to fight my way if necessary back to the stair up to the Queen's rooms, but the wee man was just standing watching me. "You're from up there?" I nodded. "And you want out?" I nodded again. Could he be sympathetic? "Aye, small blame to you. I'm not keen on stayin' here meself, girl."

He sighed, and shook his head. "A fine business, this! Is she — Her Majesty — is she still — you know — well? In good health? Good!" He puffed his cheeks in relief, but then looked again and took in my plain clothes. "What were you up there for?"

I gaped a second, and remembered the trimming. In the excitement, I'd just shoved it back into my pocket. I showed it to him. "I'd to take this up to —" make myself unimportant — "to one o' the maids, an' the men just came up the stair at my back, an' I couldn't get out. Sir."

"Well, you picked a fine time to do your errand, girl! And a fine way to get out, too, for there's guards on the door, and they'll not even let me out, and I'm John Taylor, the King's own valet!" In his annoyance he was quite comical, with his superior southern nose right out of joint, but I'd no time to swop complaints with him.

"How many are there, sir?"

"Eight. A minute ago, at least. Douglases all, as wild a crew as ever I've seen! No respect for their betters! I wish I was back in Hampstead! You can't get out this way, girl!" As I eased the door open a touch, his alarm increased. "Here, you can't do that! If they see you they'll blame me!"

All the guards were over at the windows, their backs to me, but side on to the doorway I'd to go through. I had to get away before this idiot's squawking attracted their attention. I slipped into the room as the poor wee man's hand reached for my shoulder, and ran over to the far door. He didn't cry out, but stood watching in an agony of indecision as I lifted the latch. I'd nearly got the door open silently when he made up his mind, and called out to them to catch me. By the time they turned to him, and then back to me, I was out and running.

A voice shouted, "Get her!" Another cried, "It's just a servin' lass!" The first voice shouted again, "Are ye sure? Johnnie, Dougie, after her!"

Here was a corner. To the left there were more guards, at the far end of the corridor, holding torches, but listening to their officer talking. I checked and turned away from them, though it was the wrong way, and round the next corner again. Had I lost them?

A hand grabbed my wrist and I was violently jerked to a stop, and hauled into a dark window embrasure. I opened my mouth to scream.

My attacker's other hand clamped over my mouth, and a voice hissed in my ear, "Wheesht! No a sound!" Sandy!

When I'd got my heart back out of my throat — "Are ye tryin' to give me a fit, ye big gowk?" I gasped. "Are ye all right?"

He drew the curtain closed in front of us. "I was just goin' to ask ye the same," he whispered, "but I hear ye are. Are those men chasin' ye?" To my horror he stuck his head out, and as the men pounded up, and I tried not to breathe, said innocently, "Are ye seekin' a lassie ran by, sirs? Aye, that way!" They raced on, and my heart started again as he came back into the shelter with a half-seen grin. "Aye puts them off, that, helpin' them on their way." I could near have hit him for his complacency — giving me shocks like that! If I'd not been so glad to see him. "Now come on — it's clear out this way."

He started to pull me out of the window archway, but I held him back and quickly told him what I had to do. "Ach away, ye're daft," he argued. "There's more Douglases in the Palace than woodworm! Even if the lords isnae killed or arrested already, they'll never get out!"

"I must try, Sandy," I insisted. "It's the Queen's own command!"

He sighed, and squatted down to think. "Where's Huntly's rooms, anyway?"

"At the back, on the first floor," I said. I told him how I'd been instructed to get there, and he nodded.

"Aye, I went a message round that way once. Now — I wonder. . . Did they say how far the rooms were from the back corner o' the house?"

"They said it's the fourth door from the end." Why was it so important?

"Aye, that's no so bad," he muttered. "Now mind what I tell ye, keep the head, an' we'll maybe all get out o' this carry-on alive!"

I clamped down my temper, shut my mouth, listened carefully to his plan, and we darted out of our hiding-place to go seeking our separate goals. It was a wrench parting from him.

In spite of my instructions, I got lost twice dodging soldiers, once had to claw my way clear of a pair, and once bought myself off with a kiss all round and thought myself lucky to get bye; well, I couldn't fight six of them. But at last I found the right door. I fair thundered at it, seeing a group of armed men stride round the corner and start to run towards me, and nearly fell on my face as the door was jerked open before me.

The servant jumped back away from me, and Bothwell leapt from his seat by the table, his sword half out before he saw I was harmless. "What in the Lord's name —?" the other lord, sprawled at his ease in a chair by the fire, was beginning, but I just whipped round to slam the door behind me.

"Help me bar it, my lords, for yer lives!" I shrieked. The soldiers' fists and spears thudded on the door, and it started to open against me. Just in time Bothwell pushed the gaping servant out of the way, kicked the door to, and slapped the bar into its brackets.

"Open up!" a voice shouted above the banging. "In the name o' the King!"

They eyed me. "The King an' the lords has killed Seigneur Davie, an' near killed the Queen, an' now they're here for you!" I panted.

"Open up! George Gordon, Earl o' Huntly! James Hepburn, Earl o' Bothwell! Open in the King's name!" the call came again outside.

Bothwell, veteran of many escapades, reacted first. "That's Kerr o' Todhole," he said. "If he gets in here we're done for. I hanged his brother for reivin' no six month back." With a heave he crashed a heavy carved cupboard down behind the door, waved to the rest to bring chairs and chests and wedge them in too, and called back, "I serve the Queen's Grace, Kerr, no the King!"

Outside there was renewed thumping and banging at the door, but the attackers couldn't get a good run at it across the narrow passage and it stood fast. At last, as we all stood waiting, the two lords with their swords drawn, their servants and I with pokers and knives, and I recovered my breath, the voice shouted, "Well, my lords, we'll just leave ye be the now! There's a guard on the door, an' there'll be men watchin' under yer window as well, so ye'll no escape that way neither, unless ye can fly. I'll see ye in the mornin', when the King'll have more leisure for to consider ye. I wish ye both a good night's rest, my lords!" The men outside laughed, and footsteps retreated. But some voices stayed, joking and shouting in the corridor.

After a minute, seeing no-one was breaking the door down this instant, Bothwell laughed round at all our grim faces. "Cheer up, my lads, we're no dead yet! I've been in tighter places than this before, an' got away wi' a whole skin — though once or twice wi'out my breeks!" The tension slackened, and as we all moved again he splashed out a glass of wine for himself and, as an after-thought, another for the Earl of Huntly.

Lord Huntly took it absently, staring at me. "Who are you, lassie? An' what's all this about Davie Rizzio?" he said. "It's no just an attack on Lord Bothwell, is it?"

"No, Geordie, I'm no that great a man that the King's after me. No yet," Bothwell grinned. "What's up, Leezie?"

They were somehow not surprised at Rizzio's death. "Aye, man," Bothwell mused, "he's been fair beggin' for trouble this last while. Aye. An overbold servant, high-stomached beyond his place, that riled all the lords. I knew somethin' was in the air against him."

Huntly agreed. "But in the Queen's presence! And her wi' child! It's monstrous!" His northern voice was shocked, but not at the deed itself. Neither of them had any sympathy for the poor wee man whose mobile face and sweet, deep voice were lost among the lavender. All their feeling was for the Queen — all Huntly's feeling, for the Earl of Bothwell just laughed.

He opened the window and leaned out. "Aye, damn him, there's a guard below us right enough! Watch well, gentlemen, an' don't catch cold! Here, pussies, have some wine! A wee gift from the mouse!" He tossed the half-empty bottle to smash and splash among their feet, and chuckling closed over the shutter again on their oaths. "Well, Leezie, ye've got yersel' in a right pickle here, lassie! Was it all for love o' me, eh?"

"It was for the Queen's command, my lord, an' no other reason," I told him firmly. "An' if we're right lucky, we're no in such a pickle as ye think."

"Aye?" He grinned at Huntly. "A rare lass, our Leezie! Can sort out any troubles, if she has the right tools! A pie, maybe, or a baker's peel! What's the trick this time, Leezie?"

"A friend, sir!" I said. "If we can but reach the end room, there's the old lion pit below the window, an' they'll not see us for the wall's too high. I'd hoped we could get out down the corridor, but since we cannae —"

"We'll just have to go another way! The chimney an' the roofs?"

"No, sir; the window! I'm telled there's a ledge ye can climb."

"An' who told ye that, eh? Some right queer friends you have! Put out the candles, Geordie, an' we'll see." He opened the shutters again, careful not to let them squeak and alarm the men below, and peered out. "Aye, see there, it runs window to window right to the end. We can just about do it."

Huntly looked out in his turn, and nodded, but his elderly manservant was horrified. "I cannae manage that, sir. It's too narrow. No, no, sir, I'd fall!"

"Then you'll just have to stay, Archie. They'll likely no harm you, no when we're away — a thump or two, maybe, but no more."

Bothwell's mournful servant agreed, mournfully. "I'll stay as well, sir. But ye'd best take the lass."

"Paris, Paris! Did ye ever know me leave a willin' lass behind in all the years ye've served me?" his master grinned.

Huntly argued. "What? It's but four-five inches wide, Jamie, and broken in parts! Look at it! She'd never manage! We must leave her."

"Leave her to the mercy o' those rogues? She'd no get off wi' a few blows! Dastard! Would ye fall, Leezie?" challenged

Bothwell, and I shook my head.

"I can climb along it as well as you, sirs," I defied them.

He nodded triumphantly at Huntly. "See? A braw lass this! Dauntless, I swear it! I'll go the first, an' when I reach the next window, I'll whistle for Leezie to come after me, an' give her a hand in. Then I'll go to the next one, an' then ye come across by Leezie, an' she'll come over to me, an' so on. D'ye understand?" He was impatient, for young Huntly was slow to grasp what he meant, but at last it was settled.

I looked down at my shoes in my hand, that I'd taken off for silence when I was running from the soldiers. I was better off without them for climbing. Oh well, I'd maybe get them another time. I tucked my hose inside them, and hid them away in a corner; then thought, 'No, I'll no leave them!' Defiantly I slipped one into each stocking and tied the hose together so that they'd hang round my neck, out of the way.

Huntly crossed himself and whispered, "Now Jesus Christ an' his saints preserve us from all manner o' evil." He was a Catholic, after all.

As Bothwell climbed up to the sill he gave his friend a slap on the shoulder. "Don't leave it all to Christ, man! I never heard he was that good a climber!" he muttered, and slipped out of sight with a chuckle at Huntly's face.

It was eerie, inching along the narrow ledge, silent as an owl in flight even when I tottered, for fear of drawing the attention of the guards below our feet. I gripped the cold stone with cool fingers, and moved light and easy.

Once as Bothwell crept out onto the ledge a bit of stone broke off below his foot and clattered. He swore under his breath, but there was a shouting and commotion at the front of the Palace that drew the guards' eyes and ears, and they didn't look up. He grinned back at me, winked, whispered, "The devil looks after his own, eh?" and eased on.

Another time Huntly, arriving in the same windowsill as me, jostled me. There was little room, for the space was only nine inches deep, not three feet long and about four high, and I'd have fallen but for my knife that I'd wedged between the planks of the shutters. He grabbed at me, and near enough sent us both over while trying to save me. It was a hard-breathing second before we were both safe, and the strain came off my wrist. I don't think he knew we'd been so near falling, for he just smiled at me and nodded at the knife blade jammed there. "Good idea!" he murmured in my ear as we rested. Good enough to save us both.

I had a queer certainty that we'd not be seen. I felt like a ghost, moving and being still, clinging and balancing in my turn, as if I could step off the ledge and drift safely on the air to the corner. I could scarce stop myself trying it. There was no ache in my calves or tremor in my clinging fingers, though the men were sweating and their faces strained.

The corner was the worst bit, for the ledge had crumbled. Bothwell at last stopped his infernal grinning as he worked his way round. But after a tense minute the breathy whistle came, and we knew he'd made a safe landing. I slid gently after him, with Huntly's whisper of "Careful, now," in my ear. Heavens, what did he think I'd be? The stone was worn and rounded under my heels as I edged round face out, but I was slim enough not to overbalance. I gripped the cracks, pressed back hard, and at last I reached safety.

There was a balcony, thank God, where King James the Fourth had stood to watch fights between his lions long ago. No lions fought in the pit now, not for many years, but the Queen had a few wild beasts in cages round it, and the door was kept locked. As Bothwell's firm hand helped me onto and then down behind the broad baluster, and he signalled to Huntly to start, I looked over. The noises of the night had disturbed the beasts, and they were chattering, grunting and pacing uneasily. "What's down there?" I asked in a whisper.

Bothwell had been listening for Huntly, and the question surprised him. "Eh? Nothin' much. An old leopard. Some wild goats. Hares an' such — old pets. Monkeys. A few parrots. Nothin'."

As Huntly's hand appeared at the corner, I saw he was coming face in to the wall. His hands had a better grip that way, but the strain on his toes and calves was worse. His head appeared, one shoulder, his fingers edged along the cracks

145

between the stones. One foot stretched round, seeking a hold. It caught the ledge, and he eased round.

His foot slipped. With a gasp he gripped at the cracks, and held. His shoe slid from his foot, and clunked on the roof of a cage below. There was a screech as whatever lived in there roused, and the noise spread to other cages. We waited; nobody came to see what the alarm was. There was no way that we could help him. After a taut while, Huntly hanging by his hands and the foot still on the far side of the corner, and gritting his teeth with the strain of it, silence returned below us as the beasts settled. Huntly took a deep breath, felt for the ledge again and finished the trip.

"Heh, heh, a near thing that, Geordie!" whispered Bothwell, helping him in. "Kerr said we'd have to fly out, but I didnae expect ye to try it! I thought ye were away."

The younger man looked up from where he'd collapsed at our feet. "I'll no say I thought different, James," he panted. He grinned faintly, his chest still heaving. "But God's good, eh?" Just the opposite of Bothwell's comment.

At last we could rest for a minute, behind the stone baluster of the balcony. We leaned back, relaxing and easing tired muscles. Bothwell, as always, was the first to rouse himself. "Well, Leezie, how do we get down from here into the pit? Climb over the cages?"

"No need, sir." I whistled softly, and Sandy's whistle came softly back.

"Who the hell's that, then?" Bothwell demanded.

"My friend, sir. My part was to fetch ye here. His was to get us a rope an' the key to the pit."

"Him that climbs round the Palace windows? I'll see this friend — he's maybe a friend o' mine, too! But from this day on, that's a sure an' certain thing." He clapped me on the shoulder admiringly. "God, what a lassie! Have ye horses ready as well?"

"No, sir, I fear ye'll have to see to that for yersel's," I said apologetically, and the pair of them started to laugh. They seemed to be near hysterics, but when I shushed them like bairns they smothered their giggles, apart from an occasional hiccup or yelp of laughter.

On this side of the Palace we were in the light of the moon, where before we'd been in deep shadow, but in my dream-like state I'd no fear we'd be seen. I leaned over and gestured to Sandy to throw up the rope. He tried, five times, but each time it fell away, bouncing off the wall or falling sideways.

"Tie a rock to it, man!" hissed Bothwell.

"No, for if it fell again it'd be heard." Huntly was right. What could we do. . . Maybe my shoes would carry. . . The linen! Sitting in my pocket all this time, thirty feet of strong linen trimming. I pulled it out and lowered one end, weighted with my shoes, as the men grunted surprise and approval. Sandy tied it to one end of the rope, we hauled up, and within three minutes we'd slid quietly down to where he was waiting — with Gordon of Huntly's dropped shoe, even. He had unlocked the door of the pit for us, and we all slipped like the shadows around us out past the cages where the mangy old leopard and the Queen's other beasts stirred and coughed in their sleep, down between the senior servants' houses, the dairy and brewhouse, the stables and stores, sheds and workshops and all the clutter of buildings that sheltered us safely, out to the far wall of the Palace grounds, over, and into a clump of trees. If anyone heard us, they stayed quiet, keeping out of the way of trouble.

"My God! I never thought we'd do it!" Young Huntly was frankly exhausted.

Bothwell stretched his fingers and chuckled. "Did ye no, then, Geordie? Well, I did, for I aye get what I set my mind on. Do you come wi' me to Dunbar? I'll raise my men there, an' send word to Liddesdale for more."

"No. I'll away north for Perth. I'll pass word to the Hamiltons, an' we'll have an army for the Queen in a week. If they don't kill her. . ."

I gasped, but Bothwell scorned the idea. "What? An' set the whole country — the whole world against them? Ye need a damn good reason for killin' queens. Though old Henry seemed to manage fine. . . They're no that daft. On ye go."

"You'll see to my mother? An' Jane?"

It took the earl a second to think who Huntly meant. "Eh? Oh, aye! O' course, man! Would I forget my own wife?" Sandy winked at me.

The young man unfastened a pair of clasps with a chain between them from his doublet, and gave them to me. "Take these as a small token o' my thanks, Leezie Sinclair. If I can ever help you, you'll no need to ask twice, for George Gordon o' Huntly's in your debt for his life, and he doesn't forget —"

"Aye, aye, man, there's no time for flowery speeches, the lassie knows fine what ye mean! Away wi' ye!" Bothwell broke in. Huntly shrugged, kissed my hand before I could pull it away, and trotted down the path.

Bothwell turned to me. "Well, I owe ye my life, it seems, Leezie."

"Me an' Sandy both," I said. I was annoyed Huntly hadn't thanked him.

"Aye, aye. Here, lad." He fumbled for a coin in his fine suede pouch, and in sudden exasperation tore it off and threw it to the lad. "Here, take the whole o' it! But for you I'd no be needin' it the morn anyway."

As Sandy caught the pouch there was a fine chinking, and his grin fair flashed in the moonlight. "Thank ye, my lord!" he said enthusiastically.

Bothwell paid no attention, his eye fixed on me again. "I've minded where I've seen ye. I never forget a face — no a lass's, anyway. My own lands at the Hermitage. Ye're Adam Hepburn's daughter, are ye no?"

My stomach froze. "No, I'm no, sir. He's but my step-father. An' if ye'd reward me for this night's deed, then just never tell him where I am."

He eyed me in the moonlight for a second, and nodded. "If that's yer wish, it's the least I owe ye, lass. Come on, then." He turned into the night.

"Where, my lord?"

"Dunbar, o' course. I have friends down the road will give us horses." He was surprised I wasn't following him.

"No, sir. I'll just away back home."

"Don't be daft, lassie! There's no time for coyness!" He

reached out to grab my wrist, but I dodged, and refused again. This time I meant it, and he finally realised that. "But if ye're no wantin' to come wi' me, why did ye come to save me?" He was puzzled.

"The Queen's order, sir. I telled ye." And something else, no business of his.

"The Queen? She ordered ye hersel' to warn me?"

"You an' my lord o' Huntly, sir."

"Aye, aye." He clearly disregarded Huntly's share, and stared through me, suddenly rapt, calculating. He came to himself with a start, and shook his head to clear it of whatever thought I'd started in him. "Aye, well, Leezie, I'll keep ye in mind. Ye'll be repaid for this night's work, I swear to ye." He looked grimly back at the Palace. "As will others."

"Aye, sir," Sandy nodded, and Bothwell grinned at him.

"Good lad!" His tone changed again as he turned back to me. "If you or yer mother can pass a message to Her Grace, tell her she'll be safe if she can reach Seton House. Could she climb down a rope ladder, if you smuggled one in? Tell her I'll have every man in the east out for her in a week. Oh, aye, an' bid my wife come after me as soon as may be."

I nodded, and before I could move, his arm was round me. "An' here's a wee somethin' to mind me by." He was going to kiss me again. I'd turn my face away, I thought. I didn't. Better than those stinking Douglases, anyway; quite pleasant, till my stomach lurched in me, as usual, and I squirmed away.

He loosed me, smiling mockingly again. "Aye, no wakened yet, Leezie? Well, I can wait. I'll see ye soon."

"God willin', sir," I replied, and he laughed and went whistling off.

I sat down on a stone, suddenly cold and weary. With the Earl's daredevil grin gone, there was no strength left in me. I remembered the scene up in the Queen's room, and the cries for help. I'd never use lavender scent again!

Ach, this was daft, for had I not seen worse in the Elliotts' raids?

"Well, come on then, Leezie, we'd best be gettin' back." Sandy's warm voice at last recalled me, and his firm arm supporting my shoulders slackened. He blethered on to cheer me. "See what he's given us! There's gold here, as well as siller! I can feel the greasiness o' it in my teeth — ten gold coins at least! We're rich!"

"You are, Sandy," I said, trying to bring my mind back to the present. "I've Huntly's chain. I want none o' Bothwell's money." I recovered myself. "I — I'll claim my own reward, when the Queen's safe again."

He stared. "Ye dinnae want any silver? Aye, well, we'll see. Come away. It'll be easy to get home. The Provost's come down wi' half the folk o' the town to see does the Queen need help. She cried out a window for help, poor wife, but one o' the men took her back in wi' a knife at her throat. Aye, while I was gettin' the rope, I seen it! The folk cannae think what to do, for they cannae risk her bein' hurt, so they're millin' about. They'll be driftin' away back home soon, an' we can just join in the crowd."

My own throat tightened again as I pictured the scene. Poor lady!

Sandy was quite right. The men were wandering agitatedly back up the Canongait, their spears and Lochaber axes and a hackbut or two waving like reeds in a gale as they argued. We joined the fringes, safe from any Douglas notice among the merchants, journeymen and apprentices, and headed home.

Halfway up the street I tugged Sandy to the side. "That's my lord o' Bothwell's lodgin'. I'd best go in now an' tell his lady he's safe. No, ye neednae come if ye'd rather stay out." He would indeed. Truth to tell, I was so tired I didn't want to go in either, but she was due to be reassured.

The door opened quickly to my knock, and I entered to face a dozen Borderers and about ten pistols. After a minute's alarm, mostly mine, I was ushered up to the hall on the first floor, where a young lady in a black robe sat quietly by a fresh fire. She frowned as I came in and made my curtsey.

"You have news? O' my husband?" Her voice was cold. She didn't seem pleased to see me.

"Aye, my lady. He's well. He's safe. He's on his way to Dunbar."

Whatever reaction I'd looked for, she didn't show it. Her face gave no slightest hint of her feelings, for relief, joy, or whatever. She simply waited for me to continue. Rather flatly, I told her what had happened, not mentioning the hair-raising climb along the ledge. Her sharp, shallow-set eyes watched me coldly until I stammered to a close. How did she make me feel small? And why?

After a pause, she nodded. "It must have been dangerous to warn my husband? Why did ye?"

I hadn't expected that. "The Queen told — told me to, my lady."

"No other reason? You didn't wish to go wi' him to Dunbar?"

This was getting monotonous. "No, my lady. He asked me that as well. But I said him no."

For the first time a slight smile appeared on her lips. "You did? That wouldn't please him, I'm thinking." It wasn't a question, and I had sense enough not to answer it. She inspected me again. "I had thought there was not a woman in Scotland wouldn't come runnin' to his whistle, but I apologise for misjudgin' you, Leezie Sinclair. That's two honest women he's met in Edinburgh." Her smile grew, malicious, not warm.

I thought about that for a minute. Did she mean she didn't love him either? Looking at her, and remembering how she'd been made to wed him, I'd not be surprised. But this was getting too awkward for me. . . "Will you be for Dunbar this night, then, my lady? I could tell your men on my way out."

She shook her head consideringly. "I think not, Leezie."

"It's what the Earl said."

"He doesn't always get what he wants. No, I'm safe enough, an' I think I'll stay a while and see can I get help to the Queen. She'll be needing it, poor lady. My mother's a lady-in-waitin'. I'll give her James's message, an' she can see if Her Grace has one for him, that I can carry. Aye, that'll be best."

She paused, thinking. Her face, like Mistress Knox's, was smooth; but there was a sharp brain active behind the calm. "A word o' advice, Leezie. Tell nobody it was you carried the word to Bothwell an' Huntly. No till the Queen is safe again, at least, an' maybe better never. The Douglases don't like to be bested, an' you must know they're ruthless when they're angered." Not the only ones, I thought, but it was good advice, and I'd pass it on to Sandy. "Now, did the Earl give you a reward? No?" She summoned her steward and gave me three hundred silver merks, before she dismissed me as coldly as she'd greeted me. She was generous, and considerate in thinking of my safety, but there was no warmth in her. Of the two, her and her man, I didn't know which I pitied more. Like the Queen and Henry Darnley.

And that was a right queer thought for a poor lass like me to think, eh?

Not so poor, though! As Sandy and I walked on up the street, we counted up in the light of the merchants' torches what we'd won; he had eight gold nobles, each worth six pounds Scots, two royals, fourteen merks, seven silver testoons and eleven halfs, five copper coins — and a fine suede pouch, worth good silver itself; I had a chain, a heavy gold chain with green jewels, maybe emeralds, on the clasps, and three hundred merks that were worth two-thirds of a Scots pound each. And I'd done a great favour for the Queen.

Matthew Kerr, ye'll be seein' me soon, I promised myself. But a good sleep first, for it had been a long, long day.

The Mews

Did I think I'd get a night's sleep? Huh!

Sure enough, I went straight up when we got in, to fall into bed beside ma, who was still sound asleep. But Sandy told the edited story we'd agreed on to Mistress Martin and Ina, who had been waiting up for us. She told the neighbours. They told their friends, who told their friends, who told the bailies, who told the provost.

At about three o'clock in the morning Sandy ran up the stair to call me down to speak to the provost himself. I struggled to master my sleepy thoughts and give a sensible story of the murder only. Then the questions; yes, I was sure Rizzio was dead, yes, I thought the Queen was safe for the moment, yes, I'd seen someone fire a pistol at her, yes, Bothwell and Huntly had escaped — not a word about how. I blinked owlishly at Sandy's grin.

At last the crowd started to leave, arguing fiercely on both sides of the case. Mistress Martin chased out the last ones and barred the door again. "My certes, lassie, ye do seem to get yersel' into all the trouble that's goin' about!" she commented. "My, what times! Murders an' rebellion, an' they Douglases — did ye hear the wee friar's dead, that yer ma tried to help? They broke into his house an' finished him in his bed, even! What'll

153

the minister say about it all, eh?"

We soon found out. Next day John Knox was preaching in the High Kirk, to a packed congregation. Never mind 'Love thy enemies' or 'Thou shalt not kill', and no thought of the Queen's well-being; it was 'a just act an' worthy of all praise'. He gloated about the death of Goliath, as if poor wee Seigneur Davie was a giant, and the thirty or so Douglases who had attacked him while he was unarmed in the Queen's presence were a puny David; the Douglases were the Israelites destroying the Philistine, the wrath of the Lord, Heaven's judgement on the idolator. The cheering would sicken you.

Ma was in the palace courtyard, trying to see the Queen, when a messenger went out to call in the midwife, and ma insisted that if the babe was due she must be at hand. She managed to get in to the Queen's outer apartments and speak to old Lady Huntly. The Queen had more sense than climb down a rope ladder to escape, in her state of health. She would find a way herself. Meantime, ma thought, the Queen was recovering, although she complained of pains for her guards' benefit.

I knocked to tell Kate all about it, but the door was locked. Babs said she and Alice had left before dawn, with a great bundle of luggage, and she swore that she didn't know where Kate had gone. Wise she was, for that very afternoon Master Patterson came in to see me, stern and righteous, to demand Kate's whereabouts, and ma and I could put our hands on the Holy Bible and take oath in all honesty that we'd no idea. Clearly Master Knox hadn't forgotten her, and already, even in the midst of his triumph over Rizzio's death, he was trying to put his hand on her.

Master Matheson, who had come in to see how ma was, firmly ushered the disappointed and resentful elder out of the door with, as he said, an itch in the toe of his boot. He brought us the news that the Queen's half-brother, the Earl of Moray, had come back from England, where he'd been since his rebellion. "An' she falls on his neck an' calls him her dearest brother, as if he'd rescue her! You'd think she didn't realise he must have known all about it!"

"Moray?" Ma was quite horrified. "He knew it was planned?"

"How no? It was his friends did it. O' course he knew."

"Ach, poor lass! No a soul she can trust, no even her husband nor her brother, an' hersel' a prisoner an' in poor health — what can she do?" Ma was near distracted.

"She's got just two choices. Escape, or stay their prisoner an' do what they tell her. Pardon them, an' that. Till she can escape, at least."

"But will they believe her, sir?" I asked.

"Pray they do, lass," he said gravely. "For if they don't, I couldn't say what would come o' it."

Next day we heard she promised to pardon them, as Master Matheson had prophesied. But the morning after, the town woke early, to a buzz of incredible news. The Queen had escaped to Seton House!

With the help of some loyal servants, Mary and her husband, who had apparently decided he was safer with her than with the lords, and not far wrong either, had slipped away. Darnley, they said, terrified of being caught, had lashed Mary's horse on, nearly unseating her. When she begged him to consider her condition and go more carefully, he yelled at her that if she lost that child they could have others! She told him to ride on and save himself, and in panic he did so.

The town was split. Many cheered her; others wept in rage. Within a few days the conspirators, hearing that the Queen was approaching the town with an army, all left, some for England again, some, including Knox, for the Highlands. And the same day that Mary entered Edinburgh in triumph, Bothwell and Huntly at her side, Darnley trailing behind, Kate reappeared, with a sweet smile for Master Patterson's scowl and absolutely no explanation of where she'd been. "At a friend's house," she said, her huge black eyes wide and amused at my frustration. "You must allow me my wee secrets, Leezie! Do I ask yours?" How did she know I had any?

I took thought, and went over to the tailor across the wynd. I was almost certain I'd get into the mews now, and my old breeks were a perfect disgrace. A new suit, plain brown from head to foot, of firm thornproof cloth; a plain doublet, breeks to the knee, two pairs of shanks, a coat, a flat cap to hide my hair, and boots as well, and all for less than a sixth of the money Lady Bothwell had given me. With Kate's dress, I now had so many clothes I had to buy a chest to keep them all in!

And at last the day came that I'd been praying for. Peter Matheson, with a huge smile, presented me with a summons to appear before the Queen at eight in the morning of Monday the twenty-fifth of March, at Lord Herries' house in the High Street where she was staying, for she couldn't yet bear Holyrood. Kate helped me dress, in my black, of course, with Lord Huntly's gold and emerald clasps. "Just perfect, lassie," said Alice, and I felt I could never look better.

Mary received me in her bedroom. It was bright with tapestries and painted panels, but there was a carpet on the floor instead of sweet herbs. John Lauder was there playing softly on his lute and winked to hearten me, and there was a small group of folk at the back of the room.

I had expected her to be in her bed still; I had the idea that great folk never rose till late. But she was up and dressed except for her gown, wrapped in a great furred robe over her yellow satin petticoats while her maids were dressing her hair. I found them distracting, but she sat still on a velvet stool as they worked round her, paying no more heed to them than if they had been flies. "Come away in, Leezie, my dear, and let me thank you again!" Her warm smile wiped some of the strain off her face. She held out her hands to me as I knelt smoothly in my braw black gown. "Mon Dieu! My dear, how you're elegant! Turn round an' let me have a wee look at you. My, my, Seton, is this no a change? Ah, how would you know, you never saw her before! What have you done to yoursel', Leezie? It's like magic!"

In my politest voice I told her a bit about Kate, and she said she knew her, had heard her singing and playing at several houses. "But I never knew she was such a dab hand at turnin' a gawky goslin' into an elegant swan!" I blushed, delighted. Ma saying that would have set my back up; the Queen saying it was pure pleasure. "Maybe I should hire her to teach some o' my young attendants a thing or two!" As if she needed to!

At last she came to the point. "How can I reward you, Leezie? You saved two o' my dearest an' most loyal supporters, at the risk o' your own life. What can I do for you in return?"

I shook my head. "There's nothin' I want, Your Grace, but what I wanted before. Just to be 'prenticed in your mews. If you think what I did for you's a good enough reason for you to interfere. . ."

She laughed delightedly. "I could see that stuck in your craw when we spoke on it at the table," she smiled. Her face went blank for an instant as her mind flew, like mine, to what had happened a few moments later. . . But then she brought herself back to the present and nodded briskly. "It's what you asked for, for savin' my hawk. Now you've saved two o' my lords, an' you ask nothin' else? Are my lords worth no more to you than my hawk?"

I smiled, seeing that she was just joking. "Tell you true, Your Grace, they're not. I'd save a hawk before either o' them."

All the maids smiled, and Mary Seton burst out laughing with her mistress. "Mon Dieu, I must tell James he's o' lesser value than a kestrel! Can you see his face!" chuckled the Queen. "What do you think, Master Kerr?"

With a start I spun round. The Master of the Mews stepped forward out of the corner behind me, and I sank into a curtsey, cursing my knees for wobbling. I was more nervous of him than of the Queen.

"A very natural judgement, Your Grace," he said stiffly. As they all laughed again, he frowned down at me, and turned to the Queen. "If it's Your Grace's command that I take the lassie in, I must obey you," he said stiffly.

She looked at him steadily, no longer smiling, until he met her eye. "Master Kerr," she said, and somehow her quiet voice was changed to a trumpet call; "Master Kerr, this lass has done me and my country — our country, yours an' mine — a great service, an' has risked her life in the act. I do not command you, though as your queen I could do so. I ask you, as a favour to me, as a reward for the dangerous service she has performed for us both, to accept this lass into your service. She has set her

157

heart on this single thing that is in your domain, not mine; I ask you to try her, on the same terms as the lads that you take in. If, in your honest judgement, she turns out unfit to work wi' your hawks, tell her so an' send her back to me, and I will console her as best I can. But give her a fair trial; this I request o' you, for my sake, as you are an honest an' loyal servant o' your Queen."

His jaw set, and his shoulders sank. He knelt glumly before her. "Aye, Your Grace. I'll give her a fair try." The words were dragged through his teeth.

Her smile was glorious, and she offered him her hand to kiss. He took it, and as he rose she rose with him, as tall as himself, her long fingers light on his huge brown fist; "You have my thanks, from my heart, Master Kerr." At last his face cracked into a faint smile in answer to hers.

He turned to me, and beckoned with his head. "Come on, then. If Your Grace will give us leave?"

"Aye, on you go, Master Kerr, I mustn't keep you from your duties!" she smiled. "An' good luck to you, Leezie!"

His shoulders stiffened again in front of me as I curtseyed my way out behind him. It looked as if I'd need all the luck I could find.

When I looked back, going out the door, the Queen had already turned all her attention to the problem of which ruff to choose, gold, silver or white, and never a glance after us.

In the hall Master Kerr turned to me. "Outside." No waster of words, and where was the ease we'd had at the start? Well, I mustn't expect him to be happy about it. I'd known it would be hard. Sometime soon I d win back to it. As we walked out of the house he didn't stand back to let me precede him, and drew an odd look from one of the men waiting to see the Queen. But he was my master now, I must remember. For a second I regretted Kate's teaching me to look and act like a lady. Then I firmed my chin and hurried down the hill after him, my petticoats bouncing and billowing to my long stride.

He didn't look at me as he talked. "You've other wear? Suitable?" I nodded, and as he seemed not to have seen, said, "Aye, sir." At that he stopped dead, so that I had to skid to a halt to avoid bumping into him, and glared at me. "I'll do what the Queen says. No man, nor even you, shall ever say to me that I didn't give you a fair chance. But I'll tell you now, I'll never accept you fully. One mistake, just the one, an' you'll be out!"

I didn't feel it was the time to protest that that was scarcely giving me a fair trial on the same terms as the lads. I nodded.

His lips tightened again. "You'll be called Sinclair. You can't stay in the 'prentices' dormitory. But wherever you sleep, you'll be in the mews by five every morn, ready for work, hail, rain, snow or shine." Maybe he thought that would be hard; with Ina's booming tocsin at four, I'd have time to reach Leith by five, let alone the White Horse Lane, and if the Netherbow was shut still, I could drop off the wall. "An' I want no complaints. The lads are as happy as me about you comin' in. If they're too rough for you, you can aye leave."

So there was the warning. I'd have a hard time of it. It was up to me to bear it, or give up. And I love you too, Master Kerr, I thought resentfully. You'll not stop me — nor all your bullying apprentices!

In fact, it wasn't too bad at all. The mews was a world of its own, unconcerned with anything except the feeding, training, and general well-being of the hawks that were kept in it. Their actual owners were considered rather a nuisance, always wanting to take them out themselves. We preferred it when they decided to play golf, or archery, or tennis, for then we could fly the hawks and falcons ourselves. And that was the whole centre of our existence.

The Queen had several falcons for herself and her husband; six peregrines from Norway or Orkney, three Manx gyr-falcons, four sakers from Africa, even an eagle — more for show than anything, it was a useless hunter — and eight casts, each of two birds, of her favourite merlins. She also kept several birds of different kinds for the use of her visitors, ambassadors and such, who might not bring their own. That in itself made a fair number. As well as that, lords coming to Court often brought their hawks with them, and if they had no room for them, and in the jam-packed town few had, they'd leave them with us; for a fee, of course. And sometimes country folk brought us extra eyasses — young hawks — or adult hawks caught on passage, and we'd quietly train them for sale privately, though I didn't discover this for months. We never knew from one week to the next how many we'd have in. Anything between thirty and ninety. Some days I'll swear Master Kerr had them perching on the rafters above the beds.

It wasn't that we were short of space, either. There was the big mews room that I'd seen before, that would hold over twenty birds, and a slightly smaller one. There were an open weathering shed, stove rooms for sick and moulting birds, hack rooms under the roof where young hawks were kept till they could fly well; the kennels for the hounds that put the quarry up for the hawks; three bedrooms, one for Master Kerr, one for John Fraser the journeyman and his wife, and the dormitory for Rab, John's son, who was head apprentice, and the other four lads under him; and the kitchen to cook for all. There were furniture rooms for the piles of old hoods, bags, gloves, lures and so on, that silted up all the corners; storerooms, workrooms, the mouse room where we kept mice and chicks for the hawks. Outside was the weathering green and the long training run beside it. The White Horse Mews was a big establishment.

There were more folk than the falconers and austringers, too. There were the cadgers — the men who ran with a square frame slung over their shoulders, to carry six birds each when the Queen went out hawking. To call a falconer a cadger was the ultimate insult, I found. There were the kennel boys and trainers, with their own places among the kennels. The outsiders, the snarers who caught birds and brought them in to be released for the hunt, the mouse and rat and coney-catchers who sold us food for the hawks, were in and out all day, and one old man sat muttering and sniffing over a stove in a wee room all by himself working dogskin into fine strong leather in brilliant colours for hoods, leashes and jesses, and chasing anyone who let a draught of cold fresh air into his smoky, stinking haven.

It took me a while to find my place in all this. It was difficult for everybody; I was female, so they didn't want me, loyally adopting Master Kerr's attitude. But I'd been sent by the Queen herself, so they couldn't show their anger and dismay too freely. My brown suit was fine — a bit too fine, being new, but it would do. I ignored the jeers and name-calling till they withered out of boredom, didn't turn my back on them, kept a sharp eye on my things, carefully avoided tripping boots and spilled ale, and when they tried a sly pinch at my breeks I made sure it wasn't repeated.

I was older, and taller, than most of the apprentices, who had come in at nine or ten years old. I soon found I was acting like a mother to Alan, the youngest, for John Fraser's wife who should have cared for him was a mean-minded, lazy bitch. When the bigger lads, Patrick, Jacob or Rab — usually Rab — tried bullying me, I found I could beat any one, and hold my own with any two of them. Master Kerr said nothing about our bruises and black eyes, either; and the day they treed me in the dormitory and he came in to find me up in the rafters, kicking Rab's teeth in as he hauled at my feet, he just glared and called us out. He did seem to be trying to do as he had promised, and give me a fair trial; at least, he whipped us all equally.

I took in some of Babs Martin's broken pies. Not too often, but when I'd had a good day, with no bother, I'd reward them with a pasty. They were all growing lads, the cook was appalling, and without my ever saying a word they soon learned. That maybe helped me more than anything.

With time out at night, I could relax and ask ma or Master Matheson for advice on how to handle situations. Peter was particularly helpful. He told me about the 'long stand' that I might be sent for, to be kept waiting about for hours. Or they might play Huntigowk on me; tell me to take a message to somebody who would always just have left the last place I was sent to seek him, so that I'd be running about after him all day from one end of the town to the other. When Rab sent me out with a note the very next day, and at the kennels I was told Master Long had just left, they thought for the kitchens, I carefully opened the note; sure enough, I spelled out, 'Hunt the gowk along!' I was so pleased Kate had taught me my letters! I had a fine time that day. I went climbing round the Castle crag, and found a wee patch of almost level grass on the south side, where I could relax in the spring sunshine. When I got back near sunset, with the note to show the journeyman to excuse my absence, and found them sniggering at me, it was me had the last laugh.

I aye got on well with lads, better with lads than lasses, and after a month or two we had settled down fairly steady. Once they'd discovered I could, and would, fight them, and didn't intend to kiss them, mend for them, or clean out their fusty wee beds, the lads started to forget for longer and longer that I was a hated, despised female, and I began to learn the arts of falconry.

The day always started with examining the birds' castings. These were the skins, bones and feathers which the birds were given in the last meal of the day to keep their digestions working properly, and which were thrown up in a little oval pellet during the night. Any bird that hadn't cast was not moved, fed or bathed until it produced its casting.

Then Master Kerr checked the condition of each bird carefully, feeling the muscling of its chest, weighing it in his hand, studying its eyes and feet and the set of its feathers. Hawks had to be sharp set with hunger or they'd not return to the glove or lure, but would fly away. Half the art, I learned, was to judge when a hawk was at its right weight; lean and hungry enough to be recalled, but strong and fit enough to fly and hunt its strong, fit, wary quarry. The difference between a fit hawk and a weak one could be less than an ounce with the smaller birds, and I was lost in awe of how Master Kerr kept track of their condition.

Then the birds had a bath. Not all of them bathed every day, but the chance to splash in the basin indoors or the scooped-out log on the weathering green had to be offered to them. One of them seldom did more than dip her talons in the mews, but if she didn't do that, as soon as she was released outside she simply sailed off till she found a stream or puddle and soaked herself; and then, of course, she was too wet to fly well. We had to know their individual quirks.

After the bath they'd be set outside on the perches and blocks to weather for at least three hours. Without this time to preen and stretch they'd not fly well. The dogs were let loose then and trained among the hawks, for they all had to learn to know each other, work together, not frighten or attack each other. The hawks soon learned to pay no heed to the dogs, while any dog that couldn't learn to ignore the perched hawks was quickly turned into meat and leather before it upset the birds; very few, actually.

This was the time for training new hawks to the fist and hood, for cleaning the mews, for brewing medicines and seeing to any that were sick. Young birds were fed now on the glove or perch, for they needed two meals a day. And this was when Master Kerr tested the skill of any visiting falconer by the state of his bird; "Aye, a grand peregrine — but a good bit light, sir! An' look at the length o' her talons! Either you've no skill, or no pride, or you should be turned from your master's door as an idle cadger!"

In the afternoon most of the made — trained — hawks were taken out to fly at game, whether by their owners or by us. This was when the snarers were needed. Every falcon had to be flown nearly every day, at the quarry it was entered for, to keep it fit and keen. The short-winged hawks, the sparrow-hawks and goshawks — whose trainer was called an austringer, not a falconer — could go three or four days without hunting, for they were short-flight birds, going like an arrow from the fist after rabbits or pigeons, jinking and dodging through trees and bushes after their prey; and often enough getting lost if they caught it and sat tearing at it. We had to put bells on their tails as well as their feet, so that we could find them in the undergrowth. Gosses even liked to sit in a tree and have partridges driven under them, so that they could simply drop on their prey. Lazy brutes, and no great thrill to fly, though productive for the pot; the goshawk was called the kitchen hawk.

But the long-wings, the falcons proper, the peregrines, gyrfalcons and merlins, both the female falcons and the smaller males, the tiercels, had to have the training for their high towering flights and magnificent stoops, and the only way to get it was to do it. And when we had maybe sixty falcons to train and muscle-up, we hadn't the time to go far seeking larks or starlings for the merlins, or ducks, grouse or heron for the larger birds. As Master Kerr said, it wasn't sport, and he disliked it, but there was nothing else for it. I hated it. I felt so sorry for the captured birds, shocked and dazzled, bundled out into danger. I often felt like cheering those that got away, as more than half did, instead of cheering on the hawk.

Two or three times there was trouble when the training birds went after the carrier pigeons that some of the lords, and some merchants too, kept in the town, and once even the queen's own white fantails. Master Kerr got a testy message from Holyrood that time, and passed it faithfully on to us, and we stayed well clear of the town from then on.

All day, the hawks in training were taught to come to the fist or the lure, first on a creance, a long, light line, then flying free; to come down from a tree, to come to a whistle. I most enjoyed swinging the lure to draw them direct to land high on my fist, instead of dropping the lure on the ground for them, and practised till I was better at it than any of the other lads; no-one could better Master Kerr, but the birds learned to know me and come to me readily. Every time, they had to be rewarded with a tiny scrap of meat, and each one's lesson finished when it had eaten enough to blunt the edge of its hunger. "You must stop while she still obeys you," I was told firmly. "Feed her the rest o' her meat afterwards, when she's back on your glove, that she'll be glad to come to you. But never go on callin' her till she's so full she'll disobey you. That's no the habit you've to teach her."

It was wonderful to work with the lovely birds, never ever forgetting that they were not pets, nor even tame; they were fierce, dignified partners in the wild hunt, and you were their servant at least as much as their master.

That spring the local folk round Edinburgh brought in news of nests of goshawks, kestrels, merlins, the smaller hawks, and we had an exciting time climbing for them. The lads finally accepted me then, for I was better on the crags than any of them. John Fraser and Rab went off as they had done for the last two or three years to the islands of Shetland and Orkney, to bring back young peregrines. They came back that year with eight eyasses, more than normal, there were two more gyrfalcons from the Isle of Man, and we had over two dozen assorted smaller birds. I wasn't allowed to touch the gyrfalcons or the peregrines, but when the first merlin eyasses were hacked — allowed to learn to fly in freedom, but fed regularly to keep them coming back, and then caught up as soon as they were ready for training — Master Kerr let me have one to man on my own.

I called her Mab, for the queen of Elfland, she was so tiny and fierce. I started out by getting her to sit on my fist. She learned quickly that I wasn't going to harm her. After only three days' flapping and trying to fly away, being brought up short by her jesses in my fingers, dangling and being picked up and set back on the fist again — and oh, how my arm ached, even with her minute weight — she would sit quietly on my hand as I went about my tasks in the mews, and let me slip her hood on and off readily. Within another day or two she would jump to my hand to be fed, and after only ten days she was flying twenty feet on the creance, from a post in the field to my lure. Master Kerr was quite pleased with me.

He'd accepted me at last, I thought, and there was no word of my being sent back as unsuitable. It helped, of course, that I was still so skinny that in my breeks I looked like a lad. But I'd started filling out the top of my black dress that I sometimes wore at night, when I had energy to visit Kate. I wondered how long I'd be able to go on dressing as a lad. Well, I'd face that when it came. I bandaged my chest flat and was glad all was going well so far.

The first day we flew my wee merlin free I was so terrified she'd just fly off that I nearly begged Master Kerr to let me keep her another day or two on the creance. But I saw him studying me again, and realised I was still on trial. My judgement, as well as my willingness to work. Was she ready? I'd thought so yesterday. It was just nerves that made me uneasy today. I called her on the creance once, and she obeyed sweetly. So I perched her back on the post, prayed, untied the creance and walked away. She roused and warbled at me, shaking herself to loosen her feathers and raising and stretching her wings, and for a second my heart stopped, but she settled again. I took the lure again and swung it, whistling to her. To my heart-stopping delight she leapt and glided for it without hesitation, and thumped solidly to the grass, tearing busily at the scrap of rabbit as if she'd been trained for years. And as I sighed in delight and release from fear, and went in quietly to pick her up, Master Kerr nodded and turned away without trying to hide his smile.

That same afternoon, we went out to the park, the same place where Rab had lost the merlin Diana a few months back, and when we saw some larks I set Mab flying. As she swept up, seeking her prey, I bit my knuckles; as she saw them, tilted gracefully in the air, and swooped like a tiny thunderbolt to her first kill, my heart leaped, and Master Kerr nodded at my joy. I lifted her, gave her the lark to eat, and we went back together, his hand on my shoulder.

I'd done it! I'd won him round! And I'd flown my own hawk! Life was marvellous!

That night I fairly raced home to tell everyone what I'd done. I belted up through the gate, ran up the High Street, swung into the wynd, into the shop, and with a quick cry of, "I flew Mab! She's grand! Tell ye later!" I charged up the stair. Sandy called something after me, but I lost it in the clatter of my boots on the steps.

The lamplight under the door showed ma was in, and I thrust it open, bubbling with my wonderful news.

A tall man rose from a stool by the fire, where ma sat stiffly in her chair. He bowed to me, a curious half-grin on his brown, bearded face.

"Well, Leezie?" he said jovially. "Have ye no a word to say to welcome yer dad?"

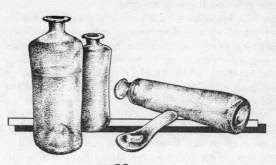

Illness

Dad only stayed about half an hour, and it was all very quiet and civilised. It was a wonder to me how we three, with the desperate hatred fair sizzling round us, could yet talk so politely.

He was quieter than I remembered him. He was working now as porter and messenger to Sir James Balfour, just up the wynd from us, and had arrived in Edinburgh only the day before. No, Bothwell hadn't told him where we were. He'd spoken to Katie's Tam, and got all the gossip of the wynd. He didn't mention pigs' guts, or broken arms, or anything about Liddesdale. He took a glass of claret that I offered, more for ma's sake than his, for she was taut with fear. He listened with interest as I told ma about flying the hawk — it fair spoiled it for me — praised me rather too much, and then took his leave politely, bowing to us both as he left. He might as well have been Master Patterson.

But there was a gloating satisfaction in him, a smirk, a constant wee smile that never touched his eyes. My hair crawled when he looked at me.

As the door shut behind him, my stomach heaved, but as ma shivered and held out her hands to me for reassurance that we were still safe I held it steady, and wondered all the time what dad would do next.

Peter Matheson was furious. For a moment, watching his angry frustration later that evening as he swore uselessly, I felt a satisfaction of my own, but then realised I should be ashamed of myself; which didn't make me feel better. As ma's friend he had no standing, while dad had the whole strength of law, religion, and social opinion on his side. Who would support a wife who left her man, that she had promised before God to love, honour and obey? Ma could be pursued in the courts if she didn't return to dad, aside from any threat to her in the street or even in her room here. If dad just seized her and dragged her to his room in Sir James Balfour's house, or if, more likely, he forced his way in here, no-one would have any right or, except for Peter, any wish to object. We could only be thankful he'd shown no desire to do it. So far.

After a few minutes' rage, Peter started to think again. "You're safe settled at the mews, Leezie, are ye no?"

"I think so, Peter. Master Kerr seems to have accepted me. If I don't do anythin' too dreadful!"

"Aye, well, just take care you don't! Now you, Janet." He hugged her comfortingly as she clung to him, near as distressed as she'd been when we left the farm. "Sure the Queen would protect you, if the worst came to the worst!" Well, maybe. But as we looked doubtful, a thought came to him and he thumped the table in glee. "Never fret, my dear love, you're safe!" We both stared at him. A grin of delight spread over his cheery face. "Aye! When's the Queen's bairn due? No more than a month?"

Ma's face mirrored his joy in sudden comprehension. "I must set up the nursery at the Castle soon anyway! I can start it right the morn, an' he'll no can reach me, for he's no right to enter there!"

"Exactly that! But I can get in, for that I'm an officer o' the Queen!" They were holding hands now, gazing smiling into each other's eyes like a pair of daft youngsters in their calf-love. Then they leaned together and kissed.

I was so embarrassed for them! Had they no dignity at all? At their age, they should surely be past all this? I sat squirming

168

on my stool, trying not to look, till a thought sidled into my mind. "But ma, what about me? I can't stay here, in rooms by mysel', all on my own so near dad. What'll I do?"

It broke them apart. We all looked at each other, baffled. "Babs can maybe suggest somethin'?" said ma doubtfully.

Peter opened the door and yelled for her down the stair-well. "Babs! Can you come up a minute? We've a wee problem."

Her voice echoed up in exasperation. "No, I cannae. I'm busy, an' I'm no gettin' any younger. Have yer knees stopped bendin' that you cannae come down?"

We trooped obediently down the stair. Mistress Martin and Sandy were packing next day's meat and currants into pots, with a good pour of ale. "It's the dregs o' the ale-wives' casks. I barter it for broken pies, an' it fair improves the flavour," she said as Sandy started reaching the pots into the warm oven. He winked at me; it must have been his idea.

Ina gave us a big grin and a grunted greeting that with Sandy's constant encouragement had actually started to sound like speech. "Guh e'en!" She sat back contentedly as we all replied "Good even!" to her. That was the second time, for all of us, but she was so proud of her new achievements that we enjoyed giving her her pleasure. It was little enough she had, poor wife.

"My certes, this flour'll never rise wi' all the chalk an' chaff in't! It's a fair disgrace! Now, lad, what ails ye?" Babs and Sandy got on with the work as they listened. Alice, Kate's maid, coming in from the wynd, stopped to listen too. They all perfectly understood our worries at dad's appearance, ma's delight at getting out of his reach, and my own fears at staying alone. "For he could still claim ye, for all he's no blood kin," Babs nodded.

"An' demand you return to him, if you've nobody to see to you," Alice agreed. "Pity you're no wed, or betrothed. Or could he put a bar on that?"

"I think not," said Peter. "I'm no advocate, mind, but I think as he's but her step-father he'd have to show a by-ordinary good reason to bar her weddin' — if it's to a reasonable man." He looked at me quizzically. "Have you nobody in mind,

Leezie?" They all laughed as I hastily denied it, and the whole atmosphere lightened. "Besides, you're o' full age now, lass, are you no?"

"Sixteen next week, sir," I said.

"There you are, then, lackin' close male blood kin you can pick your own man, an' he can't stop you that easy. But while you're still unwed — well. . ."

Alice suggested, "I could ask my mistress — there's room in the kitchen wi' me. But —" with a side glance at ma — "it mightn't be suitable."

There was a lot left unsaid in that, and she wasn't surprised when ma shook her head decisively. "Thank you kindly, Alice, but I'd rather no." I wasn't surprised either, but I was a bit disappointed. It would have been grand to stay with Kate. Our singing was being badly neglected these days, for I just hadn't the time. And my hands were a disgrace; Alice had winced at them.

As we sat puzzling, Ina grunted again, her eyebrows twisting and hands waving as her heavy tongue struggled to form the words. At last Sandy nodded. "Aye!" He turned to us. "Ina says why does Leezie no bide in here, in the back room wi' Mistress Martin? There's place for another pallet. What say ye?"

Babs sat like a corn-stook while ma argued against herself. "It's too much to ask!" she insisted. "We couldn't put so much on your shoulders. What if my man made trouble? No, no, you're kind, but it would be too much. . ."

"Blethers!" the old wife snapped. "I'll decide for mysel' what's too much, thank ye, Janet! Leezie's a fine lassie, an' we owe her a deal o' gratitude for what she did for Ina. If it would help her, to stay a while wi' us, it's the least we can do. An' it's no trouble, for she'll be company, an' for rent, well, she's aye buyin' pies for the laddies at the mews, an' that'll be enough." As we all sighed happily at this happy solution, she added, "An' we'll just see the peel's aye stood ready by the oven door, in case her dad does come seekin' her. I'd no like her to lack her favourite weapon!"

And so, in laughter, it was settled. Ma moved up to the

Castle, just a week before the Queen did so herself for safety during the birth of her child. I moved into Babs Martin's back room, sleeping on a truckle bed that rolled on wee wheels under her own bed during the day. Our rooms were let to a lively young brewer, Jaikie Fraser, and his new wife, who fell foul of the Pattersons the very first day by inviting them in for a pint or ten, and gave us some rare laughs with their continuing feud. And dad, next time he called for ma and was disappointed, lost his smile for a second, Babs said, and then went off up the wynd smiling again, but with eyes like coals of hell. "Aye, lass, ye're well clear o' that one," she said, her mouth twisting with dislike.

I went back to the mews with relief. I was so wrapped up in my work, I scarce noticed the world outside. Even when the Queen's bairn was born in the middle of June I was too busy to heed the cannons. When young Alan ran in with word it was a boy, I literally had my hands full with a tiercel peregrine. He had been tied on a perch too near a goshawk, which had clutched his wingtip and damaged the feathers so badly we had to imp four of them. We had cut the replacement feathers and glued the pegs into their hollow shafts. Alan burst in on us just as I was holding the wing spread and steady while John Fraser trimmed the broken primaries and fitted and glued in the new ones. It was a fiddly job, the hawk was none too happy about it, and the last thing we needed was a boy jumping in yelling, "It's a laddie! A prince! Ha-hey!" Poor Alan left the room near as fast as he'd come in, with his ears a sight redder.

Later, drinking the babe's health by the bonfires, we heard all the news. We laughed at the Countess of Atholl trying to transfer the Queen's pains to Lady Reres by sorcery. And we frowned at the Queen's bitter words to her sullen husband; "My Lord, God has given you an' me a son, begotten by none but you. An' he is so much your son I fear it will be the worse for him hereafter."

As the weeks went by I heard the gossip about Darnley's behaviour going from bad to worse, but more important to me was that I never saw ma. She was aye on duty in the Castle, for the Queen took long to recover from the hard birth. When Mary was at last better, the nursery was moved to Stirling, where the Countess of Mar took up her hereditary post as Royal Governess.

Peter Matheson could visit ma whenever his work took him up that way, and came down to see me, sometimes at the mews, with news of her. Once he was in full red uniform, carrying his staff of office; he'd just been witness in a case in the Law Courts. All the lads were impressed, and my standing went away up, but I was glad he'd not come earlier, for it would have looked as if I was seeking his help, and would have made it harder for me in the unwelcoming company. It was all right now, for I'd found my own feet without him. Then it dawned on me that that was why he'd not come down before, and I realised, not for the first time, that he wasn't anybody's fool.

In the middle of October, the Queen went off on her Justice Eyres, judging cases all round the Borders. The royal nursery moved back to Edinburgh, to Holyrood, and Peter brought me a message from ma; would I like to come next day and see her? I'd likely see wee Prince James, too. I jumped at it, of course, if Master Kerr would let me out. But he did, and even came with me; he had a gift for the Prince, and would take this chance to present it, he said.

About an hour before noon, then, we walked down the two or three hundred yards to meet Master Matheson at the Palace gates. He and Master Kerr liked one another, I was pleased to see.

Along a corridor on the south side, past guards and serving-men who all nodded in a friendly way to Peter, we turned in by a narrow door into a large, low-ceilinged room. A gable headdress lifted among the dozen caps that turned to us, and Peter addressed the over-rouged lady under it. "Give you good day, Lady Reres! Master Kerr, Master of the Queen's Mews, and Mistress Sinclair's daughter Leezie, come to visit her and the Prince, with your goodwill?"

The florid lady looked at my breeks, and bellowed red-mouthed with laughter, her jewels flashing. "Daughter?

172

My God, what'll Sinclair do when she's a son, eh? Put him in skirts?" It had never entered my mind to wear a gown. I flushed in annoyance, her laugh roared again, and a wail started in the next room. "God's wounds! There's that lad wakened again! Will he ever sleep more than five minutes? Aye, aye, Matheson, take them in. I'll give you leave, since her High an' Mightiness isn't here." That must be the Countess of Mar. As we bowed and headed for the door, she was reaching ring-crowded fingers for a bowl of sweetmeats and wondering aloud, laughing, what the Countess might be doing, and who with. Her teeth were as rotten as her breath. And her mind.

In the next room a lutenist I didn't know was playing, and a lad rocking a huge carved cradle was protesting, "But I never stopped, Mistress Sinclair! That laugh o' Lady Reres' would wake the dead!" Ma tut-tutted at him, lifting and cuddling the baby, humming gently with the lute. She had a new red gown, and a three-inch ruff. She looked happy, relaxed in spite of the screaming baby in her arms; fulfilled. This was her perfect place, her perfect task.

She turned and suddenly saw us. "Ah, Leezie! It's good to see you again, my dear! How are you?" Still hushing the baby, she came and kissed me, which was embarrassing in front of Master Kerr. When I introduced him to her they greeted each other with respect. She just smiled at Peter, as if she needed do no more. The little jealousy rose again, but I shoved it down.

"Is the Countess o' Mar no here, mistress?" Master Kerr asked, his deep voice producing a hush among the women fluffing up the cot's pillows and straightening the sheets and purple and gold velvet coverlet.

"No, sir, a messenger came for her. Were you wanting her special?"

"It's just —" he fidgeted under all the female eyes — "I have a wee gift for the bairn. The Prince. Prince James. I thought best to give it to her. . ."

She raised an eyebrow at him over the baby, and lifted a tiny pink hand out of the fine knitted shawl to wave it at him. "A gift from the mews, sir? He'll no be fit for hawking for a year or two yet, I'm thinkin'!"

He flushed at her merry smile, and smiled back, uneasily, more used to men's company than women's. "No, no, it's no a hawk — though I've got an idea for a style o' hood — no. But I heard the babe was restless, an' I thought this might please him." He fished inside his tunic and brought out something I'd never seen before; a pretty silver ring about four inches across, with a dozen bright leather tassels, little ivory balls and tinkling hawk bells fastened round it. "See, ye can tie it up to swing an' chime for him, or give it to him to bite on when he's teethin'. . ."

"Alice!" Ma called across the room. "All o' you! Come see this!" The girls flocked over to exclaim over the gift. She held it up in front of the baby's face. The sharp little eyes, puffy with crying, focused, and there was a pause in the wails and wriggles. Everybody held their breath. Another long wail; another pause, as the bells tinkled. The crimson faded from the baby's face, and he gazed intently at his new toy. She smoothly laid him down in the cradle, nodded to the boy to start rocking it again and hung the rattle on a knob at the top of the carved canopy, where it swung ticking and tinkling above the baby's face. There was a blissful silence; and a relieved sigh.

Ma waved to the lasses to draw back and leave the baby alone, and they settled again round the fire to their ironing and embroidery. She drew Master Kerr slightly to one side, away from the throng. "Did you make it yoursel'? An' I'll swear it was your own idea, too." He flushed awkwardly, nodding. Ma laid her small hand, all white again now, on his huge brown one. "Sir, I've never seen such a bonny thing. It takes a man of real kindliness of heart to think on such a lovely gift for a bairn."

He'd not been as scarlet even when I'd angered him that first day.

"Is the wee Prince weakly, then, ma?" I asked.

She looked up at me in surprise. "Weakly? No, no, not that. He's just a bit fretful. Takes a lot o' carin' for. He's no a big lusty laddie, mind, but when you think on what his mother

174

went through to bear him, we should be glad he's alive at all. He'll do fine." With her to look after him, of course he would.

She turned to the lasses. "Alice, he'll want feeding again in an hour or so. You'd better take another drink o' milk an' ale."

The big lass, the Prince's wet-nurse, smiled confidently. "Aye, no bother, mistress. I'll be ready." She eased the fullness of her loose bodice.

"Come sit you down by the window," ma was starting, when the door swung open and a tall, upright woman stepped firmly in. She cast a glance like a whip round the room. The girls leapt to their feet by the fire, and ma curtseyed deeply. Peter bowed, and Master Kerr and I copied him.

"Sinclair!" Her voice cut like her glare. "Who are these people?" Her face softened not a fraction as ma explained about the silver ring on the cradle. "Aye. Well, now that you have made your gift, sir, there is no need for you to remain. Visits here, in the chamber of your future king, will no longer be allowed except in my presence. I will speak to Lady Reres after." The lady, behind the Countess, turned pure white at the tone, then red as fire. Master Kerr was furious. Peter Matheson beckoned with his head to us to come away. There was no mention of my being ma's daughter; had she not had permission?

The lady was speaking again. "We must take special care o' the babe now, Sinclair." Waving a dozen guards in, to take station round the walls, she went on, delighting in the drama of the announcement, "The Queen is gravely ill. It's no expected that she will live. The babe may already be the King o' Scots!"

As we left, the first nobles were already crowding into the outer room.

A Messenger-at-Arms was going down the corridor. Peter seized him, dragged him into a corner with us, and demanded, "Archie! What's happened?"

Indiscreet or not, the man was dying to talk about it. "Aye, well, what we've heard is that the Queen's near death, Peter!" he whispered. Everybody, it seemed, was whispering round us — those that weren't crying openly. "You know the Earl o' Bothwell was hurt? Three weeks back the Elliotts raided his

175

lands, an' he rode out after them. He caught them, an' Jock Elliott wounded him sore."

"Where? How badly?" I'd heard nothing of this.

"In the arm, an' it went bad. He was right sick. So yesterday when the Eyres was done Her Grace rode over from Jedburgh to see him, wi' Moray an' a score more. It was a hard twenty-five mile, an' then the Hermitage couldn't take them all in, so they had to ride right back again. Her Grace was tired out, an' she went into convulsions, an' they're feared she'll die. An' Darnley'll no go to visit her, for fear o' catchin' whatever she's sufferin' from, an' the wee Prince losin' both parents. Fatherly love an' consideration. He says." He looked round to see that no-one was listening. "Typical!" he whispered.

"An' if she died, the bairn would be King." Peter's voice was quiet. "An' who would be Regent?"

None of us answered. The idea was too sickening.

The Queen did, in fact, live, though we heard that at one point she was thought to be dead. Her French physician's skill saved her and she slowly recovered most of her health. When she was on the mend, her husband finally went to visit her, a week after Bothwell had struggled to do so.

She was well enough to have her son christened at Stirling that Christmas. Darnley refused to attend the Roman cere-mony, sulking in his rooms, and then, afraid of the lords he'd betrayed to Mary after Rizzio's murder, he rode off to his father's estates near Glasgow to sulk some more.

I was having the time of my life. The senior falconer, John Fraser, left the mews to become falconer to Lord John Hamilton, and took his big son Rab with him. The last of the bullying stopped and I could finally settle deep into my job. A badly hurt tiercel goshawk was brought in one day, and I nursed it back to health. When Master Kerr praised my work, I near burst with pride. And he started to let me fly the great peregrine falcons. With that and my wee merlin Mab and the gos, life had no more to offer me. I called the goshawk Geordie, for its greedy, beady wee eye reminded me of Geordie Tod.

It was a strange thing, then, that just after the New Year I saw the man, Geordie Tod himself, in the High Street. Or he saw me; the first I knew of it was a slap on the back that knocked me slipping into the icy kennel. Shaking my foot angrily, for it wasn't cold enough to freeze the filth right down, I turned to see who this was that had attacked me, and saw the wee fat man cowering exaggeratedly back. "Forgive me, Leezie!" he begged. "I just forgot mysel', I was that pleased to see a friendly face!"

"From the back, Master Dalgleish?" I asked him, starting to grin. Somehow I could never stay angry with him.

"Well, ye're showin' the world a fine pair o' cheeks!" he chortled, and to my annoyance I felt my face grow hot. He roared with laughter. "Dod, Leezie, ye've changed! Ye're too finicky now for this world, ye that used crack a jest to make a tink blush! If ye cannae take a wee joke wi'out reddenin', ye'll do better to stay in yer skirts — if ye have any!"

I was peeved. "I have so, Geordie Tod! I cannae stop now — ye've heard I'm in the Queen's mews? Aye, well, I'm just out on a wee errand. But come in to see me the night, at the pie shop in Blackfriars' Wynd."

He held me back, his smile fading. "Is that no near Balfour's, where yer dad's in service? You mind yersel', Leezie, lass. He was fair ragin' about the pig guts. Ragin'. Then he went all silent, for near a month. An' then he comes up, no even at term day, an' says he's givin' up the land, I could do what I liked wi' it — an' you bein' so fine now I'll no tell ye what he said I could do wi' my rents bills — an' he just vanished off the face o' the earth. An' next day a lassie he used visit at Langholm was found beaten to death. There's no proof, Leezie, but. . . If I was you, I'd take heed." He seemed honestly — if you could use that word of him — concerned about me for a second. Then the wee dimples returned to his chubby cheeks. "But what am I sayin'? Here's the lass that's got her wee cuttie all ready for anythin', eh, Leezie?"

I considered him steadily. "Aye, sir," I said at last. "I must thank ye." He looked embarrassed. "Will ye come round the night?"

"Aye, aye, lass," he nodded briskly, and laughed again as I

bowed politely — well, what was I supposed to do in my breeches; curtsey? — and ran off.

I fair knocked his eye out that night, though, in my grand black gown and gold clasps, and a new French-style cap. Most satisfactory.

Geordie was in town to serve Bothwell, of course. French Paris, who had been the Earl's valet for years, had left his service to join the Queen's, and Geordie had come to take his place. Not that he knew much about clothes, but he was ready for any skulduggery. "I can slit a throat that sweet the man'll no know he's dead till the deil claps his shoulder!" he boasted, laughing.

"In civilised Edinburgh?" I commented, and he laughed even harder.

I sharpened up my knife, and took care in the streets when it was dark. I'd no wish to end up with no proof of who killed me. But somehow I had the feeling dad had something else in mind for me than that. Something worse.

Two stories started the rounds. King Henry was ill, the doctors said, with the smallpox; but the gossips said that wasn't the kind of pox he had, and considering where, and how, and with whom, he'd been spending most of his nights, everyone knew which story they believed. Kate had developed a convenient cold for whenever he called on her.

And Peter Matheson had heard that Mary had discussed with her advisers how to rid herself of her treacherous, impossible, dangerous husband. Divorce or annulment were impossible. What did that leave? But Mary had told them she'd do nothing that might lay any spot on her honour or her conscience. "Aye," he said, "but maybe they think she's as great a liar as theirsel's."

"Is she no, then?" I asked. "Knox is aye on about her craftiness."

He thought for a minute. He never answered me like a bairn, or a foolish gossip, but aye tried to give me an honest reply. "Well, she's no saint. But her motto's 'Loyauté me lie'. French for 'Loyalty binds me'. If you're honest wi' her, she'll be honest wi' you. An' that's how she's aye acted. She promised never to persecute the Protestants, an' she hasn't. It seems to me she's honest as any o' them, an' a sight more than most. She'll play on words, mind, that you think she says one thing an' she really means the other. Like when she promised to pardon the lords as killed Rizzio, but later when she felt better."

"Well?" I said. "She has done it. In spite o' them no bein' that loyal to her. An' daft to do't, I think. I'd have hanged the whole jing-bang o' them."

"I have no doubt o' that, but Mary's no like you," Peter said. "But she didn't mean to pardon them at all when she said it, that's for sure." I had to agree. "Aye," he said, "maybe they think she's doin' it again. That —"

"That what?" I asked. "That she means she'll no agree to nothin', but they can go on an' murder the King, as long as official-like she knows nothin' about it so her conscience is clear? Well? Are they right?"

He considered. "We'd better stop this, Leezie," he said. "You don't know, an' I don't know. Best leave it." I still wondered, though.

I wondered even more when Mary, who we all knew loathed her husband now, no blame to her, went to visit him in Glasgow, and he came back to Edinburgh with her. If I had heard the rumours, surely some servant or friend must have heard them too, and warned him. But then, he was a fool. His face was covered with a mask of taffeta to hide the scars left by his disease. He wanted to stay in Holyrood; the Queen refused, for her baby was there, and she'd not risk the bairn catching ill. She wanted him to go to Craigmillar Castle, but it was too isolated; he demanded to be near her, where he felt safe. They compromised, and he was settled in the old Provost's Lodgings, in Kirk o' Field Square. The house belonged to Sir James Balfour's brother.

It wasn't a big house, but could quickly be made comfortable, with a bath, and Mary's favourite tapestry, of coney-catchers, which made me laugh when I heard about it. He ordered his own purple velvet bed brought up from Holyrood for him, for the black velvet one the last tenant, the English

Ambassador, had left was too shabby. His bedroom was built out onto the town wall, and had a pleasant view south over an orchard to the Burgh Loch and the Pentlands.

We had a good time that week in the mews, for the weather was bright and frosty, with a scatter of snow, just grand for hawking, but all the lords and ladies were dancing attendance on the King and Queen. But in the town and court there was a nasty feeling in the air. One day the Queen's brother, Lord Robert, quarrelled violently with Darnley and warned him that if he didn't leave Edinburgh at once it would cost him his life. The Queen was furious, for that night the King had a right bad turn, and she said the quarrel must have upset him. I remembered ma's saying that the Queen had a soft spot for sick folk, and wondered if it was at work again. She spent several nights at Kirk o' Field, playing cards with her husband, and slept in the bedroom below his.

I kept remembering 'Loyauté me lie'. Loyalty? Darnley had over and over betrayed her trust and love. Or was I imagining things, and she was really trying to start again with him?

Now the Prince was older and stronger, ma had been able to run up to the pie shop for an occasional blether, saying what a relief it was to get away from the Countess of Mar for a while. She was aye cheerful and bright, and even when she saw dad in the shop once, when he'd come in to collect a special oyster and mushroom pasty that his master had ordered, she just nodded politely to him and passed by, hiding her shudder.

That was the night Sandy fell sick, with a griping in his belly and a high fever, his mind wandering. Poor Ina was fair distressed. Babs tried all she knew and he improved for a day or two, but then he grew worse again, vomiting, crying out in the fever and not knowing us, and eventually she called in a physician to examine him.

He felt Sandy's neck, looked at his eyes, tasted his water, and frowned. "Has he perchance eaten fungi, that the unlearned call mushrooms, this past week, dame?" he asked, sniffing and shrugging his big black gown easier on his narrow wee shoulders. He shook his head doubtfully when we said no, but then Ina grunted and nodded, and Babs remembered Sir James's pie.

"Aye, maybe, sir," she said. "He made a pasty for a special order a day or two back — just before he was taken ill. They wanted mushrooms, an' for that we had none the man gave us some dried that we could use, an' Sandy steeped them in wine, an' — here, was there some o' them no' what they should be?" She was white at the thought that Sir James might be sick as well, for even if it was his mushrooms that had caused the trouble, she'd be blamed for it.

"Who was it? Sir James Balfour? Well, dame, per bona fortuna, or by good luck, ye may disencumber yersel' o' inquietude, that is care, for there's none o' his household has taken sick. It's no that, then. But it's strange. Peculiar in the extreme. Superficially, that is to say, on the surface, it's similar to the signs an' symptoms o' a wee taste o' the Destroyin' Angel, as the vulgar name a kind o' toadstool that's a killer if ye but lick yer digits, that's yer fingers, after pickin' it. An' ye cannae easy tell it from the good, or bona fide, ones. If ye void or vomit it up sans hesitationis, at right away, that is, ye may feel amelioration, or relief, for a few days, but in finis, that is to say in the end. . ."

"In the end?" she said.

He nodded portentously. "It kills ye. Dead." And sniffed again.

"Well, sir, that's the only mushrooms that's been in this house since — ach, since October. I use them when they're in season, but I dinnae store them."

The doctor eyed her carefully, but she was obviously telling the truth. "Aye." He paused, thinking hard, pulling the end of his nose that didn't need lengthened. "The word gets round, ye'll be aware. Among physicians, that is to say, men of science. There's but one man ailed recently in this way in the town, an' that's —" He suddenly stopped, and his tone changed. "Well, then, dame," he gabbled, "ye must just do as ye're at. Keep him warm, but no hot, give him plenty warm drinks, milk maybe but no ale, pray for him, an' he'll mend if it's God's good will." He wouldn't even

181

wait to prescribe any medicine, though she told him she was quite prepared to pay for it. He just pulled down his cap, wrapped his scarf round his neck against the frost and raced out, scarce even pausing to collect his fee.

And that, as Babs said, wasn't a lot for her silver testoon, even allowing for the fancy language.

Murder!

At noon on the ninth of February two of the Queen's favourite servants got married. Ma had the evening off, and came up to tell us about it. Queen Mary had attended the wedding, and after a visit to her husband at Kirk o' Field was due back at the palace that night, for a masque to celebrate both the start of Lent and the wedding. "Saves siller, eh?" ma joked.

Sandy seemed better that day, starting to know us when we gave him a drink and trying to talk. He was sleeping in my wee truckle bed, so that Babs could see to him in the night and the customers couldn't see him during the day, and I was using his bed under the counter. When ma and I got in from the Kirk, for it was the Sabbath, he smiled up at us, clearly on his way back to health, and we were all so happy we ended up having quite a wee party to ourselves, like the Queen.

Babs had some gossip about Sir James Balfour and Rab Ormiston; there had been a constant coming and going at their houses this last day or two. Far more folk than usual seemed to be in and out, and not one stopping in to buy a pie; "Damned rogues, every one o' them," she commented. "Bothwell an' a cousin o' his, John Hepburn o' Bowton, an' one o' the Hays o' Tala, wild lads them. Ina says yer dad's been busy these days as well, runnin' up an' down the town like a caddie, an' a many o'

Bothwell's men wi' him. That man Dalgleish that was in to see Leezie, he's aye about. An' French Paris."

"But he's in the Queen's service these six months now," ma said.

"Well, he's been in about wi' his old friends again," Babs said. "An' here's a queer thing. Ade Murray was in here no an hour bye. He said he went in last night to pay Black Ormiston a wee debt, but was sent off sharpish, wi'out payin' his siller. Is that natural? They're plannin' some villainy, I'm feared."

On her way to entertain at the wedding masque, Kate paused by the door to put on a furred cloak against the blowing sleet, and agreed. "It's maybe against you, Janet. Take care," she said soberly, the huge white plumes of her mask nodding in her hand, contrasting with her gold and red Moorish costume.

"Ach, what for would all they grand folks be botherin' about me?" ma said comfortably. "It'll maybe be somethin' for the masque the night. My, that's a grand gown, Kate." Kate still looked worried, and ma stood up. "Never fear for me! Here, I'm due back. I'll walk you down to the palace for company. It'll be a fine show. The lords'll be plannin' a surprise for the Queen the night, just."

True she spoke, without knowing it; for just after Kate came in, about two hours after midnight, there was an explosion like a hundred cannon that shook the whole town. I leaped up, forgetting whose bed I was in and thumping my head on the table above me. When I recovered, Ina was waving out the door, her mother shouting at her side. "Away, ye rogues! What have ye been at, eh?" she screeched. "Did ye see them, Leezie? Men runnin' up the wynd as if the devil was after them! Come on, hear the shoutin'?"

We dragged on our clothes and ran out. A crowd was heading for the foot of the wynd, and joining it, Babs and I came down to the Kirk o' Field buildings, and stood horrified, shivering in the snow flurries.

The Old Provost's House was destroyed. Just a pile of rubble. Blown up.

We dug frantically in the rubble, hoping to find the King. We found the cook, dead, but no-one else. Then we heard a hoarse shouting, and along the top of the town wall itself staggered a tattered figure. It was the King's porter, Nelson. He was beckoning and pointing down outside the wall, sobbing and near collapse. I was among the folk that climbed the wall to help him, and leaped down to find out what he was pointing at.

In the little orchard on the far side of the wall lay two bodies, their nightshirts soaking in the snow. A dagger, a cloak and a coat were laid out quite neatly round them, and a chair lay toppled nearby. One was a small man. I'd only seen him briefly, and scarcely recognised him in the flickering torchlight; it was the King's valet, wee John Taylor.

The other was his master. Henry Darnley, King of Scots.

Not a soul in the town got a wink of sleep that night. That night? That week. Rizzio's death was nothing in comparison. Bothwell, as Sheriff of Edinburgh, was charging officiously about the streets with his men. The bodies were examined by physicians, and Darnley's body was placed on a board to let folk see it; no mark of violence at all, no bruises or stab wounds, no singed hair, no sign of blast; how they had died was a total mystery. A huge reward, £2,000, was offered for the capture of the criminals.

Babs told the inquiry what she had seen; eleven men, hurrying up the wynd towards the High Street. Or towards Rab Ormiston's, or Sir James Balfour's, but nobody said so. "Aye," the old wife added excitedly, "An' I cried after them, 'Traitors!' I cried. 'Ye've been at some evil turn!'" I didn't remember those exact fine words, but then my head had been ringing from hitting the table.

Mistress Crockett opposite confirmed every detail. "An' I stopped one man, holdin' to his silk cloak, askin' what the noise was, but he didnae answer me!" A silk cloak? No commoner, then.

Bothwell had been seen about the place, and his men carrying heavy barrels down by Kirk o' Field. But Bothwell had witnesses that he'd been at the masque, and then about the palace soon after the explosion, in his nightgown.

Johnnie Galloway at the Netherbow created an uproar. "I was wakened after midnight by some men sayin' they was friends o' the Earl, to let them out in a hurry into the Canongait, an' I'm sure — well, almost sure — Bothwell himsel' was one o' them!" Was that before or after the explosion? And would the Earl be daft enough to go openly like that to the gate? He could easily have got out as I had done for months, by dropping down over the wall. "Well, maybe his wounded arm was still weak for climbing!" Or maybe Johnnie was drunk?

"Geordie Dalgleish, Bothwell's man, he bought candles after the curfew, when all decent men are indoors!"

"I'm a friend o' Bothwell's porter, an' he warned me special to stay off the streets that night!"

"We live down by the Kirk o' Field, an' we heard the King screaming, 'Pity me, kinsmen, for the sake o' Jesus Christ who pitied all the world!'" But few believed the old gossips, for they never mentioned it till two days later.

We remembered Ade Murray, sent hastily away from Black Ormiston's; why?

Hints, not proof; all pointing towards Bothwell. But working alone? We doubted it. A many lords had wanted the King dead. Including half his family.

The day after the explosion, Babs and I were settling Sandy for the night, and wondering whose illness had scared the doctor off. "The only man o' note I know that was sick that week was the King himsel'," Babs muttered as we washed Sandy's face, "an' he was gettin' better."

"Aye," I agreed. Then it struck me, with horror — "But d'you no mind he'd a wild quarrel wi' Lord Robert, an' had a relapse, they said, that same night? Maybe it wasn't the quarrel made him fall back? If that mushroom pasty was sent to the King, but he misliked the taste — would he no have been sick, like Sandy, and then seemed to recover? An' then died o' it in the end?"

"Ach, away!" the old wife scolded me. "If this an' if that! Blethers!"

But Sandy must have heard our whispers, for that night

Babs called to me in distress. Sandy was moaning and struggling in his sleep.

"Sandy! Sandy, be at peace!" I joined in with her, trying to hold him down on the bed, but with crazy strength he heaved us off, and staggered naked out of the door. "Vengeance!" he started to yell. As Babs and I dragged on clothes against the bitter cold, he suddenly raced off up to the High Street. We could hear his voice echoing weirdly through the closes. "Blood! Innocent blood! Lord, open the heavens an' pour down vengeance on me, that have destroyed the innocent!" We followed his bare footprints in the snow up and down the wynds for minutes before we could come up with him, frantic, crying pitifully, howling for vengeance, while the townsfolk lay shuddering silent and fearful around us and the watchmen called to hearten each other down in the Cowgait.

At last we caught him. I slapped him hard across the face, as Peter Matheson had once done to ma. He jumped and staggered, and I feared I'd hurt him; but his fit faded, and he let us wrap a cloak round him and lead him home, while even the beggars huddling in the corners of the closes kept clear.

As we tucked him up in the bed again, chilled and shivering, a warm stone from the oven at his feet, Babs clutched my hand. "Is he clean crazed?"

"No," I reassured her, though I was none too sure. "He's sick, an' repeatin' the last sermon he heard at the Tolbooth Kirk. Two-three days an' he'll be fine." But it was another week of night watches, and four more desperate chases through the black streets, before at last he recovered.

The ministers preached that he was the voice of the Lord, calling down justice on the murderers. We never told the truth to a soul, for fear of questions. But I had a hard time keeping awake in the mews.

Darnley had a rich funeral in Holyrood, and the Queen showed little grief — not that we honestly expected it, but she needn't have left off her mourning within three days of the death and gone to play golf at Seton. They said the doctors insisted, for the sake of her health; "Aye so?" said most folk. Placards appeared on the Tolbooth door, accusing Bothwell, who swore he'd wash his hands in the blood of the writers. But as fast as he tore them down, new ones were nailed up, starting to accuse the Queen with him.

In the mews we got little work done for days. The weather was too bad to go out with the birds, and we were too excited to turn to making and mending. But Master Kerr took us in hand, and for a month we were held down to it, till the whole mews was gleaming with whitewash and fresh sawdust, all the woodwork repaired and scrubbed, the screens replaced, all worn furniture for the hawks mended and polished or thrown out, and we had settled again.

We paid notice, though, when the Earl of Lennox, Darnley's father, accused Bothwell, and brought an army of three thousand men to back his case in the Privy Council in April; but when he heard of Bothwell's army of four thousand Borderers waiting for him in Edinburgh, he went back home. A right riot all the wild mosstroopers caused in the town, too. I met a couple of old friends — Danny again, with a new sheepskin, who didn't recognise me; I didn't know whether to be pleased or annoyed. The Council heard evidence, but with no-one accusing Bothwell, he was formally acquitted. "Aye, so?" we all said.

I wondered. Did Mary truly believe Bothwell innocent? Or was she dazzled, as ma had been by dad, while she was still weak from her illnesses, tired and depressed, and surely in distress? With his strength and cocky bravado, and the loyalty he'd always shown her, he'd cheer and support her. 'Loyauté me lie.' But she must see he was only loyal to his own interests, surely?

Again I remembered ma and dad. Was Mary one that needed a man? Did she not allow herself to see Bothwell clearly, for she knew in the back of her mind that if she let herself know the truth, she must lose him?

Or did she know all about the murder beforehand? She had cause enough to hate her husband, and wish him dead. Had she helped plan it, and persuaded Darnley back to be killed? I didn't know.

The town was fair boiling. Rumours spread fast as the

plague. "The Queen's in love wi' Bothwell, an' means to wed him!"

"Aye! An' the most o' the lords has signed a pact to support him!"

"She helped Bothwell murder her husband, to get him out o' the way!"

"But how can the Queen marry a commoner? An' him wed already?"

I knew that his wife would probably be quite pleased to see the back of him, but for him to look to wed the Queen! But the look in his eyes just after Rizzio's murder came into my mind. Had he started then to think, to hope, to dream, to plan? He'd boasted he always did what he set his mind to; he never refused a challenge. This could be the greatest challenge of all.

And then — "The Queen's mad! Or bewitched! Ye heard she went to visit her son, in Stirlin'? Well, on her way back, Bothwell met her and carried her off to his castle at Dunbar! An' she went quietly wi' him, an' refused rescue!"

So the rumours were true.

Within three weeks Bothwell's divorce was granted. The Queen made him a duke, for that was the lowest degree she could reasonably wed. Rab Ormiston was knighted the same day, for no good reason anyone knew; Sir James Balfour, Bothwell's friend and old ally, was made Captain of Edinburgh Castle, to hold the strongest fortress in the land for the Queen and her new husband. Rewards — for what? we asked.

Four days later, on May the fifteenth, the Queen and Bothwell were wed. It was the gloomiest, saddest wedding anyone had ever known. Even during the ceremony, Mary wept. She knew already this was a fatal mistake; but whether for need and weakness, or love, she could not alter it.

The folk of Edinburgh were so angered that Knox dared to return in June and preach against the Queen, demanding her death in every sermon, "for greater abomination was never in the nature o' any woman than is in her!". Darnley, whom he had condemned so bitterly before as a heathen, Catholic, liar, profligate, was now "a martyr, an innocent youth sacrificed by that monstrous slave o' Rome, that blasphemous Jezebel. . ."

And much, much more. The hour-glass was turned at least once in every sermon, and the people cheered him.

Even Babs. "Sure it's better Moray should rule!" she argued. "Anythin's better than Bothwell! He's more arrogant an' takes more bribes than Rizzio! An' why should a Queen no' be burned for murderin' her man, like any other wife?"

The Protestant lords, who had agreed to help Bothwell, now felt the popular support. They rose in revolt against Mary; and when she and Bothwell sought safety in Edinburgh Castle, his 'friend' James Balfour refused to let them enter. She had to flee again to Seton and Huntly for help.

A month later, the two armies met at Carberry Hill. The ministers and people were fierce against the Queen and Bothwell, and though Mary's army had more noblemen, her ordinary soldiers had no heart to fight. Many just drifted away. The rebels promised her honourable treatment and obedience if she and Bothwell parted. To prevent the bloodshed of a battle, she surrendered to them while Bothwell rode off, promising to raise another army to rescue her.

The Kirk lords, many of them as much involved in the murder of Darnley as Bothwell, did not treat her with the honour they had promised her. They dragged her into the town as a prisoner, through a jeering, screeching mob throwing stones and filth, urged on by the ministers, shouting, "Murderess! Kill her! Burn her! Whore! Drown her!" Her face was dirty, her red skirt stained and torn, her hair straggling down her neck.

My heart near broke for her, as I remembered her riding through these same streets, these same people, elegant and smiling amid approving cheers. How different from this tear-stained, battered, helpless woman, sometimes trying angrily or desperately to argue with the crowd, more often silent in exhaustion and defeat. I remembered her kindness, her consideration.

I turned and fought my way out of the riot, angry and disgusted. Whatever she had done, whatever she had known or suspected or allowed or refused to admit to herself was happening, from now on I knew I was wholly on her side. If I could help her, I swore to myself I would, gladly, whatever the cost.

I never saw her again.

She was taken away by night to the Castle of Loch Leven, where she fell ill again, and was forced at knife-point to sign papers of abdication in favour of her year-old son. Her half-brother Moray was to be Regent. The baby had indeed been her greatest threat. In July he was crowned King James the Sixth. Knox preached the triumphant coronation sermon.

The mews was a haven of peace for me, for not a soul in the place but sympathised with the Queen, even Master Kerr, in spite of being a strong Kirk man. It was a refuge from the malice and ill-feeling throughout the town.

Then one evening in the High Street someone seized my arm. It was John Knox, his wife at his side, as white of face as he was red. "Strumpet!" Heads turned all round us. "Get yoursel' into seemly women's garb, you disgrace to your sex, an' pray the Lord to forgive you in His infinite mercy! I know you, Leezie Sinclair, as claimed kinship wi' me! No kin o' mine would appear so, lewd an' shameless in the open street! I'm no forgettin' ye, mockin' at the Lord's humble servants, you an' that hell-black harlot! Mend your ways or I'll see you driven out like Hagar from among the concourse o' the godly!"

His wife, still-faced, not even looking at me, touched his sleeve. "Husband, you'll do yoursel' a mischief, ragin' like this." He nodded to her, controlled himself, glared at me again and stumped off up the street beside her. All the bystanders, staring, drew back from me as if I had the plague. I was shaking with rage and distress as I ran up to Kate's, to warn her.

My hands were trembling, to my annoyance. She sat me down on one of her fine padded stools and gave me a glass of sack, sweet and strong. "Never fear, lassie, I'm ready for him. But I didn't expect him to take so against you. We can't let him spoil everybody's life just for his righteous revenge on me."

"But how can you stand against him, Kate? He's — he must be the most powerful man in Embra the now!"

"Away, lassie, who told you that? Himself? He's the noisiest, sure, but he's but a Kirk minister. I have friends worth a dozen o' him."

I couldn't believe her. "That's no what you said before, Kate! Are they worth him an' the whole Council? For he has the backin' o' all the bailies —"

She patted my shoulder. "Sup that up, lass, an' don't fret. He took me by surprise last time. I've no intention o' lettin' him arrest me for witchcraft, or anythin' else. Nor you neither. Now, hold your wheesht a minute till I think." She walked up and down the room, humming gently, running her fingers lightly over the citterne strings, shuffling the cards, settling her cap absently before the panel of mirrors. Finally she nodded decisively. "Aye. Leezie, can ye ask Master Kerr for two hours off the morn's morn?" She hugged me. "Never fear, lass, we never died a winter yet!"

I was comforted by her assurance, though she'd tell me nothing — now that I thought about it, she never did tell me anything important.

At the agreed time Kate, in her dark blue, respectable gown, was nodding approval of me neat and tidy in my brown suit. She whisked me out, up a set of stairs in a close near the High Kirk, in through an oaken door. A fine young man in a black kirk gown like a minister rose from behind a desk to greet us.

"Mistress Lenton! You're before your time, mistress. It's no a thing that the ladies are well known for, neither." He was smiling.

Kate returned the smile widely. "But then I'm no lady, Master Sharp! This is a young friend o' mine, Sinclair, that's concerned in this matter as well." He bowed again, his eyes sharp as his name. "You do understand, Master Sharp, that I require absolute secrecy about this? I have your sworn word on it?" He bowed, smiling graciously and patronisingly. "It's no laughin' matter, sir!" Her voice was stern. "There's lives could depend on it! Aye, sir, that's true. Now, you remember what we arranged? I can hear him on the stair!"

We were swiftly ushered into an inner room, and the door left a crack ajar. Kate whispered in my ear, "He's an advocate, one o' the best! John Sharp, a risin' lad! Now wheesht, an' listen." Uneasily, I wished I knew what was happening. Babs Martin aye said the only honest lawyer was a dead one.

Another visitor was being shown in and seated with his back to our door. I knew the voice; Master Knox himself! Kate hushed me before I could speak.

"Well, sir, where is this person you say needs my advice?" The old man's tone was irritated, and he was panting a bit from the stairs. "Why did he no come to see me himsel', eh? If it's a matter o' the Lord's work, I'm at the disposal o' any o' the Lord's children, an' no lawyer need be concerned."

Master Sharp was respectful but firm. "I'm given to understand, sir, that it is a matter o' some conflict between a lady's legal an' her spiritual duties, an' she wishes to have advice from both o' us togther."

Knox's voice rose slightly. "In any conflict, sir, the spiritual duty must aye come first! For man's first duty is to the Lord, to fearlessly bring every soul into His light o' truth an' justice, wi' no consideration o' rank, money, position nor power." He coughed slightly. "But ye say it's a woman, sir? Ech, aye, then she'll need all the help we can give her to appreciate this duty. For women are weak vessels, sir! Their minds are ill fitted to comprehend the great verities, as are the minds o' men. Aye, a poor, feeble thing, the mind o' a woman! You'll mind the great John Calvin himsel' said they were like cows, fit for two things only; to bear children, an' die. An' I must admit —"

But Kate could bear it no longer. Her jaw had dropped, and then clenched. She rose, drew a deep breath, gestured to me to stay where I was, and gently, quietly, like a cat, pushed open the door and came in on the men.

There was a short pause, as Master Sharp enjoyed Knox's expression. I wished I could. Then he was all geniality, and Kate all soft, yielding meekness, smiling and nodding, thanking them both respectfully for their consideration in agreeing to see her at such short notice. Master Knox said not a word.

Seating her by the fire opposite Knox, the lawyer stood back. "Mistress Lenton, would you care to explain the matter on which you wish our advice?"

She bit her lip, as if shy, and reached inside her cloak pocket.

"It's this letter, sirs, that — that came into my possession a few days back. I'm wonderin' whether I should make it known to the Privy Council, that's inquirin' into the foul murder o' the late King Henry Darnley."

The lawyer frowned. "Has it a bearin' on the case, mistress? Does it tell, plainly or by inference, who was responsible for the deed?"

Master Knox interrupted him. "We know who was responsible, sir! That Popish devil-worshipper, that abomination o' her sex, as was Queen until by God's help she was cast down from the throne she had defiled too long! An' her accomplice, the triple-damned warlock pirate, Bothwell!"

"Aye, he's been playin' the devil wi' the shippin' round about Arbroath," agreed Master Sharp. "But maybe this letter has fresh information about it?"

Kate had been waiting patiently for them to let her speak. "I believe it may, sir, though it's no that clear," she smiled. I couldn't see what there was to smile at. "It seems to be from a person o' great importance in the town, sirs, a man that's looked up to an' respected by — it's no lie to say by thousands o' folk. An' it seems to show that he knew about the plan; that he was less innocent than he'd wish folk to think him."

They paused, considering. There were a good few men like that in the town; if it was a powerful nobleman, and they advised her to tell, it could make them a bad enemy. The lawyer pursed his lips; "But does it actually add to our knowledge o' who did the deed, mistress?"

"I'm no sure, sir," she said. "It's just — if I'm right, this man is deceivin' all the good folk o' the town. I don't know whether I should speak out, sirs, wi'out respect to rank nor power, as Master Knox said himsel', for it may be my stern duty before God to bring this sin an' this sinner into the light o' His truth an' justice. But then, I might be wrong in what I take from the letter, an' that would discredit an honest man. Would you advise me, sirs, for my woman's mind —" her voice was pure honey — "is too weak to decide."

There was another pause. "You can scarce expect us to give you advice in general, when the actual letter is at hand," the young man said. As she hesitated, he added, "I'm mindin' I'm sworn to absolute secrecy, mistress."

Knox sniffed irritably. "I haven't my eye-glasses wi' me," he grunted. "Read it out, Master Sharp, an' be sharp about it. I'm due at the Tolbooth."

The lawyer opened the letter, flattened it on his desk, and cleared his throat. "Well, it's no long. 'To the right noble the Earl o' Bothwell,' it's addressed. M'hm. 'In the matter which your lordship did open to me in December, I have prayed for guidance, an' I believe it is God's will. While no Christian man can readily approve the wilful death o' any o' the Lord's creatures, it may well be that the takin' off o' one may be acceptable as a sacrifice for the good o' the many, an' the said H. D.-' H. D.? Henry Darnley? Maybe. Er — 'H. D. bein' a blasphemer an' a heretic is fittest o' all men in Scotland to be put away for the triumph o' God's holy cause. My lord, your designs an' those o' the Lord are not aye in accord; but here it seems to me God intends that our ways may run together for a while. As my forefathers supported yours in years past, so in this one matter I believe it is the will o' the Lord that I should support you. May the Lord bless this your undertakin', an' bring it to success. Yours, in the service o' the Lord o' Hosts.' The signature — " He stopped, put the letter down on the desk, and stared at Knox. "The signature, sir, is J.K."

J.K. John Knox! Knox himself! Approving, agreeing to the murder that he was trying to have the Queen executed for! Condemning Darnley, that he was now praising! Oh, marvellous Kate! I bit my knuckles to keep quiet and hear.

Knox was standing, glaring at Kate. "It's no mine! It's a devilish forgery!" he snarled, his stick thumping the floor.

She sat meekly on her stool, smiling up at him. "I'd never claim other, sir; but who am I to say? The writing can be compared wi' other letters. There's many o' them about."

Master Sharp searched abruptly in a box on the shelves behind him for a paper, and studied it and Kate's together. "They seem the same," he said drily.

"Exactly, sir. You see my difficulty," Kate murmured.

"This about his forefathers supportin' Bothwell's — you said that a while back, Master Knox. I heard you mysel'." The lawyer's voice was cold.

"It's no true. It's a plot o' Satan! I've been in Ayrshire all this while —"

"No, sir. You came into the town for the Kirk Assembly in December."

"As God is my witness it's a lie!" Knox sank back to his stool, panting.

"The hand is identical wi' yours, sir, an' the style. It mentions things folk will mind on you sayin' an' doin'. But you may be believed. I cannot say. You'll know yoursel' how eager folk aye are to tear a man's reputation down."

After another aching silence Kate, as if regretfully, said, "Well, sirs, I'm in your hands. To me it seems the letter may well be false, an' gives no real information to aid discovery o' the murderers. But should I hold it back on that account, when cleverer minds than my poor weak woman's one might find enlightenment an' — interest in it?"

The lawyer studied Knox, who studied the floor. At last he said carefully, "Mistress Lenton, I believe I cannot advise you here. The man to do that is Master Knox, for it's him that's the expert in matters o' sin an' conscience."

Knox never lifted his eyes. He must have been seeing in his mind's eye the likely reactions to the letter. His enemies would leap on it with delight. He would be ruined. No-one would ever again believe a word he said. His power would be gone. His voice was half choked. "No. I dinnae believe it is necessary for you to take it to the Council. For —" he dragged a deep, gasping breath, as if it hurt him — "for it would but damage the — the person folk would believe — wrongly believe — wrote it, an' do no good to the town."

Kate smiled at him. "I must say that was my opinion as well, sir. I'm glad we're in such kindly agreement." You could practically hear his teeth grinding. "But I've another worry, sirs. I've heard a rumour — maybe mistaken — but it is possible I may be questioned about a wee false charge that was made against me in malice a while back. Now I'm thinkin' I'd best give this letter to one o' my friends for safe keepin'. I'd no like it to fall into the wrong hands, you'll understand. Is that no fair, Master Sharp? But if I was accused, then my friends, bein' honest folk, would surely feel duty bound to give it in to the court, an' tell what we've decided here together, as evidence o' my good character. Or if any o' my friends, Leezie Sinclair for example, was attacked, maybe I'd be that upset I'd forget to keep it hid. An' I'd truly no want that to happen, sir, just from a nasty wee man's spite at me. Do you think it's likely?"

At last, Knox lifted his head and looked long at her, then glanced at Master Sharp. "You swore secrecy?" At the lawyer's nod, he nodded slowly in return. Rising heavily, leaning on his staff, he faced Kate. "No, Mistress Lenton. It's no that likely." Suddenly he whirled, thrust out his staff and knocked open my door to reveal me blinking in the blast of light. "Aye. I thought so." He paused at the stair-head. "May the Lord judge your black soul as it deserves, Kate Lenton," he said longingly, as if it was a curse.

Undaunted, she smiled sweeter than ever, and curtseyed. "I'm sure He will, sir. And yours." He left to the sound of her soft, deep chuckle.

Master Sharp was frowning. "How did ye come by this letter, mistress?" he asked sternly.

"Why, Master Sharp, you don't expect me to tell you all my secrets?" she answered him as she'd answered me. "Did I say one illegal word?"

He shook his head in admiration — I think. "Not one. Is it —?" He stopped.

She smiled again, without replying, tucking the letter away safely in her cloak. "Come round this evenin', sir, an' I'll see about payin' your fee," she murmured. "I settle my affairs promptly. I hate to bide in any man's debt."

He bowed, smiling in return. "I can see ye're a good woman o' business, mistress," he said. "I'll look forward to it." He kissed her hand as if she was a court lady, which made her laugh out loud, and ushered us out.

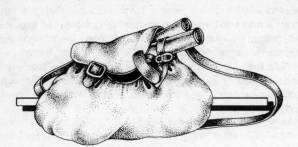

James Balfour

That spring Mary lost even her man. Bothwell sheltered from a
storm in a Norwegian port. But the King hadn't forgotten him,
nor had his niece; and the Earl was imprisoned for breach of
promise. The Queen's own health was slowly improving in the
quiet of her captivity at Lochleven. Since her abdication she
had clothes and embroidery threads sent her, and had her own
servants and rooms. Her jailer, Sir William Douglas, Moray's
half-brother, one of the best of the clan, made her as
comfortable as he could.

All summer the wee folk involved in Darnley's murder were
hunted down, questioned and executed; but not the great lords
who had encouraged Bothwell and were now trying to shift
their guilt onto him and the Queen alone. His servants
confessed they'd brought in the gunpowder and hidden it in
Kirk o' Field, actually in the Queen's bedroom below
Darnley's. If Mary had slept there as she'd intended she must
have found it, but her councillors had insisted, very strongly —
oh, aye? we thought — that her servants would be disappointed if she missed their wedding masque, and after it she had
gone to bed in the Palace. The fuse had been set alight when all
was quiet, and Bothwell had just had time to get back to
Holyrood — by the Netherbow, Johnnie Galloway was quite

right — in time to put on his nightshirt and pretend he'd never been out.

"It's no right!" Babs said. "There's only nine men named, and I seen eleven. Who were the other two, eh? An' just how did the King an' his man die?"

"No-one can say, Babs," Peter said. He was in for a warm and a pie one damp night, and we'd all gathered by the oven door to pass on the gossip.

"No-one will say, ye mean," objected Sandy, and Peter shrugged.

"Maybe. Is it likely? Moray's in trouble enough without that, for Elizabeth o' England's no pleased about him forcin' Mary to abdicate."

"Little wonder there either. She'd no want deposin' queens to become a habit," said Kate. "It could be her next."

I was perched on the stair above them. "What makes me mad," I offered, "is to see all the lords I know fine were in on the plot walkin' about free."

"An' sittin' in Parliament! Ye're no alone there," Babs agreed. "Moray's on right shaky ground. He needs some proof Mary's guilty, an' soon."

"Keep this quiet," said Peter. "He's got it."

"What?" I nearly fell off the step onto Sandy, putting pies in the oven.

"Aye. Providential, eh? Sir James Balfour — aye, him again, Bothwell's 'friend' — he sent word to Moray that Geordie Dalgleish was in the town."

I was surprised. "Wee Geordie Tod? I thought he'd run."

"He came back. He was arrested today, an' threatened with torture."

"Huh! Money would have more effect on Geordie Tod than threats!" I said.

"Maybe, but. . . He's confessed the Queen's friends sent him to Sir James — aye, the same man — to get an important casket. Sir James gave it to Moray. Moray says there's love letters in it Mary wrote to Bothwell, provin' she knew of the plan, agreein' to help in it by bringin' Darnley to Edinburgh, away from the safety o' his father's lands near Glasgow. It's no common knowledge yet, an' nobody but Moray's seen them. Now keep it quiet, or I'm in trouble."

We gazed at him. "Is it true? The letters?" Babs asked.

"Who's to say?" said Kate. "There's as many forgers in Embra as in London." Well, she should know. "If Mary did write the letters, she was daft no to burn them after; but then, she was daft to wed the man anyway. Whether or no, she's done for now; she'll never sit on the throne again."

"Maybe," said Peter. "But the Borders, the west and north are still mainly for her, and the Hamiltons are fair mad at Moray for takin' the Regency."

"Well, there's damned few in Edinburgh wants Mary back," said Babs.

"Sure Moray doesn't; he's just sold the Queen's black pearls to her cousin Elizabeth. She bid more for them than Catherine de Medici, her as was Mary's mother-in-law. Bitches both. An' keep that quiet too!" said Peter bitterly.

The Queen wrote to Moray, demanding to see these letters and face her accusers in Parliament, to find out the truth; but the lords refused her.

Wee Geordie Tod was one of the first to be executed. Fit for any villainy, he'd laughed; and see where it led him — and his master. I went down by the gibbet, to give him the comfort of one friendly face at the execution, and Sandy came with me, to give me comfort. Geordie waved to me, and grinned; but his eyes haunted me after. Dad smiled, with his mouth, when he met me later.

Hawking went on as usual with the lords, Regent Moray and his friends, but we resented them. Never mind the rights and wrongs; there wasn't a soul in the mews but preferred the Queen, who knew us all by name, smiled and was gracious, to this sour-faced or over-hearty gang of hypocrites, arrogant, inconsiderate rogues. When the Queen had kept us out late, or in the wet, she thanked us with silver or a flask of wine. This lot never gave us a thought. During that autumn all the Queen's own merlins flew free, even my wee Mab. We kept the seven that we'd manned that spring, for she had never put a hand on them; but all the others that she loved so well, we took off their jesses and bells and hacked them back down the wind. And Master Kerr never said a word.

One cold, damp day in April, young Alan was out with Master Kerr and me, up on the Pentlands with Morton, some Douglas lordlings, and an unusual guest, Sir James Balfour. We'd been out for three hours after partridges, nesting or not, and had halted to change horses. The servants came up with flasks and baskets — not a bite for us, of course — and the lords scattered through a nearby wood to take their ease. I slipped off to find a sheltered bush.

While I was still crouched down, I heard men moving on the far side of the bushes from me. I cursed my being female, and hoped the Douglases wouldn't spot me, or they'd tease me daft. I stayed where I was, frantically hauling at my breeks, tying my points and looking for a path away that didn't lead me over the rustling, giveaway bracken. I didn't know the voices, and was too embarrassed to pay much heed till I heard an English voice say, "Cecil says Her Grace is sure to believe them, Sir James." I froze to listen. 'Her Grace'? The Queen? And Cecil? I didn't know any Cecils. I knew a Sir James, though.

Papers crackled. "Aye," the other man said consideringly, "I'll need to study them further, but they seem perfect. An' I know the very man to finish them. . . I've no leisure now. Put them away again, an' I'll see them later." They walked out round the end of the bushes where I crouched hidden, glad my suit was dull brown. I knew one tall, angular back; Sir James Balfour, right enough. The other was a messenger, tucking papers away into a big, worn deerskin bag. It had a long shoulder strap and two wee buckles, much like my hawking bag.

Like my hawking bag. If this was a plot against Mary — and if I dared. . .

Check, first. "Alan!" As I came out of the wood, not near the men, I jerked my head to call the lad over. "Who's that wi' Sir James?"

He knew, of course; if you wanted to know anything at all in the town, you just asked Alan. "It's a messenger from England,

Sinclair. He came up just as we stopped. His name's Jackson, an' he's got a big black cuddy, see there!"

I thought hard. He was a sharp wee devil, and a good actor. And he'd be at no risk. Right. "Alan, I'm thinkin' there's a letter in that bag would harm the Queen." His eyes grew round, staring up at me. "Will you help me find out?"

Never a moment's hesitation. "How?" If I'd asked him to cut his hand off he'd be reaching for his knife. From my bag I fished out my bit pie.

"Here's my piece. Aye, take it, but don't eat it, ye daft wee gowk! It's no for you! Wander down there among the hounds an' unbuckle a couple, quiet-like so nobody sees you. Then drop the pie in among them, an' get out quick — an' mind, when they ask you, it's your pie! An' here — don't look so innocent! It's as good as a shout!" With a wink and a thoughtful look — I'd given him some interesting advice, I realised — he sidled away down the hill.

I sauntered up by where the messenger was sitting against a tree above and behind the rest where he could see them all, his bag on the ground beside him. As the rumpus erupted, the hounds and Alan all yelling and fighting, the man leaned forward to see better. I reached gently round the tree, laid my bag down and lifted his, and while he was still laughing I sauntered away again.

Had anyone noticed? No, thank God. Quick, back into shelter, and open the bag. There were a dozen letters. Some sealed; can't risk breaking them open. But one bundle were folded together in a wrapper, the seal broken. Blessing Kate's lessons all winter, I struggled to make one out.

'To Her Grace, Mary, Queen —' I skipped a lot of long words. It said Queen Elizabeth was dying, and had named Mary as her heir! Mary was hereby invited to Carlisle or Berwick, where she would be escorted to London 'to meet if it be God's will with Her Majesty of England and be confirmed in this your great and high position. As sign of the truth of this, we send you a token, the which you will recognise.' It was signed 'Burghley' and half a dozen names more.

My grin near split my chapped lips. Our Queen to be Queen

of England as well! Let the lords try to keep her in prison now!

What did the next one say? 'To Our Dearly Beloved Cousin, Mary, by the Grace of God Queen of Scotland and France, Greetings.' I glanced at the signature. 'Elizabeth R.' What? It advised Mary to stay patiently in Lochleven, for Elizabeth was gathering forces to persuade Moray to free her. But how could Elizabeth be writing letters and raising armies if she was dying?

The next one said there were ships awaiting Mary at — a space — to carry her wherever she wished. Again signed 'Elizabeth R.' What was going on?

I struggled to grasp the rest quickly. One called the Queen to come to Edinburgh, where — a space — held a chest of gold for her. One invited her to come to London, and assured her of help against the rebels. One told her to go to Ireland, one to trust Elizabeth's friend — space — and do as he arranged. All were different; all except the first were signed Elizabeth R; every one spoke of a token; none was dated.

There was a small velvet bag in the satchel, sealed, with two lumps in it. The token, clearly, and something else. I felt through the thick cloth in vain. No, it wasn't safe to break the wax, I decided regretfully.

Shouting rose as the hunt was called together again. I hastily folded the papers back into the bag, and hurried through the trees. Damn! The messenger was already getting up, my bag slinging to his shoulder. No time to think; I started to run, as if afraid of being late — and not far wrong, either. I swung round the tree-trunk and cannoned into the man, clutching at him to steady myself, falling — surprisingly hard, that was — and pulling the bag from his arm. I rolled over it, staggered to my feet and held his own bag out to him, panting an apology, and turning without pause to run on. As I reported to Master Kerr, I watched from the corner of my eye as the courier stared after me, and quickly opened his bag to check on its contents. For a split second I had a horrible fear that I'd given him my own bag again, but no, mine was on my shoulder. The Englishman rebuckled his bag firmly, hoisted it back to its place, and mounted to follow the hunt without, I hoped, any idea that his letters had been read by an enemy.

I was on my way home that night before I could get peace to think, so late that Johnnie Galloway had to shout to me to hurry or he'd close the Netherbow gate on me. He laughed at me, and cuffed my cap off. My plait of lengthening hair slithered down red round my shoulders, and I'd have sworn at him the year before. It suddenly struck me that though I ran miles every day keeping up with the mounted men, though I was tougher than ever in some ways, I was softer in others. I hadn't hit anybody, not seriously, for almost a year.

This wasn't helping me think. Ach, this was beyond me. Right, who could I ask? Kate. And Peter. Babs Martin had turned against the Queen; better not.

Luckily I saw Peter in the High Street, and asked him to come up with me, and Kate was in; I poured out my tale with a sense of relief. Another thing that I'd grown soft in, I thought, was in judging what I could handle myself. Or was I just getting some sense?

They stared at each other for nearly a minute without speaking. Then Kate sat back from her table and sighed. "My God, lassie, you do set rods in pickle for yoursel'! But this beats all. Spyin' on Balfour an' the English! Your head's rockin' loose on your shoulders."

"Never mind that, Kate, what do we do about it?"

"How many letters, Leezie? Seven or eight? An' each one sayin' somethin' different?" Peter was pulling at his lip as he thought.

"Aye, sir, stay in prison, escape, come to Embra, come to England, go to York or Ireland — all sorts o' things."

"An' near all signed by Elizabeth?" He looked over at Kate. "A trap."

"Just that," she nodded. "To get the Queen to go just where they want her. It would just need a wee man to pass her the right letter, somebody she'd trust, an' she could be tricked into doin' whatever suited them best."

"But what good would they do?" I asked. "The Queen's fast in Lochleven Castle. She can't go anywhere."

Kate smiled at me. "Aye behind the news, eh, Leezie? Willie Douglas's wee brother's just put out o' Lochleven Castle for that he was plannin' to rescue Mary. He near did it, too. An' if he had —"

"When he does." We stared at Peter. "Aye," he nodded, "an' Sir William maybe no that hard to deceive, neither, for bein' jailer to a Queen's no easy on the purse nor on the conscience. I doubt the Laird o' Lochleven's young brother'll try again, an' succeed. Think on it! Willie Douglas is Moray's own half-brother; their mother'll be mad at him if Mary gets loose, but they'll no be all that hard on him. But if he just accidental-on-purpose-like turns a wee blind eye to somebody, his young brother maybe, slippin' her out from under his nose, an' then she gets back to the throne, think how grateful she'll be! He's a lot to gain, an' no that much to lose. But if we can see it, others can an' all. That's maybe why they've sent up all these letters."

"I'd credit anythin' o' Blasphemous Balfour, but would Elizabeth do such a thing?" Kate asked. "Trick her own cousin? What good would it do her?"

"Keep Mary from claimin' the English throne," Peter said. "Did the man no say 'Cecil', Leezie? That'll be Sir William Cecil, Lord Burghley. Him as you said signed one o' the letters. He's Elizabeth's chief adviser. Maybe the signature's forged an' she doesn't know, but I'd no wager on it. An' Balfour would get Moray's friendship, an' a share o' the gold. Enough for him to do't."

"Aye. One o' the greatest villains in Scotland. 'Neither fear o' God nor love o' virtue,' Knox said o' him, an' he was right that time, anyway. Betrayed his friend Bothwell just when it suited him. Now he'll be lookin' for a new profit." Kate's voice was like lye, that would burn the skin off your hand.

"But what can we do, Peter?" Talking was all very well, but. . . "Get word to the Queen no to trust any letters from Elizabeth? Would she credit us?"

He considered again. "Maybe no. She's aye thought Elizabeth would come to her aid in the end, for that Mary's her cousin an' heir, after all, an' Elizabeth can't openly support rebels against Mary wi'out givin' her own unfriends a bad example to follow. No, Mary'd no believe a warnin' wi' no proof. They've exchanged gifts — rings, it was."

"Rings? That could be the token in the wee bag! She'd know her own ring."

"Aye — an' the other thing was most likely a seal." One problem solved.

"Who would use them?" Kate mused. "Lennox? He's no love for Mary since his son Darnley's death, but then would she trust him? Maitland's for England — aye has been. Or Argyll? He's Mary's good-brother, but he's Moray's friend, an' a damned rogue. Ach, who knows? But how could Balfour get the letter to the man? I can't see how they'd work this."

We talked round and round it and got nowhere. Even if Sir James gave his agent in Mary's train all the letters beforehand, how could he tell the man which one to use without arousing suspicion?

It all seemed a waste of time, for the Queen was still in Lochleven.

A week later she escaped, just as Peter had said. Young George Douglas and a wee cousin of his slipped her away on the second of May.

Within a week more than half the nobility of Scotland were milling about round her at Hamilton, swearing their loyalty and squabbling about precedence. Some of our Edinburgh men slipped out to join Mary's army; others marched to join Moray. Master Patterson was one of these, and his wife took the children back to her mother in Tranent, looking happier than she'd done in months.

As it happened, ma came home next day, dismissed by the Countess of Mar, in charge of the baby King's nursery, for being too soft with the babe, and then arguing that that was her charge from Queen Mary. The Countess had her out of Stirling Castle for impertinence within the hour. Ma wasn't too upset about that; having been nurse to the Prince, she would be in demand by half the mothers in Scotland. But to leave the babe with the Countess worried her. "Love's no in the woman!" she lamented. "Poor wee bairn!"

Babs was delighted as I was to see her back. The Frasers, with their new baby, moved across the landing into the Pattersons' rooms, which were bigger. Ma and I settled into our old ones as if we'd never been away. And if the Pattersons came back — what a pity!

At the mews we were having problems. My goshawk Geordie had fallen sick, and passed it on to the rest. He was now recovered, but all the other gosses were huddled bad-temperedly in one of the stove rooms, the air stinking with camphor — I'd be bad-tempered myself in there, but it was the best cure, Master Kerr said. We were getting on grand now, easy and happy together, and I was learning fast. He was a great falconer, and a great teacher. He was helping me with another problem; a young tiercel saker I was training. When we took him out to teach him to wait on, flying above us as we walked with the dogs to put up duck or grouse for him, he'd started raking off on his own after pigeons. We had been most unlucky; five times, when we thought we had a clear field of grouse, pigeons had risen or flighted in nearby. He'd gone after them and actually caught two, which was unusual, pigeons being wary and tricky fliers. We decided to put him right back to training on the practice field for a while. If we couldn't sort it quickly he'd aye be unreliable.

It was maybe that that made me take note when one evening, as I was coming in from the mews, I saw a group of folk leaving Sir James Balfour's door; he'd been replaced by now as captain of the Castle, and was back in his own rooms above the corner of the wynd. One man was the English Ambassador, one was Willie Gray, hell mend him, and the third was dad.

As they reached the High Street they looked up to the window, where Sir James's shadow loomed like a black spider in its web against the yellow candle-light behind him. They lifted a farewell hand to each other, and the Englishman came down past me while dad and Willie turned away up the hill.

As soon as I got over the jump and grue I always felt when I caught sight of dad, I saw Willie had a fair-sized oblong basket on his head. I heard pigeons as I turned into the wynd. My mind wandered. Pigeon pie. No, these were live birds. Fancies — fantails or tumblers, maybe. Or carrier pigeons. We'd not caught any of them this year. . .

Carrier pigeons. Messages. Swiftly and secretly. James Balfour.

A note of which letter was to be given to Mary. By somebody already with her. Somebody who could get hold of a carrier pigeon and send it in to Edinburgh, or who knew somebody who kept them here already.

Ach, surely not. This was ridiculous. You couldn't rely on getting a handy carrier pigeon loft wherever the Queen went. Unless you'd known where she'd go... because you advised her... but the sender would need a bird from each loft you might be near... a lot of pigeons... a basketful...

My feet had turned me and taken me back to the High Street, but dad was gone, and though I ran right up as far as the Castle I couldn't see him or Willie. They could have turned down any close or wynd, and gone up any tenement. There were enough attics in Edinburgh, and enough pigeons about the place, that a man could keep a dozen carriers without anyone noticing.

What could I do? Even if I was right? Nothing.

When might it be sent? Think. Dad had come out of his master's house with the pigeons. Sir James had the letters. Or had had them. Mary faced a battle within a day or so. She'd lost the last one. If she lost this one, she'd be ready to accept advice, help, a letter given her by someone she trusted.

Soon, then, for if she lost she'd have to flee, and they'd not know for long where she'd be. Tonight? Too late, it was growing dark. Probably at first light tomorrow. Tonight the bird might settle for the night and forget — did pigeons forget overnight? — or be taken in a tree by a polecat. Or an owl. Or a hawk.

A hawk. That saker! He might as well do something useful! And Geordie. Pity all the other gosses were sick. The merlins were too small, and the gyrfalcons too large, but there was a peregrine falcon I'd been allowed to fly several times this last month...

No, I couldn't. Catch a single pigeon, out of the hundreds round the town, alone? It was impossible. Even if I was sure there would be a carrier pigeon, and I wasn't, it was impossible. And maybe lose or ruin two or three hawks to do it? Ridiculous. Master Kerr would turn me out, and I'd deserve it.

Could I ask Master Kerr, then? No; he was a strong Kirk man. Or anyone else? No-one else would understand. This was for me alone. Could I do it?

For the Queen? I'd been ready to risk my life for her when they were killing Rizzio. I'd sworn to help her, whatever the cost.

But hawking? My one delight? My love? My life?

Never again thrill to watch the lovely, deadly birds balance and swing on the air, climb in power and grace, and stoop in a heart-stopping dart to the tiny explosion of feathers of a perfect strike. Never again charm a wild, wary killer into a fragile, delicate partnership, that could be lost by a moment's carelessness. Never again nurse a sick bird from an untidy, coughing jumble of feathers back to a sleek, elegant efficiency, bright-eyed and arrogant, lifting to your hand in neither affection for you nor gratitude, but a burning spirit that accepted all your care, all your knowledge and attention and love, and tossed it away into the sky in fierce elation, and your soul with it.

Could I risk losing it all? For a Queen who might well be a murderess?

Of course I couldn't. I'd be mad.

Next morning I was at the mews by four o'clock. I took a cadger's frame and lifted Geordie, the saker tiercel, and with a shrug, the peregrine falcon. As well sink my boat thoroughly. I had to carry Geordie, for gosses were never hooded, and a gos on a frame would attack the others. The sun was still not risen when I started up the far end of the Castle Rock. It would have been an ideal place to watch for the pigeon if I'd been sure it was coming this side of the Rock. I wasn't. Well, it was a stupid idea anyway, and no great loss if I picked the wrong side, for even if there was a pigeon, and even if it was loosed that morning, I'd not get it anyway. This was all for nothing.

No; for the Queen.

It was an awkward climb to the wee flat patch of grass I'd

found the year before, just below the wall of the Castle. I could look down left to the town chimneys and right towards Falkirk and Glasgow, and Hamilton, where the Queen was. The hawks were uneasy. Their routine was upset. They'd not been bathed or allowed to weather. I hoped that they'd not rake off to find water. And that if they stooped on a pigeon and missed, they'd return to my whistle and lure instead of chasing away after it. And that if they killed, they'd stay on the quarry till I could get down to retrieve them later, and not be stolen. And that nobody would see me from the battlements away above my head, and send soldiers to chase me, or shoot down at me, or shoot the birds. Oh, well. . .

I lifted Geordie first on my glove, and let him look about. A flight of pigeons fluttered among the rooftops below us, and he roused his feathers, interested. He warbled, stretching his wings up and back, and settled again. I gently scratched under his chin, which he loved, and loosed the leash from his jesses. He was as ready to fly as I could make him.

The sun rose suddenly. All the hawks seemed to breathe deeply and stretch in the warmth. A single pigeon rose with a clatter of wings from the rooftops, circled once and headed our way, just below us, steadily and straight. It could well be a carrier. I lifted the gos to let him see it. He tensed, and shot off.

Suddenly the pigeon saw the goshawk, and you could practically hear its thoughts. Dive? Turn away? An old bird and experienced, it watched Geordie come; at the last fraction of a second it tilted in the air. He missed by a foot and swung back, screaming in anger, but already the pigeon had dived among the chimneys to safety.

I whistled hard and he rose to the lure, to my relief not going after the bird. He wasn't fully well yet, or he'd not have returned so easily; or at all. I hoped it wasn't that pigeon. Forget it. Try to, anyway. Look for the next.

Twice more he leaped out at pigeons for me, missed, and rose back panting to my call. I was glad I'd spent so much time practising drawing the hawks in to my fist, for on the Rock there was no flat ground except the square yard where I stood. On the fourth strike he chased the pigeon away round a corner of the Castle walls out of my sight.

One lost. My job lost too. Don't think about it.

I unhooded the saker, a swift young bird. Usually he was one of the easiest to handle, once he'd had his bath, but today, unbathed, he was fidgeting and griping, even bating once right off the glove. Maybe he was upset by my own emotions. If it hadn't been for the Queen, I'd not have flown him at all. But when another pigeon came steadily out our way I had to launch him, hoping he'd settle once he was on the job.

He didn't. He rose unsteadily, flapped in an irritated, unhappy way, found his balance, and climbed more strongly. The pigeon approached fast. Did he see it? Whether or not, he ignored the pigeon, ignored me, and fluttered down into a tree just outside the West Port. Immediately a host of small birds gathered to mob him, swearing and jeering at him, and he sulkily shifted from tree to chimney to tree away down towards Lauriston and out of sight. Two lost.

With burning despair, last dregs of hope, deep regret, I unhooded the falcon. She was the finest bird of the three, and the one I might damage worst. She might not even pay any heed to the pigeons I flew her at, being well entered for far better quarry. But I had to try. For the Queen. As I gentled her I saw another pigeon swinging up from the Cowgait roofs, and held her up to see it. She stared, gave me a look of sheer unbelief — you want me to chase that rubbish? — and almost disdainfully launched herself. When it dodged her stoop, she screamed in surprise and annoyance. Insulted, she went after it, away to the south-east, climbing and swooping vainly as it twisted and dived before her to vanish in the woods of the Burgh Muir.

I had failed. Failed myself. Failed Master Kerr. Failed the Queen.

I had never been nearer weeping. I had always known this was a forlorn hope. That didn't make failure, ruin, any easier to bear. I sat down on the grass and seriously considered stepping off, to crash to my death on the rocks far below. But I'd likely just break a leg, which would be ridiculous.

As I sat, another pigeon came west from the town, straight

as an arrow. I watched it, with certainty growing in me that this, of all the birds I'd seen that morning, was the one that carried the message I was trying to stop. And now it would go straight through, safe and unharmed. I was so drained I couldn't even rouse myself to care.

The pigeon flew past me, almost level with my face. Dully I watched it go.

Suddenly a black streak flipped over the castle wall and smashed the pigeon down among the rocks. As quick as that.

I gaped, and gasped, and cheered! Geordie, my beautiful, blessed goshawk! He must have lost the bird he was after, and been raking about freely to find other quarry; and he had! At that second I'd have died for that bird.

I slid down the rocks to find them, in a deep cleft, by the sound of the hawk's bells, and found a tiny silver tube fixed to the pigeon's wing. With trembling fingers I opened it. Inside, on a scrap of paper, was written 'IV. JB' Letter number four? James Balfour? It had to be this one! It had to be!

I laughed and laughed, crazy with shock, the sudden whiplash from despair to triumph, the success that wonderful bird had snatched from my utter defeat. I giggled and snorted till the tears of joy ran down my nose, trying to control myself, while Geordie glanced up at me wonderingly from the pigeon's body, a feather sticking sideways from his beak, and his blank expression set me off again.

I'd done it! Whatever happened now, it was worth it, for we'd done it! We'd saved the Queen!

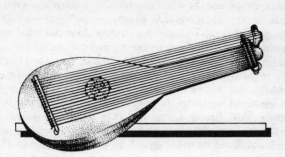

Betrothals

At last I sobered up. Well. Triumph or not, back to the mews. Collecting the frame, I went off towards the saker's latest perch by a chimney, marked by a cloud of chittering sparrows and a crowd of chattering lads. I told the biggest of the lads that that was the King's hawk — I nearly said the Queen's — and he'd get a reward if he watched it and told the man who'd come along that evening to catch it exactly where it had perched. He swore he'd not take his eyes off it. That was something. Now for the peregrine falcon.

Three minutes later, as I was not very hopefully heading out to the Burgh Muir, the laddie pattered after me with the saker grasped fluttering and cursing in both grimy hands. "I jist shinned up an' snicked him," he grinned. "Aye, I fell aff, but never fear, I taken care the hawk didnae get hurted." Hooding and soothing the agitated bird, I gave the lad a bawbee for his scrapes and bumps, and he raced yelling in delight to share his good fortune with his friends.

The peregrine falcon was even easier to catch. She was soaring above the Burgh Loch, and when I whistled and swung the lure she swooped sweetly, straight down to the scrap of meat on my glove.

My heart felt near bursting with joy. I'd stopped the

message, in spite of the odds against it — hundreds to one, they must have been — thousands to one! — millions! — and was bringing all the hawks back! I even started to wonder, rather hysterically, with the luck throwing itself at me like this, if I could return them without being found out. But when I pushed gently at the door of the mews, Master Kerr himself opened it for me.

He gestured me into the big room, examined the hawks minutely, and firmly sent the other lads, grimacing with sympathy to me behind his back, to set the birds out with the rest. He sat down by the fireplace, folded his big hands quietly on his knees, and without looking at me at all said, "Well, Sinclair?"

I couldn't lie to him. I liked and respected him too much. Besides, what reason could I give for borrowing three hawks? Stammering, I told him the truth, my joy withered in me. I waited to see what he'd do. I knew, of course.

He sat still, considering. It was just an hour before noon. Sometimes a bark or a whistle came through the sacking windows, but most of the time there was no noise at all. Suddenly my knees trembled under me, and I sat down on the other stool without waiting for permission.

After what seemed a long, long time he stirred. He took a deep breath, sat up straighter and shook his head regretfully. "You can't stay."

It was what I'd expected, after all. I nodded. "I know that, sir," I said.

"No, you don't," he denied. "When you came here, I hoped — I was certain you'd fail. I thought after the novelty wore off you'd lose patience, or slip somehow wi' the birds, an' I'd have fair reason to dismiss you in good faith."

"I knew, sir," I said again. Why was he bothering to explain all this?

"But you didn't, Sinclair. Like I said the very first time I set eyes on you; you've as good a way wi' the hawks as anybody I've ever seen. They'll sit quiet when you handle an' physic them. You seem to know what they're thinkin', an' they obey you as if you bewitched them. I've never had a lad like you. I was — I was that proud o' you! An' now — I can't keep you."

It seemed to be hurting him to say it. I felt guilty for letting him down. I tried to remember that it was all worth it, I'd saved the Queen. But I looked round at the long perches that I'd never see again and my heart ached like ice.

"Could you no beat me, sir, an' still let me stay? Please?" A vain hope, and he shook his head. I rose drearily. "I'll clear my things from my shelf."

He didn't look as if he understood; then held up a hand to stop me. "No, Sinclair. Sit still. I can't let you go just like that." He swallowed, and cleared his throat. "Sit down, lad. Lass. There's somethin' I must say to you."

Puzzled, scarce heeding him, I sank back. Anything, to put off the moment of leaving. The hood I'd been making yesterday lay on my shelf. The last one ever. I'd made a right cobble of the plume.

Master Kerr opened his mouth twice to speak before shooting to his feet, the most abrupt movement I'd ever seen him make. I started to pay more attention. He looked — he looked embarrassed. Shy, even. He spoke to the fireplace. "Lassie. I was wed when I was younger, but my wife died when our bairn was born, an' the babe — my wee son — died no an hour after. Well, the Lord's will be done. I've never wed again. Never wanted to."

My mouth opened by itself, and I found it hard to breathe. He couldn't mean. . . I swallowed as hard as he did himself before he forced himself to go on. "Wi' all the folk about the mews, cooks an' that, I've no needed a woman to look after me. An' my Maggie was a grand lass, an' I never met anyone I liked half as much. No till now."

He cast one glance over at me, apparently happier now he'd got started. "I know I'm older than you, lass, but I'm no fair done, eh? I'm this side o' fifty yet. I've been head falconer here this five year past. It's a good job. Respected. An' I've a bit siller put by, an' a good room here in the mews — I could get my own house if I wanted it — an' there's aye the hawks."

Suddenly he sounded pathetic, and I couldn't bear to hear him. I jumped up, but he caught my wrist. "I know you think much o' the birds, an' you've never thought o' me, but think now! If you wed me, you'll no lose the hawks. You'll be here wi' them all the time. Think on it, Leezie! You'll no do better."

I stood still in his grasp, though my stomach was churning inside me. But I had to know; "Why did you no ask before, sir?"

His grip was red hot. "It — I — I don't — Ach, damn it to hell!" He spun away from me and threw himself down onto the stool hard enough to break it. Then he drew a deep breath and swung back to me, trying to make me see. "How could I, when you were my own 'prentice? I'd have been the mock o' the town. I couldn't do't. I wanted to, but. . . Or how could I keep you on here after what you've done? Did you expect it?" I had to shake my head. "No. But now — now you've got to leave, it's more than I can do to stand by an' see you just walk out. Lose you. Forever. I had to speak. An' I know fine what they'll say, that you're too young, an' that, but I don't care. I — I love you, more than I care for anythin' anybody can say. Think, Leezie. Will you — can you wed me?"

I stood frozen. He'd never given me the slightest sign. What could I say? I couldn't — I couldn't. I felt sick.

After a while he sat wearily down on the stool again. "No. I'm too old for you, lass, I know that."

I couldn't leave him like this, in pain and humiliation. I couldn't bear it for him. I knelt by him. "Sir," I said. Slowly he looked round to me. "Sir, I've never thought o' this. Never had any idea. It's too sudden for me to have an answer for you, just like that. But I respect you, an' admire you." It was very hard to go on, to find the right words. "I like you for yoursel', an' we get on well together, an' there's nobody I'd rather wed." As his face brightened, I drew back. "I can't tell you aye or no now, sir. You must give me time to think about it. Please?"

He held a hand out to me, and rather doubtfully I put mine into it. "How long, Leezie? How long will you be, thinkin'?" he pleaded.

This was dreadful. "No more than a week, sir." That was surely long enough to speak to Kate, and ma, and make up my mind?

"An' you'll come an' tell me, whether it's aye or no?"

"Aye, sir. I — I owe you that."

My throat was closing on me. It was so hard; harder than he could ever know, just to speak of it. But he was rising to his feet again. "A week, then, Leezie. You'll give me fair trial, as I gave you?" I nodded, dragged my hand from his great fist that didn't want to let go, and fled.

All day I wandered the town, out by my old haunts past the Burgh Loch, up to the Castle, right round Holyrood Palace. There was the ledge I'd climbed along with Bothwell, and the wood where he'd kissed me. I'd felt sick. Master Kerr was a better man than Bothwell any day. Kind, and honest, and gentle. He was older than I was, but less than John Knox and his bride, and they did well enough. It was true, I'd never find a better match. Or anyone I respected more, or liked better. And there were aye the hawks. But — could I? And would I not disappoint him? I couldn't cook, or sew, or keep a house; but then, he knew that. Oh, God, please help me! I turned in to the High Kirk, and sat on one of the benches, praying for guidance. All I got was cold.

At last I dragged back home to the shop. With the downs and ups and downs of the day I was fair exhausted.

Ma was standing in Kate's door, having a good laugh as Alice and Kate bustled about inside. When I peered past her, I saw Kate's great chests open in the middle of the floor, and ma turned to me with a smile. "Here you are at last, Leezie! D'you see this? What d'you think — Kate's leavin' us!"

"Leavin'?" I could scarce take in the idea.

"Aye, lassie!" Kate's wide grin was even wider and whiter than usual. "I'm away next week, to — come on, guess where!"

I shook my head. I didn't know what to say. In her news my own dismals lifted for the moment. "Where, then, Kate? The Low Countries, like you said?"

She hugged me in her excitement. "No, lassie! The Spanish has started the Inquisition there, an' I'll no risk it! Never that! Nothin' that'll put me in more danger than I am here."

"But Knox can't harm you — wi' the letter an' all —" Drat

it, ma looked intrigued, she'd be asking me about it later.

"Knox can't live for ever, lassie. An' the letter's losin' power wi' every day that passes, but the Kirk's gainin' more. No, I'm off to London!" She kissed me, laughing at my astonishment, whirling away to sweep a cloak out of Alice's arms and toss it to me. "Here! I'll get new in London! An' these sleeves! I've a lad in the English Ambassador's train that fancies me. He's got me a passport, an' offered me a room in his house, an' his good word, till I'm settled."

"Are you gettin' wed, then?" I bundled the things up, and the gown and head-dress she tossed after them. Would red suit me?

They all three burst into laughter. "Wed? What for should I wed? No, lass, if I'd wanted to wed I could have done it long ago. I've had offers enough!"

"I'll warrant you have!" Ma, even ma, was smiling, her arms full of velvets and damasks, laughing at Kate dancing round the room.

Kate reached me a hand and drew me to dance a pavane with her, singing her answer to me. "Marry a man — just one single man — when I can have all the pleasure o' many? Do I want bairns — or a settled house — when I can get gold, an' music, an' dancin', an' fine gowns —" she broke off as the rhythm staggered, and flung her arms wide. "My brother's wed, the dull dog, an' my long-tongued sister, an' they both disapprove o' me. But I'll no be ordinary — I'm somethin' special! My grandam was a princess o' Ethiop! An' my grandsire was a king! Aye, there's for you, now! I'm a cousin o' Queen Mary's! No that she's likely to own to me! There's no a man in Embra to match me! What can a husband give me that I can't get wi'out tyin' mysel' down to one man? I can get the better — get the best — o' all o' them! An' that's why I'm for London."

Her arms swung wide. "Who is there here? Dry, dull Kirkmen, hypocrites all, like Moray, or Morton, or Mar, or any o' the other lyin' scoundrels, all in pious black, on their knees all day prayin' for strength to stab each other in the back at night! I'm fair sick of the whole jing-bang o' them! Forbye they're dead set against all the things I love, an' now the Queen's gone there's none to bring light an' joy to the town. I'll no be dull an' sad, just because the Kirk elders thinks it's how the Lord wishes all men to be — an' that means all women as well! No me! I'm for light an' colour, an' gaiety! I'll take my songs an' my dancin' down to them as can appreciate them, an' pay me well for them. An' if it means hell-fire for me after, at least I'll have good company!"

Ma, pretending to be shocked, ran giggling up the stair. Alice looked up from the chest. "Well, will you get on wi' sortin' what you want to take to hell wi' you, mistress! There's a pile o' fans over there, an' stockin's wi' the moth in them. If you spend all day gabbin', we'll no be ready by Martinmas!"

Kate kicked out to knock Alice over as she danced past, laughing. Alice rubbed her backside, pretending to scowl, but the excitement kept breaking through. Kate picked up an armful of feathers and lace to sort out, but tossed it high. "Ach, it can get to hell by itsel'! We'll leave it all to Leezie here!"

Oh, God! I suddenly realised I was losing her. On top of everything else! Kate's grin faded. "Here, lassie, what is it? I've never seen you weep before! Who stole your scone? It's not me leavin', neither — you've no been like yoursel' since you set foot in the door."

They swept a heap of bonnets off a stool, sat me down by the table, gave me a glass of sack and insisted that I tell them everything.

They approved my attempt to help the Queen, and cheered my triumph. "This is the note? J.B. — aye, I'll swear you're right, lass, that's Balfour, the black-hearted rogue! Well done, my dear, truly!" But as I went on to tell them about Master Kerr's proposal, they grew sober again. When I'd finished hiccuping into the wine, for they'd not watered it and it was strong enough to make my eyes blink, Kate sat back on her heels beside me. "Well, Leezie. I never — never ever — met such a lassie for tyin' hersel' in knots. Why d'you no just say aye to the man? An' thank God fastin', that you can do so well? For face it, Leezie, you'll no do better for yoursel'. You're bonny enough, but there's no cocky young laird goin' to see you an' fall smack dab in love wi' you. He's a good man, Matthew Kerr, kindly an' settled, wi' enough siller to keep a wife, an' you'd have your hawks. What more d'you want? If I was you, I'd grab him."

I shook my head desperately. "I know all that, but I can't — I can't!"

Alice murmured something to her mistress, and went off into the kitchen. Kate rose slowly, considering. She perched beside me, up on the table top, thoughtfully disentangling her citterne that lay there under the piled silks. "Is it that you're no in love wi' him?" It was a way out. I nodded. "Love? My God, Leezie Sinclair, just how many folk do you know that wed for love? An' if they do, how many make a good thing o' it?" Her voice was scathing. "Would you look at the Queen? She wed Darnley for love — I've never seen a lass as soft as she was for him. An' then she fell in love wi' Bothwell after. An' see where they got her! Or your ma? Why did she wed your dad? Love! My God!" The citterne played a sharp discord to point up her words. "Fallin' in love's like leapin' a dyke when you can't see the far side o't. You may find a fair field o' flowers, an' be happy ever after; but you're just as like to end up to your bum in a midden. 'Madly in love'! If you're mad, is that no the worst time o' all to make such an important decision? Do you like him? D'you laugh at the same things? Wed for laughter an' likin', that's best; or sense, or siller. They last longer! An' love may grow as well, in time, if you work at it."

She eyed me sternly. "But that's no all, is it?" At last, as she waited long for my reply, I had to shake my head. "No. What is it, my dear? What is it drives you turn a cold eye on any lad comes near you? I've seen you wi' my friends. You were aye frozen; you'd let none o' them lay a finger on you. We all knew it. It was why your ma let you come to me. I thought you'd relax a bit wi' time, when you saw nobody wanted to harm you, but you're aye the same. Why?"

There was another long pause. I wished Alice would return, to break the unbearable moment, but she stayed in the kitchen. I couldn't — I couldn't. . .

Kate's strong fingers pressed my chin up, so that I had to

meet her eye before I twisted away again. "It was your dad, eh? Am I no right?"

It took me all my strength to nod. I couldn't have spoken.

I don't know what I expected, or hoped, for her to say. I sat there, limp as a knotless thread, and waited for her to speak. To be shocked. To condemn dad — or me. The guilt, the misery, drowned me.

She lifted my chin again and said dryly, "Well? What of it?"

I thought she'd not understood. Suddenly the jagged words tore their way out. "He — he — in the byre, five year back — he said if I told he'd kill me — an' ma — an' he said whenever he wanted — an' he beat her — near killed her — an' he made me — over an' over — for fear he'd murder her — an' I couldn't tell her — till I got my knife — an' then — he had to sleep sometime, I said — an' — if a man touches me — or I think — I feel that sick — I — I — Oh, dear God!"

Alice was there with a bowl, just when and where I needed it. When I'd finished, she gave me a cold wet cloth to clean my face, and after a long, long while I whimpered to silence. I felt such a weight off me!

Kate sat still, like a judge, all this time. She stared out of her window, waiting for me to be ready to speak to her again. When Alice finally took the bowl and cloth away and shut the door behind herself, her mistress turned a big dark eye severely on me. "So he's beat you, then?" she said.

"Beat me? Aye, often."

"No like that!" she snapped, exasperated. She over-dramatised. "He's ruined your life! You'll never can live like a normal woman! All for the terrible thing he did in the byre!" Her tone changed, to cut me. "He's beat you!"

"What d'you mean?" I was taken aback. I'd expected shock, horror, disgust; hoped hopelessly for sympathy. This sharpness — it was me was shocked.

"D'you think you're the only one it ever happened to? It's common, lassie! It happens to a many lasses, an' they don't all make such a tirrivee about it. Aye, it's no what it should be; neither's starvin', an' there's folk does that every day. Nor it's no the right way to behave — away an' complain to Master

221

Knox. It's no fair. Life's no fair — see God about it. But things happen every day that's worse. You could have died o' smallpox, or been blinded, or been born crippled. But you've fought back, an' survived, an' you've your strength an' health, an' you're away from him now. You've won. It was what — a hundred? five hundred? — bad times; well, think on it like bad dinners. You've had the belly-aches, but they're by now, an' you'd no fear eatin' another meal for that, would ye? Well, then, you've won! But if you let it spoil all the rest o' your life, then he's won, beaten you, d'you no see? Face it, an' think! D'you want that?"

Slowly I shook my head. Yes, I saw, and no, I didn't want dad to have beaten me. "But — no — no — I can't —"

"You must! Ach, it's no easy, lassie, I know it's no as easy as eatin' another dinner. But every time you turn from a man for no reason but what your dad did, he's beat you again. Where's your smeddum, lass? Where's your courage?"

I tried to brace my shoulders. My heart. It wasn't so hard — I'd been a fighter all my life, I knew how to fight, I'd not let him beat me — I could fight this. . . Could I? Fight dad? The thought of him. . . The stink of him. . . The guilt. . . No, please no. . . Oh, God, please. . . Aye. . . Aye! Aye, I could! I must!

I gave Kate a smile — a rather watery one. She drew a deep breath and smiled back. "That's my gallant lassie! Face him! Fight him! Never give up!"

"Then you think I should, Kate? Wed Master Kerr?"

Now the wide mouth showed disgust. She snorted at me. "Huh! It's no advice you want — it's a book o' instructions. Well, you'll no get it from me. You've a mind o' your own — away an' make it up for yoursel'. Just don't let your dad make it up for you!"

I sighed. I was scared, and I still didn't know what to do. "Can I no come to London wi' you, Kate?" At her irritated glare, my own eyes sank again.

"Ach, stop that!" she snapped at me. "You look like a whipped spaniel! No, you can't come, for you'd just be a misery. I'll no take you, an' that's flat." Her voice softened. "Look, Leezie. There's three things a woman can do. She can be like me, an' entertain all men — for a price. You'd no enjoy that, an' you'd fail. She can wed, like most women, an' be a good wife to a single man; you could do that, wi' your man at the mews. Or she can find a way o' earnin' a livin' for hersel'. Could you do that? Wi' your hawks, maybe? Think about it, eh? Just you make up your own mind which you'll do! Now clear out o' here an' let me get on wi' my packin'. Alice! Where's that lazy jaud got to now? Alice!"

It didn't help me to decide, but it was strangely cheering and bracing.

Next day Peter slipped in, in haste, to bring us the news of the fateful battle at Langside. "The Queen's lost again! Her general — Argyll, Lady Jean's man — you mind on the ribbon? He fainted as Moray's men advanced." He spat in disgust. "An' her men ran. Mary rode out to try to rally them, but they struck her aside to get by."

"Oh, no!" But somehow I'd expected it. "What can she do? Where'll she go?"

"God knows. Head north, to Huntly, if she's any sense. She still has more men than Moray, if she can but find a general for them. She's the best man o' the lot o' them!" He hurried back to the Palace.

At least, I thought, listening to the hymns of triumph ringing in the streets outside, she wouldn't be deceived by any false letters from Elizabeth. And I prayed for her, my debonair, gallant Queen, to keep on fighting.

My own fight was going well. Fairly well. I'd tried to face my fears and horrors. It was hard, for I'd aye shut my mind off from it before. But now I forced myself to look straight, and could see how twisted I had become inside me. I'd started to fight the darkness and sick weight of guilt. It had even come to me that some day I might find the thought of dad as a belly-ache funny. Not yet; but some day. I could consider Master Kerr almost calmly, with only the slightest twitch of my stomach.

What else could I do? Help Babs Martin? I'd not want that all my life. No hawks. Get a place as falconer in another mews? Gordon of Huntly would maybe help. But he was away

223

fighting with the Queen, and had no time for hawking. Start on my own somehow? I had silver. But did I know enough, after only a year? No, I couldn't do that. Then how could I continue to fly hawks?

Master Kerr, came the answer every time; Matthew Kerr.

But I don't love him!

So? I liked him; we laughed at the same things. We could work together. I respected and admired him. Was that not enough? Better, even?

That evening, Babs called ma and me down. "My, listen to the party!" ma smiled as we passed Kate's door. "That's two days it's no stopped now! Ach, well, nobody'll notice, with the celebrations all over the town." Victory bonfires blazed in every open space.

"Aye," I said. We both sighed a bit. "She's sayin' farewell to all her friends. I'll need to get another chest for all the clothes she's given me!"

In the shop, Babs was laughing till her wrinkled face looked more like a March apple than ever, and her grey eyes fair sparkled. "Come away down, wife! Shout on Kate, Leezie! I've news for ye! What d'ye think? It's Ina an' Sandy! They're betrothed! They'll sign the papers the morn an' wed in three weeks!"

Ina, in a new dark-brown gown, a fresh white bonnet over her grey hair, and only two shawls, grunted and nodded happily, and Sandy, startlingly well-dressed in dark blue broadcloth, bowed, both grinning, as ma took a hand of each and laughing with them wished them many years of happiness together. My face froze in its smile. I managed to say what was right, though I can't remember what it was, and I turned to the stair to hide my expression.

When I broke in on Kate and her friends to tell her, she was as delighted as ma. She brought her friends down, and wine, to drink health to the happy couple. Her citterne appeared, the neighbours stuck their noses in at the music, and stayed, Katy's Tam rolled in a keg of ale, more musicians arrived, more people stopped by. Someone gave Ina a pewter spoon as a wedding present, and that started a shower of gifts, for they were both well-liked. Ina's face flushed deep, patchy red as she grinned and bobbed, struggling to thank everyone. The counters were dismantled and a dance started up.

After a while Sandy swirled Ina onto the floor. He'd made her a new chair with big wheels, so that she could move herself about a fair bit now with her strong arms. He twirled the chair about among the dancers while she laughed, and we all laughed in kindness with her. It was really too big, though, and he soon set her back beside the oven, out of the way of the main swing of the night. Then he asked her if he could join the dance, and she agreed happily. She sat proudly waving her big hands almost in time to the music while he danced with Babs, Kate, ma and then me, taking each of us up to the chair for a word with Ina, which was kind, before swinging us into the crowd. I'd been up for every dance, and by the time Sandy had bounced me round the flagstones once I was crimson as my new gown, one of Kate's. I pulled him over to the door for a breath of air.

He was glad of the break too, and stood by me easing his new high-ruffed collar and gasping in the cool air of the wynd. It was just starting to grow dark, and the shadows were deep already across the narrow passage. A couple were kissing beside the door, and he leaned out and told them to move either in or away, before they shocked the ministers. He was good-humoured about it, and we all laughed before they returned to the dance.

"Quite the master o' the house already, Sandy," I commented. I didn't mean there to be any spite in my voice, but he glanced sideways at me.

"What's wrong, Leezie? Are ye no pleased for me? Or for Ina? For we're grateful to ye. It wouldnae have happened but for you."

I bit my lip. How could I say what I felt, without hurting him too much? "When — how did you come to think on it, Sandy?"

He nodded at the memory, smiling slightly. "That day Babs was in tears because Ina would be left alone, if Babs died first. I'd no chance then, I was just a scullion in the shop. But then, wi' Huntly's siller, thanks to you, and the extra Babs paid me — it all mounted up. An' at last I spoke to her an' Babs, an' found they were just waitin' for me to make up my mind. Aye, Leezie, it's a good match for us both. I'll look after Ina, an' I'll inherit her mother's shop. An' the half o' the land as well, for she's part-owner o' the tenement."

"Aye, an' I'm a burgess o' the town," Babs's voice squeaked behind me. "Budge over a bit, lass, an' let me get a breath. I'm fair meltin'. Aye, when I'm away he'll inherit that as well. Burgess o' Embra! No bad for a penniless laddie, eh? Who would ever have guessed it? Was it no a good thing I let ye know how we were placed, eh?" She grinned, coughed, poked me in the ribs with her elbow and chortled happily. "Aye, no flies on old Babs, eh? An' my sister Bessie'll be fair ragin'. It's grand!" Scarlet and grinning, her thin white hair trickling from her tousled cap, she turned back to the dance.

"But Ina — she's — well, like she is. An' she's old, Sandy," I muttered. "Can you stand that?" He was but a year or so older than me.

"Ach, that's no great matter," he assured me kindly. "It's just a marriage on paper. But she'll never suffer from me, in body or mind. I'll look after her well, an' keep her happy. An' did ye know it's her keeps the accounts? In her head, just? Aye, she knows every penny in an' out the shop. She's no daft, Ina! It's a good bargain, that suits us both. We'll deal fine together."

At last I could smile. "God's blessin' on you both, then, Master — here, what is your second name, then?"

He opened his mouth, and then stopped with it still open. "Well." He sounded absolutely dumbfounded. "D'ye know, I couldnae say! It's that long I'm just Sandy! No, I cannae think on't! Ach, well, I'll just take Ina's name. Master Martin — Burgess Sandy — no, Burgess Alexander Martin, I'll be! That'll please the old dame, my good-mother, eh?"

He went back in, smiling, as Ina called him. I looked after him. He'd been kind to her, taking her out to the kirk, helping her talk, spending time with her, bringing life to the poor hulk that I'd found when I came, and had pitied as a daftie. Even before he'd had any idea of wedding her. Aye, it was a good match, for both of them; if you excepted love.

But Ina fair doted on him, and he cared for her; maybe they had love, in their own way? Not like ma and Peter Matheson, perhaps — I realised suddenly that I'd quite accepted that now — but strong, and good enough for them. It seemed there was more than one kind of love.

Was there any love between myself and Master Kerr? Of any kind? Yes, there was; but was it enough?

As darkness grew the party broke up. We tidied the shop. Sandy tied on his apron over his good doublet to fire up the oven for a few minutes and ready the pots for the night, and Ina rolled her chair over to sit by the warm glow, smiling and sighing happily, contentedly waving her hands and head in time to the music still lilting in her mind. Kate saw her friends off, and ma and I were just following her up the stair when there was a banging at the street door.

"Ach, we're shut!" called Babs, but it didn't stop. We paused to see who was so impatient. She wearily shrugged and reached to lift the bar for the visitor. He shoved the door wide, pushing her back against the wall.

It was dad, with that evil wee half-smile on his face, and his eye on ma.

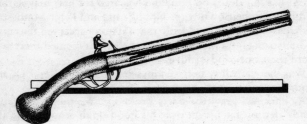

Dad

Dad smiled up the stair, eyes and teeth glinting in the light of the lamps and the oven. "Janet," he said quietly.

She stared down at him. "Adam," she acknowledged him, her voice faint.

"I've come for ye, Janet. Ye're my wife. An' it's time ye minded on it."

My jaw was clenched with fear, but I suddenly realised it was for ma, not for myself. That gave me a little courage. And Kate, close enough behind me for me to feel her warmth, touched my shoulder. Don't let him beat you! Fight!

"The Queen will no be that happy, sir," I said. My voice was almost firm.

He grinned up at me. "The Queen? Queen Mary? If ye're lookin' to her for aid, Leezie, dinnae hold yer breath. She's away for ever."

I smiled. My jaw felt as if it was cracking, but I smiled. And the thought of beating him again, not just with pig guts while he was unconscious but here, awake, alert, in public, was so sweet! My heart rose glorious in me. "Why do you say that, sir? Are you so sure she'll no be back?"

Suspicious now, he glowered up under his heavy eyebrows. Ma and Kate were statues by me. Babs and Sandy were hovering protectively beside Ina, but he cast no glance towards them. "Aye, I'm sure! Certain sure."

"Would you be relyin' on a letter, sir? A letter from the south, maybe?" As his face changed, I drew from my pocket the tiny note from the pigeon's wing. "That this was the sign for? I fear ye'll be disappointed."

He stepped forward and reached up for the scrap of paper. My fingers scalded at his touch. Let him see his mistake clearly, and know I'd beaten him!

"How did ye come by this, Leezie? Ah — ye're in the mews, are ye no? Ye didnae kill the bird this came from?" I nodded, elegant in my triumph. Inside, I was jumping up and down on him, singing and cheering, gloating, childishly making faces; but outside I was calm and restrained. The flame of the wee lamp in my hand glowed quite steady and still. I was proud of myself.

He raised his eyes and eyebrows to me, less shocked than I'd expected. "Aye? Well done, then, lass." I smiled my thanks. "An' where are the others?"

My breath stopped and lamp oil splattered on the stair. Others. Others. More than one. Of course, of course they'd not trust it to just one bird. Oh, God, he'd done it, he'd done it, the Queen was tricked, and ma had no shelter from him, and he'd won, and all my delighted triumph and confidence shattered round my heart in piercing splinters.

He was coming up the stone steps towards us. "Aye, lassie." His eyes were burning. He reached out to lift ma's hand from its grip on my arm. "Others. She's away to England now, an' our friends there'll see to it she stays there. Out o' everybody's road. Forever." I'd thought I was past feeling, but I wasn't. "Now. I pray ye come up wi' me to — our room." The stress he laid on 'our' rang like a mourning bell. Oh, ma! "For we must discuss — our future. Yours an' — ours." Every time, it was a knife slashing at my mind.

Knife. Knife. I wasn't wearing it, in my new red dress with the tight cuffs. It was up in the bedroom, under the pile of clothes. But if I could just get in there, I could set my hand right on it. And then. . .

He led ma up the stair past me like a cow to the slaughter. I turned to follow, passing Kate wide-eyed at her door. She hissed behind me, "Sandy! Get out o' here an' find Peter Matheson. Move, you gowk!" The scrape of the door and the receding patter of flying feet were a tiny comfort.

I sat on the wee stool where I was told and listened to dad laying out his — our plans. He was going to move in. Sir James was happy to let dad live out, so near his work. "An' like he says, it's no a good an' proper thing for a wife an' her man to be separate." Dad sounded quite pious.

"Proper?" I was getting my second wind of courage, thinking of my knife just a few feet away, and Peter coming as soon as Sandy found him. Keep fighting. "What would Blasphemous Balfour know about what's proper?"

Dad had found ma's small stock of wine. "Mind yer tongue, Leezie." He rose from ma's chair, and almost casually lounged across to me and slapped me hard, watching me closely. When I didn't attack him, he reached out and gripped my arm, checking that it was true, I'd not my knife hidden. He twisted and lifted me cruelly. "Where's yer wee tickler, then, my lass?" he sneered. Then his gaze sharpened. "Aye, where is it?" He twisted my arm even harder, but dropped me as he saw I'd not answer. "Man, ye've aye been a stubborn bitch. But maybe —" He reached out to ma, and she screamed as her arm near snapped again. "Aye, that'll draw ye! Fetch it here!"

What could I do? I found the knife and handed it to him, in despairing rage. He grinned, and tossed it out the hole in the shutter. "Just as well, lass. This is Embra. Ye'll no get away wi' murder here. Now or later. If I'm found wi' a knife-hole in me, you'll hang. Mind on it!"

"Ma told me no to carry it, near a year back," I muttered, wiping the blood off my lip. "That's the only reason Willie Gray's still alive!"

"Oh, aye!" he nodded. "Willie's a handy laddie — a hard, hard worker for the right man, Leezie. But no great friend o' yours. It's a bond between us."

"I'll no break my heart over that! I fair boke at the very sight o' him," I said with emphasis. "Or the stink!"

He laughed, pulling the cork from a second bottle with his strong fingers. "Aye, but ye'd better learn to like him," he grinned. "He'd make ye a fine husband, Leezie, an' if I ordered it ye'd have to wed him. Would ye no?"

My stomach nearly heaved as usual; but no! Now I had a shield. "Aye, sir, if I wasn't promised already." His jaw dropped. "I'm to wed Master Kerr, the Master o' the King's Mews in White Horse Lane." It was a lie; or was it?

Ma, entranced with fear beside him, didn't react at all, and he hit out at her to wake her. "Is this true? Janet, ye jaud, is this true?" His blow sent her sprawling, and he kicked her. I sat still; I knew from experience if I went to her aid he'd just kick us both, harder. She lay still, too, under his feet, and after a minute he gave up and sat back down. Now I could go to lift her back to her stool, shuddering and blank-eyed, paralysed with the old terror.

As I stepped back from her, he caught my wrist again and tugged me towards him. I fell on my knee before the chair, and one long hand clipped my throat and began to tighten. "Is it true?"

I took a deep breath — it might be my last — and said, as steadily as I could, "As God's my witness, I swear Master Kerr has asked me to wed him."

Suddenly, overwhelmingly, I knew what would be — must be — my answer.

My free arm tensed, ready to claw dad's eyes if he tightened his grip. What else could I say. . .? "An' he has the ear o' Moray, an' Morton!" Well, he could speak to them, even if they'd not heed him much. . .

It was enough, just, to put him off throttling me, and he pushed me away angrily. He was well into the second bottle now. "A pity that. Aye. A right rogue, Willie. It was him sicked Moray's men on Geordie Tod, when they'd lost him in spite o' me tellin' them where he was. An' he looked after the birds fine. But he wasnae in on the big thing. No, he missed that."

Geordie? They'd betrayed wee Geordie Tod? As well as the Queen? Dear God, I'd kill him! Peter must come soon. Keep dad talking, now he'd started; while he was speaking he wasn't hitting ma. Or me. Or worse. "What was that, then?"

He looked sly, and tapped the side of his nose knowingly. The wine was working enough in him to make him talkative, thank the Lord. "Can ye no guess? An' yer callant down the stair here near dead from it? The mushrooms! We gave the pie to the King's cook, an' glad he was to get it, the lazy rascal, for the smell fair drowned your teeth — aye, he's a grand baker, your laddie! It would have worked, too, but the damned fool threw it at his man for spillin' the wine. They just scraped it up an' threw it out. A right waste, eh? Aye. Darnley. King Henry. If he'd eaten that pasty, he'd have died nice an' quiet; just a sudden relapse. An' if there was any question, you an' the old bitch down the stair would have taken the blame. . . An' me an' French Paris wouldnae have had to humph all that damned gunpowder up an' down the town."

He stretched back in his chair. Ma was watching him like a bird before a snake, and he smiled gloatingly at her. "A damned queer thing, though. Ye know he didnae die wi' the explosion? But nobody laid a hand on him. No a single finger. We was watchin' in the orchard, Sir James an' me, when we heard the lads as had lit the fuse come out, an' run away up the street to report to Bothwell. An' right after, does the King no come clamberin' out his window in his nightshirt an' drop into the orchard no twenty feet from us, an' his wee valet cryin' after him. Out o' his mind, he was, roarin' about thieves an' robbers, an' demons burnin' him, an' wavin' a dagger. Maybe he'd heard them. Or it was the pasty after all, givin' him nightmares. Or just too much brandy.

"Well, I was ready to strike him when my master pulls me back in the shadows. 'No the now, man,' he says, an' I sees the wee valet drop a chair out the window an' climb down by it wi' a coat over his shoulder, an' the wind blowin' his own nightshirt up about his bare bum. The pair o' them runs up an' down the garden, Darnley moanin' about fire an' burnin', an' forgive me my sins, an' stabbin' wi' his dagger at the wee man that's cryin' about cold an' freezin', an' his teeth rattlin' — an' I'll tell ye it wasnae warm — an' tryin' to make him put on his coat an' climb inside again before they both catched their death. It was better than a play. We was laughin' fit to split.

"Sudden the whole house blows up in front o' us. Barram! An' Darnley looks up at the bits flyin' through the air, an' he just sits smack down in the snow. There's a cloak floats down, gentle as a snowflake, an' lands just by his feet, an' he stares at it. 'My God!' he says, clear as anythin'. 'My God!' An' he just puts a hand to his heart an' lies back in the snow an' dies. Nothin' else. He just dies. An' then the wee man, he runs about half demented, tryin' to gather his wits an' squeakin' for help. But he stops to try to lift the King. An' he cannae do't, see? He gets him up just so far, an' then he slips in the snow, an' Darnley comes crack down on him. He struggles up an' crawls a wee bit, an' then falls on his side an' lies still, like the King. They dinnae budge an inch, an' the snow drift-driftin' down on the top o' them.

"Well, we watch them lyin' there for a minute, an' my master says, 'Go over, Adam, an' see how His Grace is.' Darnley's as dead as ever I've seen, an' the wee man's hit his head on a tree root an' is unconscious. I've my knife out to help him on his way, when my master says, 'Just leave him be, Adam. In this cold he'll likely no last long, an' he's no seen us anyway. An' we can swear to it on our Bible oath we never lifted hand to them, wi' a clear conscience.' A clear conscience, eh! We laughed till we could scarce walk. We just left them, for there was folk stirrin', an' climbed the wall where it was broke, an' up the street just behind Bothwell. It was my master's cloak Mary Crockett caught; God, what a voice that wife's got! Next we heard was that they was both dead, an' no sign o' how. Well, that's how." He chuckled cosily.

I stared, near as stiff with horror as ma. "But — are you no feared I'll tell?" It was maybe daft to ask, but I couldn't help it.

He chuckled again. "Tell? Tell who? Moray? Morton? Huntly? Mary? Bothwell, the damned fool? Knox? Come an' I'll tell you somethin', lassie; there's no one o' them didnae know. No, no even Lennox, the King's own faither. That's a fact." I wondered how much of it was truth indeed. He grinned unpleasantly at me. "There's no a soul ye can tell, nobody as matters, that'll listen. My master's one o' the great men o' the

State now, an' there's letters he has, signed letters, that'll keep him safe from every man in the Government. The letters in that daft casket! They're nothin'! Nothin'! Who's to accuse him, that he cannae prove was in it as deep as himsel'? Talk away, lass. Blether away all ye like. Nobody'll heed ye. But before ye do, think on. There's many a wee accident can befall a young lassie that's a nuisance. Or her mother. Just you mind on that."

He laughed, standing up. He was a big, powerful man, his hair touching the rafters, his shoulders broad, his beard full and curly. At first sight anyone would have judged him a fine, hearty man; only his deadly eyes showed the truth. "Come away through, then, Janet," he said, raising her with one hand at her shoulder. She lifted like a rag doll. "I'm for bed. Are ye comin', Leezie?"

He laughed at me again. What could I do? Nothing. He'd betrayed the Queen, and the King, and if I fought he'd hurt ma. Nothing, nothing, nothing!

Then someone knocked at the door.

"Who is it?" dad asked, dropping ma again to fold like wet silk at his feet, his hand on the long knife at his belt.

"Leezie, Ina's fallen!" Babs's voice was anxious. "An' Sandy's no here. Can ye come give us a hand to lift her?"

My heart leaped. Stop! Think! I looked at dad for permission before I moved. He nodded. It sounded a reasonable request; but I knew better. It wasn't that hard to lift Ina; they didn't need me. It had to be help.

Sure enough, as I unbarred the door and it opened, Peter Matheson stepped quietly in, his sword ready drawn.

I'd thought dad would be taken aback, but he just grinned at Peter over ma's head. "Aye. Ye're late, man!" he murmured quietly. He'd been expecting Peter, waiting for him! Suddenly he bellowed, "Get out! Ye've no business here, comin' between a man an' his wife! I'll have the law on ye!" But he was still grinning. He didn't expect Peter to go. He was just putting himself in the right, for when he'd killed Peter and the bailies were investigating.

Peter was in uniform, his bag on his shoulder, clearly just off duty, panting from running. Dad's blade, still in its sheath, was a foot shorter than Peter's. "Run him through, Peter! Now!" I begged him. He hesitated. The advantage was all his, but he couldn't strike a man with no weapon in his hands. As Bothwell had once done to me, dad laughed in his frustrated face.

Suddenly dad scooped up a stool and threw it at Peter to knock aside the sword blade, diving right after it, drawing his knife. They hit the door together. It slammed over and the bar fell, shutting out the excited, worried faces on the landing. Peter swung dad off him and they circled. For a minute they fenced, sword against knife. Dad feinted; Peter deflected the following thrust and stepped in to strike.

He trod on ma's ankle. His foot turned under him. Dad pounced and they were down, wrestling. And now the advantage was with the shorter weapon.

They rolled over and struggled to their knees, then fell again, ma under them. She was still paralysed with fright, and couldn't escape; she just curled up helplessly in a wee ball. As they struggled and twisted on top of her, the knife and the sword grating and swinging just above her, she wailed faintly.

I thought to stun dad with the poker, but they were thrashing about too much, heads right in the corner. I couldn't get near enough to be sure which one I'd hit, and if I hurt Peter — or even distracted him. . . Could I catch the blades with a blanket? Again, I might just get Peter's. . . As I danced round, poker in my hand, trying to get in close enough for a sure blow, I got a nasty kick from a hard boot that drove me back from them, and my foot caught in the strap of Peter's big satchel. It clunked as it dragged along the floorboards, and I grabbed it up to see if there was a dagger in it.

There was better. There was his pistol, Betsy. The big, heavy, double-barrelled pistol, that he always carried loaded.

Could I remember how to use it? It was over a year since he'd shown me. Pull back the flints. Here were the lids that held the powder in the pans; lift them. I was panting with tension. A blade, Peter's blade, clattered out of the roil of their fight, and I nearly reached for it; but they rolled over on it, snarling and grunting with the strain, and I stayed with the pistol. Where was the safety catch? Here? Oh, pray God I had it right, and the powder was dry!

I clutched the pistol butt as the fight moved away from the fireplace, spinning the chair across the room. The two men were locked together, straining and twisting, using every trick, every foul blow and grip learned in years of rough fighting, to disable or kill each other. They rolled clear of ma, and I thought now my time had come; I could fire without risk of hitting her. I firmed my grip, but relaxed after a moment; for Peter was winning.

They were on their knees. Peter had dad's knife hand twisted away out to one side. Dad was trying to get free, but Peter, gasping and straining, was gradually turning the wrist, as he'd once twisted mine. Slowly, slowly, the strong fingers were forced to open, and the knife clattered to the floor. Still Peter held that wrestler's grip, and dad started to grunt with pain as his wrist creaked. I was near cheering with joy at Peter's victory.

Suddenly ma began to struggle up behind them. Instead of just lying as she had been, curled up and still, she hysterically tried to fight her way clear of a battle that had already left her. One swinging arm hit a stool that had been knocked into the corner, and she grasped it and started to flail it about. I shouted at her to be still, but she was beyond sight, beyond hearing. Hair flying, mouth gaping, eyes blank, gripped by fear and desperation, she screamed and struck mindlessly. The stool swept round at the full length and force of her arm, and glanced off the back of Peter's head.

The hard pad half stunned him. He lost his grip on dad's wrist, and fell sideways, shaking his head, trying to regain his wits, to carry on fighting... Too late. Dad had a finger dislocated, sticking up out of his hand like a pen, but he seized his chance. Before Peter could recover, dad had grabbed up his knife again. Peter instinctively gripped dad's knife wrist with both hands as he thrust. Dad kicked and heaved. Suddenly he was at Peter's back, with a choking grip on his neck with one arm, while the other strove to bring his knife round and down. As I watched, Peter began to lose the little strength he had recovered, and his clasp on dad's knife wrist was failing. Dad grinned beside Peter's ear, twisted his hand free, and flung his arm back to drive the knife home.

I fired.

The pistol kicked wildly in my hands. Ma screamed. Dad shouted and flung himself back as the ball passed his ear, and Peter knelt gasping on the mat.

Coming to herself too late, ma dropped down beside Peter, taking him in her arms. "My love! Oh, my true love! I've killed you!" she sobbed.

Dad, black murder in his face, the long knife in his hand, looked down at them, his wife and the man she loved, kneeling at his feet. His hand twitched. Then he looked at me, and froze. I stared back over the pistol. The second barrel waited to be fired. I could kill dad, here and now, and he knew it.

I waited for the red mist to fill my mind as so often before, to shut out everything but the flat certainty of what I had to do, right or wrong. It didn't come. The berserk fury that used to give me such strength was gone. I had to pull the trigger to kill dad in full awareness of what I was doing.

I couldn't. In spite of all, I couldn't. If he didn't move to harm Peter or ma, now that he was helpless and at my mercy, I couldn't.

Civilised Edinburgh.

"Get out." I could only whisper it. "Get out, an' never come back."

The fury and fear in his face died, and a sneer grew on his lips. "Back? Aye, I'll be back, my fine lady! Wi' friends! An' we'll see then!" he hissed. My finger started to tighten on the trigger in a fury of my own, in disgusted rage at myself, in hatred and despair and shame, and he stopped and drew back from what he'd been going to say, in case it drove me over the narrow edge into murder. He slammed his knife into its sheath, turned, tugged open the door and limped out. The stair-head was empty.

Peter lifted his arms round ma, and they knelt together. "Oh, my love!" she whispered again. He drew her to him and they kissed, gently and lovingly. I wasn't embarrassed. But I didn't envy them their love.

Down the stairs there was a shout; a thud; silence again. Dad was away.

I put down the pistol, unlocking my fingers from the butt with some difficulty. Peter stood up, with ma's help and mine, and I lifted the big chair for him. "I'm sorry, Peter," I said.

"Sorry mysel', no to get here earlier." He was wheezing, from exertion and the grip on his throat. "What should you be sorry for?"

"That I didn't kill him. Then you an' ma could have wed, an' all our problems would be by, an' we could all be happy. But now —"

"No," he whispered. "Murder. Same's the first time. I'm —" He stopped. He couldn't quite bring himself to say he was glad.

"Leezie! Janet! Come down! Peter! Come down, all o' you, right away!" Kate's voice echoed emptily up the stair-well to us. What could she want?

We trailed slowly down, the Frasers agape behind us. Kate stood still by her door, looking down the steps. Babs was motionless in the centre of the shop, Sandy over by the oven door. Ina sat in her chair, not by the oven where she had been, but near the foot of the stone stair. And at her feet, beside the wheels of the chair, lay a heap of brown leather and wool, splashed with blood.

Dad.

We stopped, still as the others.

Ma was the first to move, to go gently down and kneel by him. "Aye, he's dead. May God have mercy on his soul," she whispered.

"An' on us all," someone murmured.

After a long moment, Kate lifted her head to look up and round, gathering our eyes. "He fell," she said clearly and slowly. "He came to visit Mistress Sinclair an' Leezie, an' met wi' Master Matheson here." She went on, picking her words carefully. "They were lookin' at Master Matheson's pistol together when it went off." True. Not the whole truth, but true. "An' Master Hepburn was just comin' down the stair on his way home when he fell. His head's split. That's what we

238

say; just that. No need for more. It's none o' other folks's business, an' would just confuse them. That's what we tell them." She looked down at Babs and Sandy and Ina, who looked gravely up at her. Not a head moved; but I'd have sworn as their eyes met they nodded to each other.

"Aye, mistress," said young Master Fraser. "That's all. We heard nothin'."

"The shot, aye, but nothin' else," his wife agreed firmly, and he drew her away up the stair.

"How did he fall?" Peter asked.

They all looked up at him. Kate spoke first. "He slipped. On the oil there, see? An' wi' no rail. . ."

"Aye." Sandy turned quietly to feed the fire again. His apron was blotched with red. Maybe he'd knelt by dad. The bundle of sticks had a couple of fairly thick bits of wood stuffed into its centre. The handle of the peel, broken. It had been beside the oven. Like Ina. He glanced up. "He fell."

Babs assented briskly. "Ye can see where his head hit the step there — there's blood on it. He fell."

And Ina, as all our eyes turned to her, and there was a knocking at the outside door, where curious neighbours and the bailies would soon crowd in to gasp and wonder and question, Ina slowly, deliberately nodded her ponderous head. "Aye. He feh. Theh. On 'tep." And the strong hands on her great, powerful arms clumsily moved the folds of her new skirt to hide a dark stain.

Three days later we all gathered in the wynd to see Kate off. She was watching her carved bed, all dismantled, and her chests and bundles being roped on the backs of a dozen mules for the long journey south, and Alice was hopping about like a hen on hot tar and screeching at the men to take care.

"She'll have her neck wrung before they reach Dalkeith if she keeps that up," Peter muttered to me. It was good to be able to laugh with him again, at last. Beside him, ma was in black, formal mourning for her husband; very pretty she looked too, and they'd not wait long before being wed.

Two young lords in front of us were talking above the

chatter and gleeful comments. "Aye, she's in Carlisle. They say the Governor's in a rare tirrivee at havin' a Queen arrive on his doorstep wi' no warnin', an' no even a change o' chemise." Mary? I pricked up my ears. The young man seemed to have all the news. "Nobody knows what persuaded her to go to England. All her men advised her to stay, go south to the Borders, they're solid for her, or up north — Huntly's raisin' more men for her there. But she would have her way, same as aye. Maybe she's right, an' Elizabeth'll aid her, an' we'll see her again wi' an English army at her tail, but I'd say it's no likely." He noticed me eavesdropping and turned away with a snort of irritation.

"Never you fret, lassie!" Peter, also listening quietly, soothed me as I bit my lip in grief for my failure. "You did your best. There's no a soul in Scotland could have done more for the Queen. If your quest didn't succeed — well, the Stewarts are a misfortunate family. If it's the will o' the Lord, lassie, she'll be back, an' you can maybe help work for it, eh? If it isn't, she'll no, an' you must just abide it." I frowned, shrugged and sighed. There was really nothing else to do.

Suddenly there was a swirl in the crowd, as Alice, finally satisfied that the boxes were safe, was heaved to her seat behind a groom. The guards and horse-boys straggled away in an irregular procession down to the Netherbow with the led mules and ponies. Babs popped up out of the throng, and Sandy pushing Ina in her chair, all excited and flushed by the stir, and Kate started her last farewells. A shake of the hand for this one and that, a hug, a kiss — a lot of kisses.

She came round to where we, her 'family', were standing at the entrance to the wynd. "Babs, my dear — Leezie — Ina an' Sandy — an' Janet an' Peter." She studied us a moment, and laughed. "Half the world's gettin' wed! Leezie, mind what I've taught you, now! An' keep fightin'! Be happy, my dears! I love you all." She kissed us each. Something flat slid into my pocket. "You'd better have this, eh, lassie?" she whispered in my ear. "I'll no be needin' it. Keep it safe, now. An' tell nobody where it is!" She winked to me as she drew back.

Her white mule was led forward. The young Englishman

who was her escort put her up smoothly and elegantly to her gilt-tasselled saddle. "Give us a song, Kate!" someone called, and laughing she gave them a verse of 'John, come, kiss me now.' As the lad did so, smiling, they cheered, and then joined in the chorus, she conducting them with a red-gloved hand. I remembered the Queen's white pony, and the red gloves she had worn when I first saw her... And the King, Henry Darnley, singing that same song at me... last year... so long ago... standing on the stair...

I slipped forward to put an imploring hand on her bridle. She was waving goodbye to everyone when she saw me there and leaned down. "What is it, lass?"

"What happened, Kate?" I whispered. "What really happened to dad that last night?"

She gazed a second. "What do Babs an' the others say?" she murmured.

I bit my lip. "They just say he fell. They'll no speak about it. But what did happen?"

The beautiful black face smiled blandly, with a flash of white teeth and rouged lips. A delicately plucked eyebrow rose. "He fell," she said in faint surprise as she gathered up her reins, their bells tinkling musically. "What else would you have me say? Leezie, you're aye seekin' secrets. It's a bad habit. Have you no noticed, it can get you into trouble? He fell."

She blew a last round of kisses, smiled to me specially, turned her mount and rode away.

I took a deep breath to steady myself, and slipped into the crowd. It was time I went, with mingled apprehension and relief, to give Master Kerr his answer.

GLOSSARY.

argy-bargy — argument
avaunt — go away
aye — yes; always

bailie — magistrate
bairn — child
bawbee — halfpenny
besom — scold, unpleasant woman or girl
bide — stay
bird — woman
bittie — little bit
blatherskite — over-talkative
bleezin' — blazing drunk
blether — talk, chatter
bodies, pair of — stiffened bodice or corset
boke — vomit
bonny — pretty
boozy — drunken
branks — scold's bridle; metal cage to fit over head, with bar to
    press down tongue
braw — fine
braws — best clothes
breeks — breeches

callant — young man
citterne — kind of lute
clairty — filthy
commonalty — common people
coney — rabbit
creance — long, thin tethering line for training hawk
cry, cried — call, named

cuddy — horse
cuttie — knife

daft, daftie — stupid, idiot
dastard — coward
deil — devil
De rien, monsieur — Don't mention it, sir (French)
dinnae — don't
Dod — God
dottle — fool

ell — measure of length, 1.3 metres
Embra — Edinburgh
eyass — hawk taken from the nest before it can fly

finicky — delicate
firkins — small barrels
flesher — butcher

gangrel — tramp
glowerin' — frowning
gob — mouth
gormless — brainless
gowk — fool
groat — copper coin, two pence Scots

hammerman — smith
hizzy — hussy, slut

ill-thoughted — dirty-minded, malevolent

jaud — slut
jesses — thongs on hawk's legs to hold it by
jing-bang — party, affair, bundle

kirk — church

lassie — girl

Martinmas — St Martin's day, 11th November
masque — play, performance, acting
Merci du compliment — Thank you for the compliment (French)
merk — silver coin, 13 pence sterling
mind — remember, take care
mosstrooper — Scottish Border raider

-nae, eg doesnae — -n't, eg doesn't
ounce — 25 grams

passage hawk — hawk caught and trained as an adult bird
Patey — Peter
plack — copper coin, halfpenny
plaid — length of woven cloth used as coat/cloak/shawl/blanket
presently — now, at this present moment

reivers — raiders
royal — gold coin

sack — sherry
shanks — stockings, often of same cloth as breeches
siller — silver, money
subscrivit — signed

take heed — take care, pay attention
testoon — silver coin
tirrivee — upset, state of alarm
tod — fox

whiles — sometimes
wynd — narrow lane

ye, yer — you, your

Other Kelpies by
Frances Mary Hendry

Quest for a Kelpie

It is a crucial moment in Britain's history: Prince Charles Edward Stuart's attempt to regain his grandfather's crown from the Hanoverian King George is in the balance.

Jeannie Main is warned that she will make a king and break a king. But how could a wee fisher lass do such a thing?

What will bring her four times into the shadow of the gibbet? And why should she risk her life by riding the Kelpie, the most dangerous monster in all Scotland?

This fast-moving tale won the first BBC Scotland/SLA "A Quest for a Kelpie" competition in 1986.

"...a remarkably accomplished first novel.... the packed, realistic story of a girl from a fisher family caught up in the '45 rising." *The Guardian*

ISBN 0 86241 136 X   £2.95

Quest for a Maid
Frances Mary Hendry

With the Scots King murdered, the path to the throne is now clear for the ambitious Lady de Brus and her son Robert. But there is a rightful heir to the throne -- an eight year old princess -- the Maid of Norway. As powerful forces of witchcraft, sorcery and wealth plot her destruction Meg and her loyal friends, Peem and Davie, risk their lives for her safe rescue. Their crucial mission is dogged with danger but the fragile young princess's life is in their hands -- and with that they hold the key to the peace and destiny of a nation!

"... a terrific novel, wholly engrossing... fast-paced, exciting and great fun." *The Sunday Times*

"I ended this novel with a rare sense of disappointment that there was not more to come! A truly remarkable novel." *Junior Bookshelf*

ISBN 0 86241 315 X   £2.25

Look out for...

QUEST FOR A QUEEN TRILOGY
The Lark
Frances Mary Hendry

More adventures spanning the lifetime of Mary Queen of Scots are in store for you in *The Lark:*

Young Jean is in for a surprise when the Commander of the Scots Guard chooses him to be "whipping boy" to the French dauphin, future husband to Mary Queen of Scots. Scarcely knowing what lies in store for him, he finds himself at the French court amidst a strange selection of characters -- the Serpent Queen, Chicot the evil dwarf, and the dauphin himself -- a sickly bad-tempered boy who delights in the suffering of others.

Adventure and intrigue follow on thick and fast for Jean who finds himself caught up in the furious course of history.

Have you read...

Black Swift
Josephine Pullein-Thompson

Born at Radstock Castle during the Civil War, Black Swift is the fastest filly in Sir Thomas Wakefield's stable. Taller and stronger than any horse in England, she is the first of a new breed with which her owner hopes to repair his battered fortunes. But before she can be put to the test, Black Swift is stolen by Bernard, Sir Thomas's younger son, and taken to the heart of the battlefield.

Written by the famous pony novelist, Josephine Pullein-Thompson, this book brilliantly evokes the wild and lawless time that followed the war as well as the great spirit of hope that it brought forth.

ISBN 0 86241 339 7   £2.50

Dogsong
Gary Paulsen

"You must leave with the dogs. Run along and find yourself. When you leave me you must head north and take meat and see the country. When you do that you will become a man."

Inspired by the Eskimo shaman Oogruk, Russel Suskitt takes a dog team and sled to escape the modern ways of his village and to find his own "song" of himself. He travels across ice flows, tundra, and mountains, haunted along the way by a dream when, to save himself and a pregnant Eskimo girl he has rescued, he must kill a polar bear in the ancient way learned in the dream.

It is a rigorous journey for the boy and his team of dogs, but in a combination of wills, their spirits soar as one to survive in this unforgettable run toward self-discovery.

"There is enough gritty realism to satisfy the most adventure-hungry readers. A remarkable book."
School Library Journal.

ISBN 0 86241 323 0   £2.50

Alf's Secret War
Donald Lightwood

The colourful world of the music hall suddenly falls apart for Alf when his father is arrested during a show for ignoring his call-up papers.

With his father now a reluctant soldier Alf has to confront his confused emotions. He thinks the world of his dad but knows there is an enemy to fight. When his mother leaves him to entertain the troops, the hurt he feels can only deepen.

Alf takes charge of his own fate and finds a strange sense of security when he takes a destitute family under his wing. Slowly he comes to realise that his father too must be feeling the hurt of rejection.

He sets out on a foolhardy journey through war-torn Britain to find his father. His brave quest provides a thrilling finale to this wonderful story.

This is Donald Lightwood's second novel for children. His first, *The Baillie's Daughter,* won the "Quest for a Kelpie" competition in 1989.

ISBN 0 86241 383 4   £2.95

The Green Gang
Aileen Hunter

A school conservation project turns into a
frightening adventure when Donna and her friends
find a poisoned buzzard on the hillside.

Furious at the farmer's cruelty, the children decide
to take action: "It's illegal... and it's what we
should be basing our project on... the needless
slaughter of a bird of prey."

But their plans bring trouble when the farmer's
son seeks revenge and turns their friends against
them.

Which side is Ally on? Will the jealous and
spiteful Karen ruin their project? The odds are
against them, but Donna is determined not to give
in...

The Green Gang is Aileen Hunter's first novel. Her
exciting story provides a fresh look at how children
today are acting positively to protect wildlife and
our environment.

ISBN 0 86241 364 8   £2.50